DEVIL'S DEFENSE

DEVIL'S DEFENSE

A Fischer at Law Novel

LORI B. DUFF

SHE WRITES PRESS

Published 2024

Printed in the United States of America

Print ISBN: 978-1-64742-736-8
E-ISBN: 978-1-64742-737-5
Library of Congress Control Number: 2024913130

For information, address:
She Writes Press
1569 Solano Ave #546
Berkeley, CA 94707

Interior design and typeset by Katherine Lloyd, The DESK
She Writes Press is a division of SparkPoint Studio, LLC.

To my parents

Wherever they are, I know they're proud of me.
I'm honored to be your daughter.

CHAPTER
ONE

———

Coach Wishingham pulled a stapled-together pack of papers out of a folder and plopped them on Jessica's desk. On top of the stack was a telltale pink sheriff's service of process paper. Ah, so. The famous Coach had been served with a lawsuit.

"Six o'clock in the morning the doorbell rings, and there's a deputy standing at my door with this nonsense." Coach's incredulous tone begged Jessica Fischer to be just as mystified by this turn of events. How could the Great and Powerful Coach Frank Wishingham III be served with a lawsuit in the wee hours of the morning like a regular peasant? Jessica kept her face neutral. "He apologized to me, said there was nothing he could do, he had to do his job. I asked him who I should call. I thought it would be good to have a lady represent me under the circumstances. He said he wasn't supposed to tell me, but he told me to call you. Said you were a real pistol and would be discrete."

Jessica's first reaction was to be surprised that any of the deputies knew her name, much less had a favorable opinion of her. Then, after a second's thought, she realized she must stand out as one of the only women to make an appearance in Ashton's courts. She reserved the debate over whether or not being called a "pistol" was a compliment for later.

Jessica knew that in the town of Ashton, Georgia, the order

of worship was first Jesus, second America, and third the high school football coach, with the second two interchangeable if it were a winning season. It was often a winning season. And here was the high school football coach, in the middle of a winning season, sitting in her office.

She was relatively new to Ashton, having moved there just three years ago from the Atlanta suburbs. On paper, it had looked easier to open a law practice here. The rents were cheap, the layperson-to-lawyer ratio was good, and she was the only female lawyer in town. She was only just now realizing what that meant in practical terms, and unsure how she felt about it.

Her paralegal, Diane, had knocked on her doorframe about a half hour earlier. "Tripp Wishingham is going to be here in a moment."

"What's his deal?" Jessica asked.

Diane pointed a manicured finger at Jessica. "Coach Frank Wishingham the Third, aka Tripp Wishingham, of the Ashton High School football team?"

Jessica sighed. "I don't care about football. What does that have to do with me?"

"Honey, honey. If you want to make it in this town, you will care about football. Anyway, I don't know exactly; he just called and said he had an emergency."

"Mmph. Everyone thinks it's an emergency." She checked the time. Ten minutes before he was supposed to show up. "Well, he's employed, so his check will probably cash."

Diane shook her head and left Jessica's office.

At 4:25 p.m., when she heard Coach come into the building, Jessica refreshed her lipstick and fluffed her hair. She looked at herself in the front-facing camera on her phone, trying out different expressions, seeing which one would make her look older and more knowing than her twenty-nine years would allow. Whatever the Coach's issue was, if he were as well-known as Diane said he was, representing him could open up a world of business for her. If she could be the lawyer to the cool kids, her business would thrive.

Remember, she told herself, while doing one last check for any remnants of lunch between her teeth, *don't undersell yourself.* She knew what other lawyers charged, and she knew she was worth at least that, no matter how odd the numbers felt coming out of her mouth.

Diane brought Coach Wishingham back at 4:40. Jessica could have taken him on time but didn't want him to think she was just sitting at her desk. She was a busy and important lawyer, wasn't she? Not just waiting for clients to walk in.

Coach Wishingham strode in through the door, taking one step for every two of Diane's. Jessica took an instant dislike to him for the same reason, she supposed, that everyone else liked him. He was a good-looking giant of a man in his midthirties with dark, slicked-back hair and blue eyes that actually twinkled. Twinkled! It might have been the twinkle that Jessica distrusted the most.

Still, Jessica plastered on a smile and held her hand out across her wood veneer desk to shake his hand. She'd need a few more Coaches to hire her before she could afford solid wood furniture. Coach didn't seem like the kind of guy who would notice particle board, but you never knew.

"Jessica Fischer. Good to meet you." She made a point of looking him directly in the eye, insisting that she, too, was an alpha dog, despite the fact that she wanted to slink away with her tail between her legs. For all the classes she'd taken in law school, it was her theater training from college that helped her the most in these moments. She wasn't Jessica Fischer, inexperienced lawyer just on the brink of competence. She was someone else who knew exactly what she was doing, and she owned this stage.

Coach Wishingham leaned forward as he crushed her hand. She was almost bowled over by the combination scent of Right Guard and Old Spice. "Frank Wishingham," he said in a gravelly baritone. "Everyone calls me Coach. But I guess you know that."

Then he put his other hand over hers and winked—actually winked!—and continued to hold eye contact with her until she pulled her hands away. A beam of light came in through the window and highlighted the dust swirling in the air around his head.

And now here she was, looking over the petition he'd handed her. She licked her lips and settled back in her chair to put some distance between them. When she looked up, the twinkle in his blue eyes had gone icy. She felt the ice pierce a spot in her forehead.

"Do you want me to explain this to you?" she asked.

"I get the gist, but yeah."

"This says that you are the father of a sixteen-year-old girl. I assume you're aware of this? Her?" She looked up at Coach. His eyes hadn't thawed any, but he nodded, so she continued.

"The petitioner, a lady named Sarah James, asks to establish legal paternity, which means for the court to declare that you are officially the father, wants you to pay child support going forward and also back child support, and cover her health insurance."

"How do you get me out of it?" Coach hooked his hands behind his head and leaned back, crossing his ankle over his knee. His posture seemed studiously relaxed, and his face was pointed toward the ceiling. Jessica couldn't imagine what was going through his head at that moment. The only way she could have these conversations was by rushing through a dry recitation of facts and then bracing for the reaction. When there was no reaction, like this, it made her nervous. She understood emotion. She didn't understand this casual flatness.

Without other options, she answered the question she was asked. "Well, the easiest way to get you out of it is if you aren't this girl's father. Are you her father?" Jessica heard Darth Vader's voice in her head. *Frank, are you her father?* She suppressed a giggle.

"If I am, this is the first I'm hearing about it."

"Hold up," said Jessica. "You all both live in this little town for however long, and this morning is the first time anyone tells you that you might be this child's father?" This was too much.

"I didn't know shit about it until this morning. They don't live in Ashton; they live in Parksville. I'm not saying I was a saint sixteen years and nine months ago, but I am pretty sure I never had sex with—what's her name?" Coach Wishingham took the set of papers from Jessica and read the name off the top. "Sarah James."

"Do you know who she is?" Jessica asked the question knowing good and well that Coach knew exactly who Sarah James was. He struck her as the kind of guy who had binders full of game stats in his office.

"Well, yeah. I went to high school with her, but she doesn't really stand out in my memory."

"Do you know why she would be saying you are Francesca's father?"

"I mean, look. I was the quarterback in high school. You know what it's like around here." He paused for her nod to his all-but-rhetorical question. She knew it was the answer he expected, so she gave it. "It wasn't like I had to work too hard to get a girl if I wanted her. I know I'm a big fish in a small pond, but Sarah is living in that small pond, and she wants to land that big fish."

He didn't seem the least bit humbled by what he was saying.

"Why now?" Jessica asked. "Do you have any idea why Sarah would wait sixteen years to get child support and health insurance and see you every other weekend for visitation exchanges?"

"Visitation? I don't want anything to do with this girl!" Coach's transformation from tabby cat to tiger was so quick Jessica wondered if he'd been body snatched.

"Even if she turns out to be yours?" Jessica had not gone to law school to cheat a teenage girl out of the opportunity to have a father. Then again, who knew if Coach really was Francesca's father? Maybe he was the victim of some deluded unpopular woman who wanted attention. She reminded herself to keep an open mind. Rent had to be paid, and someone had to represent this guy. It might as well be her. Once they had more facts and everyone had a chance to digest all this new information, maybe they could have a different conversation.

"She's not mine! Look, I slept with a lot of girls in high school. Find me a football player that didn't. So sure, I may or may not have been at some party that I don't remember with this Sarah chick a whole lot of years ago. Does that make me some girl's father? A father is a whole lot more than some shit I did drunk after a game. I'm hiring you to get me out of this, understand?"

"Got it," Jessica said. "I'll see what I can do." Looking for a way to take control of the conversation, she turned to the back page of the paperwork. "She's being represented by Eric Crabtree. He's a friend of mine. Let me call him and see if he's in the office. He might be able to give some insight into all of this."

Jessica turned toward the phone and dialed Eric's number. Breaking eye contact with Coach made her realize how captivating he was. Not necessarily in a good way, but in a powerful way. Turning toward the phone was like breaking out of a tractor beam. Somehow the air felt fresher.

Although she wasn't above lying to a client to make herself sound more in the know, she hadn't lied to Coach. She did like Eric, and they did have a good working relationship. They'd never seen each other outside of professional settings, but they'd sat next to each other at plenty of networking events and while waiting for interminable calendar calls in courtrooms. She enjoyed his company. He wouldn't lie to her. He might not tell her everything, not if it would hurt his client, but what he did tell her, she could count on. Plus, he was a competent lawyer, which made every experience with him something she could learn from, not that she'd ever tell him that fact.

When Eric picked up the phone, she said, "Hey, Eric. I've got Coach Wishingham in my office. He got served this morning. I was wondering if you might tell us what inspired Ms. James to file this now." Jessica listened to Eric. Coach stared at her as Eric gave her the quick and dirty. Jessica could have a good poker face when she needed it, but she decided not to turn it on just now. Let Coach sweat her expressions.

When she hung up, she looked directly at her new client. "Turns out that Ms. James was never really sure who Francesca's father was. She was at some party near the end of senior year in high school and got very drunk. She passed out on a bed in a back bedroom. A couple of guys came in. You, she thought, and some other guy she thinks was called 'Jazz.' Maybe someone else. She's not sure."

Coach Wishingham's dimpled chin was frozen in a Golden Age of Hollywood smile. Jessica wouldn't be surprised if he'd studied 8x10 black-and-white portraits of Cary Grant and Humphrey Bogart to get that exact blend of charm and impenetrability. He laughed. "Yeah. Jazz O'Reilly. His real name was Jeff. We called him Jazz because when he was about to catch a ball he looked like he was doing jazz hands." Coach imitated jazz hands and then cocked his hands in a limp-wristed gesture. "Ha! What a faggot!"

So funny, Jessica thought dryly. "Right," she said, ignoring the floor show. "Sarah says she remembers the guys saying something crude and pulling off her pants and having their way with her. She barely felt it, wasn't even sure it happened. Then she found herself pregnant, so clearly something happened. A few months ago, she did the Gene Pool genetic testing kit thing on her daughter—you know, those things that everyone is doing to find out their ancestry—and got a hit on you."

"Damn." Here, Humphrey Bogart would have stuck his face into his hand cupped around a cigarette lighter. Deprived of that option, Coach licked his thumb and looked down at his boat shoe, polishing off an invisible scuff.

Jessica kept staring at the space where Coach's eyes would have been. "Damn is correct. Eric said he had a heck of a time convincing her not to file rape charges."

Coach's head jerked up. Jessica was surprised to see genuine confusion there. "Rape? I never raped anyone!"

"Didn't you? Did she give you consent?" Jessica reminded herself to lower her voice and keep it professional.

"Did she say no?" Coach's palms were up and his hands were spread wide. Jessica tried to remember what her theater teacher called this pose, but it was supposed to convey openness and truth-telling. This entitled asshole really thought all women were his for the taking unless they tried to fight him off.

Jessica took a long breath through her nose, paused, and counted to seven, then breathed out through her mouth, counting to eight. It helped a little. This was not the time for a lecture on the subtleties of consent. She reminded herself that it was her job to convey her client's position, not her own.

"Listen, you're not charged with rape at the moment. Here's my question. For her to get a hit on you through Gene Pool, you had to have done it too. Did you?"

"Yeah."

"So? Did you get a hit on her?"

"I have no idea."

"Can you check? I thought the whole point was to find out who you were related to."

"I can check," he said, taking out his phone and poking at it. "I never really looked at it after I found out what I wanted to know. We can trace our family back generations, of course, but there were rumors that my adopted great-grandfather had *Black* blood in him." Coach Wishingham whispered the word "Black" in the way that Jessica's grandmother whispered the word "cancer." Like it was a horrible thing you could speak into existence by saying it loud enough. "I always thought that was nuts. This genetic thing proved he didn't. That's all I wanted to know. I didn't bother going back to read anything else."

Coach Wishingham swiped at his phone a few more times, then said, "Hot damn." He pushed the phone over to Jessica, showing her the notification on the Gene Pool app: "Relative Finder notification: Francesca James. Relation: daughter."

Jessica gave him a minute to digest the information, then said, "Do you want to think about what you want to do?" This seemed simple from a legal standpoint. He was the father; the law proscribed what he had to do. Emotionally, though, the guy had to be in turmoil, no matter what kind of a dick he was.

"What's there to think about?" he said, sliding his phone back into his pocket. Jessica arched an eyebrow, as several possible things to think about crossed her mind. "I don't want a daughter. I sure as hell don't want a teenage daughter, and I'd rather keep all my money. Can't I sign over my rights? I want you to fix this for me."

"I don't have a magic wand," said Jessica. "I can't make all this go away." They'd only been talking about a half hour or so, but a lot of information had been exchanged. Surely he couldn't have processed much of it. She needed to figure out how to stall to give him the time to be thoughtful instead of reactionary. "I can, however, see what I can do to minimize the damage. I don't know how reliable these spit-in-a-cup genetic test things are. We can do a more legitimate DNA test before we take a real stand. Give me a day or so to do some research. In the meantime, brace yourself. This is all public record, and we live in a small town. Someone is going to call you and ask what you think. Promise me that whatever the question, you say your lawyer advised you not to comment on pending litigation, but that you wish nothing but the best for Francesca no matter what happens. Refer them to me for specifics."

As soon as Jessica mentioned the possibility of publicity, Coach seemed to jump back into his own skin, or at least the skin of his own making. The matinee idol light was back in his eyes. "I'm not afraid of talking to reporters. I talk to them all the time. They love me!"

"I don't give a crap." Jessica had to let him know on the front end that she was here to get the job done and was impervious to his charms. "They love you because you win football games. This has nothing to do with football. Reporters love a good scandal, and there is nothing that the press loves more than seeing a hero fall. Trust me on this one. Say nothing."

CHAPTER
TWO

Jessica sent Coach Wishingham on to Diane to check out. She shut the door to her office behind him and sank back down in her chair, staring up at the ceiling. Objectively, getting him as a client was a good catch. His hefty retainer would go a long way, and representing him well would enhance her reputation. Still, it was no small task representing someone she didn't like on a gut level. They'd have lots of arguments before this ended, no doubt. Ah well, all for the greater good.

Diane came into Jessica's office without knocking and clicked in on four-inch heels. Jessica had no idea how tall Diane actually was. Jessica, at five foot five, towered over her. Diane couldn't be more than five feet tall, but she always wore shoes that made up for the fact. She flounced into Jessica's client chair for the postmortem, her usual habit, her full skirt billowing up. Diane picked up one of the stress balls Jessica kept in a basket on her desk and tossed it from hand to hand.

Jessica needed these conversations. Diane understood the world differently than she did, and she helped Jessica frame her cases in a larger context. She was an excellent sounding board. Still, she wanted Diane to think these conversations were all about Diane's need to know rather than Jessica's need to organize her thoughts, so she always made Diane speak first.

"He's just as good-looking as he was in high school," Diane said, her eyes glinting.

"You think so?" Jessica said. "I didn't find him the least bit attractive."

"Liar," said Diane. "There's not a woman on earth who doesn't think he's handsome."

Jessica laughed. "He's handsome, I guess," she conceded. "But handsome isn't the same thing as attractive. He is repellant. He *thinks* he's handsome, and that's gross."

"You think you're so smart," Diane said, miming throwing the stress ball at her.

"But I *am* smart," Jessica said, grinning despite herself.

"Well, he *is* handsome," Diane answered.

"Touché," Jessica said, pausing to consider what made it okay for her to think she was smart but made it not okay for Coach to think he was handsome. "But I don't think being smart gets me any special privileges. He expects the world to fall over and do whatever he wants because of his chin dimple."

"That's because the world *does* fall over and do whatever he wants," Diane said, then grinned at Jessica again. "I would."

"You don't think personality has anything to do with attractiveness?" Jessica countered, never missing an opportunity for a debate. It was a quality that had served her well in school, but hadn't always been the best for her personal life.

Diane only grinned bigger. "Honey, I'm not asking him into my bed for conversation."

"Oh, shut up," said Jessica, tossing a stress ball shaped like an egg that she got from the Kroger at Diane, missing her by a good foot and a half. It bounced uselessly on the floor next to her. Diane's need for gossip appeased, Jessica chose to move on to more practical concerns: getting Diane up to speed on what was going on and what needed to be done.

"I feel like I need a shower," she said, after she'd explained the whole sordid story. "Talking to assholes who would take advantage of drunk teenagers up close and personal is the worst. It wouldn't surprise me if he did rape her." Jessica picked up her water bottle to take a drink and wash away the poison from her earlier conversation as best she could.

"Well, he didn't rape Sarah James," Diane said with a matter-of-factness that surprised Jessica.

Jessica put down her water bottle and gaped at Diane. "Say what?"

Diane shrugged. "There's just no way Tripp Wishingham raped anyone."

"And you know this how?" Diane couldn't possibly know, but of course, you never knew with her. Despite the age difference between Coach and Diane, it wouldn't entirely shock Jessica to find out that Diane had been at that party all those years ago. Diane seemed to know everything and have been everywhere.

"Look, I was a secretary in the high school back then. I knew who they were. Sarah was this plain, mousy girl, and Tripp was *Tripp*. There wasn't a girl in the school who wouldn't have given her left leg to have a chance at him. For a girl like Sarah to score a guy like him—that was not rape, that was a victory."

"Come on, Diane."

"I'm serious! What happened at those high school parties was no secret. Only a fool would get pass-out drunk and expect nothing to happen. The whole *point* of getting pass-out drunk in high school is hoping something happens. It was for me, at least," she said, giving Jessica an over-the-top wink. Jessica grimaced. "Look," Diane continued, sighing, "I'm just not buying that she didn't know till now that it was Tripp. She named her daughter Francesca. Frank. Francesca. Get it? Who names a kid after their rapist? No one, that's who."

Jessica could not believe Diane was defending this creep. Never in Jessica's life would she get pass-out drunk to make herself easy prey for a football player. She hadn't thought her morality sheltered her until she became a lawyer and she had to suddenly find a way to see the world from the perspective of people who did things Jessica would never consider. That's why Diane was invaluable. She kept Jessica out of her own ivory tower. Truth was a matter of perspective. It wasn't Jessica's job as a lawyer to argue her own opinion. It was her job to argue her client's position to the best of her ability and within the bounds of the law and ethics. It was the judge's job to sort through all the different perspectives and arguments and find some semblance of objective truth. And anyway, they were both just guessing at what was going on in high school Sarah's mind. All they knew was that her lawyer was saying it wasn't consensual here, now, in 2018. Whatever the case, she couldn't wait to get home to scrub the afternoon off her back with a high-quality loofah.

"You don't have to like the guy, but he did just pay you to represent him, and I'm going to appreciate the eye candy going in and out of the door. This is a high-profile case, missy. You do a good job, more come in the door and I get a raise. Go home. Tomorrow we'll get to work."

Because she knew what was best for her, Jessica took Diane's advice.

CHAPTER
THREE

J essica liked baths in theory more than she liked them in reality, but she kept trying anyway. One of the things that had sold her on her house in Ashton was the huge claw-foot tub in her bathroom. She had images of herself soaking away stressful days in lavender-scented water with her hair piled on top of her head.

What actually happened was that she sloshed around in water that was either too hot or too cold, dripping oily water on the floor as she leaned over the side to get a drink of water. Mostly she was bored. She couldn't figure out how to read without dipping the edges of her paperback in the bath, and she wasn't one for staring at the ceiling.

She hauled herself out of the tub, trying not to flood the tile, and wrapped herself in a towel. She stood, huddled underneath it for a moment before gripping the corners and pulling them back and forth to exfoliate her back with the rough loops of the terry cloth. Her purple fluffy bathrobe waited on a hook for her—she threw the towel on the floor to sop up the water on the tile and gingerly stepped over to the hook, trying not to slide and fall on the wet ceramic.

Jessica pulled some dental floss out of a drawer and sat on her bed, methodically scraping the surface of each tooth. Truly, it hadn't been a bad day at work. Her escrow account had grown considerably with Coach's retainer. She was running a for-profit business, after all, not a social service agency. It was critical that she earned enough to pay Diane's salary and her own, as well as rent on her office and the mortgage on her house.

She wasn't yet at the point in her career when she could pick and choose clients. Still in her early years, she had to hope they would pick and choose her. Coach was a local celebrity. No doubt representing him would get her picture in the paper. In a town where you had to drive a half hour to find a movie theater and even the fast food restaurants shut down at 9:00 p.m. on the weekdays, there wasn't much to do besides gossip. No such thing as bad publicity so long as they spell your name correctly, right? With any luck the *Ashton Post* would give her some free advertising while they speculated about high school Coach's sexual prowess.

It had only been a dozen years since Jessica was a high school senior. She'd never been to one of the football parties—whatever kind of a mouse Sarah James might have been, she clearly had more social standing than Jessica herself had. Jessica would never in a thousand years have gotten drunk at a party around those assholes, mainly because she'd never have been at a party with those assholes.

Her mother taught her to value strength and control—alcohol made you weak and out of control. Feminism, her mother said, was about choices, and how could you choose if you took away your reason? It had all made sense at the time. Then Jessica went to college and took women's studies classes and learned that her mother had allowed men to define her choices: she decided what she could and could not do based on how men would react to it.

She came home in the summer full of fire and fury, arguing with her mother in a way she hadn't when she was fifteen and nonstop argument was expected. She didn't come home the next summer, taking an internship instead, and then came home only for the briefest of visits until her senior year when her mother announced she had breast cancer.

Jessica shook her head. How did her train of thought travel from Coach Wishingham to her mother's breast cancer? She didn't like thinking about those sad years, the ones she missed and the ones she tried to make up for. Of course, she didn't like thinking about Coach Wishingham much either. What would Donna Fischer have said about Frank Wishingham?

Stop, stop, stop, she told herself. She got off the bed, tossed the dental floss into the trash, and went back into the bathroom to brush her teeth. The bathroom still smelled like lavender. She closed her eyes and inhaled, trying to fill her brain with the scent instead of her thoughts.

Jessica slipped into bed and picked up the book on her bedside table. Better she think about someone else's stories, she told herself, pulling out her bookmark and settling into the pillows. She read herself to sleep like she did most nights.

CHAPTER
FOUR

At about three o'clock the next day, Diane announced that Bobby Turnbull from the *Ashton Post* was on the phone. Her heart quickened a few beats knowing she was going on record. The few conversations she'd had with Bobby in the past were brief and substanceless. This was her first on-the-record interview about a case. She waited a few seconds before she picked up the phone so Bobby would think he'd interrupted some important task.

"Hey, Jessica, it's Bobby from the *Post*. I just spoke to Tripp Wishingham, and he said you were representing him. Is that true?"

"Yes, it is." Okay, that was a softball. She knew the answer to that one.

"Great, that's good. Coach said that this whole thing is just a ploy to distract him from the playoff game this weekend, that this girl—Francesca?—goes to Britt High, who Ashton is playing, and that the timing seems awfully coincidental to him. Is that your official position?"

Jessica was glad that Bobby couldn't see her smacking her forehead with her palm. She swallowed and focused on keeping her voice measured. "We don't have an official position yet. We're still investigating all possibilities and haven't ruled anything out. This is all new and, of course, very shocking to my client."

"Is he Francesca's father?" Bobby asked, like Jessica had known he would.

She and Diane had spent the better part of an hour coming up with a response to this question that was both neutral and seemed like she was answering the question. Jessica put on her lawyer voice. "Anything is possible. At the moment, we just don't have enough information to say one way or the other. Our hearts do go out to the poor girl who is caught in the middle of this adult drama. Whatever the outcome, we hope it is the best possible resolution for her."

Jessica hadn't hung up the phone all the way before she yelled out to Diane in the next room, "I'm going to throttle Tripp Wishingham with my bare hands."

Diane appeared in Jessica's doorway. "If anyone gets to touch Tripp Wishingham's bare flesh, it's me."

Jessica had a quick flash of an image of Diane in a catsuit, slinking around Coach's legs before latching onto his throat with her fangs. She suppressed a grin, masking it with an exasperated sigh. "The *one thing* I told him not to do was talk to the press, and then he immediately goes telling Bobby Turnbull that this lawsuit was just filed as a distraction for the playoff game because Francesca goes to Britt."

"Ooooh," said Diane. "I mean, you have to admit—that's a brilliant plan!"

"Are you kidding me?"

"Not in the least!" said Diane. "Look, that's great PR." Jessica raised her eyebrows, and Diane continued. "And the timing *is* a little odd. Why wait sixteen years? Why wait until right before playoffs? Now he looks like the victim. Never discount the court of public opinion."

"The court of public opinion doesn't matter inside of a courtroom," Jessica said, but she faltered. Truth, justice, and the American way had to count for something, didn't it?

"We were assigned to Judge Brandywine. Seriously, Jessica. Think," Diane said. Jessica did her best to ignore Diane's condescending tone. "You don't think Judge Brandywine reads the *Post*? Reelection's coming up. He won't make Ashton's local hero look bad if he can help it." Diane got out of her chair and walked over to Jessica and patted her on the shoulder. "Honey, you are smart, super-smart with all of those books, but you have absolutely no idea how the world actually works."

I don't, thought Jessica. This was her greatest weakness, she knew, fighting hard for the world to be what she wanted it to be instead of recognizing it for the cold place it was. She grabbed Diane's hand and leaned her cheek against it. "You live in a completely different reality than I do, don't you?"

"Honey, you see what you want to see. I see what is. You need me. Without me, you'd make brilliant legal arguments and then be surprised every time you lost a case."

CHAPTER
FIVE

—⁓—

Jessica was mostly grateful that it was Eric Crabtree on the other side of this mess. On one hand, he was crude and brash and completely convinced of his own brilliance, but on the other, he was at least honest and had a decent sense of humor. He wasn't into playing stupid lawyer games, making things difficult because he could just to pile up billable hours. Eric cooperated with the DNA tests, and agreed, after much whining and begging on Jessica's part, not to do much of anything until the results were in and they'd talked. The fact that she could whine and beg on a five-minute telephone call instead of having to file motions and do legal research to figure out obscure procedural reasons for delay was one of the many reasons she liked Eric. He'd made her work for the professional courtesy, but it was all in good fun. They'd also agreed to postpone the reams of paperwork associated with formal discovery, such as asking for years' worth of bank statements and tax returns, until the end of football season.

Eric called Jessica a few weeks after their last conversation, and when she picked up, he hooted into the phone, "Who's yo' daddy?"

"Shut up."

"Okay, not yo' daddy, *per se*, but my client's baby daddy."

"Frank Wishingham the Third," Jessica said, in her best Thurston Howell the Third voice.

"The one and only. DNA results came back, and Wishingham is a match."

"Shocked. Shocked, I tell you," deadpanned Jessica. She may not have known anything about Coach a few months ago, but she was a girl who did her homework, and it didn't take much research to learn about his reputation.

"So," said Eric. "How many thousands of back child support is he going to pay? Is he picking her up this weekend so my client can finally get a weekend off?"

"Well, let's see there, Eric. Even assuming you're telling me the truth about the irrefutable DNA evidence naming him the father . . ."

"Oh! Oh, Jessica! I'm wounded. Are you saying I'm a liar?"

Jessica froze. Had she gone too far? She thought they were friends and he knew they were joking—of course if there were a DNA test saying Coach was the father, then he was the father. Why would Eric lie about something that provable? She was trying to be light and fun. Dammit, she was no good at fun. She huffed out air through her nose in frustration. Enough banter. Back to lawyering. "No, Eric, of course you're not lying. If the lab tests came back that Coach is the father, then he's the father. But back child support? Please. Let's base child support on what he was making sixteen years ago when she *should* have brought this up—what was that? Minimum wage in 2003 was what? Five bucks an hour and change? He was a college football player, so he couldn't work more than say, twenty hours a week, so that would be about a hundred dollars a week, which is only fifty-two hundred dollars a year, assuming he never took a day off. Let's base child support off of that."

"Ha ha. Seriously, what's his offer?"

Jessica mentally punched herself for her inability to express herself properly. It was only when she stopped joking that Eric thought she was being funny. "Seriously, how in the hell would I know? You've only just told me that the DNA test came back. Do you have something official you can send me? I'll get him in to talk about it and then let you know."

Jessica placed the handset in its cradle gently, as if it might explode if she were too rough with it. She stared at her computer screen, hoping there were answers there. She contemplated asking Siri how to break the news to a volatile guy whose sole focus was prepping his team for the playoffs. *Oh what the hell*, she thought, and typed, "How do you break bad news to an alpha male?" into Google. She was instantly bombarded with ads for erectile dysfunction medication. She rolled her eyes—even Google assumed she was a man worried about her dick.

Deprived of AI help, she called Diane into her office.

"Okay, my friend, we have to figure out how to tell Tripp Wishingham he's on the hook for child support."

Diane clicked her acrylic nails on her front teeth, then, with a jolt, transferred the clicking to the surface of Jessica's desk. "Hmm . . ." she said, eventually, "I think the best way for me to tell him would be after sex. Bad news goes down best during pillow talk."

"Diane!" Jessica had no interest in her mental image of them in a four-poster bed with satin sheets, Diane's tiny body curled around Coach's huge form, her hand buried in his chest hair.

"Just kidding, just kidding! Unless you think it would work . . ."

Jessica cut her a side eye that answered the question. "I think clinical is the way to go," she said, shoving the prurient imagery aside and shifting into business mode. "Just lay down the facts. Don't give him any room for maybe this or perhaps that. You're the daddy: daddies pay child support. The only questions the judge is going to concern himself about are: 'How much?' and 'Is there any back support to be paid?' The first question is easy, but the second is brutally hard." Jessica fell back inside her own head, stripping away the drama from the case and seeing it for its essential legal simplicity. Child support was a calculation on a worksheet. Not much to it but learning what everyone's income was. Whether or not back child support had to be paid had more to do with the judge's discretion and a sense of moral obligation. Now the only trick was to get her client to see it as clinically as she did. That was the part that tripped her up the most.

"It seems like you know what you're doing. So what do you need from me?" Diane's voice startled her.

"I don't know," Jessica said. "Sounding board?" She rocked back and forth in her chair, talking to the ceiling as much as Diane. "Do I just email him the results and ask him to come in? Or do I get him to come in and show him the results here? Do I call him and tell him? Do I get *you* to call him and tell him?" Jessica hoped Diane would pounce on this idea, knowing that while she'd much rather never have to talk to Coach again, she couldn't relegate this job to Diane. For all Diane's talk, Diane's silence here meant she knew this too. With a sigh, she stopped rocking, planted her feet on the floor and her hands on the desk. Time to be resolute. "Okay, here's what I'm going to do," she said, the plan forming in her mind even as she spoke. "I'm going to email him the results, so he can get all the asshole things he's going to say when he reads the results out of his system before I have to hear them. Then he can come in so we can discuss what to do next. Sound good?"

Diane stood and saluted. "Aye-aye, Chief. Glad I could be of service."

Jessica smiled and raised an eyebrow at her. "Don't you have work to do?"

"You want me to get the discovery out on the Rodriguez case, don't you?" Diane said as Jessica nodded, and went back to her office.

CHAPTER
SIX

⟶

"The hell, Jessica," Coach barked into the phone.

"Excuse me?" Jessica squeaked, her voice higher than she would have liked. She shouldn't have been surprised by the phone call, and yet, here she was, surprised.

"I told you I wasn't dealing with this shit until the season was over, and the season is far from goddamn over. Are you the only person in this shithole town that doesn't know that?"

Jessica's mouth opened and closed twice before her voice rose from her throat. She'd imagined a number of reactions Coach might have to the news, but mad at her for telling him the news at all was not one of them. This made her indignant, which made her mad at him, which made it easier to speak up. "The world does not stop turning during football season. The DNA results came back. What kind of lawyer would I be if I withheld that information from you?"

"The kind of lawyer who wants Ashton High to have a winning season."

This was such a ridiculous thing to say, Jessica could think of nothing to say in response, and so she said nothing. Coach filled the silence on his own. "So, here's what's gonna happen. I'm gonna pretend I never got that email. You're gonna resend it to me when the season's over, and when I see it then, I'll be seeing it for the first time. Got it? Great."

Coach hung up the phone before she could answer.

Jessica picked up one of her stress balls, the dark blue one shaped like a brain with the logo from a neurologists' office printed on it. She squeezed it hard until it disappeared inside her fist. She breathed in through her nose, held it, then let it out as slowly as she could through pursed lips. Then she called Eric.

"Hey, buddy," she said when he answered. "New development on the Wishingham/James debacle."

"You're giving in to all our demands?"

Jessica chuckled silently. Oh, how she wished she could say yes just to end it. "Yeah, no. Well, maybe. Well, whatever we're doing, I don't know what it is, and we're not doing it until the end of football season." Once again, she thanked Fortuna for putting Eric on the other side of this case. She could be honest with him, and not have to make up some cock-and-bull story that would allow for procedural delay.

"Are you serious?"

"Dead. Coach is apparently too busy getting his team through the playoffs and beyond to give this matter the attention that it deserves. He is not making any decisions without being able to focus fully on the situation on hand, and believe me, you don't want him to either. This is not a guy who can multitask." Jessica bounced the eraser of a pencil on her desk like a drumstick on a snare drum. The reality of what she'd just said didn't make it taste any better in her mouth.

"You realize the level of bullshittery you're throwing at me, right?" Jessica couldn't see Eric over the phone, but she knew him well enough to know that he would be carving finger-sized canyons in his gelled hair. You could always tell how stressful Eric's day was by how intact his hair was.

The fact that Eric was correct only served to frustrate Jessica more and make her dig her heels in. "And you realize that you can call it what you want to call it, but it ain't gonna change, right?"

"We're going to get this on a calendar and let the judge deal with it."

"Fine," said Jessica. "Be my guest. By the time you get a court date, football season will be over and you will have pissed off Coach Wishingham beyond reason or negotiation. You don't think Judge Brandywine isn't watching the playoffs along with the rest of the county?"

"This is bullshit!" Eric's voice was getting louder.

"So you said." She couldn't deny the fact, but she couldn't agree on the record either. She silently begged Eric to understand this. Surely he did. Surely. Time to try to lighten the mood. "You realize, don't you, that the pioneers used dried cow pats as fuel for their stoves. They kept warm with it and cooked their food over it. Basically, bullshit built this country. Bullshit is patriotic. As is football. Suck it, Eric. Your client waited sixteen years; she can wait another few weeks."

Jessica could practically hear Eric deflating. "Fine," he said. "But it's still bullshit."

"God bless America," said Jessica before hanging up. She looked up at the ceiling and apologized to the universe. It really wasn't fair that a football game was taking precedence over this poor girl's life. But she wasn't being paid to be fair. She was being paid to represent Coach Wishingham. Even if it did make her a little ill.

CHAPTER
SEVEN

———

F riday afternoon, at about three o'clock, Diane asked Jessica what she was doing that evening.

"I have big plans to be braless on the sofa with a box of wine and Netflix." Jessica had been looking forward to this evening all week. What with Coach yelling at her for doing her job and then having to call Eric to delay the case for bullshit reasons, and the thousands of other things she'd had to do for her other clients throughout the week, she deserved a boozy night on the couch in solitude. "I'm excited about it."

"That's not what you're doing," said Diane.

"No?" Jessica gave Diane a suspicious once-over. Whenever Diane got bossy like that, there was great potential for disaster Jessica had no way of getting out of.

"No. You're going to the football game. Ashton is playing Parksville at home."

"Uh-uh." Jessica lifted her foot and stomped it noisily. "I am literally putting my foot down. I hate football. The bleachers are uncomfortable, the beer is crappy, and the game is boring." Jessica peered into Diane's face, searching for a motive. Then it dawned on her. Coach Wishingham would be there, and Diane wanted her to see him outside of the lawsuit.

"The bleachers are uncomfortable, I'll give you that much,

but it's a high school game, so there's no beer, and the game is actually a lot of fun if you know what you're looking at."

"No beer? No way I can watch sober."

"That's where you're wrong," said Diane. "I've gotten stoned on plastic nacho cheese. You can do that and support the PTO at the same time."

"No."

"Yes."

"Why?" Jessica whined, as visions of her peaceful night at home with reruns of *Friends* faded away. It was a losing battle, she knew, but Jessica hated losing, so she gave it one more whiny "Why," this one topped with puppy dog eyes.

"Because you have a bug up your butt that Coach Wishingham is just this useless piece of meat. You don't like anything about him."

"That's not true!" Jessica protested, even though it was. When she thought of Coach, she invariably thought of all those assholes in high school who never gave her the time of day.

"Isn't it?" Diane put her hand on her hip and cocked her head. "You've never said anything even remotely kind, or even neutral, about him."

"People are complex," Jessica conceded. She didn't *hate* Coach, that was too strong a word, but she didn't see anything she *liked* about him either, certainly not enough to spend her precious free time in his company. Still, there had to be something redeeming in that barrel chest of his. "No one is a hundred percent bad."

"Then tell me what you like about him." Diane arched an eyebrow, a smile playing at her lips. She wasn't going to let Jessica off easy, that much was clear.

"He's . . ." Jessica scrambled to think of something. "He's always well groomed."

Diane gave Jessica a Disapproving Mommy look. "I'm supposed

to be the one focused on his looks, not you. Tell me something about him as a human."

Jessica pressed her lips in a line and finally said, "He's confident?"

"You need to see him in his element. You need to see why everyone else falls all over themselves to please him. All you see is this case, and if that's all you see, then yes, I get why you don't like him. But there's more to him. Trust me. I've known him since he was a teenager."

Jessica huffed, seeing there was no way to win this. When it came to the citizens of Ashton, Diane was omniscient. "Fine."

"Also? You spend too many Friday nights with a box of wine. You're too young for that. I'll pick you up at six. Wear red."

"Fine," Jessica said again, feeling like a teenager giving in to her mother's demands.

Diane arrived precisely at six o'clock. She was decked out from head to toe in Ashton red, including a red hat and scarf. She looked at Jessica, who was wearing jeans and a white sweatshirt with red flowers. "Mm-mm, baby girl. No. You have got to change."

"What? Why?" Jessica tugged on the hem of the sweatshirt. She thought she looked cute.

"I told you to wear red."

"I'm wearing red!" She pointed to the flowers on her torso. "I'm just not trying to camouflage myself in a murder scene the way you are."

"Don't you have anything solid red? Or do we have to run by the Kroger to pick you up an Ashton sweatshirt?"

"Seriously?"

"Seriously. You'll stick out otherwise."

Diane grabbed Jessica by the shoulders, spun her around, and marched her toward her bedroom. Several rejected outfits later,

Jessica was wearing a red cardigan atop a black-and-red-striped T-shirt with red ballet flats.

"I don't understand why I can't wear tennis shoes." Jessica looked at Diane's feet, which were strapped into three-inch red wedges. "How do you even walk in those things?"

"Get in the car," Diane replied.

The Ashton High School stadium could put some college and even some minor league ball arenas to shame. The high school itself might have had a leaky roof since Diane herself was a student there, but the Ashton Red Devils played in a shiny, new stadium.

"Do you know how many tubas the money that built this stadium could have bought for the school? Or state-of-the-art science labs?" Jessica said when they pulled up. "This is insane."

"It's business," said Diane.

"Business that favors one kind of kid over another." Jessica remembered begging her mother's friends to buy crates of oranges and ad space in the programs to have enough money to buy plywood for theater sets, resenting like hell the district-funded construction of the alternate practice field for the junior varsity football team so they wouldn't have to compete for time with the varsity team.

"Business that attracts attention and donors. Look up there." Diane pointed to the electronic signs that ringed the seating, all flashing the names of local businesses. "How much do you think those businesses pay to have their names up there? Every butt in every seat pays ten dollars admission, then another fifteen or so on drinks and snacks. The more attention these kids get, the more likely they are to attract colleges that'll hand them scholarship money."

Jessica looked at the people streaming all around her. Diane was right—again. About everything, it seemed. About the stadium paying for itself—you sure weren't going to get this many people to pay ten bucks a pop to see this year's production of *A Chorus Line*—and the fact that Jessica's initial outfit was inadequate. All the Ashton fans were dressed head to toe in red. Women and girls were dolled up as if they were going to a five-star restaurant instead of eating chili cheese fries served up by a sixteen-year-old conscripted by the PTO. There were tented booths lining the walkway to the bleachers selling pom-poms, colored hair spray, face paint, shirts, scarves, hats, ponchos, giant foam fingers, and all manner of noisemakers. Other booths sold boiled peanuts or snow cones. Some sold nothing but gave you candy and an invitation to church on Sunday morning.

Jessica had lived in Ashton for three years now, and while she'd been *aware* of the high school football fanatics, she had never known it consisted of this many people. Suddenly, she was glad Diane had dragged her here, to see something that was so integrally part of the fabric of her relatively new hometown. Before now, Jessica had thought the football mania was a joke everyone was in on, but now she realized she'd been the only one laughing at the spectacle and she felt a little bit ashamed.

Snare drums echoed off the stands, beating through the noise of the crowd. People swirled in every possible direction. Jessica held on to Diane's elbow for fear of losing her in the sea of blood-colored humanity surrounding them.

They took their seats on the forty-yard line behind the Ashton bench just as a voice boomed over the loudspeaker to introduce the team. The band played the school fight song, and the crowd stood and cheered as if Justin Timberlake himself had taken the stage. Some cheerleaders dressed far too scantily for the chill November air rolled out a red paper banner with "ASHTON" written on it in white script. An oversized blow-up football helmet crowned the exit of a red vinyl tunnel, and teenage boys larger than most men Jessica knew burst out of it and through the paper banner, running onto the field.

Before each boy headed to the home bench, he went to Coach Wishingham, who tapped each boy on the shoulder twice and looked them all in the face. Diane had led them to a seat only a few rows back, so Jessica had a pretty good view of their client. She had to admit, there was something about him, something larger than life. As spectacular as this whole event was, he outshone it all. Her eye was drawn to him. He wore pressed red twill pants, a red long-sleeved shirt, and a red windbreaker with the Ashton logo embroidered on the breast and back. The band of an earpiece stretched across his otherwise perfect hair. He carried a red plastic clipboard in the crook of his left elbow. As the announcer introduced the Parksville team, a group of boys in green and white, Ashton's starting players huddled around Coach for final instructions.

The team captains headed to the center of the field for the coin toss. Jessica was surprised to realize she was excited when Ashton won and elected to receive. The teams lined up on their respective sides of the field, and the Parksville kicker began to loosen his leg with impressively high kicks. At the kickoff, Ashton's receiver caught the ball and ran it to the thirty-five-yard line before being sunk underneath a pile of green-and-white jerseys.

And the game was on.

Jessica had been to enough football games in college to know what was going on, but the game itself didn't interest her that much. Coach Wishingham, however, was fascinating to watch. She'd never paid much attention to coaches during football games. On television, you either saw them yelling at referees or players, or gazing intently and seriously off into middle distance. The images were packaged to make good visuals and didn't necessarily reflect what a coach actually did. Jessica wasn't sure what Coach Wishingham was doing, but whatever it was, was intense. No one seemed to do anything without checking with Coach first. Everyone nodded gravely at his instructions. Occasionally, he'd grab a player by the shoulders and lean his forehead against the young man's. The player would tuck his helmet under his arm and walk away just a little bit taller. Other times he wouldn't touch the young man at all. Those boys would shrink.

Just before halftime, Ashton was up 14–7 and Jessica was surprised at how quickly time had passed. Coach stretched his neck left to right and looked at the clock, then down at his clipboard before barking some instructions to his assistant coach. Jessica felt a tap on her shoulder and jumped.

"Sorry. Didn't mean to startle you."

Jessica looked up and saw Bobby Turnbull settling onto the bleacher next to her. "Hey, Bobby. No worries." She turned back to the field, but then realized something, and faced Bobby again. "Wait. Shouldn't you be in the press box?"

"Nah," he said. "We've got a sports guy who covers that. I'm just here watching the game." He lifted his bottle of Coke and took a long swig.

Diane leaned over Jessica and said, "Hey, Bobby."

"Hey, Diane."

Jessica put her hands on her lower back and stretched, feeling her joints aching. "All the money for this stadium and they couldn't put backs on the seats?"

"You're not supposed to sit back and be comfortable. You're supposed to stand up and get excited," Bobby said.

"You're also supposed to be seventeen years old," Jessica said.

"You're basically seventeen years old," Diane said.

"Shut it, old lady," Jessica replied, grinning at what had become one of her and Diane's running jokes.

"Ouch!" Diane said, punching Jessica lightly in the arm.

"Break it up, ladies. Do I need to call security over here?"

"We'll behave," said Jessica, folding her hands in her lap and doing her best to look innocent.

"So why are you here?" asked Bobby. "I've never seen you at a game before."

"I decided that if she was going to represent Coach, she needed to see him in action," Diane said, answering for her. "He needs to be more than a case, you know? She doesn't know the Coach that Ashton knows."

"That's a great idea," Bobby said, looking at Jessica. "I mean, what would life be like without knowing the Great and Powerful Tripp Wishingham?" Bobby's face was neutral, but there was more than a touch of sarcasm in his monotone. Jessica wondered what the backstory was behind his tone. "Anyway, I'm going to get back to my buddies, but we always meet up at the Waffle House on Route 186 after for a postgame party. If you ladies want to join us . . . ?"

"Maybe," said Jessica, already yawning. As much as a Waffle House trip seemed fun, she was exhausted. "This week kinda kicked my ass. We'll see how tired I am."

"We'll see you there," Diane said. As soon as Bobby was out of earshot, which wasn't far, given the noise of the stadium, she turned to Jessica and grinned. "That boy likes you."

"Oh, bull," said Jessica, but she blushed despite herself. Bobby was cute, no doubt, but he was a good old boy, wasn't he? Ashton born and bred. Not the type to be into her, and not the type she generally liked. Bobby was a nice guy, about her age, but she honestly hadn't considered him that way until Diane brought it up. But then again, Diane had a habit of seeing things she didn't. So maybe she should consider it. He wasn't bad looking at all. About five foot ten, reasonably well-built with a head of thick, curly brown hair, he had a guileless look that was appealing. Still. "Yeah, I'm gonna pass on that one."

"Why?" Diane asked, pouting. "He's single, employed, and doesn't have a criminal history that I know of, and you know I'd know. What's wrong with him?"

What was wrong with him? Aside from some assumptions, nothing really, except, well, no one in this Podunk town had paid her much mind so far, why would Bobby be the exception? Besides, wasn't there some kind of conflict? "He works for the paper."

"And?"

"And he wants information about Coach's case. Dating him has the appearance of impropriety."

"And *you*, my dear, have the appearance of someone who needs to get laid."

Jessica looked toward the heavens for help. "How do you know Bobby anyway?"

"He went to Ashton High when I worked in the front office."

Before Jessica could respond, a trumpet blasted loudly and snare drums echoed around the stadium. A roar went around the crowd, and the players ran off the field. It was halftime.

With forty-five seconds left at the end of the game, the score was tied 21–21. Coach Wishingham called a time-out, and Jessica could see helmets bobbing in their huddle as he pointed to his clipboard. They all put their hands in the center of the circle and shouted before splitting up and taking the field. The center snapped the ball to the quarterback who hopped back a few steps, cocked his arm, and threw it in a perfect spiral down the field. Out of nowhere, Parksville player number 42 shot up. He looked like he was going to snatch the ball out of the sky. The amount of anxiety in Jessica's gut surprised her as much as the relief she felt when it sailed through his hands. Ashton player number 17 grabbed it through the Parksville 42's arms and hit the ground running. He threaded through Parksville player after Parksville player, red and green weaving together like a Christmas wreath, eating up the field until he reached the fifteen-yard line. There, a Parksville player grabbed his legs and pulled him to the ground. There were ten seconds left on the clock. Ashton set up for a field goal and made it. Ashton won.

Jessica and Diane began hopping along with everyone else in the bleachers. The noise was deafening. The players all stormed Coach Wishingham in celebration before lining up to shake hands with the Parksville team. They all trotted off to the locker room to do whatever it was that boys did in the locker room after a win.

The drain of adrenaline after the excitement at the end of the game only further served to exhaust Jessica. She wouldn't have gone to Waffle House, but Diane was driving, and she didn't have it in her to argue. She found herself squashed into a booth with Diane, Bobby, and three of Bobby's friends. Bobby, seated next to Jessica by way of Diane's careful finagling, introduced her to a long, lanky guy named Lee, and two of his coworkers at the paper, Tyler and Wade. Bobby and his friends did most of the talking, rehashing the game.

There was much debate over whether Coach did the right thing.

"I don't understand why we're having this argument. We won. Who cares how?" Wade said.

Bobby shook his head. "It's not about the individual games. What are the guys on the team taking away from this? Always play it safe?"

Lee slapped his hand lightly on the table. "Dude. You have always been like this. Tripp could win a Pulitzer, and you'd say it's because he didn't put himself out there for the Nobel committee."

A slight spot of color showed on Bobby's cheeks. "Tripp Wishingham is an asshole. Always has been." Lee nodded agreement, conceding this point. "The one good purpose he serves on this earth is supposed to be giving us a good game to watch on a Friday night. Playing it safe with the field goal at the end instead of letting the boys try to run for another touchdown is not only dull but teaches them to only take the path of least resistance. That wins can and should be easy."

"You're reading too much into his strategy, Bobert," Lee said.

"He's all talk, that guy. Doesn't have the stones to actually do anything."

Lee shook his head. "He wins games, Bobby. You've hated him as long as I've known you. Get over it."

Despite the fact that Jessica couldn't see the point of debating a successful strategy when they'd won, she was happy to sit back and listen. Besides, she was sure her opinion on the matter wouldn't be welcome anyway. More interesting was observing the group dynamics. Diane was in full flirtation mode with Lee, who seemed to be about ten years too young for her—not that that stopped her from looking at him through her lashes and slapping his shoulder every time he spoke. Jessica gathered that Bobby had known Lee since they were boys: every other sentence seemed to be a private joke that referenced an event that happened decades ago. Every time she heard Diane giggle at something Lee said that was only marginally funny, she'd nudge Bobby and they'd share a rolled eye.

After the third nudge-and-eye-roll combo, Jessica wondered if Diane was right, that Bobby had a thing for her. His thigh was pressed up against hers, but it couldn't not be, the booth was so small and tight. Their forearms brushed as they ate, and Jessica felt a little charge each time.

Jessica was so unused to having a love life that she'd stopped considering having one. The last real boyfriend she'd had was in law school, and Keith had left her when things started getting rough with her mom. She didn't blame him—between changing adult diapers and reading case law to keep up with her classes, she had no time at all to devote to a relationship. Still, it was when she'd most needed a friendly face and someone to hug that she'd lost the friendliest face and the arms in which she found the most comfort.

She'd found, however, an inner strength she didn't know she

had. After the flood of tears had subsided, she knew the universe had given her the gift of independence. Her mother had done just fine on her own after her father had left them and then moved to Arizona; she could do just fine on her own too.

But just because she could, did that mean she wanted to? She honestly hadn't considered the question in years. She'd come to Ashton not long after graduation, and Ashton was not exactly brimming with single, educated prospects in her age bracket and sharing her worldview. Bobby calling Coach an asshole had definitely piqued her interest—perhaps he wasn't such a good ol' Ashton boy after all. Disliking the golden boy didn't smack of conformity.

Diane was pushing this, something Jessica couldn't ignore. Diane's outer brashness belied a knack for keen observation: she had to concede that Diane usually ended up on the side of right on personal matters. Perhaps she should open that window and at least *consider.* She had no idea, and the thought of it scared the ability to consider rationally right out of her head.

She could sum up anyone else's life rather neatly, read any set of facts and apply any law to it. Her own? Not so much. There wasn't anything inherently wrong with dating a reporter; she just couldn't talk to him about work. Which she shouldn't do anyway because of attorney-client privilege: nothing that was not in the public record should be discussed as a matter of course. It was all academic anyway. There was no way Bobby had any interest in her. *Besides*, she thought, *the real question is whether or not I'm interested in him.*

Jessica turned her head and looked up at Bobby. He was lifting a forkful of scrambled eggs to his mouth. Her shoulder bumped up against his, the eggs rolled off his fork, and with a fluid motion, Bobby attempted to catch them midair. He missed, following their trajectory to her left leg with his hand. They both looked down at his hand on her thigh. Bobby's cheeks flushed.

"I'm sorry, I just tried to . . ." He lifted his hand up and saw that in his haste he had ground the eggs into the fabric of her jeans. "Argh. Let me . . ." He yanked a handful of napkins out of the dispenser.

Jessica grabbed his wrist to stop him. "Bobby. Stop. It's okay. Eggs come out in the wash." She kept hold on his wrist as he met her eye. She felt a zap of energy that scared her a little.

"I didn't offend you with my horrible table manners and touching your thigh without express permission?"

"No, you're good," she said, letting go of his wrist and patting his knee, wondering if touching his leg was crossing a line she couldn't uncross. "Eat your waffle and keep your syrup away from me. Diane won't let me in her car if I'm sticky."

Bobby went back to his plate. Jessica's thigh was still warm where his hand had rested. She felt Diane's foot pressing on top of hers under the table, as subtle a "you go, girl" as Diane was capable of giving. Jessica focused solely on the rest of her hash-browns, afraid that making eye contact with anyone would betray the cracks in her heart.

Back in the car, Diane grabbed Jessica's shoulder and shook it. "I told you he liked you!"

"We're not even out of the parking lot, Diane," Jessica said, pretending to be annoyed but unable to keep the grin off her face. "He's standing twenty feet away from the car. Can you keep your voice down until we're sure he can't hear?"

Diane peeled out of the spot without looking behind her. "Did he ask you out?"

"No, and I doubt he will." The idea that Bobby had felt the same electric jolt, and that feeding that energy was a good idea all seemed too much.

"Oh, he will."

"How would you know?" Jessica said, desperate to change the subject. "You were too busy trying to cradle-rob Lee."

"Well, this *cradle-robber* was asked to dinner for tomorrow night. Some men like a woman with enough experience to know what she's doing." The glow from Diane's smile practically lit up the interior of the car.

"Di. Anne. You cougar! How did you manage that at a table full of people?" Jessica was genuinely impressed with Diane. The thought of merely flirting with Bobby, who she already knew, had her insides twisted, yet Diane could be introduced to a man and carry the whole thing to being excited about a first date in a span of an hour. She thought about what Bobby had said about Coach—how he disdained someone not willing to take risks. Wasn't that her all over?

As Diane began to talk, Jessica tuned out, reveling in the joy of her friend's chatter. Looking down at the light stain on her jeans, Jessica realized she was smiling. *What the hell?* Did she like Bobby? Was getting involved with him any kind of wise? What would happen if he found out what a coward she was? What if Diane was right—like she usually was—and he called her? What would she do?

CHAPTER
EIGHT

On Monday morning, Jessica sat at her desk with a cup of coffee, wishing she could start work on the James versus Wishingham matter, but until Coach was ready to engage, they were just circling. It would be another month or so before football season was over, and that was if they didn't make statewide playoffs. Instead, she looked at a stack of invoices and check stubs on her desk and decided it was a good morning to work on bookkeeping. She opened QuickBooks and set to work. Jessica didn't hate bookkeeping as much as a lot of lawyers she knew did. The orderliness of it made her happy. Everything had its place. The satisfaction of a balanced general ledger made her smile. Life was messy. Accounting was not.

The chimes of the front door alarm sounded, and Jessica looked up as Diane walked in, the distinctive *click-click* of her heels providing the percussion to her enthusiastic impression of Rod Stewart's "Do Ya Think I'm Sexy."

"Someone's in a good mood," Jessica called out.

Diane twirled around Jessica's doorjamb like it was a stripper pole. She shimmied down and up and asked, "How was your weekend?"

"Like you care how my weekend was," Jessica said, smiling and shaking her head. "You want to tell me about yours."

Diane flounced into the client chair and grinned. "Ask me how dinner went on Saturday."

"How did dinner go on Saturday?"

"Oh, the food was fine, I guess. We just went to Chili's. But afterwards . . ." All the weight of the world landed on the word "afterwards."

"You didn't take advantage of that poor boy, did you?" Jessica asked, knowing the answer to the question. What would it be like to be that free? Diane's ability to live in the moment mystified Jessica.

"I took advantage of nobody. That young *man* knew exactly what he wanted, and I allowed him to have *some* of it." Diane fished a nail file out of her purse and buffed out a spot on her left hand. "Never give it all up right away. Always leave 'em wanting more."

"I don't know what to say," Jessica said, laughing.

"Nothing to say, dear, nothing to say. Just be happy for me."

Jessica shook her head, impressed by Diane's ability to close a deal. "I'm happy for you." She was happy for her friend. Diane was pretty and fun and deserved all the good things. Jessica remembered Diane batting her lashes up at Lee in the Waffle House booth and tried to imagine herself doing the same thing with Bobby. She would just look ridiculous. Diane was infused with charm; Jessica had other attributes. Diane was an extrovert who needed constant activity and company; Jessica was an introvert who lived inside her own head. That was okay. The world needed different kinds of people to make it a different kind of place.

Diane leaned over the desk. "You don't look happy."

"I am." Jessica waved her off, suddenly aware of the silence of her internal reverie. "I'm just trying to finish this pile of billing so I can see if I get paid this month. But enough about that—you gonna go out with him again?"

"Oh, I don't know," Diane said. "He was fun to play with, and I'll probably see him again, but he's not long-term material."

"I have no idea how you do that," Jessica said. "How you just . . . play like that."

Diane leaned toward Jessica's desk, resting on her elbows. "Listen, honey. I had my true love. When David died . . . I'm not getting two of those, and I know it. Boys are toys and no more now." She rose to her feet, seeming to shake off her memories of David. "Coffee time! Gotta be perky when the phones start!"

As if on cue, the phone rang, and Diane clipped off on her heels to answer it. Jessica watched her go. She knew Diane's husband had died young of pancreatic cancer, but beyond that detail, Diane never much talked about him. So much of her was an open book that when she closed off a subject, Jessica thought it better not to ask about it. All Jessica knew was basic facts. Diane and David had been childhood sweethearts. They'd married right out of high school. David went to college and then got a job teaching at Ashton High. Diane had followed him to the front office. When he'd died, Diane had lost her mind a little bit— this much Jessica knew from Spencer Jacobsen, the lawyer she'd worked with when she first came to Ashton. Diane holed herself up for a few months, then came out roaring, sleeping with any guy who would have her. She quit her job and used David's life insurance money to go back to school and become a paralegal.

Jessica couldn't imagine being in her midthirties and having her husband die of pancreatic cancer. She'd been twenty-four years old when her own mother had died, and that had been hard enough. Picturing her mother now, only in her late fifties and shriveled and wasted, half out of her mind, Jessica still railed at the unfairness of it all. Even then, it was natural, normal, and expected to have your parents die. But a young husband? Jessica didn't know how she would react. Keith leaving her that terrible third year of law school had felt like a mortal wound, but Keith still existed in the world. It wasn't the same. She didn't dare judge Diane's reaction. All she knew was that it came from a place of unfathomable pain.

To think about Diane losing her husband so young and refusing anything but physical love was more than Jessica could manage on a Monday morning. She went back to her number work. She thought about how appropriate the word *numb*er was. It made her numb in a good way. It occupied her mind so that she couldn't think personal thoughts.

By 10:45, Jessica finished her bookkeeping with a sense of accomplishment and put the three-ring binder she kept her receipts in back on the shelf. She moved on to tackle a motion to suppress on the results of the Intoxilyzer machine for a DUI case she had coming up. Jessica—or, more to the point, her client—was trying to say that she was too drunk to understand when the officer explained that she had the right to refuse to blow into a machine that would say how drunk she was. If she could convince the judge that her convoluted reasoning was correct, then no one would ever hear the evidence proving that her client was, to use a technical term, shit-faced. Jessica felt okay with this, morally, because she knew her client was currently sitting in an inpatient rehab facility. This would do more for her than prison or community service in the long run, and cost her more than any fine. Jessica also knew it probably wouldn't work. Legally, voluntary intoxication, that is, drinking pitcher after pitcher of margaritas after work with friends and then driving one's self home against the advice of everyone else at the table, wasn't an excuse for what came next. Didn't hurt to try, though.

When she finished with that, Jessica opened up her email, her most dreaded task of the day. Her inbox cheerfully informed her that she had over three thousand unread emails. She set a timer for twenty minutes, because if she didn't set a time limit, she would be sucked into the vortex and never emerge.

Just as she deleted yet another ad for penile enlargement sup-plements, Diane appeared in Jessica's doorway again, this time with a shit-eating grin on her face. She coughed to get Jessica's attention. "There's a phone call for you, m'dear. Line one."

Jessica raised her eyebrows. "Did you ask who it was?"

"It's a Mr. Turnbull from the *Ashton Post*. He *says* he's calling on business."

Jessica's heart thumped. She breathed in through her nose and counted to seven before picking up the phone. She had been suc-cessful at shoving Bobby out of her brain every time he popped in it over the weekend, which was annoyingly often. Damn him for popping up in person, forcing the issue. "This is Jessica Fischer," Jessica said in her best professional lawyer voice.

She shooed Diane away with her hand, but Diane stayed rooted to the doorframe.

"Hey, Jess, it's Bobby." When Jessica didn't respond immedi-ately because, not that he knew it, her dry throat stuck to itself, he stammered, "Bobby Turnbull? From the *Post*?"

Jessica coughed to get things moving. "Yeah, Bobby, of course! How are you? How was the rest of your weekend?" She took a sip from her water bottle to clear the rest of the cement from her throat.

"Oh, good, good. Didn't do much. Mowed the lawn. Drank some beer. You know."

"Yeah," Jessica said, and sat in dumb silence for what felt like twelve years while Diane watched, her eyes wide and pleading for details.

"So, I, um, I meant to ask you . . ." he said, then trailed off.

"Yeah?" Jessica coaxed. Realizing what she was doing, she thought, *I guess I have my answer.*

"Did the DNA tests ever come back on Coach Wishingham? It seems like there's been plenty of time for them to come back."

As many thoughts flooded Jessica's mind as there were emails in her inbox. She shoved her unhelpful, if interesting, disappointment aside.

What should she say to Bobby about the DNA tests? She was not fond of lying. She could not, however, disclose that the DNA tests had come back because her client would not want her to. She was beholden to him. Normally, she could fudge an answer, but Bobby had asked her a direct yes or no question. She could say, "No comment," but wasn't that an answer? And that certainly wouldn't encourage other, more personal questions.

This, dammit, was why dating someone like Bobby was a bad idea. She chastised herself for being disappointed that his interest was solely professional. What if they were a serious thing and they'd been lying in bed after two glasses of wine and he asked her a question like that?

"Well," she said, stretching out the word into four or five syllables like a good southerner, stalling for more time. "Why should I tell you?" *Oh Lord*, Jessica thought. Why had she just said that?

Bobby laughed, thank the heavens. "Because I'm cute?"

"Why, Mr. Turnbull," Jessica said, adding molasses to her voice, doing her best Scarlett O'Hara impression, "are you attempting to suggest that I might violate attorney-client privilege simply because of that curly hair of yours?" She felt a zap of electrical short circuit in her brain, and everything went dark for a split second. Abort! Abort! Rewind! Who was this girl talking about curly hair? She had to get back to thinking about the law. Refocus! She squeezed her eyes shut and thought of a legal question. Was the information about the DNA test even protected by attorney-client privilege since Coach hadn't told it to her? Never mind. It seemed a good enough shield to hide behind for the moment. She busied her frontal lobes with puzzling out that ethical quandary so she wouldn't have to think about how insanely flirtatious she'd just sounded.

"Is it gonna work?" Bobby said, sounding every bit as flirty as she had a moment ago. This cat and mouse game might very well lead to her untimely death.

"I'm afraid not."

"Please?" Bobby wheedled.

"Have you ever heard that joke?"

"What joke?"

Jessica cleared her throat. "A piece of string goes into a bar and orders a beer. The bartender says, 'Hey, we don't serve string in here.' The string is offended, but also really, really thirsty. So he goes outside and ties himself into a knot and beats himself against the brick wall of the bar. Then he goes back inside the bar and orders a beer again. The bartender says, 'Aren't you that piece of string that was just here?' And the piece of string, acting all offended, says, 'I'm afraid not.'" When she didn't hear a response, she said, "Get it? A frayed knot?" Jessica laughed far out of proportion than the joke warranted, more from nerves than anything else.

"You're a nut."

"Maybe, but every single time I hear that phrase, *I'm afraid not*, I think of that joke."

"So you're not telling me about the DNA test?" Bobby pressed, clearly not going to be derailed from his mission.

"Nope."

"You're a *tough* nut."

"The toughest."

"But I can assume that *if* the DNA test came back, and *if* the DNA test showed that your client was not the father, I'd know. You'd be contacting our advertising department to take out an ad on the front page of the paper to announce that fact."

Jessica pressed her lips together in a tight line. Bobby was not wrong, but she was not telling him that either. "You can assume whatever you want, but I will neither confirm nor deny diddly-squat."

"I'm going to quote you."

"Be my guest. There's no such thing as bad publicity so long as your name is spelled correctly. Make sure you put the 'c' in Fischer."

Jessica could hear Bobby take a deep breath, and she wondered if this was it—if Diane was right, if he was going to ask her out. She couldn't let that happen. Not until she knew how she wanted to handle it.

"Anyway," she blurted out, "good talking to you, Bobby. Gotta go. Bye!"

Jessica hung up the phone before Bobby could respond. She rubbed her face vigorously with her hands and looked up to find Diane still planted in her doorway. Diane looked at her through raised eyebrows.

"What?" Jessica groaned.

"What my fanny. You cannot flirt with that boy like that and then just hang up."

"I don't know what you're talking about." Jessica turned back toward her computer and opened an email from the bar association inviting her to a sure-to-be-boring cocktail party where she could kiss some Very Important Backsides.

Diane, however, was not one to let work get in the way of an interesting conversation. "You might fool yourself, girlie, but you can't fool me. Poor Bobby likes you so much and you lead him on, and then *wham*—you just paint his balls blue."

"I didn't lead him on," Jessica said, a little indignantly. "A little innocent flirtation is a great distraction technique. I believe you're the one who taught me that nugget of wisdom."

"Not when you're young and cute and so is he, and *especially* not when he has a monster of a thing for you." Diane turned to leave, as if that finished the argument.

"Get back here, lady," Jessica said, suddenly feeling the need to blow all her frustration and confusion out at once.

"What?" Diane spun around on her heel, making her skirt billow like a figure skater's.

"Just because *you* have some kind of vicarious crush on Bobby and want me to have some grand romance so you can live it through me because . . ." Jessica thought better of saying the real reasons why. Diane started this mess by driving them to the Waffle House; it had to be her fault. Diane had this ridiculous belief that all of Jessica's problems could be solved with the right man. Ridiculous. Men only complicated things—how had Jessica's mother's life been made better having to raise her alone while her father went off to Arizona with a new wife? How had it been easier for Jessica to nurse her dying mother while she was grieving the only serious relationship she'd ever had? Meanwhile, Diane avoided relationships of any depth because she claimed to have been-there-done-that with her dead husband? It didn't make any sense to Jessica. "Because I don't know, it's more fun to watch than a soap opera?"

"You don't know what you're talking about," Diane said. "I can smell your pheromones from here, and you spent more time flirting with Bobby than talking business. Why would you do that if there wasn't more to come?" Diane coughed. "No pun intended."

"Or, and I know this will sound crazy to you, but there's a lot of ground between innocent flirting and 'more to come.' I may or may not even want to come more." Jessica realized how bad that sounded the second it came out of her mouth, and the twelve-year-old boy looking over her shoulder tried not to giggle. She couldn't deny she liked Bobby anymore, but she still wasn't sure it was a good idea to take the relationship anywhere. Even that short phone call was fraught with ethical quandaries. Any other reporter would have gotten a terse "no comment," and it would have been over. She couldn't let her feelings get in the way of her obligations to a client.

"Like hell you don't," Diane said. "There's not a person on earth who doesn't enjoy a good orgasm. Even you, Little Miss Chastity Belt." A lascivious grin crawled across Diane's face.

So much blood rushed to the surface of Jessica's skin she feared an aneurysm. In theory she thought women should own their sexuality, but she wanted to own hers and keep it private. The thought of Diane imagining Bobby bringing her to climax was humiliating. "Of course I do. But . . . but . . . well, I just see men . . . especially Bobby . . . as more than vehicles for my next orgasm."

"What are you implying?" Diane's face no longer looked friendly and teasing.

What? Why was Diane mad? Jessica was the one being tossed into bed with Bobby. Jessica was getting tired of this conversation and the whiplash-inducing trajectory of its moods. "I'm saying that since you want to have this vicarious romance with Bobby through me, the only thing you can think of for me to do is to hop into bed with him. Like, what else would I do on a date? Talk to him?"

Diane looked like she'd been slapped. "You watch yourself. I'm a grown woman who can do what she wants with her body."

"Absolutely you are. And so am I." Jessica tried as hard as she could to sound reasonable and conciliatory. "Which includes not doing stuff with my body that I don't want to do."

Diane huffed out a breath through her nose, all the animosity going out with it. "Then you shouldn't imply that you want to. Listen, m'dear, I don't think you'd be half as agitated as you are right now if you didn't really like Bobby."

The correctness of Diane's observation blindsided Jessica. She couldn't process it right now, so the only thing she could do was change the subject. She took a deep breath and blew it out, wishing she could blow away their previous topic.

"Did we ever hear back from the DA's office on the Stuckey case?"

Diane laughed. "Whoa! Way to change the topic! Segue much?"

"I don't want to talk about boys anymore," Jessica said.

"What if I do?" Diane raised an eyebrow, implying she had something to say.

Jessica sighed. "I don't want to talk about boys as they relate to me. Please?"

"What about boys as they relate to me?"

Jessica rolled her eyes. "You're impossible."

"Impossibly attractive." Diane was smiling again. Jessica dug through the basket of stress balls and found the one she was looking for. It was from the local power company, and it was shaped like a magnet. She tossed it to Diane, and it bounced off Diane's shoulder.

"Huh," Jessica said. "I would have bet my paycheck that would have stuck."

CHAPTER
NINE

~

It was easy enough for Jessica to keep herself busy for the next few weeks. The courts came to a grinding halt between Thanksgiving and New Year's Eve, and so everyone scrambled to get what they could done in late October and early November. Jessica filled her mind with trying to get as many clients out of jail as she could before the holidays, and resolving as many custody disputes, at least on a temporary basis, as was possible so that she wouldn't be getting tearful telephone calls the day before Christmas Eve about how a child's father "kidnapped" her and wouldn't let her mother have her for Christmas.

She hardly had the brain space to think about Coach Wishingham, who definitely wasn't worth thinking about, and Bobby, who probably was.

She stopped by the Kroger in mid-November one Sunday to find something to eat for dinner. She settled on a rotisserie chicken, which, after she picked on it as is, could then be scavenged to put atop a salad and thrown into canned soup. While waiting in the checkout line, she saw the *Ashton Post*'s headline: Abelard 28–Ashton 14. The great Coach Wishingham and his team had lost at State. She threw the paper on top of her groceries to read later.

At home, she spread the paper out on the kitchen table to

read as she gnawed the meat off a chicken leg. She wished she paid more attention to her father, who had a way of folding the paper in a complicated origami so that he could hold it up and read it as he ate without having to hunch over. It had been a good number of weeks since she last spoke to her father: she reminded herself to call him later in the day. He was unlikely to call her, but she still felt some kind of filial obligation to call him from time to time.

She skimmed the article about the football game. The description of the plays held no interest for her. She only wanted to know what Coach Wishingham had said to the reporters and whether or not he had made her job more difficult. Thankfully, no one seemed to much care about anything but football, and all his quotes seemed pulled directly from every hackneyed sports movie Jessica had ever been forced to see. "We lost our focus." "Abelard was a strong opponent." "We will come back stronger next year." "I'm proud of these young men." Blah blah.

She turned the page of the paper. The pages were so large she had to stand up to do it, and her chicken-covered fingers left a greasy handprint on the page. Why did newspapers make their pages so large? Wouldn't they be easier to read in a smaller format? Hell, they were easier to read online, which is probably where they were all going anyway. Still, there was something about the smudge of newsprint and the smell of the ink that made her think fondly of those few years when her father spread out the Sunday paper, her mother read a book on the sofa, and she lay on the floor with a box of crayons and a coloring book, trying hard to stay in the lines and make her pictures perfect.

On the next page was an article titled, "City Considers Roundabout; Citizens Weigh In," which wouldn't have interested her in the slightest except for the byline: Bobby Turnbull. She'd managed to keep Bobby out of her head for a few weeks, but there he was, on her kitchen table. She cringed thinking about their last conversation and how flirtatious she'd been. Where had that come from? It wasn't the kind of thing she'd normally say. She wasn't sure of its origin—had she said it because she genuinely wanted to flirt with Bobby, or was she just trying to deflect from the question he'd asked and that was all she came up with?

She closed her eyes and pictured Bobby. He did have nice, curly brown hair, and in a vacuum, running her fingers through it did seem like fun. He was a nice guy, and he'd been good company at the Waffle House. She could still scare up a sense memory of his hand on her leg when he'd dropped his scrambled eggs, and the warm feeling seemed like more than just the natural heat of his hand.

Jessica picked up the chicken leg and sucked on the end of the bone. Honestly, it didn't matter at all what she thought of Bobby, and whether or not dating him would put her in any professional quandaries. It had been more than two weeks, and he hadn't called her since she'd oh-so-humiliatingly mentioned that she wouldn't mind running her fingers through his hair, then hung up on him, and she'd gotten nothing but radio silence ever since.

Of course, nothing had happened on Coach Wishingham's case since then either. Clearly, she was just a source of information to him and nothing more. So be it. Life was easier that way anyway. Jessica eyed the other chicken leg and tried to decide if she should eat it or save it for another day. She pulled it off the chicken and bit in.

The next Tuesday, Coach Wishingham was back in Jessica's office. It was the first time they'd spoken since she'd emailed him about the DNA test, and, true to his word, he pretended like he'd just heard the news.

"Congratulations on your winning season," she said, shaking his hand quickly.

"We lost at State," was all Coach said in response. He seemed like he wanted to change the subject, but it seemed odd to Jessica not to talk about it, at least superficially.

"Yes, but you made it to State," Jessica offered, trying to get in his good graces by looking at the positive side. She was about to have a difficult conversation with him, and she needed him in a good mood.

"And lost. In the end, we lost because we lost focus," Coach said, sounding more like he was at a postgame press conference than meeting with his lawyer about a paternity suit. His shoulders relaxed, as if he realized he wasn't on the record and he could speak more freely. "Too many errors. Charlie Kicklighter—our only quarterback worth a flip—is so obsessed with his damn girlfriend that his head wasn't in the game. Abelard didn't out-play us; we beat ourselves."

"Right," Jessica said, and smiled, having reached the end of what she knew about Ashton's football season. "Shall we get to the case?"

Coach shrugged, as if he didn't care one way or another.

"Well, as you know, we got the results back from the lab DNA test, and you are Francesca's father. I know you talked about signing away your parental rights, but I have to tell you, that really isn't something you can do unless it is in the child's best interests."

"What about *my* best interests?" Coach Wishingham pounded a meaty fist on Jessica's desk so hard that her coffee cup jumped off the coaster. Jessica tried not to show her surprise. "Doesn't anyone give a crap about my best interests?"

"Honestly? No," Jessica said, secretly enjoying the look of disdain on Coach's face. "Look, right, wrong, or indifferent, better lawyers than me have litigated this issue before and the law is clear. The law says that as an adult, you can deal with the consequences of your actions, but Francesca is a child. She shouldn't have to deal with the consequences of actions the adults in her life took before she was born. She has the right to have parents, more specifically, the financial support of parents. Parents can't just duck out because it is inconvenient. It doesn't matter whether you're only now learning about her or whether you had her on purpose. You can sign away your right to visitation and whatnot, but you can't sign away your right to support her."

"So Sarah gets a big ol' pile of money just because she got drunk back in high school?"

Jessica struggled to keep her voice measured. She was not going to let herself be intimidated by him. She hadn't spoken to Sarah, hadn't even gotten her discovery answers because they'd all agreed to wait for Coach's stupid football season to be over. There was nothing to talk to Eric about over the past few weeks. But she didn't need to talk to any of them to know that Sarah had spent untold thousands of actual cash dollars taking care of a baby that Coach made just as much as she did and deserved at least a little reimbursement. How could he not see this? Such a typical bully—thinking if he said something loudly and forcefully enough people would just capitulate. "No. First of all, it's Francesca that gets the money, in care of Sarah. You had a drunken orgasm sixteen years ago that you forgot about. One of many, I assume," she added, reveling a little too much in the flash of anger in his eyes from her slight dig. "As a result, Sarah spent those past sixteen years raising a child. She spent sleepless nights with a crying baby. She took off work when Francesca got sick. She changed—and paid for—thousands of diapers. She bought food. She paid for day care and shoes and ballet lessons and I don't know what. Now she's asking for you to pay for your share and let Francesca take advantage of some pretty nifty state-sponsored health insurance that you get because you're a teacher."

"Whose side are you on, anyway?" Coach asked, looking at her like an unfaithful lover.

"Yours! Of course, yours." She was, actually, on his side, though she understood why he didn't know it. She was trying to get him to see right, to prevent him from looking like an asshole in court. How could she explain that without telling him flat out that he looked like an asshole *now*?

"It doesn't sound like it." Coach Wishingham rose out of his chair and leaned over the desk, towering over her.

Jessica imagined poor, drunk, teenage Sarah James flat on her back on a stranger's bed, this body looming over her. She swallowed hard, knowing she was toeing the line between her personal opinion and her legal obligation to her client. It was sharper than a razor blade and was starting to cut her feet.

"Look, Coach," Jessica said, in the most neutral voice she could muster. "One of the most important jobs I have in representing you is to predict what I think they're going to say. If I were her lawyer, that's what I would say. If you're on the stand and that's how you react, it isn't going to play well."

Coach sat back down. "Oh ho ho. Very smart." He touched his head and gave Jessica a conspiratorial look. She wasn't sure she *liked* that he thought they were of one mind, but at least he didn't see her as the enemy. "Like how I watch videos of other teams to try to guess how they'll play against us."

"Exactly," said Jessica. "And you just played right into my fake." She swallowed hard and made a promise to herself to donate to a domestic violence agency to atone for that lie.

"So how do we get around it?" Coach asked.

"I don't know that we *can* get all the way around it." Jessica took a large sip from a cup of water on her desk. Oh, how she wished the DNA tests had come back showing that Coach wasn't Francesca's father so she'd never had to have this conversation. She had hoped to avoid it, but no such luck. "Judge Brandywine isn't going to let you sign away your rights. Francesca stands to gain too much from you becoming her legal father—Social

Security, inheritance rights, health insurance, all of that. If you sign your rights away, she doesn't benefit. Generally, judges only let that happen if you're a child molester or predator or something awful like that. You're not, are you?" Jessica pulled off what she thought was a realistic-sounding laugh. "Besides. Even if you sign away your rights, you still have to pay child support, at least until she becomes an adult. It wouldn't do you any good."

"That's a terrible law," Coach grumbled, looking like he'd lost at State again because of bad referees.

"Hey, I don't write the laws; I just tell you what they are. I can tell you who our state senator is if you want to call him and get him to do something about it."

Coach waved his hand dismissively. "Bruce? Ah, I know him. I'll call him later."

Of course you know him. Jessica forced a smile. "It's not all bad news. They want sixteen years' worth of back child support. I found some case law that can limit your exposure since they did wait so long." She looked up at him. "Do you care about the reasoning behind that?"

"Nope."

"Okay, so we can try to cut that back, and maybe get you on a payment plan instead of a lump sum to make it more doable. Will you agree to that?"

Coach nodded and sighed. "If I have to. Honestly, I'd rather write one check and get it over with."

"Great," Jessica said. This was going better than she'd hoped. "I've got both of your financial affidavits, so it's just a matter of plugging the numbers into the child support worksheet. You get a credit for adding her on your health insurance. That's all easy. The tricky part is this: they really want you to meet Francesca." Coach had said he didn't want to meet her. Jessica didn't know why, didn't really care why at the moment, but if this was the issue that was going to screw up her resolving this case, she needed him to agree to meet Francesca. Besides, the optics of Popular-Coach-Wants-Nothing-to-Do-with-Love-Child were horrendous.

"No. Absolutely not." Coach made a ref's "pass incomplete" signal, waving his hands one on top of the other. He was not catching that ball. Jessica did not know a lot about football, but she knew a number of referee's gestures—her father loved to second-guess them on Sunday afternoons, standing up and yelling while repeating the movements when he thought they were wrong.

"They wanted me to show this to you." Jessica put a photo of Francesca on the desk. She was wearing a blue sparkly homecoming dress, the same color as her eyes. As Coach's eyes.

Coach picked it up and studied it, then put it back down on the desk. "She's hot. If I was ten years younger and not her father . . ."

Coach's lascivious tone brought bile to her throat. "That's disgusting!" Who could even think such a thing about his own daughter, much less say it out loud? Even if he were joking, that was no excuse. Lord, this man was a letch.

"What?" Coach asked, looking genuinely perplexed.

"She's your daughter *and* she's sixteen, for Chrissake!"

The irony of splitting his skull open with one of the Wonder Woman figurines on her display shelf appealed to her, but Jessica refrained.

"That's the age of consent." When Jessica didn't laugh, he threw up his hands. "You women have no sense of humor. Look, she's a pretty girl. She looks a little like me. She looks a lot like my mom." Coach looked down at his lap, a brief moment of silence.

Jessica looked at the top of his head. Was he honoring his late mother with a moment of silence, or was he coming up with something else gross to say?

Coach cleared his throat. "But that's a hard no. I don't want a relationship with her."

Jessica was actually starting to agree with him. She didn't want him having a relationship with Francesca either. Still, it made for bad theater, and she was the director of this play.

"So when they tell the *Post* that the Great Coach Wishingham has completely rejected out of hand the daughter he fathered in a rape sixteen years ago, I'm supposed to say . . . ?"

"How the hell am I supposed to know what you are supposed to say?" Coach said, all red-faced anger again. "Isn't that your job, to figure out what to say? Look, I didn't rape anyone. A nothing girl like Sarah James would have been happy to score someone like me in high school. If she didn't want to do anything, she should have kept her legs together. If she's going to lie there all splayed out for the taking, how is that my fault?"

A fire lit in Jessica's chest. She could get behind the idea that she didn't have to agree with her client, but did he have to make her job so bloody difficult? Did he not hear how offensive what he was saying sounded? Not just sounded—was! "Don't you think you bear any responsibility? You think it is entirely her fault because she was, what, wearing a short skirt?"

"Teenage boys can't control themselves. Hell, grown men barely can. That's right there in the Bible. You don't see King David getting chastised for succumbing to temptation, do you?" Coach sputtered, not letting Jessica get a word in. "No, you don't. You see the women getting their comeuppance for being temptresses. If girls don't want to be touched, then they shouldn't put themselves in a place where the touching is easy." When Jessica tried to speak, he put his hand up and rode the rumble of his baritone right over her soprano. "That's just common sense. Like you wouldn't park your car on the street with the window open and leave your laptop on the seat. That's just begging for your laptop to be stolen."

There were so many different shades of wrong in what Coach had just said that Jessica wasn't sure how to begin to approach it. The apples-and-oranges of the laptop analogy only scratched the surface. All she could do was stare open-mouthed: Jessica couldn't have spoken plain English if she wanted to.

Coach Wishingham, on the other hand, didn't seem to have that problem. He didn't seem to think that he'd said anything more controversial or irrational than two plus two equals four. "You just come up with something that makes me look good and tell that to the *Post*." He tapped his hand twice on her desk, a punctuation mark to end his sentence.

Jessica took a sip out of her water glass, her nostrils flaring with every breath as she tried to pull in more oxygen to her brain. Finally, she said, "I'll come up with something. In the meantime, I'll get those numbers together and run them by you before we propose them to the other side."

"Good girl," Coach said, and Jessica's head almost exploded. He might as well have scratched her behind the ears and given her a liver treat.

He walked out of her office and down the hallway toward the exit. When she heard the door close, she walked out of her office, Coach's file tucked under her arm. Diane was in the hallway, watching the door. Jessica looked at her, trying to bore past her hair spray and her skull to see into a brain that could find Coach attractive. What did Diane see? What else was there to this awful man? Jessica reached over and grabbed a tissue, handing it to Diane. "You might want to wipe the drool off your chin."

"That is a good-looking man."

"He's vile and disgusting."

"Oh, lighten up, Jessica. He's beautiful and charming. So what if he had a one-night something-something back in high school? He could have a one-night something-something tonight over at my house, and I'd stay sober so I'd remember it."

"Enough!" Jessica's roar froze Diane in her tracks. Jessica yanked the picture out of the file and shoved it in Diane's face.

"He looked at this picture of his daughter—*his daughter*—and basically just said, 'I'd tap that.'"

Diane took the picture from Jessica's hands. "Oh, wow," she breathed. "She *is* a beautiful girl. She looks just like him."

"Then he says he doesn't want to meet her, not now, not ever. He doesn't care what kind of psychological impact it has on his daughter, how it's going to affect her to have her father completely reject her like that."

Diane sighed and Jessica tried not to resent the sound. So often Diane downplayed Jessica's opinions, and it was really starting to get on her nerves. "Look at it from his perspective. He's had a pretty good life so far, except when his mom died his senior year of high school. Oh, that was so sad, but it made him even more popular. The girls doted on him. *Poor Tripp, let me comfort you.* Then he went on to play college football, came back a hometown celebrity, got to coach his high school football team to success. Everyone loves him, and then *bam*—this wrench gets thrown in the works."

"Some people might say this 'wrench' is an actual human with feelings that could enrich his life. Francesca is a girl who needs a father. And it isn't like he can't afford to pay child support," Jessica said.

"You do have a point there. Money's money, and it's nothing to him. But having a teenage girl in his life is a huge sea change. You can't expect him to welcome it with open arms. Lord knows his fiancée, what's her head, Emily Jenkins, wouldn't allow for that—she's closer to Francesca's age than his anyway. Besides—you have no idea. How do you know Francesca even wants to meet her father?"

"Well, Eric said she did. And how could she not?"

Diane sniffed in a way that made Jessica want to punch her in the nose. "You project your own feelings on every case you get. Want me to list the reasons? Maybe she's pissed off that he didn't reach out for sixteen years. Maybe she knows about his reputation and thinks he's an asshole and doesn't want to be associated with him. Maybe she's sixteen, and like every other sixteen-year-old on the planet, the less parental involvement, the better. I don't know. I'm not in her head. All I know is that just because Eric said she wanted to meet him doesn't mean anything. It means that Sarah wants her to meet him. Or maybe just that Eric knows that Coach doesn't want to meet her and so he's pushing for it just to keep Coach on the defensive. Look—everyone was happy before this mess. They can go back to being happy after it's resolved. Nothing has to get all crazy and rearranged, right? Coach just says that pervy stuff to distance himself from it. He can't let himself get emotionally attached to the girl." Diane paused, her expression changing from lecturing parent to sympathetic sister. "I mean, no one is that much of a jerk. Not really. They can't be. There's got to be a softer part of him inside."

Jessica was not in the mood to concede Diane any points, though she knew she'd have to give her some of them when she calmed down and thought about it. Instead, she focused her mind on a violent fantasy of slitting a tied-down Coach from throat to groin and reaching her hand in to find those softer parts in his rotten guts.

The next morning, rested and caffeinated, Jessica picked up a message slip Diane had left on her desk. Bobby Turnbull. Just seeing his name made her stomach clench. She hadn't spoken to him since she humiliated herself a few weeks ago. Jessica put the message slip underneath a stack of paperwork, promising herself she would call him back when she uncovered the slip.

It took her a while to do it, and by then she was so immersed in reading discovery responses and forwarding newly received motions to other clients that she had almost forgotten about it.

She toyed with the idea of reburying it, like she had buried daffodil bulbs in her front yard the evening before, using unnecessary force to hack away at weeds and stubborn roots in her way with a hoe. She had worked until it was too dark to work anymore, then found herself pleasantly sore and out of breath, covered in Georgia red clay. There was nothing like a shower when you were that dirty. She watched the streams of mud go down the drain, wishing she could wash away the unpleasantness with Coach just that easily.

No, she told herself. She had to be a big girl and call Bobby back. She'd just pretend that last conversation had never happened. Jessica thought of her professional brain as waffle shaped, with rows and rows of squares with high walls. She had gotten good at throwing things she didn't want to think about over the wall into a square of the waffle to deal with later. She'd toss that conversation into the back of the waffle and just deal with the square up front: the phone call. Besides, it was 12:30. He was probably out to lunch.

Dammit, he answered the phone, his rich brown voice filling the earpiece and giving Jessica a thrill she definitely didn't want because she didn't know what to do with it. "Thanks for calling me back," Bobby said. "I only have until three this afternoon before I have to turn this in."

"I'm not trying to avoid you," Jessica said.

"I know. Just . . ." Bobby trailed off.

Not wanting to give him the chance to complete his thought in case it was "Then why did you wait three hours to call me back?" Jessica launched into her prepared statement. "Coach Wishingham is still getting used to the idea that he is Francesca James's father. He wishes her nothing but good and happiness in her life and will assist her from where he stands. He's not proud of his behavior as a teenager and hopes that everyone understands that it doesn't reflect the man he has become. He also does not wish to disrupt Francesca's life any more than he already has. Coach Wishingham hopes that once the media has finished feeding off of this poor girl that they can all go back to living the lives they were living before this all began."

Jessica braced herself for the questions that she would ask if she were the journalist on the other end of the phone. *So you're saying Coach Wishingham wants nothing to do with his daughter? So you're saying that he gets to throw his great-granddaddy's money at this problem, and Sarah James gets stuck with the day-to-day fallout of having to deal with a heartbroken girl whose father rejected her? So you're saying boys will be boys, and we should just shrug our shoulders and move on with our lives?*

Instead, Bobby said, "Thanks, Jess. That's great."

Jessica's heart pounded at the way the informal *Jess* sounded in his voice. The *s*'s whispered in her ear and sent chills down her spine. Bobby's voice was surprisingly low. He'd have made a good radio journalist. "You're welcome," she said.

"Hey, are you going to the chamber of commerce's Casino Night on Saturday?"

"I guess," she said, her mind spinning into overdrive. Was he asking her to go with him? Was he checking to see if she'd be there to know if he should avoid her? She didn't know what to say, what he wanted her to say, so she told him the truth. "I bought a ticket because Nancy Trujillo was giving me grief about it, but I hadn't decided if I was actually going to use it."

"Use it," Bobby said. "I'll see you there." He switched into a very fake Italian accent. "I'll be da one wid a pink carnation in my lapel."

After they hung up, Jessica collapsed her forehead against her arms on the desk and breathed. She had other, better things to do than deal with the likes of Bobby Turnbull and Coach Tripp Wishingham and how they made her feel. Her feelings were penny-ante things compared to what was going on in the world.

She had important things to deal with, like the termination of parental rights case she was appointed on in juvenile court, and the domestic violence divorce she was working on at a cut rate in the hopes that the judge would award attorney's fees down the line. *Breathe in, breathe out, move on*, she thought, and picked up a different file.

Jessica got into work even earlier than usual the next day, feeling more energized than she had in weeks. She made herself coffee and checked her email. There was one from Coach Wishingham, which said, "Great job with the paper. Read the *Post* article. Perfect response." The article had been an absolute puff piece indicating that Coach could do no wrong, and Francesca should just count herself lucky to have such fabulous genes. It had made Jessica's bile rise, but still, she was proud of the work she'd done. It was great for her client. Professionally, that's what mattered.

She wondered if Bobby wrote the article the way he did because, well, because that was his way of flirting back. Surely Bobby was smart enough to probe a little deeper into the other side of the matter. Why hadn't he? Should she be grateful that her client looked good and was happy with her? Well, yes. But this was all the more reason why it was a bad idea to get into a relationship with Bobby. Her social life should not affect what gets published in the paper or have jack squat to do with her job. There were too many ethical quandaries like this one.

She decided to simply focus on the minor victory that was the article and get on with her day. Truly, she didn't know Bobby well enough to understand his motives for writing the article one way or another. Maybe that's really what he thought about things. If so, he wasn't anyone she needed to worry about. What would happen at Casino Night would happen at Casino Night, and she could deal with it then.

She was stacking the files on her desk in order of priority when Diane slumped into Jessica's office chair without her usual flair. "My sister is going to have to come in and see you with her daughter," she said, in lieu of a greeting or introduction.

"Okay," Jessica said, putting the filing down and looking up at Diane. She was startled to see Diane's eyes swollen with tears. "What happened?"

"My niece is pregnant." Diane's frosted hair was sprayed into such submission that it didn't fall forward even when she hung her head. "Kaitlyn. She's only seventeen. Just a baby! Babies having babies!"

"Oh no! What does she want to do about it?" Jessica scrolled through the options for why Kaitlyn might need to see her. There wasn't much she could do about anything legally until the baby was born, unless Kaitlyn wanted an abortion and Kaitlyn's parents were opposed and she was trying to get the court to give her permission despite that, and Jessica had never done that before, but she knew how academically . . .

"Not you too!" Diane shouted, interrupting Jessica's train of thought and making her flinch. "That's what her dumb-butt boyfriend said. Charlie. He wanted her to have an abortion. Like she would kill a baby like that."

Jessica backtracked. "Adoption?" Prebirth adoption contracts were complicated, but surely she could find a friendly lawyer to give her a template to go by . . .

Diane looked at Jessica as if she understood nothing about the world. "There's no way she could carry a child for nine months and then give it up to some stranger." Diane pulled a tissue out of the box on Jessica's desk and dabbed at her eyeliner with it. "Charlie. I'm gonna strangle that kid. How dare he! He's graduating in May and then he'll be gone, off to college, and he's going to have nothing to do with the baby or Kaitlyn. You know how it is. We've seen enough of those parade through this office. He's trying to go to West Point. I thought they only let the best in there. Officer and a gentleman my fat fanny. Gentlemen do not get their teenage girlfriends pregnant. Can you imagine?" Diane looked up toward the ceiling, clearly trying hard not to let the tears spill out and ruin her makeup any further.

Jessica had already said the wrong thing twice, so she said nothing. Her thought that only the rare high school senior hadn't had sex with his girlfriend, and Charlie was just unlucky to have one slip past the goalie was surely unwelcome.

After a few sniffles, Diane spoke again. "Kaitlyn is so naive. We kept her so sheltered. She met him in church camp. Church camp! We thought he was a good kid! Quarterback of the football team, goes to church every Sunday. Says please and thank you and yes ma'am and no ma'am. She couldn't possibly have known he would take advantage of her like that."

Typical Eddie Haskell type, Jessica's mom would have said. Jessica would have guessed Diane would have been able to see right through that if it were true. More likely than not, however, Kaitlyn would have a different story to tell.

Diane reached across the desk and took Jessica's hand. Jessica squeezed it.

"Can we file statutory rape charges?" Diane asked.

Jessica shook her head. "Honey, the age of consent is sixteen. She's old enough to consent."

"She couldn't possibly have consented! She's so naive! Can we file regular rape charges? Child molestation charges?"

Jessica jumped back into lawyer mode. Diane seemed to be running away with pure emotion, and Jessica needed to get her back on track before she did something rash like call the police on the poor kid for acting like a typical teenager. "Does Kaitlyn say he forced her?"

Diane shook her head.

"Then no."

"This is ridiculous." Diane stomped her foot under the desk. "The law doesn't help anyone."

"That's not true," said Jessica. "Once the baby is born I can help her get child support; I can make sure he is declared the baby's legal father so the baby can get all of Charlie's military benefits if he really does join the military. There's lots we can do. We just can't file rape charges. The law says Kaitlyn is old enough to decide if she wants to have sex with someone."

"She's just a kid! She had no idea what she was doing!" Diane roared.

Jessica knew that Diane had started dating her husband, David, much younger than at seventeen. Although seventeen-year-old Diane had to be a different creature than forty-something Diane, she was still the same person at her core. When had Diane lost her virginity to David? Probably about the same age—hell, they were married not long afterwards. Jessica herself had been eighteen, and she'd been one of the last of her friends. Jessica tried to think of someone else Kaitlyn's age that she knew, and Francesca James came to mind. Jessica waited a few beats, debated whether or not she should say it, then said quietly, "Didn't you say that poor, intoxicated Sarah James knew exactly what she was doing?"

Diane pulled her hands back and stood up, all in one motion. "That's entirely different!"

Jessica stayed quiet and calm. "Is it?"

"Go to hell!" Diane spat, slamming Jessica's door on her way out.

Jessica's hands shook, and she wasn't sure what to do next. Part of her wanted to chase after Diane and apologize. But apologize for what? For telling the truth? For pointing out the hypocrisy in Diane's attitude? If she was guilty of anything, it was poor timing. Not that there would ever be a good time. She heard the front door open and slam closed. Diane was gone.

If she were a real boss, she'd fire Diane for insubordination.

There was a good chance Diane would quit and never come back. Jessica hoped not. For all her uncomfortable attitudes about life, Diane was smart and good at her job, and she was a good foil for arguments. And she was a good friend. She called Jessica on her own bullshit, which meant she recognized the bullshit for what it was. She understood Jessica in a way few did. Diane would probably calm down and come back, Jessica told herself. There was nothing more to do about it now. She picked up her cup, but the coffee in it had gone cold and held no more comfort.

To keep herself busy, Jessica buried herself in work. She had a motion for summary judgment to write on another case, a long, tricky document with piles of research to collect. She let the phones go to voicemail and spread paper all over her desk and the floor. She immersed herself so deeply in her work that she didn't hear Diane come back in and sit down. When Diane said, "I brought you a Boston Kreme donut," she startled.

Jessica took the bag from Diane like there might be a bomb in it and pulled out the donut. She took a large bite. As she chewed, she searched Diane's face for clues about what to say. They continued to look at each other for a moment more, as if they were meeting for the first time and sizing each other up.

Diane spoke first. "You're right, you know."

Jessica smiled, relief washing over her. She realized she'd been more worried about Diane not coming back than she'd thought. So as not to ruin the moment by saying something wrong, she waited for Diane to tell her exactly what she was right about.

"I want to think of Kaitlyn as this little girl, the seven-year-old I used to take to get her nails painted and to Build-A-Bear. Not the seventeen-year-old I was in high school. I mean, gosh, David and I were already together and . . ." Diane took a big gulp from the Starbucks cup she held in her left hand. "Here's the thing. Kaitlyn is responsible for whatever foolishness she got into. But that doesn't make Charlie any less responsible. She wouldn't be pregnant if he hadn't done his part. He doesn't get to just skip away to college and leave her holding the bag, changing all the diapers and crying along with a colicky baby at three in the morning."

"Exactly," said Jessica.

"Just like Tripp Wishingham left Sarah James and Francesca sixteen years ago."

"Right," Jessica said, biting off "that's what I've been saying."

"Well, *now* I get what you've been saying. All of a sudden, I want his testicles in a bag."

Jessica fought the urge to lean over the desk and kiss Diane square in the middle of the forehead.

"Now," said Diane, the gears in her capable head clearly turning. "Since we can't do anything about Charlie till the baby is born, what do we do about Coach? How do we make him pay?"

"We don't," Jessica said, wishing she had a different answer.

Diane jerked back as if Jessica had slapped her. "Hello? You're the one who's been saying how awful he is. Now that I'm finally on board you mean we still go on telling the *Post* how great he is?"

"That's exactly what I mean."

"Why? I know people. We could do *a lot* of damage."

Jessica held back a grin. She liked this vengeful version of Diane, wanting to stand up for damsels in distress. "We won't. Look, I don't like the guy. At all. I think he raped Sarah James, and I think he's a reprehensible human being for refusing to meet his daughter. But I represent him. We can talk shit about him all we want in between these walls, but in public? Ethically, I can't do or say anything that can damage him in any way. I have to represent him to the best of my ability. That's what I intend to do. Since you work for me, that's what you're going to do too."

"But he's horrible!"

"Correct."

"How could you represent him if you hate him so much?"

"I believe in the system. Everyone deserves fair representation, and so someone was going to represent him. Someone was going to take his money. Might as well be me. At least if I represent him, I can use the money to pay you and the rent and cover expenses. This way I can do cases I actually care about, but that don't pay much, like appointed work in juvenile court. Besides, I've already talked him into paying her a few years of back child support in exchange for not filing rape charges or having an ugly trial. He'll pay child support going forward, and Francesca'll get his great teacher's health insurance."

Diane scoffed. "That's it? Money doesn't mean squat to him."

"That's our first offer. We'll offer two years back support. They'll come back with ten, and we'll end up compromising at around five. That kind of lump sum will pay for Francesca's college. Then he might—*might*—once things have calmed down, be willing to meet her down the road since we didn't burn down any bridges." Most of this was wishful thinking and educated guesswork on Jessica's part. The first offer was never the last offer. She knew how the game worked and where it usually landed. As for Francesca, that was all hope. She still had no idea what Francesca herself wanted, but she couldn't help projecting her own feelings. She remembered her father becoming more and more absent as her parents' marriage crumbled, and when he left the hole in her middle felt unfillable. When he moved to Arizona and became not much more than a voice on a telephone, the hole became a chasm. Her mother helped her fill it in with bitter feminism, covering it over with platitudes like "Women need men like fish need bicycles." But what she wouldn't have given for her daddy to come back, to read his Sunday papers and watch his football and go to her school plays.

In Jessica's perfect vision, Francesca wanted that, too, and Coach could give it to her. Easily. And maybe he would when he calmed down. She was proud of the work she'd done to keep that bridge intact. She told Diane, "If some other jerkwad was representing him, it might have turned into a much uglier show— name-calling, mudslinging, thousands thrown away on useless depositions and vengeful motions. Francesca and Sarah would have been a whole lot more hurt for essentially the same outcome, which is inevitable. Francesca gets what she needs, maybe down the road she'll get some more, and Coach thinks he won."

Diane looked at Jessica for a few beats. "You're smarter than you look, kiddo."

Jessica took Diane's hand and held it against her cheek. "Really? Because I was thinking I looked pretty smart already." Diane patted Jessica's face and went back to sit in the client's chair. "Charlie's last name isn't Kicklighter by any chance, is it?" Jessica said, remembering something from Coach's ranting the other day.

"How did you know?"

"Because, if it makes you feel any better, Coach is pretty pissed at him. Blames him for losing the playoffs."

"Small consolation."

"Take it where you can get it. And tell Kaitlyn and your sister to come in whenever. You're in charge of my calendar. I don't even know why you would ask me. Since when am I in charge around here?" Jessica's peace offering was larger than Diane's donut. Possibly more delicious too.

"I like to pretend that you *are* the boss," Diane said, faking a toss of her immobile hair. "It keeps you in line."

CHAPTER
TEN

~~~

J essica did go to the Casino Night sponsored by the chamber of commerce. She wore a red dress, along with red patent leather pumps that were about a half-inch higher than comfort allowed. She *didn't* go, however, because Bobby had told her to. Or, at least, that's what she was telling herself. Everyone who had anything to do with earning money in Ashton was going to be there. It was politicking. It was showing your face, being seen, and making sure that your elbows were rubbing up against the elbows that mattered.

Jessica had no interest in rubbing her elbows, or any other body part, for that matter, up against anyone else's, but she recognized the importance of networking to grow her business. So she parked her car and made her way across the Ashton Country Club's parking lot, wondering how Diane managed to walk on her toes like this every day without limping by the end of the afternoon.

Jessica spotted Nancy Trujillo working the check-in desk along with Kimberly Johnson. Inwardly, she groaned. As many times as Jessica had met Kimberly, she never could get beyond the "Hey, how are you doing?" stage of conversation. She wasn't sure if Kimberly was capable of more. Nonetheless, Kimberly was one of those people who was universally liked. She was pretty and friendly and helpful. Jessica knew it wouldn't do to be unkind to her just because she only had two dimensions.

Nancy, on the other hand, could be overwhelming. Jessica didn't generally disagree with Nancy's opinions, but Nancy had a lot of them, and they were all loud. If Nancy could dial it down a notch or two, Jessica suspected they'd probably be good friends.

"Jessica!" Nancy shouted as Jessica approached. "The woman in red!"

"Hi, Nancy," Jessica said, a few decibels quieter than she might otherwise have said it, just to make up for Nancy's volume.

"Look at you! I never see you wearing color. I love it! Ashton red! And you have legs! Who knew? Let me see!" Nancy came out from behind the table and hugged Jessica, then pushed her away and spun her around. Jessica made it all the way around without falling, no small task on the unfamiliar heels. "You should wear heels and short skirts more often. You really do have nice legs."

"Thank you," Jessica said, suddenly aware of how naked she was from mid-thigh down. Still, she stood up a little straighter and squared her shoulders. Jessica looked over at Kimberly, who was looking up at Jessica with wide blue puppy dog eyes. "Hi, Kimberly."

"Hi!" Kimberly uncapped a yellow highlighter and crossed Jessica's name off a list. She tore a strip of tickets off rolls in front of her and said, "The blue ones are drink tickets, and the red ones are raffle tickets. You can buy more blue tickets for five dollars and more red tickets for two dollars." She also handed Jessica a plastic bag full of poker chips. "Here's your gambling money. You can buy more of these at the table too. Whoever has the most at the end of the night wins the grand prize—a weekend at the Ritz-Carlton on Lake Oconee!" she squealed, sounding excited even though Jessica must have been the thirtieth person she'd told this to by now.

"Wow, that sounds fantastic," Jessica said, trying as hard as she could to muster up half as much excitement as Kimberly. Kimberly only grinned bigger. "Um, where's the bar?" Jessica asked, to have something to say and a reason to walk away from Kimberly. If she was going to survive this night full of fake smiles and I'm-fine-how-are-you conversations, she needed a drink in her hand.

Kimberly pointed toward the corner of the room and Jessica thanked her. She turned back to Nancy to say, "See ya later," but Nancy was busy fawning over the manager of the local bank and his wife.

Once she had a vodka cranberry in her hand, Jessica felt better. She actually didn't intend to drink much, but having a drink in her hand worked well. She could always put it to her lips if she couldn't think of anything to say, and it gave her hand something to do besides fluttering around awkwardly. This was not her scene. She didn't have the history everyone else in the room did. She couldn't talk about the same third-grade teachers or the same sermons from last Sunday. Nothing made her feel more like an outsider than when she tried to make her way in.

Jessica strode over to the blackjack table. She saw one of the superior court judges sitting there, and, not wanting to discuss work tonight, she'd nearly managed to turn away when he saw her and said, "Good evening, Ms. Fischer."

"Judge Miles," she said, stretching her lips across her face in a practiced grin. "How are you?"

"Down five hundred fake dollars." He reached in his back pocket and pulled out his wallet, then took out two real twenties and handed them over to the dealer, who passed over a pile of chips.

Since Judge Miles had seen her, she couldn't very well turn away now. Jessica sat down at the table and put a chip down in front of her. She was glad for the game because it gave her an activity and a topic. Time slowed as she focused on the game. A random assortment of people came and went in the chairs beside her. She won some hands and lost some, before getting on a winning streak. She didn't want to get up, but her bladder was begging her to. She stared hard at the cards and decided that as soon as she lost two hands in a row, she'd go. On a normal day, that would seem reasonable enough, but tonight, for some reason, it seemed she could not lose. The pressure in her lower abdomen continued to distract. *One more hand.* The first card laid down was an ace. The second a king. Blackjack.

"Dammit, Jess," she heard from her left elbow, "you took my ten!"

She turned her head. It was Bobby, looking at her with a crooked grin. Her heart pounded, bouncing between glad to see a friendly—and attractive—face and embarrassed that she hadn't noticed him sit down. "How long have you been sitting there?" She looked at his hand—an ace and a two.

"Longer than you might think. You're a pretty intense gambler," he said, holding her eyes in his own.

If you had asked her before this moment, Jessica would have told you that she preferred blue eyes, or green, or even hazel, that brown eyes were common and boring. But Bobby's were full of a depth and warmth that pulled her in and made her decide, right then and there, that she didn't care about Coach, or optics, or how difficult it would be to balance her law practice with the ethics of dating a reporter. "My powers of concentration are legendary."

"I can see that."

The dealer coughed.

Jessica startled and pointed at Bobby's cards. "You have to do something with that mess."

"Oh," he said, slowly turning his head toward the table. "Uh, draw?"

The dealer handed him an eight. "Twenty-one."

Bobby put up his hand for a high five, and Jessica indulged him. She wanted to grab on to his arm and not let go for the rest of the night, but all her brain focused on holding a Kegel. She slid off the chair and gathered her chips. Bobby gave her a kicked puppy look. "You're not leaving just because I'm sitting here, are you?"

"No," she said, "I'm leaving because I have to pee. Badly." Bobby choked on a laugh, which made him cough. This made Jessica laugh, which increased the urgency of the situation. "I promise I'll be right back."

Bobby put his hand out. "Gimme."

Jessica was shifting from foot to foot. "Give you what?"

"Gimme your chips. I'll hold them. Collateral that you'll come back. Plus, you don't want to put them down on that nasty bathroom floor."

"Sure, fine, whatever." Jessica practically threw the plastic bag at him and teetered toward the bathroom.

When she got back, he was standing in exactly the same place, holding her bag of chips, plus a fresh vodka cranberry. "Cranberry juice is supposed to be good for your kidneys. From the looks of it, yours are working fine." He held out the drink.

Jessica took it, hoping her blush was hidden by the dim lighting in the room.

Bobby tilted his chin toward the corner. "Your boy is over there working the room."

Jessica followed the direction of his chin and saw Coach at one of the poker tables, paying little attention to the game and clearly the center of attention. It wasn't surprising that Coach was there—it was surprising that she hadn't felt his Great and Glorious presence enter the room. Ah well, her powers of concentration were legendary, after all.

"You wanna go over and say hello?" Jessica couldn't read Bobby's question—was he serious? Was he teasing her? Was he testing her in some way?

"Oh, God, no."

Bobby laughed. "Why not?"

Scrambling for an answer that she wouldn't mind echoed back at her from the pages of the *Post* tomorrow morning, she mumbled, "I try not to mix business and pleasure."

The sides of Bobby's mouth curled upward, and the corners of his eyes crinkled. "Glad to see I fall in the 'pleasure' category."

"Hey!" Jessica said. She tapped his chest. "You're actually wearing a pink carnation!"

"I never bluff. That's why I don't play poker."

Laughter rumbled over the room from where Coach was sitting. Jessica tugged on Bobby's elbow, eager to get out of the room before Coach caught her eye. If she was lucky, she could leave Casino Night without ever acknowledging Coach's presence. "Let's check out the silent auction crap," she said, pulling him into the next room.

By the time the evening was over, Jessica found herself the proud owner of a framed sunflower painted by one of the teenagers at the Boys & Girls Club, courtesy of the silent auction. It would look cheery in her lobby. She managed to avoid Coach Wishingham while saying hello to everyone she needed to say hello to in order to maintain her status as a Businessperson of Consequence in Ashton. Her main focus of the night was Bobby, who never left her side. As they were heading out, Bobby insisted on walking her to her car and Jessica immediately pictured the files piled on all the seats, cardboard coffee cups in all the cupholders, and receipts that littered the floorboards. Not only was it a mess on the inside, but she couldn't remember the last time she'd washed it either. But there was no turning Bobby down, southern gentleman that he was. Not that she wanted to turn him down, not after all the times he'd touched her arm to guide her and he'd spoken volumes to her just using those beautiful brown eyes of his. She just didn't want to be judged by her wreck of a vehicle.

As they neared her car, the floodlights in the country club parking lot highlighted the filth on her back window. Bobby wrote "wash me" on it with his index finger, and Jessica laughed. She hadn't realized how funny and easygoing he was. He'd just been Bobby Turnbull from the *Post* to her before.

"It's not going to work," Jessica said. "I'm not going to wash it. I think the dirt is the only thing holding it together. I've had this car since freshman year of college."

"That shows you're loyal." He was doing that thing again, where he held her eye contact longer than would have been comfortable with anyone else, but where she thought she could stare forever without blinking.

"To a fault," she said. Jessica looked up as thunder rumbled distantly. "I'd better go before it starts to rain."

"Yeah," Bobby said, putting out his arms. He leaned forward.

He's going to kiss me, Jessica thought, unsure how she felt about it. Her body wanted to kiss him, her heart wanted to kiss him, but her damn mind still wondered if it was a good idea in practical terms. Bobby just wrapped his arms around her, crushing her face into his chest. She hadn't turned her head to the side, thinking she was going to be kissed. He smelled of complicated cologne and natural musk. She liked it. He let go and she pulled back. A kiss of red lipstick was planted right above his breastbone, and she scratched at it.

"I think I got lipstick on your shirt," she said softly.

"My wife's gonna hate that."

"Wait. You're married?" Jessica's intestines froze in place.

Bobby laughed. "No. I just thought it would be funny to say that."

"It was," Jessica said as her innards melted and began to work again.

"Hey." Bobby took a deep breath. "Can I try to make you laugh another day? Without playing hide-and-seek with Tripp Wishingham? Like in a restaurant or a coffee shop?"

"Yeah," she said. "I think I'd like that."

CHAPTER
ELEVEN

—————

First thing Monday morning, Diane, Kaitlyn, and Diane's sister Denise sat in front of Jessica as if she were the Oracle of Delphi. The older women clung to Kaitlyn as if letting go would allow her to float to the sky, away from them and out of their protective grasp.

"Okay," Jessica said, pretending she had the oracular answers they thought she did. "Diane already gave me the rundown on what happened, so I'll tell you what I know and you can fill in what I missed. Before I begin, I want to reassure you that I am not here to judge anyone for anything. We are here to deal with a situation, and that is exactly what we are going to do. I won't dance around what happened; I'm just going to call it what it is. I hope we can all do the same."

The three women nodded at her. Jessica looked at them each in turn. Diane was Diane, ready to get on with things. Kaitlyn looked like a spooked fawn, ready to run. Denise looked hard and skeptical—she was the one that Jessica was going to have to win over to accomplish anything. Jessica tried to imagine poor scared Kaitlyn having to come to this judgmental face to admit not so much being pregnant, but having had sex in order to become pregnant. As scared as Kaitlyn looked, she had to have some bravery in her just to get the job done.

Jessica decided to focus her remarks toward Kaitlyn. After all, Kaitlyn was her client, and Denise needed to understand that she wasn't going to run the show entirely. "So as I understand it, Kaitlyn, you and Charlie were in a relationship and you were sexually active?" Jessica asked. Kaitlyn nodded, looking like a puppeteer was forcing her head to move. "And you both agreed to be, right?" Kaitlyn nodded again, in that same stiff way, her face expressionless except for doe-eyed fear. "And now, you find yourself pregnant." Kaitlyn nodded a third time. To encourage her to speak up for herself, Jessica asked, "When are you due?"

Denise answered for her. "March fourteenth."

Jessica looked at Denise. "Denise. I know she's your daughter and you want to help her, but she is in a grown-up situation here. She has to take the lead. You can cheer her on from the stands, but she's got to play point. Okay?" Denise was a good twenty years older than Jessica, but Jessica tried to stare her down in the way a third-grade gym teacher would a ball hog on the playground.

"She's scared and nervous. Why can't I answer simple questions like that?"

"It's not that you can't; it's that you shouldn't. Kaitlyn is about to file a lawsuit against a guy I'm guessing she whispered 'I love you' to in the back seat of a car."

"Wait!" Kaitlyn croaked, finally speaking up for herself. Everyone stopped what they were doing and swiveled to look at her. "I'm sitting right here."

"I'm sorry, Kaitlyn," Jessica said, meaning it. "I shouldn't have said it like that, and I'm getting ahead of myself. I got mad—on your behalf—and my filter broke."

"Don't you dare!" snarled Denise.

Jessica held up a hand, wishing she could rewind. "Look, here's what I'm trying to say. You and Charlie were—are—in love, right?"

Kaitlyn nodded, the fear in her eyes replaced with suspicion.

"And because your parents didn't approve of what you were doing, you had to go underground, so to speak. As a result, there's going to be a baby. You may or may not want to file a lawsuit against Charlie, and Charlie may or may not sincerely want to be involved in this baby's life, but the law is a weird thing. Unless you file a lawsuit, Charlie isn't the baby's legal father, and Charlie has no rights to the baby and, more importantly, the baby has no rights to Charlie. We'll get more into that later. In the meantime, you've created a whole human being with him. Which is why I'm trying to tell your mom," Jessica switched her gaze over to Denise, "that how you go about your day is your business and hers, I guess. But how you behave in terms of this lawsuit is my business. Kaitlyn needs to take ownership of this problem. Eventually, she'll have to show the judge that she is a fit and capable parent to this baby. She can't do that if she defers to Grandma for everything."

When Denise didn't respond, Jessica nodded and continued. "Okay, you're due March fourteenth. You're seventeen now?" Kaitlyn nodded. "When do you turn eighteen?"

Denise opened her mouth to answer, and Jessica gave her one of her patented looks, the kind she practiced in a mirror to cut down enemies with lasers.

"February twenty-fifth," Kaitlyn said. Her voice was small and high and rose at the end as if she were asking a question. She was nervous, that was clear, but Jessica was glad, at least, that she was speaking for herself.

"Good," Jessica said. "Then you'll be eighteen when the baby is born, assuming it isn't premature. Do you know if it is a he or a she?"

"No. I want it to be a surprise," Kaitlyn said, smiling genuinely for the first time since she'd come into Jessica's office.

Denise rolled her eyes and said, sotto voce, "Isn't this whole thing a surprise?"

Kaitlyn glanced sideways at her mother as Diane looked up toward the heavens and clenched her fists. Jessica assumed they'd had this conversation before and it was one of the few arguments Kaitlyn had won.

"Well," said Jessica, "we can't file anything until the baby is here, but we can have everything drawn up and ready to go. This way all we have to do is fill in the birthday and the name. Charlie has got to pay child support."

"If you will allow me to speak," Denise said imperiously.

Jessica thought of a thousand responses, none of which were appropriate in a professional setting. Instead, she raised her eyebrows and gestured for Denise to continue.

"How is Charlie supposed to pay child support? He's a child himself, just like Kaitlyn. He's still in high school, for goodness' sake. I mean, I'd like to cut off the kid's balls and sell them on the open market to pay for diapers, but realistically?"

"Realistically, that isn't our problem," Jessica said. "Someone has to pay for the baby's food and that little bulb thing that sucks out boogers and all that other crap that goes along with babies. Why should Kaitlyn be left holding the entire bag?"

"It won't be Kaitlyn; it will be me." Denise's stiff posture straightened even more.

"Exactly," said Jessica. "Why should it be you? You, I presume, will be helping Kaitlyn in the middle of the night and changing more than your fair share of diapers. Why should you also foot the bill financially? Charlie has to figure out a way to pay child support, even a token amount. The minimum amount by law is seventy-five dollars. People in prison who have no way of earning a living get ordered to pay seventy-five dollars a month. Charlie can get a part-time job and stay in high school and pay at least that, maybe more." Jessica could—and had—argued this both ways, but she couldn't argue with the law, and here it was, on her client's side. It didn't sit right with her that Kaitlyn had to find a way somehow to provide, even if it was relying on the charity of her mother, and Charlie didn't. For all she knew Charlie's mother would be as generous as Kaitlyn's, but that was hardly the point. Kaitlyn had a squirming, crying, pooping reminder of her obligation living in her house. Charlie at least ought to have a court order reminding him of his.

"He's not going to want to," Kaitlyn said, doing a much better job of standing up and advocating for Charlie than she'd done for herself a few minutes ago. "He has football training every day. He's counting on scholarships to college, and if he doesn't keep up with his training he won't get scholarships. He wants to go to West Point. Did you know that? He can't get a job. It would ruin his chances."

Jessica took in a breath and held it for ten seconds before blowing it out. She had to wait a moment before speaking or she wouldn't use her nice words. "Honey," she said. "Listen to what you're saying." Kaitlyn wrinkled her eyebrows and tilted her head as if she really could hear the echo of her words in the small office. "What you are saying is that it is okay for you and your family to take on the entire burden of this child so that Charlie can go about his life just as he planned it."

"But he's—"

Jessica cut Kaitlyn off. "But he's nothing. I don't give a crap what he is. Are you still going to be on the cheerleading team? Are you still going to be able to be on yearbook or debate team or whatever it is you do at school, or are you going to be at home changing diapers and taking care of a baby? Why does he get to live his best life if you don't get to do your thing?"

"Well, no, but I'm going to be a mom with a baby at home," Kaitlyn said. She patted her little basketball belly with no small amount of pride. It was adorable, Jessica thought, and sweet, but also incredibly naive. Poor girl had no idea what she was in for.

"Well, he's going to be a dad with a baby at home, same as you. He is no less Dad than you are Mom."

If Jessica didn't know the three women were related before, she knew it then by the way they all pursed their lips the same way: gathered up and to the left, with their right eyebrow slightly raised.

Jessica cleared her throat. "Are you and Charlie still together?"

Denise and Diane both said, "No."

Kaitlyn cut her eyes toward her mother and then said, "No?" in that questioning way she said most things.

"Charles is not welcome in our home," Denise said. "He disrespected our rules and our daughter. I do not trust him."

Jessica knew she would have to talk to Kaitlyn outside of Denise and Diane's presence. Obviously, Kaitlyn and Charlie were still an item: Denise's forbidding the relationship had just driven it undercover. "Are you and Charlie still talking?"

Kaitlyn nodded her head.

"Are you including him in the pregnancy?"

"What does that mean?" Kaitlyn asked, her question mark finally warranted.

"Letting him go to doctor's appointments, giving him updates on the size of the baby, progress, that kind of thing."

"Why would an eighteen-year-old boy go to a gynecologist's appointment," Denise asked without a question mark.

Jessica looked at Diane before she looked at Denise to answer the question. She hoped that their usual ability to communicate without speaking would do some good in this situation. Diane was usually so vocal—why hadn't she said anything in this meeting? The whole point of her being in this room was to help support Kaitlyn and wrangle her sister. Just sitting there silently, she was doing neither. Now would be a good time for Diane to pipe in with the thousand reasons why Charlie should be at his child's prenatal checkups. When she didn't, Jessica did it for her, resenting the fact that she had to be doing all the talking in this family drama. This part wasn't really legal advice—why was she giving it? "I'm going to rephrase your question so that maybe it will answer itself," said Jessica. "Why would the baby's father want to go to the obstetrician's appointment to hear the heartbeat and see the ultrasound pictures of his child and make sure his baby is healthy?"

Denise looked a lot like Diane but wasn't half as attractive. Her features were sharper, as if drawn with a finer point pen. Her hair was a shade brassier. Her chin pointed a little bit further upward. Her blue eyes managed to be the same color as Diane's but were crystalized ice instead of warm skies. She focused on Jessica with an intensity that Jessica imagined had withered Kaitlyn on many an occasion. "You don't seem to understand. This boy took advantage of Kaitlyn. Maybe we sheltered her too much, but she had no idea what she was getting into with him. I don't care what you want to call it, but I will never think anything other than that he raped her. He may have impregnated her, but he will never be my grandchild's father to me. God punished her for her weakness with that rape, but He blessed her repentance with this miracle of a child. I will not allow that boy to have any joy from this miracle. Do you understand that?"

Jessica said nothing, not trusting herself to say anything more polite than, "What the hell is wrong with you?" She studied Kaitlyn, whose blue eyes, the same color as her mother's and aunt's, were rimmed with red and overflowing. Kaitlyn did nothing to stop the river of tears that dripped silently onto her folded hands in her lap. Diane looked off into the middle distance with an expressionless face.

"May I speak with my client alone, please?" Jessica said, keeping her voice as even as possible, despite the indignant rage rising in her throat.

Diane nodded across Kaitlyn to a skeptical Denise. The sisters left the room without a word.

Jessica picked up the box of tissues on her desk and handed it to Kaitlyn. "You don't think Charlie raped you, do you?" she asked as gently as she could.

Kaitlyn shook her head.

"Neither do I." She paused. "You're still involved with him, aren't you?"

Kaitlyn nodded.

"Let's make one thing clear. I'm your lawyer, not your mom's or your aunt's. I'm super good at keeping secrets. There are some things I have to tell because they are part of the lawsuit, but there are lots of things that I don't have to tell. As far as I'm concerned, the two of *them*," Jessica pointed her chin toward the door, "are on a need-to-know basis, okay?"

Kaitlyn nodded again, and this time she was smiling.

"It's not just because I want to keep your secrets, but because I have to. There's such a thing as lawyer-client privilege. When just the two of us are talking, if you don't want me to tell, I can't tell. And if I do anyway, you can complain to the state bar and they can take away my license. I'd have no way to earn a living because I have no other job skills. Got it?"

Kaitlyn nodded again.

"Realistically, there's only so much I can do, like kick your mom out of the room. You've got to live with her, and you'll need her help. So, let's come up with a high sign. I don't mind being the bad guy, but I need to know when you need my help. Is there some word you can manage to work into a sentence or a gesture that will signal me that I need to get your mom out?"

Kaitlyn grinned big, looking relieved, and that made Jessica smile. Jessica guessed that for the first time since Kaitlyn peed on a stick, she felt like she had some control over her life.

"How about," Kaitlyn ventured, "if I scratch my elbow like this."

"That will work," Jessica said, "but only if you would never otherwise scratch your elbow like that. Do you normally have itchy elbows?"

Kaitlyn giggled. "No."

"Then elbows it is." By the power of suggestion, Jessica's own elbows began to itch, and she scratched them. Jessica leaned across the desk. "Listen, Kaitlyn, I don't know your mom all that well, but I know your aunt Diane better than just about anyone else around here, and I know she's one tough cookie. I also know how gross it feels to be on the receiving end of her judgment. As tough as she is, Diane seems a lot softer than your mom."

"Oh yeah," said Kaitlyn.

"Look, I don't have kids, so I can't know how she feels. But I don't know if any adult has told you this: it is completely normal for a seventeen-year-old girl to have sex with her boyfriend. It doesn't make you a slut or a whore or anything. Girls and boys are both equally sexual. There seems to be this idea that if a boy wants sex, it's totally normal, but if a girl does, then there's something wrong with her. That's a bunch of bullshit. You didn't ask for this pregnancy; it just happened. Things happen. But just because you're the one with a uterus, it doesn't mean that the baby is any more yours than Charlie's. The both of you made the baby. You're Mom and he's Dad. Moms don't have to sacrifice more than dads."

Kaitlyn's head nodded like a bobblehead doll. The tears came fast and furious.

Jessica had no idea what she was supposed to do next. Kaitlyn was small, like her mother and aunt, her growing belly highlighting the tininess of the rest of her. The tears made her shrink even further. Jessica had an urge to scoop her up and hug her, to stroke her hair and promise her everything would be okay. But that seemed too intimate, and maybe too much of a lie. What was Kaitlyn thinking? Was she mad at her mother? Mad at herself? Mad at Charlie? Or just so focused on being in love with Charlie and the baby and a romantic idea of playing house? Jessica imagined herself at seventeen, impregnated by her own boyfriend at the time, and shuddered at the thought.

She had to get back into lawyer mode, and she had to get Denise under control. Whatever Kaitlyn thought of what Denise had said, however used to that kind of speech she might be, it was not okay.

"Do you have any questions for me?" Jessica asked Kaitlyn.

"What do I do now?" Kaitlyn asked.

Jessica laughed softly. "Well, first thing to do is try to get your mom off your back. Take your vitamins. Put your feet up. Do your homework. Bake that baby as best you can. I'll work on the paperwork so we can get everything rolling as soon as it's born. Remember: if you start to get hassled about anything I can do something about, you can always say, 'I don't know, can we ask Jessica?' and put it off on me. I've got your back. Seriously. Use me as an excuse for whatever you need. I'm a lawyer. I don't have skin; I have rhino hide." Jessica pinched herself as demonstration.

Kaitlyn started crying again. "Thank you."

"So tell me. I promise I won't tell your mom or aunt. What is your deal with Charlie?"

"I love him," she said, and by the look that came over her face, Jessica knew she meant it. "I know everyone says I'm just seventeen and I don't know what that is, and maybe I don't, but I know what I feel and I love him. He loves me too."

Jessica fought the urge to kiss Kaitlyn on the top of the head. It seemed so unprofessional. "What does he think of the baby?"

"We talk sometimes about what it would be like if we could just run away from our parents and their expectations, and just live like a little family. He's *so* smart. He could get a job somewhere and go to school at night, and once the baby is old enough, I could go to college too, and maybe get a job. We could do it, we really could, but neither one of us wants to give up our whole families like that," she said, all in a rush.

"Charlie says if we just have a little bit of patience, in four years the baby will still just be a toddler and he'll graduate from college and then we can get married and start our lives. He'll be home on school breaks and summers, and we can go up there and visit. I can wait. I feel like Charlie is worth waiting for." Kaitlyn blew her nose, took another tissue, and cleaned the rest of her tears off her face. "Mom doesn't. She hates him, now that peanut is here." Kaitlyn gestured at her belly. "She won't even acknowledge that no matter what, he's going to be this baby's father and a part of my life, even if we did really break up."

"Have you talked to her about this?" Jessica suspected that Kaitlyn didn't have a whole lot of adults she could talk to and felt an urge to be there for her, beyond what was legally required.

Kaitlyn rolled her eyes. "I can't even say I want to buy St. Charles Place when we play Monopoly. She can't hear his name without getting totally crazy crackers."

"I don't doubt that," Jessica said. "Hopefully, she'll lighten up when she gets used to the idea."

"Hmph," Kaitlyn snorted. "You don't know her. That lady can hold a grudge. My friend Madison? When we were eleven? She slept over one night and had to go to the bathroom, and she clogged the toilet and didn't tell anyone about it because she was embarrassed. I mean, I totally get that. Mom didn't. She found it and had a fit about it, and now every time I even mention Madison's name she talks about how irresponsible and filthy she thinks Madison is. I'm like *Mom*, that was six years ago and she was just a kid. Get over it already!"

Jessica couldn't stop laughing, thinking about poor preteen Madison. She was surprised Kaitlyn and Madison were still friends. Seventeen-year-old Jessica would have been too humiliated to ever show her face in front of Denise under those circumstances. Hell, even now, twenty-nine-year-old Jessica would have a tough time of it.

"Okay," Jessica said, still chuckling, "I think I've got a pretty good lay of the land. Let me go out and talk to your mom for a minute, and then I'll bring her back in. You good with that?"

"Do we have to bring her back in?"

"Eventually, yeah."

"Ugh," Kaitlyn said. "But I'm holding you to the scratching my elbows thing."

"Deal."

Jessica left Kaitlyn holding the box of tissues and closed the door to her office. She walked over to Diane's desk where Diane and Denise sat in stony silence. They stood when they saw Jessica, prepared to walk back to where Kaitlyn sat.

"Hold up," said Jessica. "Before we go in there, I want to say something." She took a deep breath and faced Denise. "I get that you believe Charlie raped Kaitlyn. But Kaitlyn doesn't think Charlie raped her."

"You have—"

Jessica held up a hand and cut her off. "I'm not done. When you say things like that, you negate her autonomy. You tell her that the choices she made were not valid."

"They weren't valid! She didn't know what she was doing!"

"Stop it. Stop it right now. You can say and do whatever you want when I'm not around. But if you want me to help you out with this, in my presence, anyway, you will treat my client with respect."

"Your client is my daughter, and I will not have you telling me how to parent her."

They stared daggers at each other. Jessica hoped that Denise couldn't hear the loud heartbeat pounding in Jessica's ears. She clenched her fists to stop her hands from shaking. That poor girl in there needed her mother in her corner, not to baby her or to make her into a victim, but to recognize her for who she was. Jessica fought the urge to sneak a glance at Diane to see how she was reacting to this confrontation, but didn't dare be the first to break the stare-down.

The seconds ticked audibly on the large wall clock that hung above Diane's desk, each one louder than the last. Finally, Diane came into view, placing her hand on her sister's shoulder. Denise shifted her gaze to Diane's hand, breaking the standoff. "We can talk about this later, Sissy. Go in the bathroom and fix your mascara and lipstick and meet us back in Jessica's office."

Denise spun on her heel in a very Diane-like way and disappeared into the bathroom without a word.

Diane shook her head. "You may have made a powerful enemy there, girlie."

"Everything I said was right."

"You've got to learn to separate right and wrong from should and shouldn't."

Not knowing what else to say, Jessica said, "Let's go get to Kaitlyn before Denise does."

When Kaitlyn and Denise had left the building, Diane came into Jessica's office and sat down. "So, what did you and Kaitlyn talk about in the room alone?"

"You know I can't tell you that."

Diane's chin dropped. "Uh, hello? Since when don't you tell me what happened behind closed doors?"

"Since your niece is the one behind those closed doors."

Diane groaned. "How am I supposed to do my job if you don't tell me what is going on?"

"I will tell you everything you need to know to do your job, but I'm not going to tell you any more than that. That poor girl! Her mother is so hard on her."

"I know," said Diane. "I still want to kill Charlie Kicklighter."

Jessica raised an eyebrow. "I'm fine with Charlie. I want to slap your sister."

"After today, she probably wants to slap you more."

"She hasn't spent five minutes looking at any of this from her daughter's perspective. She has tons of sympathy but not an ounce of empathy." Diane opened her mouth to speak, but Jessica cut her off. "Listen, we have more important things to talk about."

"Not by a—"

"Bobby Turnbull asked me out." Jessica hadn't planned on telling Diane, but by her reckoning it was the only way she could get Diane to quit talking about Kaitlyn.

"What?" Diane shot up. "How was that not the first thing you said this morning?" She was all but shouting. "Where? When? What are you going to wear?"

"Calm down, Chief," Jessica said. "It wasn't that formal. After the chamber Casino Night. He walked me to my car. He didn't really ask me out. He asked me if he *could* ask me out, and I said okay."

"You kids are ridiculous. You never get to the point. You do these stupid dances all around the main issue. Ask if you can ask. Ha! Stupid." Diane sat back down in the chair so quickly that her skirt billowed up and showed off the fact that her underwear was red and satin.

Jessica shielded her eyes. "Diane! Don't flash me! He was sweet."

"He was sweet!" Diane mocked. "Sweet doesn't get you laid, and that's what you need, m'dear."

Diane wasn't wrong, but that didn't mean that Jessica wanted to hear it. She looked around her desk for something to throw and came up short. Her basket of stress balls was empty, the lot of them having been tossed at Diane the other myriad of times Diane was being annoying. They still lay all over the floor on the other side of her desk. "Anyway," she said, "if he calls, I'll answer."

"I'll bet you will."

CHAPTER
TWELVE

"Okay, Jessica, what's your offer?" Eric Crabtree said.

"Eric, you know as well as I do that child support is what it is, just plug the numbers into the worksheet," Jessica said. She'd been through enough with the Denise-Kaitlyn situation to play games with Eric now. "He'll put her on his insurance, but he gets a credit for the expense on the worksheet. He won't pay any back child support, but as a gesture of goodwill he'll put five grand in a 529 account for her college."

"Visitation?"

"None."

"None?" Eric sounded incredulous.

"None. He doesn't want to disrupt Francesca's life. She's gone this far without him, why start now?"

Eric's sigh was so long and loud, Jessica could practically feel it whooshing through the phone. "Coach doesn't get to decide what interrupts Francesca's life. It interrupts *his* life, that's what's what. She wants to meet her father. Get to know him. He's really saying no to that?"

"Yup."

"What a dick."

"Visitation is a privilege, not an obligation. You can force the guy to pay child support, but you can't force the guy to see her."

"How do you suppose this is going to make Francesca feel?"

This was a body blow. Jessica supposed Eric knew it. *Like shit*, Jessica wanted to say. *Like her father wants nothing to do with her. Like the ultimate rejection.* But she couldn't betray her client. Instead she said, "Eric. My job isn't to look out for Francesca; it's to represent Coach. You know that. He doesn't want to meet her. You're going to have to trust me when I say it's a no go."

"I'll run it by Sarah," Eric said, "but don't hold out much hope. That's a lot of back child support to be paid, and you and I both know it won't affect his bottom line to stroke a check."

"And you and I also both know he doesn't have to pay sixteen years of back child support."

"She held the bag for sixteen years, Jessica. You don't think he has any kind of moral obligation?"

"Since when do moral and legal obligations have anything to do with each other?" Jessica pressed. One of the things she liked about the law was how cut-and-dried it was. She liked having a rule book you could look into for answers. Morality was a gray area, always up for debate. Laws, though? Those you could count on, regardless of how you felt about them. "We're not here talking about the morality of any of this. You know the law. She could have filed this any time in the past decade and a half, and she didn't."

"You're not pulling any laches bullshit on me, are you?" Eric said. He was starting to sound genuinely mad.

"You ever wonder why they call it 'laches'?" Jessica said, trying to defuse the situation. "When I was first learning all those stupid legal terms, I pictured the latches on a door slamming shut. I don't know what it literally means. I guess it's Latin for 'You snooze, you lose.'"

"I'm serious, Jessica."

"So am I, Eric. The case law says that it's a denial of due process to require a putative father to pay child support prior to a judicial determination of paternity. Is that bullshit? Maybe. I don't know, but people smarter than me wrote those decisions. Exactly *jack shit* prevented Sarah James from filing this action before now. If she really wanted child support years ago, she could have had it. She should be happy he's offering her a five-thousand-dollar college fund."

"She should be happy he's offering her hush money? Are you serious?"

"That's not what it is and you know it." Jessica's fist made it halfway down toward her desk before she stopped it. *Do not get mad, do not get mad, do not get mad*, she told herself. It wasn't Eric's fault his client wasn't acquiescing to Coach's refusal to meet his daughter any more than it was her fault that Coach wouldn't agree to visitation. No reason to blame Eric for the fact that this wouldn't work out simply. "Just run our offer by your client and let me know."

After Jessica hung up the phone, she wished she had the ability to throw up on cue. She would feel better if she could purge the bile in her stomach. Instead, she wandered to the office kitchenette to see what her stress eating options were.

It only took Eric two hours to call her back. Jessica's heart pounded when Diane told her he was on the phone. This phone call would determine how difficult, or not, the next few months of her life would be. "Whatcha got, Eric?"

"Child support is what it is."

"Mm-hmm."

"I can probably talk Sarah into the college fund idea, though it needs to be a little more money, but there has got to be a visitation component."

Jessica's head was shaking "no" so hard she was sure that Eric could hear it across the phone lines. "Eric. That's the one thing I probably can't do."

"But she—"

"Hold up," Jessica said. "Francesca is sixteen. Does she really want to spend every other weekend with a father she's never met? Doesn't she have her own friends she wants to spend her weekends with?"

"It's not that simple," Eric said.

Nothing ever is. She sighed. "So explain it to me."

"Let me set the scene for you. Here's a beautiful young girl who was born under suspicious circumstances to a teenage mother. She not only never knew her father, but she never knew who her father was." He paused and took a sip of something. "Think of all those elementary school 'Donuts with Dad' days where she had no one to invite."

"I'm not a jury, Eric," Jessica groaned, rolling her eyes. "You can dispose with the drama."

"I'm sorry if the truth is dramatic." Eric didn't sound the least bit sorry.

"Just cut to the chase."

"She's spent sixteen years having no idea who her father is, wondering how much her father knew and why her father never tried to find her, all that. Now she knows who he is and she wants to meet him. She's got a lot of questions about his past and his family, and she has a right to some answers."

The truth of what Eric said rendered Jessica speechless for a moment. It was hardly a comparison, but how many times had she wanted to sit her own father down and ask him why he'd decided to move a half a continent away from her? Just as she opened her mouth to speak, Diane flew into her office and rapped on her desk with her knuckles. "Hang on a second, Eric. My assistant just came into my office with something important."

"Nice fake," said Eric.

"Seriously," said Jessica. "Hang on." She put him on hold and looked up at Diane. "Your timing could not be better. What's up?"

"A Mister Robert Turnbull from the *Ashton Post* is on line two for you. I thought you might want to be interrupted."

Jessica did want to be interrupted by anyone or anything. The fact that it was Bobby, well—she would definitely rather talk to Bobby than Eric at this moment. She hadn't realized how anxious she'd been that he wouldn't call until just now. "I can't talk to him now! Get his number. I'll call him when I'm done with Eric."

"I'll tell him you're talking to some other guy," Diane said. "I don't want him to think you're easy pickins."

"Diane!" Jessica called after her retreating back, then picked up the phone. "Eric? You still there?"

"Still here."

"I'll talk to him. Again. Neither of us, though, can legally force him to see her."

"Maybe not," Eric said, "but I can do this: I can advise my client of her legal rights about taking out a warrant now that she knows who her assailant was."

"You wouldn't." Surely they had gotten over this. A thousand defenses popped into Jessica's head—this was retaliatory—if it really was rape, then she'd have filed as soon as she knew who it was, not after he refused all her demands. Why did she wait all these years to file a report? There were, of course, valid answers to those questions, but they weren't hers to say. Her stomach twisted at the thought of publicly victim shaming like she'd have to do.

"Wouldn't I? I've got a client to represent, same as you."

When Jessica hung up the phone, she roared a primal, guttural noise that spoke more truths than words probably could have. The sound propelled her out of her chair. She stomped into Diane's office where she paced in small circles.

"I take it they didn't accept your offer," Diane said, spinning her chair around to face Jessica.

"Closer than I would have guessed," Jessica said. "They're okay with the money part, or okay enough, but they won't work anything out without a visitation component. Francesca wants to meet her dad."

"I get that."

"I do too, but I don't know that Coach does, and I don't know that I can convince him to meet her. Can you call him and get him in here? This is a face-to-face conversation, not a phone conversation." Jessica made a retching noise. "I do hate talking to that man."

"Yes, but his checks cash."

"True that."

"In better news, you're meeting Bobby at Le Cirque Thursday night at six thirty."

"What?" Jessica stared at Diane, torn between admiration and abject horror at her nerve.

"You kids were taking too long to get at the meat of the matter, so I just took control. He started to leave a message, tell her to call me, blah blah, and I said, 'Look, Bobby, I know you want to ask her out, and I know she wants to go, so why don't I just make the arrangements. I'm in charge of her calendar anyway.'" Diane passed Jessica a message slip. "Here's his cell phone number. I gave him yours. I was losing patience with the pace of this romance."

"How did you know I didn't have plans on Thursday?" Jessica asked, trying as hard as she could to look perturbed.

Diane looked up at Jessica through her raised right eyebrow.

"Okay," Jessica said. "Point taken."

"You're meeting him there," Diane said. "That will ensure you don't drink too much and that you end up back at your own place alone."

"Diane!" Jessica said in mock horror. "What do you take me for?"

"A red-blooded, pretty American girl going out on a date with a good-looking, red-blooded American boy. Keep your panties on until at least the third date."

Jessica just looked at Diane. She considered saying something snarky, then decided against it. Diane was one of the few people she could count on in her corner, and she couldn't risk pissing her off. Instead, she hugged Diane's shoulders and kissed the top of her head, which she immediately regretted due to the taste of hair spray on her lips.

CHAPTER
THIRTEEN

꠱

Coach would only meet after school, on Thursday, so Jessica wore her date clothes to the four-thirty appointment, not wanting to rush afterwards. That meant her cleavage was more on display than it might otherwise be for a professional meeting. She put on the cardigan she kept over the back of her chair, but it did nothing to help conceal her décolletage.

Coach sat in her client chair like it was his living room, his right ankle on his left knee and his hands clasping his wrists behind his head. He was a champion manspreader. "Well? What did they say?" he said, without any preliminaries, his eyes flicking down momentarily to her chest before returning dutifully to her face.

"Financially, they're good."

"Good then, draw up the paperwork and let's get this done."

"But . . ." Jessica began, working up the courage to say what she'd practiced. She knew that clinical was best, just say it and get it over with, but still, she knew his reaction would not be good and she feared it.

"But what?" Once again, Coach's speed surprised her. In one fluid instant, he shifted from belly-exposed prey to guarded predator.

"But their acceptance is entirely dependent on your meeting Francesca."

"NO!" Coach's response was more roar than human word. He lowered his voice. "No. That's a no go."

"Why? Why are you so adamantly against meeting this girl?" Jessica couldn't understand it. If they were demanding every other weekend that was one thing, but she was pretty sure she could satisfy them with the promise of a dinner or even a long cup of coffee.

"We've been over this, Jessica. I don't want to meet her. I don't want to disrupt her life."

"They'll say that it isn't up to you to say whether you're disrupting her life. It's up to her and her mom. They say you don't know what she can handle since you don't know her." Jessica wanted nothing more than to look at her hands or the floor or out the window, anywhere but Coach's face. She forced herself to stare into his eyes, trying hard to find the depth in them.

"No," he repeated. "I know teenagers. I work with them all day every day. They think they know what they want, but they don't. They need to be told. They need to be coached. There's a reason they aren't old enough to drink, there's a reason they don't get tried as adults if they commit crimes, there's a reason for all of that. Their brains aren't, whatcha . . ." Coach tapped his forehead hard enough that Jessica feared it might leave a bruise. "Their brains aren't mature enough, the front part, the decision-making part. They need rules. Believe it or not, they like authority. They crave it. I'm not gonna let some sixteen-year-old I've never met tell me what's best. Not for me, and not for her. No. It's a nonstarter."

Jessica had a lot of sympathy for Francesca, but Coach was making some fair points. At the very least he was giving her something to work with. "Okay," she said. "I won't push you."

"Good," Coach said, leaning back in the chair, the tension clearly still in his body.

"But I need you to think up some answers to some questions. I can't answer them for you, okay?"

"Shoot."

"At some point Francesca or someone on Francesca's behalf
is going to ask you point-blank why you don't want to have anything to do with your daughter. They are going to ask you if it
doesn't bother you that it hurts her feelings, makes her feel like
her father is rejecting her."

"Wait a minute now—" Coach started sitting up again.

Jessica put her hand up to stop him. "I'm not saying that you
are rejecting her. I'm not saying that you have any personal feelings at all about this. I'm just saying that these are the questions
you are going to be asked, because these are the questions that I
have already been asked. You are going to have to have answers
for them at some point. Yours is not the only perspective in this
story. There is a girl here, and this is how her lawyer says she
feels. You can tell me all day long that she shouldn't feel that way,
and maybe she shouldn't, but she *does* and I can't stop that."

"But I—" Coach said, and Jessica put her hand up again,
enjoying the feeling of being able to control him with a gesture.

"I know that public perception means a lot to you. There's
nothing wrong with that. You're a popular guy and for good
reason. In this case, though, a fatherless sixteen-year-old girl is
going to get a lot of natural sympathy that an adult man won't.
If you want to keep public opinion on your side, and not come
across as cold and heartless—and I know you're not," Jessica said,
crossing her fingers in her lap. Surely a client-handling lie told
for strategic purposes wouldn't subtract too much from her kar-
mic balance. "If you want to stay popular, you have to play the
game, and here, the game is couching everything in terms of
what's best for Francesca, not you."

"I want what's best for her too," Coach said, and Jessica
nodded as he went on. "And what's best for her is not to have a
relationship with me."

"Good, good," Jessica said. "And why is that?"

"Because . . . because . . ." Coach trailed off and shrugged.

"Okay, well, your homework is to think about it. Make sure you have a good, articulate answer, and soon, because I promise you it *will* come up in public conversation. Probably about as soon as I tell Eric Crabtree that you still refuse to meet her and he calls the *Post* about it."

"Goddamn nosy sons of bitches. Why is my personal life news around here?"

"You know the answer to that. Because you're a local celebrity. You know everyone, and everyone knows you," Jessica said. "There isn't a whole lot of crime, so what else are they going to print in the paper?"

Coach rumbled low in his throat and pulled his eyebrows together.

"Well, anyway, think about it." Jessica was wondering how to get Coach out of her office without directly asking him to leave when he stood up.

"Are we done?"

"For now. Remember. Think about your answer and make it a good one. I know you're good at this stuff. I can make one up for you, but it's going to sound a whole lot more natural coming out of your mouth if it's sincere and not just some bullshit I came up with."

Jessica needed to clear her head between her meeting with Coach and her date with Bobby. A little mental sorbet to cleanse her palate between courses. Diane had already left the office, so she was no use. Jessica went on Instagram, the ultimate time suck, and spent time catching up with her college friends. She still loved them, but most of their lives had veered off in a different direction. The women she'd spent four years drinking with until all hours of the night were almost all married, and about half of them were mothers. The thought of that made her shudder. After clicking like and commenting on the cuteness of all the babies, she went into the bathroom to see what her eyeliner and lipstick were up to. Finding nothing terribly amiss, she took a selfie and texted it to Diane with, *This is as good as it gets. Here goes nothing.*

She got in her car and headed toward Le Cirque in Parksville, a good half hour at this time of day. She'd been there once before. It was as fancy as things got in the greater Ashton area.

When she arrived, a teenager with a diamond nose stud manned the hostess stand. "Welcome to Le Cirque," she said, pronouncing it "Lay Surk" with little enthusiasm and as much France as a french fry. She led her toward Bobby, who was sitting a few tables back from the entrance.

Bobby stood once he saw her, took half a step toward her, then stopped. Jessica walked toward him, wondering when she should stop closing the gap between them. She passed handshaking distance and stood close enough to smell fresh toothpaste on his breath. Jessica lifted her right arm, her purse dangling off her left elbow, letting Bobby decide how their bodies would touch. Bobby leaned in and hugged her, brushing his lips against her cheek. Jessica felt the smoothness of his skin. She pictured him getting ready for their date, scraping the razor against his face for the second time that day. He had to be thinking about her while he did this, in the same way she thought about him as she checked her lipstick. He wanted to look his best for her; she melted a little. She smelled fresh aftershave, a subtle unisex smell she liked. She inhaled a lungful of it and surrendered into the warmth of his arms.

"Honestly," he said into the top of her head, "I wouldn't mind keeping you here all night, but people are starting to stare."

She pulled back as if she'd been caught doing something wrong and looked around. There were only a smattering of other people in the restaurant, and all of them were focused on their own conversations. Jessica smacked him lightly on the arm.

"Now they're all witnesses to my abuse." Bobby was smiling.

They settled in their chairs. A waiter asked if they wanted to order drinks with marginal enthusiasm. He was an impossibly tall, skinny young man with prominent cheekbones. If they were in New York, Jessica would have assumed he was a runway model.

"What kind of beer do you have on tap?" Bobby asked.

The waiter appeared put-upon, as if Bobby had asked him to brew the beer himself after harvesting the wheat. "I'll get you a beer menu."

"A beer menu! Ooh la la!" said Jessica, as soon as he shuffled away.

"Okay, but if it's just a piece of copy paper that says Bud and Bud Light on it, we're leaving."

Jessica giggled. "Deal."

The beer menu, as it turned out, was a leather-bound, eight-page menu with beers, wines, and craft cocktails. Bobby chose something unpronounceable and German, and Jessica chose something with a floating orchid in it, simply because it had a floating orchid in it. After they ordered, they stared at each other for a few moments. They'd never had trouble talking before, but this felt different. This whole thing seemed engineered and unnatural. Jessica was a trial lawyer—she spoke out loud for a living. But here, in this quiet, intimate restaurant with the first guy she'd allowed herself to be truly interested in since Keith, she found herself out of words.

Bobby cleared his throat. "So, uh . . . Diane is something else."

Jessica released tension in her shoulders she hadn't realized was there. Diane was a topic she could sink her teeth into. "Oh, there's an understatement."

"I mean, don't get me wrong, I like her, but she's a pushy broad." His smile showed all of his teeth.

"Ya think?"

"I called you at work because it was the only number I had. I could have been calling to get you to sponsor some crap for the chamber for all she knew, but all of a sudden she just lights into me. 'Listen, Bobby, I am tired of you dicking around.'"

"She did not say 'dicking around.'"

"I promise you she did." Bobby did his best to make his baritone an alto and ratcheted up his accent to imitate Diane. "'I am tired of you dicking around. I'm going to tell Jessica you called to ask her to dinner and that you took the initiative to tell her to meet you at Le Cirque in Parksville at six thirty on Thursday.'" He dropped his voice back down to its normal timbre. "Before I could pick my jaw back off my lap, she gave me your cell, asked me for mine, then hung up." He raised his right hand and tucked his pinky and thumb in his palm, leaving the middle three fingers raised. "Scout's honor."

Jessica's entire body shook with silent laughter. "I don't doubt a word of it. That tracks with what she told me."

"How did you hook up with her anyway?" he asked. "She was the front office lady at the high school when I was there; now she's your paralegal. I'm not getting that connection."

"She went back to school after her husband died. When I started here, I was renting office space from Spencer Jacobsen. She was working for Spencer. Then, when Spencer got killed in that car wreck a couple years ago—I'm sure you remember that, it was big news."

"Yeah," Bobby said. "I covered that story."

"So Spencer died suddenly, and there I was, a baby lawyer, and I kind of inherited Spencer's practice and Diane all in one fell swoop. It was rough and weird and hard, but going through that together made her kinda like my big sister. I couldn't have done any of it without her telling me what to do. I write her paychecks, but truly she's the boss."

The waiter came with Bobby's pint and Jessica's complicated drink topped with a real, not plastic, orchid. Bobby raised his glass, and Jessica followed suit. "To Diane the Boss," he said.

"The bossiest," said Jessica.

The dam broken, there were no more silent moments. They were about three-quarters of the way through their food when Bobby, chewing a piece of his coq au vin slowly, looked at her and said, "Are you one of those women who is afraid to eat dessert in front of a man?"

Jessica studied his eyes, noting they were the exact same color as chocolate mousse. "That's a loaded question. You obviously want me to say that I'm not. If you didn't want dessert, you wouldn't have asked the question. So really all you're asking is what I would order."

"Do you *want* dessert?"

Jessica had just eaten an entire plate of ratatouille and was fearful that the button holding her pants together would give way, but she couldn't turn down Bobby's excited face.

"Yes," she said. "Yes, I want dessert."

Just then, the waiter reappeared, proffering a small piece of card stock rubber banded artfully to a piece of distressed wood. "Would you care to see the dessert menu?"

Jessica nodded, already reaching for it. "How about we split the apple brandy cobbler?" she said, after scanning it. Putting both of their spoons in the same dish had a romantic "Lady and the Tramp" vibe to it.

"Excellent choice," Bobby said, nodding to the waiter. "I'd also like a cup of decaf."

"Same," said Jessica.

For the first time since she arrived, there were a few moments of silence. Jessica started to panic. Was Bobby feeling a comfortable silence, or had he run out of things to say? Should she come up with something witty? Before she decided on a topic, Bobby spoke.

"So, how are things going with Coach? You guys gonna wrap things up soon?"

Jessica's heart jumped a foot and a half down into her stomach, knowing she had to abort this topic and quick. "Hopefully." She patted her belly. "Whoo! I'm sorry if I made a pig of myself. That ratatouille was so good, it was like Remy himself made it."

Bobby waved his hand. "Is Coach going to meet Francesca? That would be a fun little feature in the paper. We could send out a photographer for the big reunion."

This, she thought. *This is why this isn't going to work.* He was a nice guy, and sweet and cute and he gave her that warm feeling deep in her gut that she hadn't remembered she missed, but she could not date him because he would of course ask questions, perfectly reasonable questions, like this. "Bobby. I cannot talk to you about my client. If we're going to go out to dinner and . . . whatever . . ." She felt her face flush. "There are some topics that are just going to have to be off-limits. Work stays at work. Not-work goes out to dinner."

Bobby's eyes bored through her, and his eyebrows knit together. He didn't say anything for a long while. The silence made her nervous. She kept her hands on her lap under the table-cloth, twisting the cloth napkin. She was grateful that they were at a restaurant that had cloth napkins. If it were paper, it would be ripped to snowy shreds.

Finally, he took a deep breath, and Jessica's heart started to pound louder.

"It's a weird line to draw," Bobby said, his expression unreadable. "I mean, if we're going to be friends or . . . whatever . . .

I'm occasionally going to talk about work. I'm a reporter. I ask questions. That's what I do. I'm a curious guy. Is what you do all day every day taboo?"

"Well, no, not exactly," Jessica said. She wished she knew him better and could read him more accurately. Was he mad that he couldn't pump her for information? Was he just trying to sort out where the line was? Was he staring at her, wondering if she were worth the effort of working it all out? Oh well, nowhere to go but forward. "But you know who Coach is, and there's such a thing as privilege. I can say, 'Oh my gosh, this random guy came in today and he blah blah blah,' and talk about my day and tell stories about stuff in the public record. But I can't tell you about a specific guy you know without his permission. I keep a lot of secrets, and it has to stay that way. We can figure it out as we go. But Coach? You can't ask me anything you wouldn't have asked me a month ago."

Bobby twisted his mouth up and made a noise that sounded like gears grinding. Was that his thinking face? Lord, getting to know someone new was exhausting. Jessica put the odds at 83 percent that she had just ruined the date. She startled when the waiter reached around her to put the cobbler on the table.

"Oh, that looks delicious," said Jessica.

"It does," Bobby said, taking a bite and making a moaning noise Jessica didn't think she'd hear until at least the third date. "It is."

Jessica laughed and mentally reduced the odds to 57 percent.

Bobby walked her to her car, tapping his finger on her back windshield where his "wash me" graffiti was still legible. He pulled out his wallet and handed her a ten-dollar bill.

"What's that for?" Jessica asked.

"Will you at least run it through a car wash?"

Jessica pushed his chest. "Shut up."

He pretended to stumble backward, laughing. "Ooh, you're a violent one. Am I going to need a safe word?"

"How about 'car wash'?"

Bobby stepped toward her, smiling. "Car wash," he said. "Let's see how safe I am." He kissed her, folding his long arms around her back. She twined her arms around his waist, feeling his ribs expand underneath her hands as he breathed. He was warm against the chill of the December air. He pulled away, keeping his arms around her. "I feel pretty safe," he said.

Jessica settled her head in the hollow of his chest and nearly purred as he stroked her hair. "Me too," she said.

"So. If I want to do this again, do I call you or Diane?"

CHAPTER
FOURTEEN

———

Jessica ran into Eric in the courthouse the next morning while she was filing some paperwork on another case.

"Well?" Eric asked, cornering her in the lobby.

"Nothing has changed, Eric," she said, keeping her voice even. "He doesn't want to meet her. He doesn't think it is in her best interests."

"Her mother thinks otherwise. And she's actually met Francesca, which I think matters."

"I get that," said Jessica. *I'm not the one you need to convince*, she wanted to say.

"And?" Eric didn't usually use his bulk to intimidate, but he was a tall, broad guy with a bit of a middle-aged gut on him. When he stood up straight, he loomed. He stood at full height now.

"And Coach thinks they've all been rocking along with their lives for the past sixteen years and they need to *keep* on rocking in the manner to which they've grown accustomed, only now Sarah and Francesca will have some more money with which to rock."

Eric's face softened, and he clapped Jessica on the shoulder. "I'm sure you tried."

"You have no idea," Jessica said gratefully.

"You're a good egg," said Eric, walking away. "Sorry I'm going to have to fry you."

— — —

Jessica barely had her foot through the door of the office before Diane said, "Scale of one to ten, what kind of kisser is Bobby?"

Jessica thought about pushing her in the chest the way she had pushed Bobby, but Diane had a much lower center of gravity and wore four-inch heels. She couldn't count on the results, though the flashing image she got of Diane teetering backward and smashing into the faux-hardwood floor gave her a frightening amount of satisfaction.

"A lady doesn't kiss and tell," she said, instead of resorting to violence. "Let me put my stuff down and get coffee and then we'll talk. I've got to update you on Coach too."

"So that means there was a kiss you don't want to tell about?" Diane asked.

"Coffee first," Jessica said, taking her time at the machine. She thrust the filed pleadings she'd gotten at the courthouse that morning at Diane. "Make yourself useful for a moment. I'll meet you in my office."

Jessica sat down at her desk and lowered her face over the coffee cup, letting the steam seep into her pores. She took a big gulp. When she pulled the mug away, Diane was sitting across from her and Jessica startled.

"Well?" Diane said. "I want a blow by blow." She giggled at her double entendre.

"Well, I think we've got the financial stuff worked out, but it doesn't matter what I say, I can't convince Coach to meet Francesca."

"Do you honestly think I give a crap about *that*?" Diane gaped.

"You should. I pay you decent money to give a crap about that," Jessica said, a little more harshly than she'd intended. Diane said nothing, but her look spoke paragraphs. "Ugh, I'm sorry, Diane. It's just that I ran into Eric in the courthouse this morning and gave him what I thought would be good news. To quote Tom Petty, however, he won't back down."

"Blah blah," said Diane, waving her hand in the universal gesture for "move on with things quite a bit faster than your current pace."

Jessica blushed, and the fact that she was blushing made her blush harder and grin wider. "We had a good time."

"Ooh, girl. That goofy look on your face tells me you didn't go home after dinner."

"I did! I swear!" Jessica held up three fingers in the "Scout's honor" sign and, remembering that Bobby had done the same the night before, blushed anew.

Diane squinted, examining Jessica more closely. She sat back down slowly and said, "Okay. Maybe I believe you. But it was a hell of a goodnight kiss."

Jessica blushed all the way back to her ears.

Diane laughed throaty and loud. "Is he going to call you again, or am I going to have to make more arrangements?"

"Shut up," Jessica said, rummaging through her basket of stress balls. Before she could pick one out, the phone rang. "*Ugh,*" she sighed.

"I'll get it," Diane said, getting out of the chair and clipping off to her desk.

Jessica took a deep breath to cleanse her soul of all things Coach Wishingham and had just picked up the stack of mail Diane had left on her desk when Diane was back in her doorway, wearing a shit-eating grin.

"It's Bobby. He *says* it's business. Also, he backs up your story that you didn't go home with him." Diane spun around quickly on one heel and left before Jessica could react.

Jessica squeezed her eyes shut and breathed through her nose.

Picking up the phone, she said, by way of hello, "I apologize for whatever it was that Diane said."

Bobby laughed. "She was surprisingly professional."

I'm still gonna kill her.

Bobby coughed. "I'm actually calling for professional reasons. That's why I called on your work phone. I'm trying to separate the sacred from the profane, as they say."

"Thank you."

"So, I just got a call from Eric Crabtree."

"Ah, crap." Jessica knew what was coming next and had no interest in it, even if she was hearing it in Bobby's voice.

"Yeah," Bobby said, clearly stalling. "Eric says that you said that no way no how is Coach willing to meet his daughter, and he doesn't care what she thinks."

"That's not *exactly* what I said."

"I didn't think so." Bobby cleared his throat again. "So what did you say?"

"I said that Coach believes that Francesca is better off without him. He wants to make sure she is taken care of financially without throwing any wrenches into her personal life."

"Mmmph," Bobby said. "Look, I know there are two sides to every story, but I need some help with this. Eric says that *both* Francesca and Sarah James want Francesca to meet Tripp Wishingham. They say it's more disruptive to Francesca's life to have her father refuse to meet her. Since Tripp doesn't know her, explain to me how what you said isn't just a prettier way of saying Tripp refuses to meet with his daughter and he doesn't care what she thinks."

If it were possible, Jessica would have reached through the telephone and throttled Bobby. Not because there was anything wrong with what he said. He had an intelligent and insightful point. She wanted to throttle him *because* he was being intelligent and insightful. Jessica had a thing for intelligent and insightful men. Especially cute ones who smelled nice and kissed like Bobby did. It would stretch her considerable powers of compartmental-ization to keep work-Bobby in one square of her waffle and the Bobby from Le Cirque in another square. She didn't know if it was possible, but she was game if he was.

"Let me put it a different way," Jessica said, channeling Coach's own words. "Coach is an adult, and Francesca is a six-teen-year-old child. Coach deals with sixteen-year-olds for a living. He knows how to bring out the best in them. That's what he's known for. That's how he gets to the playoffs every year. He knows what motivates teenagers and what throws them off the rails. He's the grown-up in this situation, and he's making the grown-up decision."

"Sarah James is a grown-up too, and she raised Francesca. Are you saying she doesn't know her? How come she doesn't get to make the grown-up decisions?"

"What? Are you cross-examining me?"

"I always wondered if I should have gone to law school."

"Based on this conversation," said Jessica, "the answer is yes."

Bobby laughed. "Well? What's your answer to the original question? Why doesn't Sarah James get to answer for her daugh-ter instead of a man who has never met her?"

"Gah. Relentless em-effer, aren't you?" Jessica took a deep breath, buying herself some time. Just at the bottom of her exhale, it came to her. "Sarah James has an agenda. She needs Coach to look bad. And don't discount Eric Crabtree—he's a great lawyer. No doubt he's behind the scenes, figuring out how to try this case in the media and using you as a tool for that. This whole conver-sation, meeting Francesca, not meeting Francesca, it makes for good theater, and they're using that. It has nothing to do with what's best for Francesca." Jessica fought the urge to fist-pump. She was a master bullshitter when she had to be. And for all she knew, what she was saying was true. That was the difference between lying and bullshit. You knew a lie wasn't true. Jessica never intentionally lied. Bullshit just didn't care about the truth.

Bobby waited a few beats before asking, "Do you really believe that? Is this you, Jessica Fischer, talking or Tripp's lawyer talking?"

"Don't ever ask a lawyer what she really believes, Bobby."

"Okay then," he said. "Can I change the subject so you're not a lawyer anymore, or should I hang up and then call your cell?"

Jessica laughed. "No, this phone is fine."

"Good. I, uh . . . I was wondering if you might want to try out one of Ashton's own fine dining establishments this Saturday."

"Ashton has fine dining establishments?"

"How about one of Ashton's less sucky dining establishments?"

"I believe there are a couple of those." Jessica caught herself twirling a lock of hair around her finger and immediately stopped it, feeling like an idiot.

"Boy, you do not answer questions. You should run for office."

"Yes, Bobby, the answer is yes. I'd be happy to accompany you to one of Ashton's less sucky dining establishments this Saturday."

Jessica heard Diane stage-whisper, "Yes!" from just outside her door.

"Is Diane on the other line?" Bobby asked.

"No," Jessica said, raising her voice so Diane would be sure to hear. "She just has no indoor voice, no tact, and a vicarious crush on you."

Bobby chuckled. "I'm glad she approves. I'm guessing we wouldn't be allowed to speak on any level if she didn't like me."

"Don't knock the advantage of a good screening committee. You have no idea how many unpleasant conversations she's saved me from."

"So when I can't get through . . . ?"

"You'll know."

CHAPTER
FIFTEEN

T he less sucky dining establishment was, at least, not a chain restaurant: Billie Jo's, a meat-and-three emporium specializing in what Jessica called the brown food group. Even the vegetables weren't vegetarian, having spent the better part of a day boiling in a bath of fatback. Still, as long as you didn't mind your meat breaded and crisp and you kept the whole thing a secret from your cardiologist, it all was delicious.

"I have to know," Bobby said, slurping from a glass of tooth-enamel-peelingly sweet iced tea. "What brought you to Ashton? No one just moves to Ashton. Most of us have been here for generations, or we married someone who did, or we got a job at the distribution center. You just showed up one day with an actual degree from a real university. Who does that?"

Jessica laughed. "I ask myself that a lot." She paused, pulling a long strip of fried chicken off the bone and stuffing it into her mouth. Bobby was Ashton born and bred, so she needed to be careful about dogging the place. When she'd swallowed and wiped the grease off her hands and lips, she said, "I grew up in Decatur. Went to undergrad at Tulane. I wouldn't have come back to Atlanta either, but my mom got sick. Breast cancer." Bobby winced like most people did, which is why she rarely mentioned it. "So, when I got into Emory Law School, I felt like

I needed to come home to help take care of her. She didn't have anyone else. My parents divorced when I was young, and my dad moved to Tucson while I was in high school. She died in the beginning of my third year."

"I'm sorry," Bobby said.

Jessica waved her hand. She really didn't want to go down that path, not tonight. "Anyway, I graduated from law school ready to take on the world and make my fortune lifting the underdog, fighting for truth, justice, and the American way, blah blah. My mom left me her house and what was left of her savings, so I had a cushion. Everyone and their brother went to law school six years ago in order to put off getting a job because unemployment was so high, so there was an enormous glut of lawyers."

Bobby nodded knowingly.

"Unless you were in the top third of the class or wanted to be a public defender, no one was hiring. I wasn't a *bad* student, but I was battling to be the valedictorian of the bottom half of the class. Just dead average. Lots of people were hanging out their own shingles and signing up to be on appointed lists. You could eke out a living that way, and I did that for a little bit, just to pay bills. But there was so much competition. Then I read this article in the *Georgia Law Journal* about underserved communities. How there are towns and counties in Georgia that don't have *enough* lawyers, the opposite of what I was seeing around me. Everyone wanted to work in Atlanta and the metro counties, but you go like fifty miles out and there's no one. Even further and there's literally no one. So, I did some research. Ashton is only an hour and change from Atlanta, and the same from Athens. I have easy access to either if I want some culture. There were only like a dozen lawyers listed here in the bar directory, and none of them were women, which didn't seem like enough to serve a population of almost one hundred thousand. If you haven't noticed, I'm not the most social person in the world, so I don't give a crap about nightlife. I said to myself, 'Fuck it. What have I got to lose?' I loaded my crap in a U-Haul and here I am."

"That's so brave!" Bobby said.

"Brave? No." Jessica shook her head. "Desperate." It really hadn't felt brave at the time. It had felt cowardly, like giving up on her chances of rising to the top.

"No, desperate is taking a public defender job you don't want. Brave is moving away from all your friends and family and just plunking yourself down in a little incestuous community like this one and hoping you could make yourself a living."

The praise embarrassed her, so she focused on Bobby. At least Bobby recognized Ashton as little and incestuous—being self-aware had to count for something. Why had he stayed? It had to be something beyond inertia.

"Hi, Jessica!" A chirpy voice interrupted her. Jessica saw Kimberly Johnson heading toward their table, her elbow hooked in the elbow of a man twice her size in all directions with impressive facial hair.

Jessica pasted her professional smile on her face and greeted her.

"Oh! Hi, Bobby! You're here too!" Kimberly said when she reached them. "This is my husband, Earl."

"Hey, Earl," Jessica and Bobby said at the same time, then laughed and both said, "Jinx! You owe me a Coke."

Kimberly looked from Bobby to Jessica and back again, then smiled and petted the eagle tattoo on Earl's meaty forearm. "Earl works over at the distribution plant. He's a shift manager." The pride in her voice was the same as if she had said, "He's a transplant surgeon who just saved the president of the United States with experimental surgery."

"Wow, great to meet you, Earl," said Bobby, who then stuck out his hand to shake.

Earl spoke in a voice so low and full of tobacco Jessica could feel it rumbling the wooden bench she sat on. "Nice to meet you folks, but we need to order before they run out of chicken-fried steak. That happens sometimes. Let's go, darlin'." He tugged on Kimberly's elbow.

"Bye, y'all," Kimberly said over her shoulder as they walked away.

Neither Jessica nor Bobby said a word until Kimberly and Earl settled into a booth that seemed designed to be as far away as possible from them. Jessica swirled her fork in her green beans as Bobby piled his mashed potatoes as high as they would go, the brown gravy running like lava toward a village of stewed tomatoes.

"Well," said Bobby.

"Well," repeated Jessica.

"They seemed fun," said Bobby. "We should double-date."

Jessica kept her eyes fixed on Bobby's. "I'll get Diane to arrange it." They stared at each other. Bobby broke first, and they laughed loudly enough for Kimberly and Earl to hear them across the restaurant. They used grease-stained napkins to wipe tears from their eyes.

"So, what about you?" Jessica asked, eager to push the subject of conversation off of herself, Earl, and Kimberly.

"What about me?"

"Why did you stay? Why aren't you working for the *Atlanta Journal-Constitution* or the *New York Times*? This place seems a little . . . small for you." Jessica assumed ambition in intelligent people. Why shouldn't Bobby have some?

Bobby took the spoon out of his mouth and chewed his stewed tomatoes thoughtfully. "I went to UGA, majored in journalism, minored in English. Journalism is at a weird place now. A crossroads. Shifting from print to online, from journalists that we all knew like Woodward and Bernstein to nameless AP and Reuters wire service reporters. I think local news is where it's at. That's what's interesting. People interest me. I like writing about people I can get to know, not just the hundredth version of some national story. I know the people here and the community. Watching what makes this community tick is fascinating. Sometimes I feel like Jane Goodall observing the chimps, making notes about who is flinging poo at whom and then getting paid to write about it."

Jessica tilted her head, studying his face as he spoke. She was so intent in listening to him that she forgot she had a piece of cornbread clutched in her fingers. She put it back on her plate. The wooden table was wide, making it awkward to reach across and grab his hand, which was a shame. She felt a need to touch him. She shuffled her feet around under the table, found one of his, and pressed her toes on top of it. He stopped talking and raised one eyebrow.

She smiled. "My foot likes your foot."

"Just your foot?" He grinned crookedly.

"Nope," she said. "My left hand, and at least four fingers on my right." She held up four fingers.

"What are you even talking about?"

"Just giving you a bare minimum. It might be my whole right hand that likes you. And some other parts too." *Holy shit*, she thought. *I've gone way too far.* Embarrassed about what Bobby must think of her now, she looked down at the remnants on her plate.

"My parts have opinions too, you know," he said to the top of her head.

She snuck a glance at him. "They do?"

"They do. I prefer to let them speak for themselves, though."

Jessica wondered how quickly they could hail the server to give them the bill so they could get out of here and let their various parts have a conversation with one another.

CHAPTER
SIXTEEN

———✦———

Jessica arrived at work early on Monday morning in a good mood, unusually motivated to start the workweek. Maybe being more social was good for her psyche. When she pulled into the parking lot, she saw a large, tricked-out Dodge Ram pickup with tinted windows idling next to her usual spot. She wondered if she should worry about who it was when Coach climbed out of the cab and strode toward her, shouting when he got about halfway.

"The FUCK, Jessica. The ACTUAL FUCK?" he roared.

Jessica's good mood whooshed out of her and was replaced with irritation. She wasn't scared of Coach—he was too worried about his reputation to do anything but yell at her, and she'd been yelled at by better men than Tripp Wishingham. Her first coherent thought was, *What now?*

Coach pulled a newspaper from underneath his arm and unfolded it, shaking it at her driver's-side window as she put her car into park.

She rolled down the window, trying not to match his shouty tone. "I have no idea what you're talking about. Let me get out of my car and in my office, and you can yell at me there." She rolled the window back up and waited for him to step aside so she could open her car door. When he didn't, she opened it anyway, prepared to smack him with the door if need be. He moved out of the way at the last possible instant, holding up his hands in a "don't shoot" gesture.

Not bothering to wait for him, she strode toward the office, unlocked the front door, and turned off the alarm. Coach, on her heels, started in on her again, but unwilling to deal with him on his terms, she whirled around and pointed a finger up in his face. "You will wait until I have a cup of coffee in my hand." The nerve of this asshole yelling and cussing at her without so much as a hello. She could feel her heartbeat pounding in her ears.

Jessica practiced her mindful breathing in the kitchenette as she made herself a cup of coffee and poured in a generous dollop of half-and-half. That done, she found Coach in the lobby where she'd dumped him and invited him into her office.

"So. What's going on?" she asked him.

"This," he said, practically throwing a copy of the *Ashton Post* at her.

She picked it up. The front page read, "Popular Coach Spurns Love Child." Glancing at the byline, she saw it was Bobby's article. It was below the fold, at least. Jessica closed her eyes. *Oh Lord*, she thought, then read on.

Ashton, GA. Popular Ashton High School football coach Frank Wishingham III has made it clear through his attorney, Jessica Fischer, that he does not think it is a good idea for him to meet his daughter, Francesca James.

James, as we previously reported, is the purported daughter resulting from a tryst with Sarah James while Sarah James and Wishingham were seniors at Ashton High School. Wishingham was allegedly unaware of Francesca's existence until the filing of a paternity suit earlier this year.

"My client and her daughter have given this careful thought," said Eric Crabtree, Sarah James's attorney.

"Francesca has missed out on the first sixteen years of having a father. She wants to meet the man who fathered her and establish a relationship with him. The fact that he refuses to do so causes a sting of rejection she may never recover from."

Wishingham believes otherwise. Rather, Wishingham "is making the grown-up decision" that Francesca "is taken care of financially without throwing any wrenches into her personal life," according to Fischer.

As of this date, no hearings have yet been scheduled in the matter.

When Jessica finished reading it, she looked up, her pulse having returned to normal. "It's not great, but it's not terrible."

"Not terrible? I look like an asshole!"

"What do you want me to do about that?" Jessica retorted, holding back, *That's because you are an asshole.* "What exactly did I say that doesn't reflect what you told me?"

Coach made a guttural noise. "Your job is to make me look good."

"No."

"No?"

"No." Jessica could feel the fury flashing in her eyes. She'd had enough of this guy, and now she wanted to choke both him and Bobby. Bobby, dammit. Just his name brought to mind a sense memory of his lips on her throat Saturday night, her hands reaching underneath his shirt and feeling the smooth muscles there. She felt betrayed. "If you want someone to make you look good, hire a PR agency. I'm a lawyer. My job is to defend you in court, to zealously represent you to the best of my ability and to the limits of the ethical rules. My goal is to do my level best to get the most ideal outcome for you in a court of law. NOT"— Jessica was yelling now too—"to make you the darling of the *Ashton* fucking *Post.* If you don't want to *look* like an asshole, then perhaps you should stop *acting* like an asshole and give me some-thing to goddamn work with!" Jessica was incapable of dealing with her feelings about Coach and Bobby at the same time. Her self-control had limits. You had to fight fire with fire sometimes, and assholery with bitchiness.

Jessica could see Coach's nostrils flaring in and out. She half expected steam to stream out of them like a cartoon bull. "I assumed," he growled at a forced-calm volume, "that you were fucking Bobby Turnbull to get good press for me."

Jessica felt sucker punched. She stood there a moment, gaping like a landed fish. Which was worse? The fact that he thought this was true or the fact that he knew they'd gone out at all? The smallness of Ashton felt like it was smothering her. When she got her breath back, she sputtered, "I am not fucking Bobby Turnbull! What makes you think my sex life is any of your busi-ness anyway?" If she could have punched him hard enough to do damage, she would have.

"Earl Johnson said he saw you and Bobby out Saturday night at Billie Jo's. Despite what you think, I am not an idiot."

Jessica watched Coach's eyes flick down to her breasts and then draw a line back up to her face. "Get. Out," she spat.

Before he could respond, she heard Diane's heels click in the room. "Hi, Coach!" she chirped. "Did Jessica offer you any cof-fee? She can be a bad hostess sometimes."

Jessica, still seething, looked at Diane through narrowed eyes and shook her head.

Coach got up, nearly knocking over the chair and Diane in the process. He marched out of the room. "I was just leaving." They heard the door slam behind him.

Diane righted the chair and then sat in it. "You want to tell me what that was about?"

"No."

"Tell me anyway. Then you can thank me for rescuing you."

"He's a fucking asshole."

"Not arguing with you, sweetie." Diane reached across the desk and patted Jessica's hand. Jessica slithered down in her chair and buried her face in her palms. "Stop that," Diane said. "You'll ruin your makeup."

Jessica groaned. "My makeup is the last thing I care about at the moment."

"There's no reason to look a mess."

Jessica looked up incredulously, her chin on her chest and her mascara smeared on her cheeks. "Lady, your priorities are completely fucked up."

"Language."

"Priorities."

Both women glared at each other, daring the other to blink.

Without moving her head, Jessica slid the newspaper over to Diane. Diane picked it up and read the article, following it with a long, low whistle. "So that's what that was about."

"Yeah."

"I can guess a lot of the middle. Wanna cut to the chase?"

"Oh, Lord, Diane, where do I even start?" She ran her hands through her hair, scratching her scalp as if answers would fall out.

"Girl!" Diane scolded. "Now your makeup *and* your hair is a mess." Diane slapped Jessica's wrist, then reached into the stress ball basket, pulled out one that was actually ball shaped, and put it in Jessica's palm. "Torture this, not your head. Now. Tell me what happened."

"He said I was fucking Bobby to get good press for my clients and wanted to know why it wasn't working."

Diane threw back her head so far Jessica suspected it might snap and guffawed. Jessica threw the stress ball at her, winging the edge of her sleeve. "What are you laughing at?"

Diane sat up but didn't stop laughing. "You got laid! You did the bomp-ba-domp with Bobby!" Diane thrust her hips back and forth on the chair. "Good for you!" She suddenly quit laughing. "Wait. How would Tripp Wishingham know that and not me?"

Jessica stood up. She had way too much adrenaline pumping through her body to remain in a chair. "First of all, I did *not* fuck Bobby Turnbull. Bobby and I went out to dinner Saturday night at Billie Jo's. Kimberly Johnson from the chamber was there with her mountainous redneck husband Earl, and Earl, apparently, is friends with Coach and they have nothing better to talk about in this backwater town but who is having dinner with whom and then jump to conclusions. Why are you laughing?"

"Sweetie," Diane said, in a singsong tone usually reserved for people under seven years of age, "if you don't want me to laugh, then you shouldn't be funny."

A surge of something unidentifiable came roaring up through Jessica's entire body, and she leapt up to stamp both feet at the same time and cried out. Diane got out of her chair and came to Jessica's side of the desk. She wrapped her arms around her and hugged her tight. Because of their height difference, Diane's face pressed into the top of Jessica's cleavage. She looked up at Jessica.

"A boy could get lost in these."

Jessica smacked the back of Diane's head, not half as hard as she wanted to.

Diane sat back down, patting her helmet of hair to make sure it was in place. "Just trying to lighten the mood. Look. The point is this, no matter what you may think of yourself, you're a very pretty girl with nice legs and a good rack." For emphasis, Diane grabbed her own boobs and lifted them up. "Pretty girl plus cute boy plus Saturday night equals hanky-panky for most people. In a way, it's a compliment: they're saying you're do-able."

Jessica narrowed her eyes. She wanted to live in a world in which fuckable was not the praise people thought it was, but knew she didn't. She gripped the side of her desk, trying to decide if she should sit down or pace around the room. "That is *not* a compliment. Bobby, on the other hand, is a decent guy. We were only on our second date. He understood we weren't likely to get naked."

"Did he at least get to cop a feel?"

Jessica thought of Bobby's long, nimble fingers skimming her hips and reaching up underneath her shirt to touch her skin. It was all want and passion and, ultimately, restraint; dancing on the edges of love. She wanted to slap Diane for making Bobby sound like a fourteen-year-old who had grabbed his first boob. Surely Diane remembered what it was like to learn the contours of David's body. How could she reduce what Jessica was experiencing to adolescent-style groping? Or did Diane just assume that was what Jessica and Bobby got up to? Maybe Jessica was taking this whole thing too seriously. She looked at Diane, her eager face waiting for the answer, and relented. Diane didn't mean any harm, even when she was doing harm. Diane was just . . . Diane. Underneath it all, she wanted what was best for Jessica. Jessica loosened her fingers from the side of her desk and sat down.

Putting a smile on her face, she said, "Yeah."

Diane clapped. "Yay!"

"But that's where it ends."

"What do you mean 'that's where it ends'?"

"I mean, that's where it ends. That feel he copped is the last feel he's getting." Jessica felt a wave of disappointment crash over her head. She let it crest over her and swam to the top. She hadn't known she felt this way until now, but as she spoke, it seemed the only way. Inevitable. "I can't do this. I told you from the beginning this wasn't going to work, and this is why."

Diane looked horrified. "You cannot let your personal life and your professional life mix like that! One thing has nothing to do with the other."

"Exactly," said Jessica. "I have to do the grown-up thing and be responsible. I can't keep them separate if dickwads like Coach are going to keep pushing them together, and I need dickwads like Coach if I'm going to make a living."

"I hate that," said Diane.

"Not as much as I do." Jessica picked up a pencil and tapped the eraser on the desk, perfecting her drumroll, trying to beat both Bobby and Coach out of her head. If she couldn't change the awful reality of it, she didn't want to think about it. "Okay, look. Nothing I can do about that now. These are work hours. We need to work. What are we going to do about this mess?" She picked up the *Post* and shook it, wishing she could shake the type off the page and into the trash can, all the letters jumbled into meaninglessness.

CHAPTER
SEVENTEEN

⟶

Coach was on the phone. "Get your ass down to this school."
"What makes you think I make house calls?" *What makes you think I do anything for you?* The last conversation they'd had ended with Jessica wanting to slap the daylights out of Coach, and now he was making unreasonable demands? Like hell.

"Fuck, Jessica. Just get here. There is a goddamn protest, and your boyfriend is here and I need my lawyer here. Please."

It was the "please" that got to her. She heard something frantic in Coach's voice she hadn't heard before. She had no interest in doing this jerk any favors, but she did have to do her job and something deep in her gut told her this was for real. Jessica could hear a lot of noise in the background. She looked at her watch, then her computer screen. "It's ten thirty. I have a one o'clock it will take me a minute to get ready for, and I have to eat lunch. I can be there in about fifteen, but I can't stay long."

"Come to the gym," Coach said, and hung up.

Jessica stared at the receiver for a moment trying to make sense of the conversation she'd just had before putting it back in its cradle. She spent another moment trying to stuff away her personal feelings about Coach and push her professional obligations to the surface before gathering her purse and keys and heading over to Diane. "I'm going to the high school."

"What? Why?"

"Apparently there's some protest going on over there and Bobby is there covering it and Coach wants me there and no one is allowed to say no to the Great and Powerful Frank Wishingham."

"Protest?" Diane's face scrunched up. "Hold up. Give me ninety seconds to make a phone call."

"Diane, I do not have time; I have to go."

Diane waved her hand at Jessica. "You and I both know you're going to make a pit stop to pee before you leave. Let me call my sources and get some intel about what you're walking into."

One day Diane would be wrong. This was not the day. Jessica left her keys and purse on Diane's desk and went to the bathroom. By the time she got back, Diane was saying, "Thanks, Barb," into her cell phone and hanging up.

"Well?"

Diane smoothed her skirt. "It's not really a protest-protest. It's three girls wearing those horrible pink pussycat hats—where do they even get those?—and carrying signs that say things like 'Rapists Shouldn't Teach' and walking in circles in front of the gym. They've attracted quite a crowd—I don't think anyone really cares about the message, but you know teenagers—any excuse to skip class."

"Jesus Christ on a cracker." Jessica closed her eyes.

"Must you blaspheme in my presence?"

"Sorry," Jessica mumbled, though she wasn't, as she gathered her things and headed to the high school.

It was a short drive, as all drives were in Ashton. She wasn't sure where the gym was when she turned down the long drive, but it quickly became evident. The classroom part of the building looked like your standard 1970s-era concrete-construction high school. Next to it, connected by a short walkway, looked like a minor league sports arena. A sea of students milled around in front of it. Jessica drove up as close as she could and then parked, probably illegally.

She texted Coach. *I'm here. Where are you?*

He responded instantaneously. *In the building. Come around the west side and I'll let you in the side door.*

She thought about asking him how in the hell she was supposed to know which was the west side but decided she wouldn't allow herself to be helpless in his presence. She opened the maps app on her phone, put in walking directions to her office so the compass would show up, and headed to the west side of the building.

Coach opened the door as soon as she tapped on it and pulled her in like her life depended on getting into a safe house.

"Jesus fucking Christ," Coach said, and Jessica wondered how come Diane never scolded him for taking the Lord's name in vain. "Did you see that out there?"

She had, sort of. She purposely hadn't looked very hard for fear of recognizing anyone—Bobby in particular. Mostly what she'd seen was what Diane had told her she would—a bunch of high school kids looking for an excuse to cut class and a few teachers standing around helplessly, looking like they were grateful no fights had yet broken out.

They reached Coach's office. This time he sat in the desk chair and she sat in the guest chair. "Tell me what happened." Jessica tried not to be distracted by the decor. She believed you could learn a lot by seeing what people chose to put on display. There were a lot of pictures of Coach with other people—many of those people nearly as large as Coach himself, some of them even bigger. Plaques filled the walls, trophies the shelves.

"I left your office, got to work, totally normal."

Jessica nodded her head.

"Then I had my planning period, so I came over here. I like this office better than my classroom in the main building. In the walkway, these three girls—I don't know who they are. Never seen them before. Not cheerleaders, I can tell you that much. Woof."

Jessica took a deep breath. Even when Coach was telling a story in which he was the victim, he was unsympathetic. Well, if he was trying to get a wink wink, nod nod, "fat chicks" laugh out of her, he was not going to get it. Stone-faced, she said, "What did those three girls do?"

Coach smoothed his hair back. "They were wearing those goddamn pink pussycat hats and carrying signs. One of the signs said 'Rapists Shouldn't Teach School.' Another said 'Deadbeat Dad.' They started shouting at me. 'Hey hey, ho ho! Sexist Coach has got to go!'" Coach rocked back in his chair. "I should have just ignored them. That's what I would have told my guys to do. These chicks were definitely not worth my time. But this is not a peer-to-peer interaction. I'm a teacher, right? I'm an authority figure. And they were disrupting the school day. So I told them to cut it out and go to class.

"One of 'em, the one with the big ass and the ratty black hair, starts shrieking at me, 'I'm not afraid of you, you coward. You're too scared of teenage girls to do anything but tell them what to do!' By this time, a crowd had gathered. It's between classes, and oh God, those fucking cell phones, everyone's got theirs out and they're filming it. I'm thinking, *Where the fuck are the other teachers? Why do we have a school resource officer?* I'm smart enough not to put my hands on any of these little bitches, even just to guide them back inside."

Thank God for small favors, Jessica thought.

"Next thing I know, your fuck buddy is here, asking me if I want to make a statement." Coach picked up a football and tossed it from hand to hand. "Little shit is lucky there were kids around, or I might have ground his face into the asphalt. Do I want to make a statement? Get the fuck out of my face. That's a statement." The football made a satisfying *smack* sound every time it landed in the other palm.

"What did you do?"

"What did I do?"

For a moment, Jessica thought Coach was going to throw the football at her. "Yes, what did you do?"

Coach clutched the football in both hands, then spun it around. "I didn't speak to him at all, came inside and called you, that's what I did."

Jessica let out a breath she didn't know she was holding. "So what do you want to say?"

Coach let out a war cry. "I don't fucking know, Jessica. I don't have any fucking idea. I know I'm good at my job, and I know my job has shit to do with this mess with Sarah and Francesca. You figure out a way to separate these things for me, okay? Say something about what a great fucking coach I am to Turnbull. Suck his dick if you have to. Just do not let these dykes own the news cycle."

Jessica closed her eyes, waiting for the red to drain from her vision. On the one hand, Coach was correct—his ability to do his job had nothing to do with what happened one night when he was a teenager. The horrible things he was saying now were most likely a product of irrational anger. Still. They were horrible things he had no right to say. She was torn between lecturing him and letting it go—she knew he was in no state of mind to hear any reprimand she had to say right now, but she also knew she might bite a hole in her tongue if she didn't say something. She filled her chest with air, imagining the atmosphere of this sweaty office to be filled with inner peace instead of toxic masculinity.

"Listen, Coach. I'll come up with something. Just promise me that you will calm down before you speak to another human being." Coach's head whipped up at her, his eyes mere slits. "I know you're just venting and you don't mean to say such crude things, but if you say them to someone who isn't as . . . as understanding as me, you'll play right into what they're saying about you."

Coach continued to stare at her, his eyes gradually softening. "Fuck, Jessica," he said, in the same tone of voice another man would have said, "I feel so lost and helpless."

Jessica made it back to her car stealthily. No one was paying attention to the west side of the gym. The crowd had gotten noticeably bigger and considerably louder, and there was a police presence. She shut the door, started the engine, and checked her phone.

A text from Diane. *Your 1 p.m. canceled.*

She wrote back: *Why?*

Diane answered: *Tell u when u get here. Long story.*

Her afternoon freed up, somewhat, she texted Bobby. *I will give you a quote from Coach's camp re: today's debacle. Come by my office in about 30.*

Bobby returned a thumb's-up.

Jessica leaned against the headrest of her car and snuck a look at the crowd. They had gotten louder. There were still only the three girls with the signs, but others had joined in with the chanting. *Stop*, she telegraphed to them. *Go to class.* Then she chuckled to herself. Since when wasn't she on the side of the girls with the pink pussy hats? It seemed natural for her to be on the side of the girls fighting against male dominance, but here she was, defending the man, wanting nothing more than for the girls to be silent and slink back to math class.

She wanted them to hide what they really thought, just like she was hiding in this car, just like she had to hide what she really thought. She banged her hands on the steering wheel. Damn Coach. Damn Bobby for making it matter that much more. Damn her for having a personal opinion.

Jessica turned the key in the ignition, ordered pizza on Door-Dash, and drove back to her office.

She was hardly at her door when Diane called out, "Ooooh, girl!"

"What?"

Diane followed Jessica into her office. "It is going *down*."

"No kidding. You wouldn't believe the chaos at the school." Jessica plucked a stress ball out of the basket on her desk and began squeezing it, leaving half-moon fingernail marks in the foam.

"Apparently it is all over YouTube. Your one o'clock canceled because—get this—she doesn't want to be associated with *that rapist*, and since you're his lawyer . . ."

"Oh, fuck me."

It was a testament to the situation that Diane didn't reprimand Jessica about her language. "I tried to explain to her that Tripp Wishingham didn't rape anyone, but she wasn't hearing it. You have got to get the word out, girlfriend."

"Bobby will be here shortly. I've got pizza on the way. I'll give him a quote, then I'll tell him our relationship is all business from here on in." Her conference room seemed like the safest location to have this conversation. She could have it over the phone, but that seemed mean. Anywhere public was out. She'd never been to his house. For that matter, she didn't even know if he lived in a house or an apartment. She assumed it was a house, since she remembered him mentioning mowing the lawn, and there weren't very many apartments in Ashton, but who knew? The fact that she didn't even know his housing situation meant that she couldn't be too invested in this relationship, right? She could give him a quote, then explain to him in the same conversation that this—*this!*—was why it wouldn't work. She didn't really owe him an explanation beyond, "No thanks." It had only been two dates, right?

But it was more complicated than that, she knew. He was still Bobby Turnbull from the *Ashton Post*, and he was still going to be asking her questions about her cases, this case in particular. He would still pop up at chamber events, and no doubt she'd run into him when she went to one of Ashton's less sucky dining establishments. Jessica smiled at the memory and then braced for the wave of sadness that she knew was coming. Everything in her gut was twisted.

Diane's jaw hung open. "You can't do this."

Jessica looked up at her. "Can't do which part of it?"

"You can't just let Bobby go. I haven't seen you smile like that since, well, I've never seen you smile like that."

"Diane, I have to. I have a professional obligation to my clients. My relationship with Bobby, whatever it is, is interfering with that professional obligation. I have never shouted at a client like I did at Coach this morning, and I wouldn't have if my personal life weren't all tangled up in it. You wouldn't believe the nasty shit he said in his office just now. I wouldn't have avoided Bobby at the school and delayed a statement if I didn't have personal feelings all mixed up in this—I could have gotten something on YouTube and not lost a potential client. I can't ruin my career over two dates. I need to nip this in the bud."

Diane narrowed her eyes. "You're wrong on this one. I mean, professionally, you're probably right, but in the greater scheme of things, you're wrong. Some things are not worth other things."

"That's not your call to make." Jessica did everything she could to drain all feeling from her expression. Her relationship with Diane was not just employer/employee and she liked it that way, but at this moment, she needed to be Diane's employer. A hundred percent business was the only way she was going to get through this day.

"Maybe not," said Diane, "but I'm not wrong. You and Bobby, there's a *thing* there. You can't just let that thing go. Things don't happen like this all the time. Trust me on this one. There's a limited number of single guys in Ashton."

"Then I'll look in Parksville. Or get cats. You need to stay in your own lane, Diane."

Diane sniffed and made a little noise that might have been confused for one a Siamese cat would make. "Yes, ma'am," she said, offended. "Do you want me to hold your calls?"

"Yes, thank you." Jessica mustered a smile that would have to do as an apology for now. "That would be great."

Bobby showed up exactly on time, a fact that only endeared him to Jessica that much more. Jessica heard the alarm chime when he came in the front door and debated if she should get up to meet him or let Diane take care of it and lead him back like anyone else. By the time she decided, it was too late, and Diane was already leading him down the short hallway.

"Mr. Turnbull is here to see you," Diane said formally, dropping into a slight curtsy. Jessica rolled her eyes. "Would you like me to bring him to your office or escort him directly to the conference room?"

"Stop it," Jessica said, then turned her attention to Bobby. "Hi, Bobby."

Bobby put his hand on her arm and leaned forward to kiss her. He was aiming for her lips, but she turned her head so he'd get her cheek. "Sorry," he said softly in her ear. "Work. I get confused easily."

Diane was still standing there looking at them, her lips drawn together. "Do you need anything? Water? Coffee? A private room? A clue?"

"Go away," said Jessica.

"Yes, ma'am." Diane spun around on one heel and disappeared into her office.

Bobby tilted his head. "That all . . . seemed a little awkward. Did I miss something?"

Jessica waved her hand. She wanted to get this over with and also never say what she had to say all at the same time. She concentrated all her energy in appearing normal. "Oh, I really can't explain the complexities of Diane Myers in one go."

She led him to the conference room where he asked her, "Do I get a real kiss in here, or is the whole building off-limits?"

Thoughts tumbled into and out of Jessica's brain all at once. She really did want to kiss him. Kissing Bobby would be a bright spot of pleasure on an otherwise shitty Monday. Bobby had no idea what was coming. He thought he was just getting a quote about this morning's chaos. Was there any real harm in putting off the bad news another few minutes? On the other hand, kissing him now and then telling him that she could never kiss him again while his breath was still in her mouth seemed the height of mixed messaging. Oh, but to feel the heat of his body and the press of his lips against hers—just thinking about it made her pulse quicken. Couldn't she indulge herself one last time?

Bobby answered the question for her. He folded her in his arms, kissing her urgently. She hugged him tightly. This was the last time she'd get to touch him: she memorized the feel of his dress shirt underneath her palms and the stubble on his chin scraping against her own. She tasted wintergreen on his tongue, smelled that same, subtle cologne and wanted to go on smelling it.

He pulled slightly away, whispered, "Wow," kissing her forehead, then resting his chin on her hair, letting her lay her head against his chest. He was breathing hard. She heard his heartbeat thumping quickly underneath her ear. His Adam's apple moved up and down against her forehead as he swallowed. They fit together nicely: the curve of her neck against his chest, the natural fall of her arms around the narrowing of his waist. She noticed her thumbs absentmindedly playing with the leather strap of his belt in the small of his back.

Stop, she told herself. *Stop. You can't do this.* Tears pricked her eyes. She tilted her head back and blinked rapidly so they wouldn't fall, focusing on the breath going in and out of her nose. She let go of Bobby and dragged one of the pizza boxes toward her.

"I didn't know what you wanted," she said, sitting down and keeping her eyes focused on the pizza. "So I got a meat lover's and a veggie." She opened one of the boxes and tore off a piece of veggie. It didn't matter. It could have had shoe leather on it for all she cared. She looked up at Bobby, who remained standing where he was. "Sorry," she said. "I was hungry."

"So was I," he said quietly, then sat down. The silence between them roared in Jessica's ears. Finally, Bobby said, "You want to give me your quote and get that out of the way?"

"Oh, get that out of the way, for sure. Write this down."

Bobby reached into his breast pocket and pulled out an honest-to-God little reporter's spiral notebook and pen, and it was all Jessica could do not to melt into a puddle. She closed her eyes to avoid the visual, but that just made it worse: her imagination conjured up a fedora with a piece of paper stuck in the ribbon around the brim. "Coach respects these young ladies' constitutional right to protest, and respects their intentions, no matter how misguided their underlying information. He is not accused of sexual assault in the courts—he is involved in a paternity suit and he does not deny paternity. He hopes the protestors will respect the rights of the rest of the students at the school to get an education and find ways to make their message known without interfering with other students' ability to learn." She opened her eyes to see Bobby hunched over his notebook, scribbling furiously. He put an emphatic period at the end of his sentence and looked up at her.

"Thanks. As long as we're talking business, I thought about running Sunday's article by you first, or at least warning you before the paper came out. But then I remembered what you said and thought, *No.* You were so adamant about keeping those things separate that I kept quiet. I hope I made the right choice." The tips of his ears reddened.

Jessica dared to peer into his Hershey-brown eyes. They were wide open, begging for forgiveness. "You did," she said slowly. "You didn't do anything wrong. But that didn't stop Coach from showing up at my office at dawn and waiting until I got here so he could yell at me."

Bobby knit his brows together in concentration. "There's been a lot of yelling today."

"Look, I just don't think I can do this."

Bobby swallowed the mouthful of pizza he was chewing and let his mouth hang open for a second while he processed what he had just heard. When he spoke it was at half speed. "You don't think you can do what?"

Jessica put her slice of pizza down. She pointed her index finger back and forth between them. "This," she said. She took Bobby's stiff hand and continued, "I like you. I like you a lot. But *this* is interfering with my ability to do my job. I shouldn't be telling you this, and I hope you'll keep it in the strictest confidence." She paused, searching his face for confirmation. Bobby nodded. "But I lost a client because of what happened at the school, and Coach came in here this morning yelling and cussing at me because after Earl Johnson told Coach he saw us out together, Coach jumped to a thousand conclusions, and is upset that I didn't have some kind of supernatural control over what you write in light of our sexual relationship."

"We don't have a sexual relationship!" Bobby blurted out, then muttered, "Yet."

The desire, possibility, hope, and sadness that all rested in the word "yet" came as close to breaking Jessica as anything ever had. "I know," she said, then repeated, "I know." All of this felt so twenty-four-karat genuine, so far removed from anything Coach stood for that it seemed insane that he had anything to do with this conversation. A flash of red that he could affect her inner life at all exploded across her brain. "I set the fucker straight on that score, not that it's any of his damn business. But that's the thing. The truth doesn't matter to people like Coach. Image is everything. Perception is king. Earl and Kimberly saw us out. Let's just give them all the benefit of the doubt and say they were all at church Sunday morning. Coach saw the article. Earl happened to mention that he saw us at Billie Jo's, and wasn't it strange that we were such great friends as to be spending a Saturday night together, yet I couldn't convince you to make Coach look better in the article. Then Coach jumped to his own horny conclusions about the rest."

Bobby rubbed his face. "So, let me get this straight. I wrote an article that told the truth about a situation that interested my readers, but which pissed off your client because the truth wasn't flattering to him. Your client is under the impression that I should conveniently forget about the fact that he's kicking this poor teenage girl in the face just because I have an unrelated personal interest in his lawyer. Now you want me to forget all about my personal interest? Never mind the fact that I have, in fact, conveniently thus far, forgot about the very sordid facts of said teenage girl's conception, something he ought to be thanking me for. Then these girls start making noise about shit that just happens to be the truth and which has nothing whatsoever to do with me and . . . and . . . and . . . I don't even know what to say!"

Jessica stared at him for a while. That was a pretty neat summary of what was going on, excepting everything in Jessica's inarticulate heart. Then she said, "That's about it."

"That's bullshit."

"I'm not disagreeing. But it's also true. I don't want it to be true. I hope you believe me about that."

Bobby stared daggers at her. "Look, we've only been out twice. I don't have any kind of claim on you. You get to decide who you go out with, who you kiss, who you have *real* sexual relationships with. A concept, I'd wager, Tripp is not familiar with. You want to talk about bullshit? Your quote is bullshit and you know it. You don't owe me anything, not even a consolation pizza." He shoved the box nearest him away. "Or an explanation. But I really thought we had something going."

"We did!" Jessica interjected.

Bobby put up a hand to stop her. "And you're going to let your desire to make money off of Tripp or the rest of this pissant town trump that. That's more important to you."

"That's not it!" Jessica protested, defensive and misunderstood.

"Then what is it?"

Jessica scrambled for the words to explain herself. It was about business, which was ultimately about money, but it was bigger than that. It was ethics, and her oath to zealously represent her clients. It was pride and integrity. It was her reputation as a lawyer, which was wrapped up in her whole identity. She could not form a coherent sentence explaining this, and found herself just stuttering, "It's . . . it's . . . it's . . ."

"Jessica, my whole life guys like Tripp Wishingham have beat me out for things they didn't deserve. They're bigger and stronger and better looking and inherently more charming. They're also assholes and bullies. Why people are drawn to them is something I will never understand."

Without another word, Bobby got up and let himself out of the office. Jessica watched him leave, unable to move or speak.

CHAPTER
EIGHTEEN

After Bobby left, Jessica allowed herself a private, fifteen-minute cry in her office, then set about work. Unfortunately, work involved refreshing Bobby's article on her computer and keeping track of the comments below it, so his name literally flashed before her eyes all afternoon. She didn't much care what anyone else thought about the article, but she knew Coach would. Any minute now, the article about the protest would pop up and there'd be some more to keep up with. A large part of her felt like she deserved some of this torture for going against her initial instinct, that she shouldn't have ever gone out with Bobby in the first place for this very reason. Somehow it felt better to be able to blame herself. If the problem were her fault, then she could fix it.

She had to meet with Coach. They needed to go on a PR offensive. Luckily, it was still during the school day, so email was the best way to get him and she wouldn't have to hear his voice. She and Diane had spent the better part of an hour coming up with a game plan. She knew she'd better execute it soon before she overthought the whole thing and chickened out.

To: fwishingham@ashton.k-12.ga.us
From: JFisher email
Subject: Ashton Post

Coach – I've been giving it some thought, and I think I've
found a way to counteract the negative PR in Sunday's *Post*
and today's protest. Can you swing by my office when you
get off work? – Jessica

Jessica read over what she'd written. Short, sweet, not too
many details. She squeezed a stress ball shaped like a banana
from the local farmer's market, closed her eyes, and hit send.
Done.

School ended at 3:30, and it wasn't football season, so there
wasn't any obvious reason Coach couldn't get to Jessica's office by
4:30, but he didn't arrive until 5:15 anyway. She'd bribed Diane
to stay late by promising her not only double overtime pay but
also lunch at the restaurant of her choice the next day. There was
no way she was going to trust herself alone with Coach.

He arrived with who Jessica could only assume was his fiancée in tow. Diane brought them back and then sat in the chair
closest to the window. A good southern boy, Coach waited until
all the women were seated before taking his chair.

"This better be good," he gruffed, crossing his arms over his
chest.

"I think it is," said Jessica, as Diane nodded. Since Coach
hadn't bothered to introduce his fiancée, she said, "I don't think
we've formally met. I'm Jessica, Coach's lawyer, and this is Diane,
my paralegal-slash-keeper."

The woman put a perfectly manicured hand into Jessica's
outstretched one. "Emily. Nice to meet you," she said, then nodded at Diane. Jessica got the distinct impression that, as the help,
Diane didn't merit her own handshake.

"I'm glad you're here, Emily," Jessica said, meaning it. "I think
you can help add some perspective to all of this." Jessica had no
idea if this was true, but it seemed to resonate with Emily, who
smiled proudly. "Right. So, I've been monitoring the comments

on the article on the *Post*, and here's the thing. Public opinion is not entirely against you. There's a bunch of folks who agree that you didn't sign up to be a dad. So long as you're meeting your financial obligations, you aren't required to do anything else. Those pussy hats are politically charged, and people don't really stop to think about the message behind them. Opinion behind the protest seems to be along political lines, and, given the politics of Ashton, you're more or less okay. I'm not so much worried about the majority opinion; I'm worried about what gets in people's heads and sticks there without them knowing it."

Jessica tried to gauge Coach's and Emily's reactions so far. Coach unfolded his arms and leaned forward, but the stony look on his face remained. Emily's face remained neutrally painted on. She was too young for Botox, but she had that same immobile smile and perfect, painted-on eyebrows.

Jessica continued. "That said, a very clear majority thinks that mamas know their babies better than dads in general. If Mama says it is best for you to meet Francesca, it's best for you to meet Francesca." She paused. Coach's features were hardened in concentration. He appeared to still be listening, though, so she went on. "I know you don't want to. And I know you must have thought this through and have some good reasons for that." Jessica mentally slipped another quarter into the bullshit jar. "So far, other than Daddy knows best—and I'm not saying he doesn't—but other than that, you haven't articulated why." Jessica was enjoying this. She thought her plan was a stroke of genius and wanted to draw out the reveal to revel in the praise that would inevitably come.

Coach shifted his weight around and said, "So what's this brilliant plan you have?"

"Christmas is just in a couple of weeks, right? In the spirit of the season, of generosity and all that, buy her a Christmas present. That's a normal thing to do. I mean, there's an argument to be made that it would be weird if you didn't buy her a Christmas present."

"Okay . . ."

"And deliver it yourself."

Emily gazed at him beatifically, a Renaissance painting of Mary Magdalene looking at her Savior. "That sounds like a—"

"No." Like every other time, Coach shifted into a predatory cat posture quicker than Jessica could see the transition.

"Hold up," Jessica said, her hand a shield between them. He was not going to shoot down her plan this quickly. She noticed Diane straightening her back in a high-alert stance. Diane had probably not seen this rapid transformation before. Emily clearly had. She scanned Coach to assess the level of threat, then returned back to what Jessica had begun to think of as factory settings, neutral and bland. "I'm not saying show up in a Santa suit on Christmas morning. I'm just saying go over to their house at a prearranged time and hand her a present. Stay for fifteen minutes. Take a picture or two for the *Post*."

"I don't want to meet her!"

"I know that. I get that." Another quarter in the jar. Anything to save this solution. "But we don't always get what we want, do we?" Jessica thought briefly about Bobby's parting words and thought, *Maybe Coach always does.* She shoved Bobby to an unused corner of the waffle in her brain and went back to the room she was in. "Look, I'm mainly concerned about the courtroom. The most the judge can do is order visitation and you don't take advantage of it. The biggest consequence of that is that you don't get any more visitation, which you didn't want in the first place. So, who cares about that? You're the one concerned about the optics. I'm here to tell you that there is no way to spin 'Dad has no interest in meeting daughter' into gold. You look good without making a whole every-other-weekend kissy-huggy deal about it."

Coach was snorting through his nostrils like a bull again. "I don't like this."

"I'm not asking you to like this." *Do me a fucking favor*, she thought. *Please.* "This isn't all about you, Coach. I'm losing actual business on account of your antics. Your daughter is getting hurt. Good Lord, how difficult is a freaking photo op?"

"Your job is to do what I tell you to do."

"Again, you're wrong about what my job is. My job is to get the results you want in court. I can do that. But you can't bully your way out of every situation. Meeting your daughter may be one of them."

"Bully?" Coach's voice was loud.

"Tripp, honey." Diane leaned across Emily, her voice dripping with sugar syrup. "Listen to me." Diane had apparently joined the cast of *Steel Magnolias* and was channeling Dolly Parton's Truvy Jones.

Jessica picked up a stress ball shaped like a mailbox from the UPS store and did a number on it. Let Diane try. Jessica's appeal to cold logic was useless; maybe Diane had some southern magical rhetorical trick Jessica wasn't capable of. She wouldn't be surprised.

"Tripp, you've known me a long time, right? Ever since you were just a good-looking kid and I worked in the front office of the school?"

Coach nodded.

"I know this town. I know the people in it. Baby, this is December. There's not a woman who lives here, except maybe Jessica here, who doesn't go to sleep with the Hallmark Channel on. They are *all about* long-lost daddies and Christmastime reunions. Putting a picture of your baby blues next to Francesca's matching ones in the *Post*? Oooh-eee, you're going to make the entire Junior League cream their silk panties."

Instead of being offended, Emily giggled. She knew it was true.

Jessica considered puking into her trash can, but she swallowed her bile when she saw how Coach fed off this treacle. She wondered, seriously, if she was ever going to make it in the non-urban South as a lawyer. What Diane was doing right now seemed like a necessary skill, and it was one Jessica didn't want to learn.

Coach laughed, putting a meaty paw on Emily's thigh. "They would lap that up like kittens, wouldn't they?"

"You bet, sugah," Emily cooed, drawing out the word taffy-like for the better part of three whole seconds.

Coach stood. "I'm not saying yes, but I'm not saying no. Give me some time to sleep on it." He nodded at Diane and turned to Jessica. "Don't ever let this one go; she knows what she's doing." He pointed a finger gun at Diane and clicked his tongue twice before letting himself out, dragging Emily by her hand.

As soon as Jessica heard the door close, she said to Diane, "That was gross."

"That worked."

"It was *gross*."

"Sugar"—Diane smiled at Jessica as she said it—"you bullshitted him when you said you understood where he was coming from when I know for a hundred percent certain that you did not. I bullshitted him by implying that the women in this town find him attractive, which they do. Which one of us is more full of shit?"

Jessica gaped at Diane, who just threw back her head and hooted, knowing she was going to have steak for lunch tomorrow at her boss's expense.

CHAPTER
NINETEEN

⟶

Come Wednesday morning, they had still not heard back from Coach one way or another. Jessica had a quick hearing for a name change first thing and was back at the office by 10:00 a.m. She tossed the name change file in the "closed" pile, got herself a cup of coffee, and settled in to check the *Post*'s website. The *Post* was the best and possibly only way to keep up with the Ashton gossip. A small local paper, it only came out twice a week, Sundays and Wednesdays. There was a daily news briefing email that mostly contained obituaries, lost dog notices, and police blotters, which Jessica read every morning. In a small community, especially as a lawyer, it was important to know who died and who got arrested.

Since this was Wednesday, the email was more substantive. It highlighted the articles the *Post* thought might get clicks. She skimmed it, not caring one whit about the construction of a roundabout near the high school. She cared a little bit more about the county purchasing new fire trucks since she wanted the fire trucks to be operational if her house caught on fire. Thankfully, the pink pussy hat protestors, having had their day in the sun, had moved on to other things, probably after getting suspended from school and punished by their parents, consequences Jessica would have fought vehemently against had she been in any other position. Then an editorial caught her eye: "You Too? When #MeToo Comes to Ashton, by Bobby Turnbull." Jessica clicked on it instantly.

One of the main reasons people like living in Ashton is that they feel safe here. Our crime indicators show that Ashton is one of the safest places to live in the state. We haven't had a murder in three years. Our violent crime rate places us in the top ten safe cities in Georgia, according to Georgia Bureau of Investigation statistics.

Of course, you know what they say. There are three kinds of lies: lies, damned lies, and statistics. Statistics are only as good as the numbers inputted into the formula. Unreported crime, by definition, doesn't count in the reports.

Sexual crimes are some of the most underreported crimes in the country. This occurs for a variety of reasons, not the least of which is the fear of exposure on the part of the victims. Victims often feel alone and as if they will not be believed. This is something the #MeToo movement has sought to undo. By highlighting the prevalence of sexual assault, women coming forward with their #MeToo stories are illustrating that it can happen to anyone and there is no shame and no blame in being a victim.

The shame and blame should be in and on the perpetrator. Yet we still, as a society, glorify the perpetrators. Look at our cultural icons, the movies and heroes we hold dear. The idea of a "baby mama" is a joke, but who is up at three in the morning changing a diaper and listening to a baby cry? Not the baby's daddy, whose only contribution is twenty minutes of pleasure and the occasional check, if Mama is lucky. How many politicians still hold office after credible claims of sexual assault? How many movie stars still make millions at the box office despite using their fame and box office power to take advantage of people without that kind of clout? Does character matter? Can we separate the art from the artist?

This paper has been covering the paternity suit filed by a local mother against a popular football coach. We've been giving you news as it unfolds, as is befitting a local paper. But should we be digging deeper? Should we be looking into the night, seventeen years ago, when this child was conceived? The mother says she didn't file suit until now because she didn't know who the father was until a genetic test identified the coach. I don't know about you, but it sounds to me like there wasn't a whole lot of informed consent going on back in 2001.

A group of girls from the high school sought to highlight these facts but were quickly silenced by school administration, law enforcement, and, likely, their parents. What does it say about Ashton as a community that we tell young people that they should not speak out when they see injustice? We should be encouraging this kind of speech instead of silencing it. Maybe these girls have their own stories to tell. Now we may never know.

But it is never too late to tell. #YouToo, Sarah James? If you want to speak up, this reporter is listening. I'll bet you're not alone.

The last line may as well have read, "And fuck you, Jessica Fischer: Yes, this is just as personal as you suspect."

Jessica folded her arms on her desk and laid her head down on them. *Think, girl, think*, she told herself. Coach might not have responded to her thoughts about getting Francesca a Christmas gift, but he sure as shit was going to respond to Bobby more or less calling him a rapist in the paper everyone read. Without lifting her head, she yelled, "Diane!"

"What?" Diane yelled from the other room.

"Come in here."

"Do I have to?"

"Diane!" Jessica yelled, louder than the first time. Jessica heard a groan and the sound of the wheels on Diane's desk chair against the plastic carpet protector under her desk.

"What do you want from me?" Diane said from the hallway as she approached. When she saw Jessica's head on her desk, she patted Jessica's hair and said, "What's the matter, baby?"

Jessica pointed at her computer screen, and Diane read the editorial.

"Mmm," said Diane. "Well. That's unfortunate timing."

"Unfortunate timing?" Jessica picked her head up and sat up straight. Diane's hand slid to Jessica's shoulder, but she didn't lose contact. "Bless Bobby's heart. He's mad at me because he thinks I chose Coach over him, and he's taking it out on me in a very public way."

Diane pursed her lips and moved them around as if chewing on some words.

"The worst part," Jessica said, before Diane could get a sound out, "I mean the very worst part is that I agree with him. The very first time I talked to him on the phone I could not believe he wasn't asking me any questions about that. I had the impression that he wasn't very interested in the story, or not very interested in making Coach look bad, or maybe even not that smart. Part of me wants to cuss him out for being such a vengeful asshole, and part of me wants to throw my arms around him for being one of the only people in this damned town who seems to have any idea that what Coach did was wrong."

Diane laughed.

"Why are you laughing? This isn't funny!"

"Oh honey, the situation isn't, but you are. Lighten up! Look, I don't know what Bobby's into, but there might be a way you can combine the two . . . cussing at him and throwing yourself at him, I mean. Some of my best sex has come after a good cussing out."

"Shut up, I'm serious."

"I know you are. Has Coach emailed you yet? I know he hasn't called."

"I don't even know. This is the first email I opened." Jessica printed out the article before closing it—no matter how mad she was, she knew to preserve evidence for the file—and turning back to Outlook. One glance at the subject line of her top email and she hurled an f-bomb: "Your Boyfriend." She opened it and read: *You need to do something about your boyfriend. What are we going to do about that crap in the paper today? I'll stop by after work, but I think it's a bad idea for me to go to the house of someone who I am falsely being accused of raping.*

"Ha!" Diane's bark was loud and piercing.

Jessica looked at her, incredulous. "What in the hell could possibly be funny about that email?"

Diane took her time walking back around Jessica's desk so she could sit. "It's not funny ha-ha," she said, arranging her skirt around her thighs, the houndstooth pattern matching the maroon upholstery on the seat of the chair. "It's funny like uncanny how Coach manages to just fall into the perfect answer for stuff."

Jessica narrowed her eyes at Diane. "Huh?"

"That's how he gets out of meeting Francesca!"

It wasn't just a light bulb that turned on for Jessica; it was a whole chandelier.

CHAPTER TWENTY

"I promise you, Jessica, I had nothing to do with that editorial," Eric Crabtree said when she called him.

"I know."

"In fact, it surprised the hell out of me that Bobby would do that to your client, what with you two being an item and all."

Jessica slammed her fist down on her desk. "Jesus Christ! Why does everyone think that? It isn't even true! We went out twice and that's it. Everyone in this whole godforsaken town has us married off with a couple of kids."

"Methinks thou dost protest too much," Eric said.

"Methinks I'm just frustrated as hell that this whole town is talking about my social life."

"First of all, it isn't like there's much else to talk about around here in between football and baseball season since our basketball team sucks. Secondly, you have to admit you and Bobby would make adorable babies."

"Shut your mouth, Eric," Jessica said, wishing she could shut it for him with her fist. She did not want any reminders of the potential future she was not going to have with Bobby, didn't need any extra pictures in her mind's eye.

Eric laughed. "You need to work on not getting riled up by this crap. You're such an easy mark! Look, I don't give a squirrel's fart who you go out with except as it pertains to my client. In this case, I don't know what you did to piss Bobby off, but you did it right good and he put it in the paper."

Jessica made a garbled sound, everything she felt about Bobby and Coach condensed into one noise.

"You called me. Wanna tell me why?"

Jessica let out a whoosh of breath. "I'm just gonna speak in the passive voice here, since the whys and whos are irrelevant and pissing me off. There has been a lightly veiled public accusation that my client raped your client back in 2001. Based on my reading of social media comments, those accusations are being taken seriously by a substantial amount of people. It would be imprudent at best for my client to be alone with your client and/or Francesca at this time based on those accusations."

Eric was so quiet that Jessica thought they had been disconnected. She was just about to check when he spoke. "Damn. I went three whole hours thinking that editorial was good for my client, that it was turning the tide of public opinion against your golden boy. Turns out you're much wilier than that."

"Never underestimate me, Eric," Jessica said, then hung up the phone before she could ruin a perfect exit line. So what if Eric thought she'd come up with all this on her own.

Diane clapped her hands. "I thought you'd lost it for a moment there, but you pulled it off! Bravo!"

Brava, thought Jessica, but figured she ought not to ruin the moment by correcting Diane's Italian.

"Of course," Diane continued, "you've sort of fed the rumor mill a little more grist."

"Huh?"

"Well, now Eric thinks that you got Bobby to write that editorial on purpose to distract people from thinking that he didn't want to meet his daughter. How could you get Bobby to do that for you on purpose unless you and Bobby are still a thing?"

"Well, fuck."

"Language."

"I'd argue the situation calls for the language."

Diane waved her hand. "What are you going to do?"

"What do you mean?"

"I mean, are you going to talk to Bobby?"

"Why would I talk to Bobby? I'd be perfectly happy never talking to Bobby again as long as I live." Talking to him meant dealing with her own feelings, and she simply wasn't up to the task.

"Eric shouldn't underestimate you, but you shouldn't underestimate him either."

"What do you mean?" Jessica asked, her brain too addled by the rope-a-dope pummeling it had taken today to follow.

Diane deepened her voice in a passable imitation of Eric's. "Seems to me what we've got here is a conspiracy against my client. Miz Fischer here and her lover are waging a public relations campaign to distract from the fact that her client is not only someone who doesn't respect women's boundaries sexually, but doesn't respect their emotional intelligence when it comes to fixing the problems he created."

Jessica reached into her purse, pulled out her wallet, and handed Diane a dollar.

"What's that for?" Diane asked.

"The four words I just thought and the quarters you'd make me put in the swear jar."

"Sweetie, you've got to talk to Bobby. You've got to get out ahead of this. If the tables were turned, wouldn't you want to know what people were saying about you?"

Jessica groaned.

"You can't avoid him forever. This town is too small."

"Stay here?" Jessica gave Diane puppy dog eyes. Diane just patted her hand. "Whaddya think? Cell or office?"

Diane looked up at the ceiling. "Office phone. This is bidness."

Jessica looked up the number and dialed Bobby on her desk phone. She had to do this now before she thought about it too much. He answered on the second ring. *"Ashton Post*, Bobby Turnbull."

Jessica attempted to speak and found her throat was stuck. She cleared it and said, "Hey, Bobby, it's Jessica."

After a moment, Bobby said simply, "Oh."

"I'm not calling to give you grief." She paused for a moment to gather up her thoughts. "I just thought you might want to know, well, we might want to talk about your editorial, and what it seems like Eric is going to say about it, and what Coach already said. We might want to present a united front about it with the local gossip mill to nip all this in the bud."

"What are you talking about?" Bobby's voice wasn't cold, exactly, but it was flat and unreadable. Diane got up and leaned her head next to Jessica's so she could hear.

To quell the shaking, Jessica slipped into lawyer mode. She centered her gaze on her wall of diplomas and told herself that she was representing Jessica Fischer, talking about her to a third party. Instantly, the words came to her. "More than one person seems to be under the impression that Jessica Fischer and Bobby Turnbull are a current item. I have done my best to stop the rumors, but you know what a gossipy little town this is. It wouldn't matter, and I wouldn't necessarily care, except the impression seems to be that the recent editorial in the paper has been planted as a result of that relationship."

"What?" Bobby said. "That doesn't make any sense! The editorial did Tripp no favors."

"That's what I thought, originally, but apparently I'm a better lawyer than I imagined."

Bobby laughed despite himself. "How so?"

"I managed to spin the editorial as an excuse for Coach not

visiting Francesca—that he shouldn't be alone with young women after being publicly accused of rape. Nor should he be alone with his accuser. That wouldn't be smart, would it?"

"That's . . . actually true. Dammit."

Neither of them said anything. Diane grabbed a pen and wrote on a legal pad, *SPEAK*. Jessica wrote back, *SPEAK WHAT?* Diane wrote back, *ANYTHING!*

"So . . . what are we gonna do?" Jessica said, weakly.

She could hear Bobby shifting around in his chair and sighing. "Jessica, look, I appreciate your calling me and telling me what everyone is saying. That's good information that I needed to know. But you made it perfectly clear the other day that there was no 'we' who was gonna do anything. I'm not sure I understand the question. What is there to do?"

Jessica looked up at Diane, who shrugged. She said, "I don't know."

"Jessica," Diane said, loud enough that Bobby surely heard it through the phone, "Judge Brandywine's office is on the phone."

"I've got to go, Bobby, the judge's office is on the phone. Bye." She put the handset in its place, then cradled her head in her arms on her desk. Diane petted her hair.

Jessica said, "Thanks for the rescue."

"That's what you pay me for, sweetie."

CHAPTER
TWENTY-ONE

For the most part, all commerce that wasn't Christmas shopping shut down in Ashton between Thanksgiving and New Year's Day. Everyone's focus was on decoration and parades and generalized celebration. Outdoing one's neighbors with what Jessica thought kitschy and everyone else seemed to think joyful noise was Ashton's favorite pastime. January was spent taking it all down and recovering.

Christmas wasn't really Jessica's thing. They'd never celebrated it in her family, since her father was Jewish and her mother was a twice-a-year Presbyterian who also thought that teaching kids about Santa was teaching them to lie. This made Jessica quite the outlier in Ashton, whose population-to-church ratio seemed to be in the neighborhood of twenty-to-one. She went to all the obligatory court and chamber holiday parties, drank a glass of eggnog in her mother's honor on Christmas Eve, and for the last three years had gone to Christmas dinner at Diane's house to stave off the loneliness. She'd considered going to church her first Christmas in Ashton, but the thought of being single in a sea of families wearing coordinating outfits was not nearly as appealing as binge watching the new season of *The Ranch* on Netflix wearing fleece pajamas, and she'd never looked back. Not for the first time, she considered getting a dog. A rescue, maybe a mutt with one eye and three legs and a tragic past.

Super Bowl Sunday was the turning point between the tail end of the holiday season and getting back to work. Jessica watched the Super Bowl for cultural literacy purposes but didn't care who won. This year, Diane was having a Super Bowl party, and Jessica agreed to go for lack of anything better to do. She baked a sheet cake from a box mix and decorated it with white icing, strawberries, blueberries, and banana slices to represent the New England Patriots colors, all because Diane had a minor crush on Tom Brady.

She gathered up her cake, and bottles of Absolut and cranberry juice so she'd have something to drink, and headed over.

Diane was perched on the couch next to Denise, whose hand was on her husband's knee when she arrived. A very pregnant Kaitlyn came out of the kitchen with a tray of vegetables, which she put on the coffee table before scrunching herself into a lounge chair. Jessica hadn't seen either Kaitlyn or Denise since Christmas, and Kaitlyn's stomach had grown noticeably in the past few weeks. Despite the size of her belly, she was still small enough to tuck her legs underneath herself, becoming quite compact under a crocheted blanket. Diane had told her that Kaitlyn would rather be watching the game with Charlie, but Denise put the kibosh on that. How long would this poor girl have to pretend she was no longer in love with her baby's father? How long would Denise pretend she couldn't see it? Jessica fought the desire to drive Kaitlyn over to Charlie's house herself.

Jessica couldn't measure the quality of the football game, but she *could* tell you that Diane's palpable levels of lust over Adam Levine in the halftime show were embarrassing. "Diane," she shouted, when it was over, and Diane was fanning herself with the fake vapors, "calm down! You're going to stick to the couch."

Diane laughed and Denise cut her eyes over to where Kaitlyn sat. "There are children here," she said, in a stage whisper.

Jessica, who was feeling her vodka and cranberry, scanned the room as if searching for cops, then spoke out of the left side of her mouth. "Are you talking about the *pregnant woman* in the chair over there? I'm pretty sure she's aware of what lust does to the female body."

Denise sniffed and started to say something. Her husband, whose name was Steve or Craig, or maybe it was Greg, something generically middle-aged, Jessica couldn't remember, cut her off by asking her if she needed another glass of wine. He'd be ever so happy to get her one. He took Denise's wineglass from her and kissed her forehead. While her face was obscured, Jessica looked over at Kaitlyn and winked. Kaitlyn smiled and snuggled deeper under the blanket.

"So," Diane said. "What's your favorite commercial so far?"

"I like the *Game of Thrones*/Bud Light one," said Steve/Craig/Greg, settling a glass of yellow wine in his wife's hand.

"I hate *Game of Thrones*," said Denise. "Someone is always dying in some horribly violent way."

"That's what I like about it," said Steve/Craig/Greg, wielding a celery stick like a sword.

She waved her hand at him, knocking the celery stick to the floor. "Now see what you've done."

"Ah, my Mother of Dragons, see what *you've* done. Ranch dressing on Diane's rug." He grabbed a napkin and began to clean up the barely visible dot of a mess.

"You just wish you were Khal Drogo, Brian," Diane said, and Jessica thought, *Brian! That's what his name is.* "Jason Momoa has a good foot on you."

"Yes," said Brian, rubbing his bald head. "But we have the same hair."

Denise just rolled her eyes at Brian. Jessica guessed she'd heard some variation on that joke a thousand times.

"I like the one with Harrison Ford and the dog that orders stuff off of Alexa," said Diane. "He just gets better with age."

"Did you know that he and Carrie Fisher had an affair on the set of *Star Wars*? She was only nineteen, and he was like thirty and married," Jessica said.

Kaitlyn mumbled, "Gross."

Diane looked at Jessica with a scowl on her face. "You are just bound and determined to ruin everything, aren't you?"

"Facts ruin everything, unfortunately."

"Did you like any of the commercials?"

"I liked the Microsoft one with the adaptive controller thingy."

"Oh my gosh," interjected Kaitlyn. "That one made me literally cry!"

Jessica guessed that Kaitlyn said the word "literally" in most of her sentences, but in this case, it might, well, literally apply. That commercial had been tear worthy, especially if you had pregnancy hormones surging through your adolescent body.

"Right? It had all the feels." Jessica felt like she and Kaitlyn were having a moment. This was the first time all night that Kaitlyn had looked up from her phone. Jessica racked her brain to come up with something to say that wouldn't sound horribly grown-up and cringey. She got out, "Hey, Kaitlyn, did you—" when Kaitlyn's phone clattered to the floor and an expression of intense pain crossed the girl's face.

Kaitlyn's face stretched in all directions. Her mouth opened as if silently screaming. Her eyes were perfectly round and unblinking.

"Kaitlyn? Are you okay?"

This caught everyone else's attention. Denise shot out of

her seat and flew over to her daughter. "Katiebug? What's the matter?"

Kaitlyn looked up at her mother. She appeared to be no more than a small girl. "Mommy? Something is wrong."

Denise smoothed Kaitlyn's hair back against her forehead and kissed the top of her head. "What's wrong, baby? Tell me what's wrong."

Kaitlyn stood up, throwing off the blanket, and a splash of reddish water fell from between her legs.

"Brian!" Denise yelled. "Call an ambulance. I'm calling Dr. Prewitt."

Kaitlyn's placenta had begun to separate from her uterine wall, breaking the amniotic sac. There wasn't any reason for it: these things just happened sometimes. She was thirty-five weeks pregnant, and the baby was measuring at about five pounds. This made her close enough to full term that inducing labor was the best course of action. Denise and Brian were in the labor room with Kaitlyn. Jessica and Diane sat in the waiting room in the maternity ward.

"You don't have to stay here, you know," Diane said. "It's close to midnight. Go home and get some rest. I'll text you if anything happens."

Jessica considered this. She wanted to be supportive and to be there for the excitement, though they'd been told it would take a good six to eight hours for the inducement drugs to kick in. She'd heard women say they'd been in labor for longer, some up to a full day, but until this very moment she'd never given a moment's thought to what actually happened during those hours. The answer, apparently, was precious little. Except for the dramatic conclusion, labor was, by and large, a boring affair. "You wouldn't be mad at me?"

"Why would I be mad at you?"

"For being a shitty friend and sleeping in a comfortable bed while you make do with these horrible chairs."

"Honey, you're not family. You don't owe Kaitlyn anything. No reason for both of us to suffer. Come back early in the morning with a giant cup of something caffeinated and sweet and a box of hot Krispy Kremes, and we'll be eternally grateful."

"Are you sure?"

There was a clatter in the hallway that made both women stop their conversation and look up. Tripp Wishingham and a boy who could only be Charlie Kicklighter were heading their way.

"What the hell are you two doing here?" Coach said.

"Hi, how are you?" Jessica chirped in an extra-cheery voice to counteract Coach's rudeness.

Diane said, "Kaitlyn is my sister's daughter."

Coach narrowed his eyes and uttered one of his noncommittal grunts. Charlie stuck out his hand toward Diane. "Nice to meet you, ma'am. I'm Charlie. Do you know where Kaitlyn is? Is she okay?"

Diane shook Charlie's hand, clearly charmed. *Charming Charlie*, thought Jessica, trying not to let her smirk show on her face. Diane was such a sucker for a charismatic man-child. Still, he was here, that was something; he wasn't shirking from the get-go. He looked worried. Was he worried about Kaitlyn? Just generalized worry about becoming a teenage dad? Why had he brought Coach with him and not his parents?

"Of course, dear," Diane said, ever the southern hostess. "I'm Auntie Diane. I'll take you to her." She got out of her chair, putting her hands on her lower back and stretching out the discomfort before leading Charlie down the hallway.

"So what are *you* doing here, then?" said Coach.

"I was at Diane's family Super Bowl party when Kaitlyn

went into labor. I just came along for the ride. A better question is: What are you doing here? Wouldn't it make more sense for Charlie's parents to be here with him?"

Coach sat in one chair, but the spread of his legs and shoulders easily took up the seats on either side of him. When he took in a breath, his chest expanded, and the space he took up in the world did too. "These are my kids. We're not just out there playing a game. We have to live together as a unit or we can't play together as a unit. What affects one of us affects all of us. All for one and one for all. Like the Three Musketeers, only there's like thirty guys it applies to instead of just three."

Jessica was surprised that Coach knew "All for one and one for all" was a Three Musketeers reference. For that matter, she was surprised that he knew the Three Musketeers were more than just a candy bar. This was the first time, she realized, she'd ever seen him act like a human who cared about someone other than himself, and she felt guilty for dismissing him the way she did. He was a college-educated man and a high school teacher. It occurred to her that she didn't even know what he taught, and a pang of guilt passed through her like D'artagnan's sword. Diane was right. There was a reason why so many people liked him. There was a reason why he was able to bring out the best in these young men on the football field. Bullying or hero worship alone wouldn't do it. Jessica stared at his face, wondering what lay beneath this pompous, meathead exterior. Maybe there were riches he was afraid to expose. Perhaps he inflated himself on purpose to cover up the fact that he felt small. Who knew?

"What do you teach?" she asked.

Coach looked up from his phone. He seemed surprised she'd spoken to him. "Huh? What do I teach?"

"Yeah. What do you teach? I'm gonna guess history." She could see him being a World War II buff, playing with G.I. Joes as a little kid.

"Nope. Physics."

"Physics? Seriously?" If he'd said, "I teach the intersectionality of gender studies and racial politics from queer perspectives," she wouldn't have been more surprised.

"Yup."

"Huh," she said. "I would not have pegged you for a math guy."

"Physics is so much more than math, you know. It's how the world works. There're rules for everything. Physics is how you get good at playing pool. Physics is how a skinny guy can still be a decent football player if he knows how to leverage himself. It's actually pretty interesting. And useful. I hate shit like English. Who the hell cares where a comma goes? How is that going to help me in the real world?"

Jessica opened her mouth to argue. Millions of dollars have been won and lost on the meaning of sentences based on comma placement, but she decided this was not the time or the place to bring that up. Instead, she said, "I was never good at physics. The math tripped me up."

"The math is just how you express it. You ever watch *Myth-Busters*? All that blowing up stuff and cool shit is physics. Teachers mess up when they teach it like math. You have to show the kids what it does. Then it makes sense. I'll bet I could have made you understand it." Coach winked at her. Jessica thought back to the first time they'd met and how his wink had disgusted her. Tonight, though, she could see the charm in it and she laughed. She still thought he was an asshole, but maybe—just maybe—he had a redeeming characteristic or two.

Coach picked his phone back up and started scrolling through it. Jessica wanted to keep talking to him, to find out more, though she couldn't think of anything interesting to say. "So who won the Super Bowl?"

"Patriots. Thirteen to three."

"Oh." So much for that line of questioning. "Um, what did you think of the halftime show?"

"I wanted that skinny little twink to put his shirt back on."

Jessica didn't want to laugh, but she couldn't help herself. "Diane didn't."

Coach shook his head and went back to his phone. So much for their intimate bonding moment. Jessica pulled her phone off the charger and scrolled Instagram for a few minutes. She thought about going home but didn't want to leave without telling Diane where she was going. It was a good forty-five minutes before Diane came back into the waiting room.

"Hoo boy," she said. "That poor kid."

"Is Kaitlyn okay?"

"Oh, Kaitlyn will be fine. Between contractions, anyway. I'm talking about Charlie."

That got Coach's attention. "What's wrong with Charlie?"

"Nothing's really wrong with him, other than the fact that he impregnated my niece." Diane plunked herself down in a chair next to Jessica and leaned her head against Jessica's arm. "Let's just say he wasn't exactly welcomed by the baby's grandparents. They seem to have forgotten their southern raising. You can hate the guy, but that's no reason to be rude." Diane's jaw cracked as she yawned wide enough to show her gold fillings.

"He can be there when his kid is born if he wants to be," said Coach.

"That's what I said," said Diane. "Don't worry. Denise gets feisty, but she's all bark. It helped when the nurse came in and said the father had more right to be in there than the grandparents."

"I'll bet that went over well," Jessica said, joining in on Diane's laughter.

"Oh, you know it. It had the benefit of making the nurse the target of her wrath rather than Charlie, though, so it worked."

The three of them sat in silence for a moment, trying to

picture the scene, when Denise and Brian came into the waiting room. You could practically see the gray cloud gathering over Denise's head. Ever the southern gentleman when the situation called for it, Coach stood and nodded at Denise, since he had no hat to tip. "Ma'am," he said.

"Coach Wishingham," she said with cold formality, needing no introduction. Everyone knew who Coach was.

Brian stuck out his hand, a goofy smile on his face. This was probably as close to a celebrity encounter as he'd had. "Hi, I'm Brian Pike. Kaitlyn's dad." The men shook hands. Brian was a good six inches shorter than Coach. He wasn't a short guy; Coach was just exceptionally tall. This meant that Brian had to look up at Coach, exposing his neck. Jessica thought of a werewolf movie she'd seen where lesser werewolves ritually exposed their necks to the dominant werewolves to prove their submission and trust. Women had pecking orders, no doubt, but she could not think of anything equivalent to this alpha-beta primal pack behavior.

Jessica felt the heat of Denise's glare before she saw it. She was not happy with Brian sucking up to anyone who was on Team Charlie.

Brian was oblivious to his wife's weather as everyone settled into chairs. "We thought we'd give Kaitlyn and Charlie some privacy. Nothing is going to happen for a while, anyway."

"Frankly, I think they've had too much privacy. That's why we're here," Denise said.

Diane patted her on the hand.

After a few moments of awkward silence, Jessica gathered her purse, stood, and excused herself, promising to return in the morning with real, non-cafeteria coffee and Krispy Kremes.

By the time Jessica got to the hospital in the morning with coffees and donuts, Coach had gone to school and was replaced with Charlie's parents. Diane made introductions and they all sat down to continue waiting. Jessica didn't have to hear the back-story to know that Charlie's parents were divorced. They sat in different rows of chairs on either side of Diane. They were cordial enough, but there was frost on the edges of each word they spoke to each other.

"I'm sorry I didn't bring you guys any coffee," Jessica said, apologetically. "I didn't know you were here."

"No worries," Charlie's mother, Naomi, said. "I had plenty before I left the house." She reached in her voluminous purse and pulled out a shiny red apple that matched her shiny red smile. "Did you know that eating an apple gives you just as much energy as a cup of coffee?"

"I did not," replied Jessica, immediately slotting Naomi in the "we will never be friends" category. "That's interesting."

Rick, Charlie's father, gave such an exaggerated eye roll, astronauts on the International Space Station could probably see it. Naomi kept her smile long past its natural expiration date, demonstrating to everyone that she had seen Rick roll his eyes.

Brian came into the lobby and made a beeline toward Jessica. "Thank God you brought coffee. They gave us two little shot glasses of undrinkable swill and some powdered creamer."

Rick stood up and shook Brian's hand, clapping him on the back. "Good to see you, Brian."

"You too," said Brian, grabbing two coffees. "You see the game last night?"

Jessica watched the men talk about the Super Bowl, envious that men everywhere could use that universal conversation starter. "You see the game last night?" You didn't even really have to follow sports to make it work. You could follow it up with something without substance like, "Oh yeah, man oh man!" and let the other guy fill in the details. You didn't even have to know what game was on last night. There was always a game on last night.

Suddenly, all of the parents' phones plus Diane's chimed at once. Naomi and Diane looked at theirs first and then looked at each other. Diane looked at the crowd. "She's pushing."

Everyone but Rick and Jessica scrambled up and headed toward Kaitlyn's room. Rick looked at Jessica. "Am I supposed to be in there?"

"I have absolutely no idea. This is my first waiting party and I'm not family."

Rick huffed out a breath and scratched the stubble on his cheeks. "I was in there when Charlie was born, but it was just me and Naomi and medical people. There wasn't space for a whole lot of other folks." Rick looked down the hallway. "There's a lot of people in that room."

"Yeah," said Jessica, unable to say what she really wanted to say, which was that a seventeen-year-old girl was going to have her legs splayed open. She probably wanted as few people as possible to be looking. They both sat there for a moment, staring at the cheery wallpaper covered in storks and wooden bassinets.

"It doesn't matter what I do, Naomi is going to think I did the wrong thing. So I may as well do what I want, right?"

Jessica was deciding if it was a rhetorical question when Rick continued. "Of course, what I want is for Charlie to have kept it zipped eight months ago or at least to have used a condom. But we can't have that, can we? So second best is for me to stay at home. Then someone brings the baby by in a few months when it learns to smile and hold its own head up. They're so goddamn fragile." Rick held up his hands. They were meaty and cracked, and his nails were stained with something dark. "These hands were meant to do brake jobs and flush transmission fluid, not handle five-pound humans. Bring it to me when it's time to teach it to fish."

Rick's face was dead earnest. He was not trying to be funny, so Jessica tried not to laugh. His black hair had a cowlick that stuck up in the back and probably always had. It was probably cute when he was younger, something that made girls want to touch his hair to smooth it down, but now that the hair on the top of his head was thinning, it looked a little odd. He had thick stubble, a five-o'clock shadow at nine in the morning. His shoulders were wide and his hips were narrow, like Charlie's, but middle age had settled around his waist and into his lap as he sat.

Rick looked around the room. "How come it's just us in here? Doesn't anyone else get born in this town?"

"I guess not today," Jessica said.

Rick clicked his teeth together a few times and nodded. "Well," he said with some finality. "An *apple* doesn't do shit for me. I'm going to find a vending machine or the cafeteria and get some coffee. Whatever it is, it can't be worse than the motor oil we drink at the shop." He stood up, jingled the change in his pockets, and left the room.

Jessica took a sip of her peppermint mocha and a bite of a still-warm Krispy Kreme, and went through emails on her phone.

A few minutes later, the door to the waiting room opened but didn't close. Jessica heard Rick's and another man's voice, this one younger and oddly familiar. They were talking about cars, so Jessica checked out of trying to absorb the details and went back to her phone. Then she heard Rick say, "Just come in and sit a minute. I'm bored off my ass."

The other man said, "I really can't, I'm on the clock."

"Come on, Lee. Five minutes. This is female central here."

Lee. Diane's boy toy. That's who it was. What in the hell was he doing here?

"Five minutes," Lee said, and followed Rick into the room. He saw Jessica and said, "Oh, hey, Jessica, what are you doing here?"

"Diane's niece is having Rick's son's baby. I'm the Krispy Kreme delivery girl. Want one?" She offered the box. Lee came over and took one. He was wearing a lab coat, so she asked, "You work here?"

"Yeah, I work in pathology. I stare in microscopes. Mad scientist stuff."

"Nice," said Jessica. "And how do you know Rick?"

"I keep his truck running," said Rick.

"Best mechanic in Ashton," said Lee.

All three of them nodded, having exhausted that conversational gambit. Lee stared down at his feet and said, "I, uh, I take it Diane is here somewhere?"

"Yeah, she's in the room with Kaitlyn, along with three-quarters of the rest of Ashton, watching Kaitlyn push a human being out of her body," said Jessica.

"Well then." Lee stood up. "I'd better get back to the lab before she comes in here. I don't think she wants to see me."

"What makes you think that?"

Lee took a deep breath, considering. "You can ask her. I've got stuff in a centrifuge anyway. You probably know more than I do. If you think she wants to hear it, tell her I said hi."

CHAPTER
TWENTY-TWO

Charles Brian Kicklighter was born at 9:38 a.m. on February 4, 2019. He was a scant four pounds, fourteen ounces and just a hair under eighteen inches long. Diane thought he was the cutest little thing she'd ever seen. Whenever Denise or Kaitlyn texted her a picture, she'd run into Jessica's office to show her. Every morning, Diane subjected Jessica to a slideshow on her own phone. It wasn't enough to look at the pictures; Jessica had to hear the story behind each one, as if "Look at him waving his little hand!" were a story with a plot.

Jessica did her best to find something cute about the baby, but all she saw was a wrinkled, bald thing. He was so tiny and skinny that he looked a bit deflated, a balloon the day after the party. His eyes stayed closed. A round pacifier usually covered most of his face, which was dotted with neonatal acne. Still, she oohed and aahed like she was expected to. Jessica felt like she was the only unmarried woman in her late twenties who was unmoved by a small baby. If she gave any hint of that, it would start a whole series of conversations she had no interest in having.

Now that Charles Brian Kicklighter had a name and a birth-day, it was just a matter of waiting for Kaitlyn to turn eighteen to file the establishment of paternity suit. It was worlds easier if Kaitlyn were a legal adult. Otherwise, her mother had to sue on her behalf as her "next friend." The law said minors didn't have the capacity to file suit: like there was any magic that was going to happen to Kaitlyn between now and a few weeks from now. At seventeen years and three hundred sixty-two days old, she was too immature and unable to make the decisions she needed to file a lawsuit, but wait seventy-two hours and *presto chango, abracadabra, shazam!* Now we have a fully functional adult who can make intelligent choices.

Gotta draw a line somewhere. At least they could get a leg up on the paperwork so it was ready to file when February 25 rolled around.

A few days before filing day, flowers showed up at the office. Diane might have gotten away with retrieving them from the delivery person and secreting them away in her car without Jessica noticing if the woman from the flower shop hadn't been so vocal. "Someone has an admirer!" she sang as she passed them off. "These are simply *gorgeous!*"

This lured Jessica out of her office to see what the fuss was about. "What—or who—did you do to deserve this?" Jessica asked, burying her face in the showy, colorful flowers to get a good whiff.

Diane fluttered her eyelashes. "What business is that of yours?"

"Puh-lease. You cannot have a bouquet like that delivered to a place I pay the rent on and not give me details."

"His name is Steven and he goes to my sister's church." Diane was grinning.

"Well, well," said Jessica. "Another notch on your bedpost? Or is this guy for realsies?"

"What do I tell you, sweetie? For old Diane, boys are toys. This toy just happens to have excellent taste in flowers."

"Well that *toy* clearly has feelings. The kind of feelings that made him drop fifty bucks or more on these flowers."

Diane scoffed. "His feelings are in his pants. He just wants to ensure that *I* keep feeling in his pants."

Jessica's heart went out to poor Steven, who'd stood at the flower shop earlier in the day choosing a bouquet that he thought would impress Diane. "You're not very kind," Jessica said, feeling rejected on his behalf.

"What? I never promised him anything else."

"Humph." Unlike contracts, whose promises all had to be spelled out in the words in the documents, in real life, most promises were simply implied. That's why Jessica liked the law. It was simpler to understand than people. "You know, I saw Lee in the hospital."

"Lee? Lee who?" said Diane, arranging the flowers in the vase just so.

"Oh, stop it," Jessica said, actually annoyed now at Diane's deliberate obtuseness. "Boy Toy Lee. Bobby's friend from Waffle House. You know exactly who I'm talking about. He seemed traumatized by the idea of running into you, like you were one of those praying mantises that bites the head off her mate when she's done with him. When I asked him why, he told me to ask you."

Diane scrunched up her face. "Nonsense. We only went out a handful of times. Then he started getting icky, so I quit returning his calls."

"What do you mean, icky?"

Diane sighed. "Well, if you must know, he started to seem like he wanted more than just a little fun, and gah! No! He's so young I could have birthed him."

Jessica shook her head. She fought the urge to say, *I told you so.* She'd said from the beginning that Lee was way too young for Diane. "Let me get this straight. He's too young for you to have a relationship with, but not too young to have sex with? You are going to have to explain that one to me. That seems kind of backwards."

Diane huffed out a breath. "Jessica. Honey. He's twice the age of consent. He's not a child. He's young and firm and fun on a lonely Saturday night. Makes an old lady like me feel like she's still got it going on."

"You're not old!"

"I'm forty-eight. That's old enough. But he's what, thirty-two? Thirty-three? That's great for my ego. He's a nice guy, but I'm not in the market for a nice guy."

"What are you in the market for? A *not* nice guy?"

"Honestly? I'm not in the market for a guy. I've told you. I had David. David loved me and I loved David, and I'm not so foolish to think lightning strikes twice in the same place. I don't even want to chance it, really. Right now? I'm just taking what I can get while men still want me for anything at all."

Jessica stared at her. "That might be the saddest thing you've ever said." Diane was one of the most amazing people Jessica had ever met. She was smart and funny and simply gorgeous to boot—the thought of anyone not finding her attractive seemed out of the realm of possibility. Could Diane actually think that no one would love her now that David was gone? Diane wasn't like Jessica—she was sociable and magnetic. People flocked to her.

"You think?" Diane said. "Which one of us just got flowers? You're twenty-nine years old. I've known you three years now—have you gotten laid in all that time? That right there is the saddest thing I've ever said." She gave a humorless laugh.

"So what are you going to do with flower boy?" Jessica asked, trying to ignore the swirl of thoughts in her head. Part of her was jealous of Diane's ability to seize the moment, her ability to attract men, and her ability not to take everything oh-so-seriously, and part of her was horrified by the idea of it all. She went on the attack so she wouldn't have to defend herself. "Screw him a couple of times until he decides he might actually like you? Then kick him to the curb?"

Diane pointed a finger at Jessica. "Watch yourself."

"No," said Jessica. "You watch yourself. You're worth more than a good lay. The men in this town are telling you that if you'd just listen."

"Until you get laid, you may not advise me about my sex life, Sister Mary Jessica. I know what I want in my life, and I've lived it long and well enough to say. You, on the other hand, are too afraid to do anything, but you think you can sit in judgment of the rest of us." Diane turned sharply away, stalking off to the kitchenette, holding the glass vase close to her chest. Jessica heard the sink run for a moment, then Diane's heels click off toward her office. The vase landed with a final thunk on Diane's desk.

The day before Kaitlyn turned eighteen, she and Denise came into the office, with the baby asleep in a blue plaid car carrier seat and enough luggage to travel to Europe for the summer.

Kaitlyn's young body had sprung back into place, though her put-togetherness hadn't. Her dark-blonde hair was pulled back in a greasy, messy ponytail, and she wore no makeup. She looked like she hadn't slept since the last time Jessica had seen her, which, Jessica supposed, was entirely possible. Her tiny body swam in an oversized T-shirt covered in a cardigan over a pair of leggings. A receiving blanket covered with blue and yellow teddy bears hung over one shoulder. When Jessica went to hug her hello, she got a whiff of sour milk. Jessica glanced down at the sleeping baby. He had filled out quite a bit in the past few weeks, but he was still tiny. His head was cradled in a U-shaped pillow. Mittens that looked like little round raviolis covered his hands. A pacifier dangled out of the side of his mouth.

"Hi, y'all," Jessica whispered. "Come on in and sit down."

"Oh, you don't have to be quiet," Kaitlyn said, louder than

Jessica had ever heard her speak before. "C.B. can sleep through anything." She shook the handle of the car carrier to demonstrate that earthquakes, in addition to noise, wouldn't wake him.

When they settled in their chairs, Jessica slid a packet of papers across the desk to Kaitlyn. "Read this over."

Kaitlyn reached over to pick it up, but Denise was quicker and she grabbed it first.

Looking directly at Kaitlyn, Jessica said, "And Kaitlyn"—pause for dramatic effect—"if it's okay with *you*, sign on the page in the back with your name on it. We'll get your aunt Diane to notarize it. That page says you swear what is on the other pages is true."

"Okay," Kaitlyn said, patiently waiting for her mother to finish reading.

Denise finished, dramatically restacked and re-squared the papers by tapping them on the desk, and passed them to Kaitlyn without looking at her. She didn't wait for Kaitlyn to read them before saying, "I thought this was all about child support. Why does he get joint legal custody? I thought Kaitlyn was getting sole custody? And why does he get visitation? Look at how small this child is. He needs his mother. He can't be away from his mother. She needs him!"

Kaitlyn put the papers on the desk. She rolled up the sleeves of her sweater, closed her eyes, and scratched her elbows and forearms in long, exaggerated strokes.

"Should we let Kaitlyn read it before I answer your questions?" Jessica said.

Denise looked over at her daughter, whose eyes were still closed. "It doesn't appear that she is interested in reading it."

Kaitlyn opened her eyes and began scratching her left elbow in earnest. "I think I'm allergic to this cardigan. My elbow itches and I can't stop *scratching* it."

The penny dropped for Jessica. She was embarrassed by how

long it took her to remember their code. "Denise, let me talk to Kaitlyn alone for a minute."

Denise did not move. "I need to know what is going on here."

"I know you do, but ultimately Kaitlyn is my client. I need her to understand what is going on. She looks exhausted and overwhelmed with premature-baby stuff. I remember when I was seventeen, and the last person I wanted around when I felt that way was my mother. I loved her dearly, but I needed to process stuff before I talked with her about it."

Denise stared at Kaitlyn, who was frozen in place, her eyes fixed on a mug on Jessica's desk that said, *Do Not Confuse Your Google Search with My Law Degree.*

Denise looked back at Jessica. "You don't know my daughter. We are very close."

"I have no doubt. You love her with all your heart and all your soul and are doing everything in your power to protect her. But you are a very strong woman. I need to make sure it is Kaitlyn who is driving this boat."

"She is a child. She has no idea what she wants," Denise hissed.

With that, tears that had been brimming on Kaitlyn's lower lids released, flowing in a silent stream down her cheeks and into her lap. If Denise saw them, she made no indication that she did.

"She is the mother of a child. In thirty-six hours, she will be old enough to drive up to Pigeon Forge and elope with the father of her child. There won't be a thing you can do about it. Wanna push her to it?"

"How dare you? I have every right to sit here and know what is going on. I'm paying for this. I'm changing C.B.'s diapers. Kaitlyn is my daughter, and we don't keep secrets from each other."

Jessica felt the last remaining threads of her self-control slipping away. She held on to just enough strands to refrain from saying that there were plenty of secrets that Jessica herself knew about. Starting with the fact that Kaitlyn and Charlie had been screwing at church camp without using birth control. Jessica sucked in a breath through her nose, counted to ten, and then blew it out through pursed lips. She spent every ounce of effort in her body to keep her voice measured. "I think it's great that you and Kaitlyn don't have secrets from each other. But you need to understand that you and I will." She and Denise locked eyes. Without breaking eye contact, Jessica said, "Why don't you go find Diane. She will get you some coffee. We just got a shipment of some excellent dark roast for the Keurig."

Jessica walked to the door, opened it, and swept her hand in the direction of Diane's desk, as if it were a mystery to Denise where she might find her. Denise hesitated for a moment, then left the room, her chin pointing a good forty-five degrees skyward. Jessica closed the door behind her. The second the latch clicked, Kaitlyn let out a sob.

Kaitlyn had folded into herself, collapsing like a contortionist within the arms of the chair, her legs drawn up and her arms around them. Jessica climbed over C.B.'s luggage and put her arms around Kaitlyn. Jessica wasn't the biggest person in the world, but she was able to clasp her hands around Kaitlyn's back and let Kaitlyn rest her head against her chest. Jessica wished she were a bigger person. She wanted something softer and pillowier to offer the girl.

When Kaitlyn's breathing evened out, Jessica reached over and grabbed a box of tissues. She handed it to Kaitlyn, then walked back to her side of the desk and sat down.

"I'm sorry I'm crying so much," Kaitlyn said.

"Don't you ever apologize for having feelings," Jessica said. "Feel what you feel. How long have you been waiting to do that?"

Kaitlyn giggled. "Since about an hour after Charles was born."

"Charles? I thought you were calling him C.B."

"Hmmph," Kaitlyn snorted, the first genuinely teenage noise she'd made since she'd gotten there. Its appropriateness comforted Jessica. "I want to call him Charles because that's his father's name. *She*," Kaitlyn said, thumbing back toward the door and rolling her eyes, "doesn't like that name *or* his namesake. Obvi. So we call him C.B. to keep her quiet."

No wonder Diane liked this girl so much. "Aha. I see. So quickly, before our peacetime expires, do you want to read this over?" Jessica picked up the stack of papers and shook it.

"Honestly? I'm too tired to read. Can't you just tell me what it says?"

Jessica read it to her and explained it. They talked about the difference between legal and physical custody, and how visitation just meant he had the right to visit.

"So when he goes off to school, and he can't visit, he won't get in trouble?"

"No," Jessica said, deciding that this wasn't the time to talk about what she thought about Charlie disappearing off to school and leaving Kaitlyn alone with the baby. "So, here's the big question. Have you told Charlie you're suing him?"

Kaitlyn sighed a put-upon sigh. "No. Oh, gosh, no. I can't imagine telling him something like that."

"It can't be harder than telling him about Charles," Jessica said.

Kaitlyn smiled. "That's the truth. I'm just so tired of hard things! Everything is so *hard*!" The word "hard" came out long and whiny. If Kaitlyn weren't so sincere about it, Jessica would have made fun of her.

"Here's the thing, Kaitlyn. The law says we have to serve him with a copy of this. We can't keep it a secret from him. We can do this a few different ways, however. I can mail it to him and ask him to sign a piece of paper saying he got a copy of the petition. The problem with that is getting letters in the mail from lawyers is scary. If he didn't know it was coming, he's likely to be pretty pissed off at you." Kaitlyn nodded. "Another way is to have the sheriff come knocking at his door and hand it to him."

Kaitlyn waved her hands. "Oh no. That would be awful."

"Right. So the third way, the *nicest* way, is if you tell him about it. Then just hand it to him. Tell him you're not trying to do anything mean or fight with him. The truth is this actually helps him out as much as it helps you. Right now, the only right he has is to pay child support. You could disappear with Charles to Montana, not tell Charlie where you went, and there wouldn't be a thing he could do about it."

"Really?"

"Really. Doing this gives him legal rights, makes him the legal father, so you couldn't do that to him. It's really better for both of you. You could explain that to him."

Kaitlyn scrunched up her face. "Would you explain it to him?" she whined.

"Sorry, kiddo. I can't. I'm your lawyer, and I represent you. If I talked to him about it, he might try to say later that I bullied him into something."

"You wouldn't do that. The only person you bully is my mom."

Jessica whispered, "That's because she bullies *you*."

Kaitlyn's face-splitting grin snapped closed when Charles issued a long squeak from his car seat on the floor. "*Unghhh,*" Kaitlyn groaned. "His Majesty wants to suck me dry. Can I go in a conference room or something?" She started to fumble with the straps on the seat as Charles's crying ramped up a few notches.

"You don't have to hide or anything. We are modern women here who support breast feeding," Jessica said.

Kaitlyn flushed crimson and stuttered a response when they heard banging on the door and Denise yell, "Is C.B. okay? Why is he crying?"

"Jeez, Mom, he's fine! He's just waking up. He's hungry!" Kaitlyn shouted back.

"Can I come in?"

Jessica looked at Kaitlyn, who nodded almost imperceptibly. She got up and opened the door to let Denise in. Denise maneuvered Kaitlyn out of the way with her elbows and knelt down. "You've got to . . . Here . . . There!" She picked up Charles and hugged him to her chest, bouncing him and kissing the top of his head. "Yes, Mommy had your little arm all twisted in the strap, didn't she?"

"Mom! I had it!"

"It's okay, baby," Denise cooed, oblivious to everyone but Charles. "Gigi's got you."

A wet stain bloomed on Kaitlyn's left breast. "Mom," she said through clenched teeth. "I need to feed him."

"Let me calm him down first."

Kaitlyn had her forearms pressed against her chest. "Mom. Please. I'm leaking." Her face was as red as Charles's.

"The lactation consultant said that he won't latch on properly if he's upset like this."

"He's upset. Because. He's hungry. And you. Won't. Let. Him. Eat." Kaitlyn reached under her shirt to unlatch her nursing bra. She reached into one of the bags and got a blanket that Velcro-ed around her neck and covered her chest. She then put a large pillow with an indentation in the middle on her lap. "Mom! Now!"

Jessica watched drops of milk falling on to the pillow, unable to look away. Finally, reluctantly, Denise handed Charles to Kaitlyn, who tucked him under the blanket. Almost instantly, Charles's crying was replaced by sucking sounds. A look of relief passed across Kaitlyn's face, and her shoulders fell down from her ears a good three inches. Denise hovered over her, her hands fluttering around as if looking for a place to land and be helpful. Jessica suspected that if Denise could whip out a breast and feed Charles herself, she'd do it. She seemed jealous that she couldn't.

Jessica wasn't sure where to put her eyes. She looked up for inspiration and saw a large gray cobweb dripping from the air-conditioning vent. When was the last time she'd dusted above eye level? Had she ever? Since the cobwebs were too depressing, she glanced at the door just as Diane peeked in. Jessica coughed to break the silence and then said, a little too loudly, "You can come on in, Diane." Truth be told, there was no one Jessica wanted in the room more. She looked from Denise to Diane and felt a pang of jealousy. They were real sisters, but Diane was the sister Jessica needed in her life. Sure, they bickered, they said hurtful things to one another, but there was genuine affection there and she felt sure that no matter what, it would all come out in the wash. Diane's support was invaluable, and if Jessica was honest with herself, Diane was right more often than Jessica gave her credit for.

Diane strutted in like it was her office. She patted her sister on the shoulder, then came up behind Kaitlyn and kissed her on the head. Kaitlyn looked up at her and smiled.

Diane looked at Jessica and raised her eyebrows, silently communicating: *Is she gonna talk to him?* Jessica waggled her head back and forth and lifted her left shoulder, the universal sign for *I don't know.* Diane looked back at Kaitlyn. "You got a free hand, baby?" Kaitlyn lifted up her right hand, which had been resting on Charles's back. Diane reached across Jessica's desk, shuffled through some papers, and placed one on a book. She got a pen and pointed. "Sign here, I'll notarize it."

"But I—" Denise started.

Diane put her hand up. "I'll explain all this later with a bottle of wine." She turned back to Kaitlyn. "You're too young for wine, but you and I will sit down with some hot chocolate and we can talk about exactly what you'll say to Charlie, okay?"

Kaitlyn leaned her head back against Diane. "I love you, Auntie Diane."

"I love you too, Katiebug."

CHAPTER
TWENTY-THREE

W *hich Disney movie was it*—Bambi, *maybe?* Jessica had a clear image she couldn't place of innocent woodland critters coming out of hibernation in the spring, holding loads of colorful flowers. Whatever movie it was, that's what this March day felt like. She'd been hibernating in her office the past few weeks. Having reached the end of productive negotiations, Coach's case was set for trial, so she'd been starting to get ready for that. Everything else still kept on going, and she was trying to keep up with her other cases, including filing Kaitlyn's suit. She'd been so busy she'd hardly noticed that the winter days had gotten longer and the days warmer. As much as she generally didn't care about cars, she wished she had a convertible instead of her ancient Corolla so she could let the top down and have her hair whip around in the newly minted sunshine.

She was on her way to one of the few chamber events she actually *liked* attending, when everyone met at the chamber offices for a day of service in work clothes and got assigned to different community service–type details. Last year, Jessica had hauled wood chips and spread them underneath equipment at the playground, and the year before that, she had worn a yellow vest and competed with her fellow volunteers to see who could bag the most amount of trash from the side of the road. She had an easier time talking to people at events like this, where there were natural things to say like, "Pass me the shovel," and "Why would anyone fling a bag full of french fries out of a car?" than at cocktail parties, where she stood around with a drink in her hand and was just expected to be charming with no conversational prompts.

Jessica pulled into the parking lot and checked herself in the rearview mirror, laughing as she pictured Diane's reaction to her appearance. Suffice it to say, her paralegal would be appalled. Jessica was wearing old jeans and ratty sneakers, a T-shirt from a 5K she ran in college under duress because a boy she liked was running it, and a zip-up hoodie because there was a chill in the air that morning. Her hair was pulled up under a ball cap, and she wore no makeup. Deciding that maybe a *little* makeup wouldn't be the worst idea, Jessica dug in the car's console and found some tinted lip gloss that had probably been there since before she moved to Ashton. She put her driver's license, a credit card, and a twenty-dollar bill in one pocket, her phone in another, locked everything else up in the trunk, and headed toward the meeting place.

When she got to the chamber building, she was happy to see a table set up with coffee and pastries and made a beeline to the caffeine. Eager to get some coffee before the supplies ran out, she grabbed a Styrofoam cup and pumped coffee out of the air pot, then turned around, nearly smacking into a wall of male chest. Startled, Jessica looked up to see Diane's boy toy—then looked down and saw that she had spilled half of her cup of coffee on Lee's shoes.

"Oh God, Lee, I'm so sorry." She turned around to see if there were any napkins, and, in so doing, managed to bump her cup and dump its remaining contents directly onto . . . Bobby, who had appeared out of nowhere. Rather than try to speak or move again, Jessica just groaned.

"Lord, Jessica," Bobby said, holding both hands up in the "don't shoot" position. "I know we didn't end things great, but I'd think by now you'd be past the throwing a drink on me stage."

"No! I didn't mean . . . I wasn't . . ." Jessica stammered. She'd seen Bobby at the chamber holiday party, but had deftly avoided any conversation beyond pleasantries. Nothing had happened in Coach's case, so there'd been no reason for them to talk about that. She didn't want their first real conversation to be her apology for being clumsy and tossing hot coffee all over him. She'd rather handle it with grace and charm, but that ship had sailed, hadn't it? Jessica didn't even want to look at him, but she had to for her apology to seem sincere.

She squared her shoulders and faced him and was instantly struck by how attractive she still found him. Dammit. Her eyes locked onto his, and she suspected that with only a little effort he could see into her soul through the connection.

Bobby laughed that throaty laugh of his and Jessica was instantly sadder than she was embarrassed, which was saying something. Would she ever hear him laugh again? "I'm just joking," he said, patting her arm. His expression and voice softened, as if he'd just noticed her mortification. "It's okay. We're all here to get dirty today anyway."

Jessica punched his arm lightly, trying to pretend like she was a normal human being, not having weird feelings for some guy she'd only gone out with twice, and that months ago. What a freak he must think she was. "You gave me a heart attack!"

Bobby rubbed his arm, laughing again. "I forgot how violent you were."

"Is Diane coming?" Lee asked, forcing Jessica to look away from Bobby and remember they weren't alone. Lee's face swirled with hope and fear.

"Oh, God, no," said Jessica, and at Lee's stricken expression, she hurried to continue. "First of all, she doesn't do *events*, not if she can't get dressed up for them. Second of all, she does not get up and out early on a Saturday morning, not for no one."

Just then, Nancy Trujillo, the Chamber Event Queen herself, tapped her pen on her clipboard and said, "Can I get everyone's attention?" She got no one's attention but Jessica's, who was eager for any distraction. She repeated herself a little louder and got only a little bit more response. She then blew a whistle, which got everyone's attention.

"We have four different projects that need completing today," Nancy shouted once everyone was listening. "Hopefully, we get volunteers for all four. If not, I'll have to assign you in groups to each project."

"Group projects!" Bobby said. "I want to be the guy who lets the smart girl do all the work and then gets an A anyway."

Jessica punched his arm again, and then thought that maybe she should stop touching him.

Bobby and Lee volunteered to clear out the old cemetery, then Lee turned to Jessica and said, "You coming with us?" Jessica could not think of an off-the-cuff reason not to, so she said, "Sure," hoping that the work itself would fill the time and the awkward gaps in conversation. After filling the bed with rakes, shovels, clippers, and other useful supplies, they piled into Lee's truck and headed over to weed and pick up trash and do other routine maintenance.

Being the shortest, Jessica sat in the middle of the bench seat, between Bobby and Lee, her legs pressed up against both of them as she straddled the hump on the floor. She was highly self-conscious of every left turn that sent her caroming into Bobby's side, and tried not to apologize. She hated every second of this five-minute ride. Bobby and Lee were both good guys. Both personable and fun to talk to, and she had gone and screwed up two of the only people her own age in this godforsaken town worth talking to against her own instincts because . . . because

. . . because Diane had talked her into it. Aw, hell. She needed to quit blaming Diane. Diane may have tipped her over the edge, but that warm feeling she got when she slid across the truck seat and touched Bobby, she didn't get when she slid across the truck seat and touched Lee. She couldn't blame Diane for her own feelings.

Feelings were such inconvenient things. So much less useful than reason.

They pulled into the parking lot at the cemetery and unloaded the truck. Lee said, "If we want to make any kind of progress, we'd best divide and conquer." He pulled off his ball cap and scratched his head, then put it back on. Jessica nodded enthusiastically, grateful for his idea. He pointed to the area near the road. "Jessica, do you want to take over there? It's mostly going to be clearing kudzu. Bobby, you take that area, and I'll take over here." He pointed in different directions. They all took the tools they thought they'd need and headed off to their assigned areas.

They worked in separate silence, each in their own section of the cemetery. This work was difficult enough that it took up most of Jessica's brain space. Thoughts only came through in pieces, but when they did come through, they were of Bobby. She could hear Lee and Bobby through the trees, grunting occasionally with effort, going back to the truck to get a different tool, and the rattling of branches as they worked. It was tough, sweaty going. Jessica sat on a bench to take a break, taking a long draw from a bottle of water. A wide, pitted gravestone was in front of her. It had a roughly carved angel at the top, and beneath it was the name *BAKER*. Below that, on the left, it said, *John, 1898–1919*. To the right, it said, *Elizabeth, 1901–1919*. In between and below them, it said, *John, 1919–1919*.

Curious, and eager for something to think about that *wasn't* how good Bobby looked doing yard work, Jessica wondered what might have killed all the Bakers in 1919. Life was so different then. She tried to imagine living without electricity or a Kroger or a car or indoor plumbing, like most folks in the rural South did back then. *Oof, no.* Then again, it was also easier. No one expected Elizabeth to do anything but marry John, pop out a few farmworkers and kitchen hands, and feed the crew.

"Spanish flu."

Jessica jumped at the sound of Bobby's voice. She hadn't heard him walk up. "Huh?"

"Spanish flu epidemic. Killed a lot of people in 1919. I'm guessing that's what got the Bakers."

"Why do you know that?" She was torn between being impressed that Bobby knew that bit of trivia and irritated that he assumed she didn't. Then again, she *hadn't* known about it. She was surprised by a wave of loneliness when she realized that no one else she'd met in Ashton would have either known the precise year of the Spanish flu epidemic or thought to tell her about it.

"I used to watch the History channel a lot before they started airing nothing but Bigfoot documentaries," he said with a shrug, then pointed at the bench next to her.

Wondering if he was just looking for a place to rest or if he had a more precise game plan in mind, Jessica scooted over to give him room to sit down. The silence that followed made Jessica nervous. She sipped from her water bottle. The loud and sticky noise of her throat closing around the liquid seemed to make things worse, so she put the bottle on the ground.

"When are we supposed to get back to base camp?" she said at the very same instant that Bobby said, "I hear you're going to court the first week in April." Then they both said, "Sorry, you go," which made them laugh.

"Really," Jessica said. "I was just talking to talk. You go."

Bobby scuffed his shoe in the dirt and kept his eye on the track it made. "I hear you're going to court the first week in April."

"Yeah, we got it specially set for spring break." She took a deep breath and realized that Coach, for all his ickiness, was at least a subject she could talk about with confidence. Despite his role in the current drama, there were facts to relay, and that much she could do. "When you're a celeb like Coach, you get to pick your court date so you don't have to miss work."

"Nice to be a privileged white guy," Bobby said, and she noticed him sneaking a glance in her direction without moving his head.

"You're a white guy, you tell me." She hoped he could tell she was joking and not making some feminist attack on him.

Now he looked at her dead on. "I'm a white guy, but not a privileged one."

Jessica could smell a dangerous shift in the atmosphere. This was more—different—than Bobby being unaware of his generalized privilege as a white male in American society. Bobby's voice was serious and dripping with meaning she could only guess at. She only had seconds, maybe less, to come up with something to say that would lighten things up. She went for melodrama. "You're more privileged than ole John Baker here, a hundred years dead in his grave with only the bones of his wife and infant son to keep him company."

Bobby shrugged. "John Baker got the girl."

Jessica felt sliced open, peeled back, raw. She missed Bobby. The longing on his face was painful to see. Sitting next to him and not touching him took extraordinary effort, but nothing had changed. She couldn't change any of the professional conflicts dating Bobby created and she couldn't soothe the sharpness of the feelings she had for him, so she stuffed it all in a square of her mental waffle and said, "What time are we supposed to be back at base camp?"

Bobby slid his melted chocolate eyes off her face and onto his watch, a large plastic-banded digital model that probably had fourteen stopwatches and could tell you the time in Barcelona and Moscow simultaneously. He cleared his throat and spoke in a wooden voice. "One thirty. It's twelve now. We still have a little time, but we probably ought to start finishing up soon."

"Yeah," Jessica said, picking the water bottle back up and fiddling with the cap.

Bobby patted his thighs, then stood up. "See you back at the truck in about an hour, I guess." He strode away before she could respond, disappearing behind a large oak tree.

It had been over three months since their two dates. There was absolutely no reason why Bobby should make her feel any kind of way, and yet all her nerves were on high alert. Alone with the gravestones, she grunted in frustration.

"You okay?" she heard Lee call out from somewhere.

"Yeah, fine. Just stubbed my toe," she called back, embarrassed that she'd been heard.

She channeled her energy into clearing kudzu vines from an old crypt with the name "Johnson" on it. She wondered if it was any kin to that gossipy redneck Earl Johnson and thought if it was, she might leave the kudzu to tear down the monument. The work made her so hot, she had long since taken off her hoodie and now wished she could take off her shirt too. Sweat dripped down her back and cleavage and left half-moon stains under her arms.

She was hunkered down, her fist wrapped around a particularly stubborn vine, playing tug-of-war with it, when Lee came up behind her. "Hey, Jess, it's a little after one. You ready to put up the truck and head back?"

"Not till I get this vine," she said through clenched teeth, enjoying the physicality of the work. Something about it took her mind off Bobby the way nothing else had. She bent her knees deeper and pulled again. She felt beads of sweat pop out on her upper lip and in the crook of her elbow, and her feet started to slip out from underneath her. Nothing else moved.

"Let me help," Lee said. He came around the side of her and grabbed on to the vine. "On three. One . . . two . . . three."

They both pulled and the vine came loose, more quickly than either of them expected. They tumbled backward, Jessica flat on her back, and Lee landing on his left arm with most of his body resting crookedly against Jessica's side. At once, Jessica burst into laughter. The whole situation was so ridiculous. Lee stumbled as he tried to roll over and anchor his right arm to get up, slipping on the kudzu vine, causing him to fall face-first into Jessica's sweaty chest.

He lay there for a small moment and then said directly into her breasts, "I wish I were less embarrassed so I could enjoy this."

Jessica shoved his shoulder and he pushed off her. They both stood up, brushing the dirt off, and letting the last of their laughter fall out of their chests. Jessica readjusted her hat.

"I'm not interrupting anything, am I?"

Jessica whipped around at the sound of Bobby's dry voice, feeling caught in the act. "No."

"We were attacked by some kudzu," Lee said, "and it knocked us to the ground and threw me on top of Jessica. She was quite the lady about it and didn't slap me across the face or anything, though I expect she'll file a sexual harassment lawsuit within the week. You know these lawyers." He cut his eyes in Jessica's direction.

"Will you acknowledge service, or do I have to send the sheriff out?" Jessica asked.

"Huh?" said Lee.

"Sorry," said Jessica. "You know, you can sign, saying you got a copy so the sheriff doesn't have to come to your house and serve you at four in the morning?" Both men were looking at her, Lee with half a smile, Bobby with none at all. "Dumb lawyer joke."

Bobby said, "Let's get the truck packed up so we can get back. I'm starving."

"Waffle House?" asked Lee.

"I don't know," said Bobby. Bobby looked over at Jessica, trying to communicate something, though what she couldn't say. He might be signaling her to put the kibosh on the idea, or he might be signaling her to give her stamp of approval. Of course, she should just say what she wanted to do, which was sink into the ground and disappear without committing. Both options seemed fraught with danger. If she said yes, was she leading Bobby on, or acknowledging that they could be friends, or was she leading herself on? If she said no, was she being a big baby about the whole thing? Depriving herself of good company for no good reason? Lord, she hated being this indecisive.

"Come on, man. I know you're tired and hungry. Wakey wakey, eggs and bakey . . ." He punched Bobby in the stomach in the way that guys do instead of hugging each other. "I'll kick your ass if you make me go home and eat a peanut butter sandwich." Lee landed another punch, and Bobby doubled over in mock drama.

"Dude!" Bobby yelled, grabbing Lee around the neck and pummeling him.

Jessica stood there a few moments, watching them pound each other, before deciding enough was enough. "Ahem. Boys!" She picked up a rake and shook it at them. "Do I need to rake you apart?"

They stood up, their arms around each other's shoulders. "Sorry, Mom," Lee said. "Can we still go to Waffle House?"

Bobby looked up at her. He was telegraphing something to her silently, but it was in a language she didn't speak. She closed her eyes. It was time to decide. *Listen to your gut.* She wanted to go. It sounded like fun, and she was hungry. Lee's presence would tame the danger of doing something social with Bobby. She said, "Fine, but you both have to clean your rooms when you get home."

— — —

They all pulled into the Waffle House parking lot at the same time. The restaurant was mostly empty on a Saturday afternoon, so they had their pick of booths. Sliding into an empty one, Jessica took care to sit next to Lee. After they ordered, Jessica focused on her food, enjoying just listening to Lee and Bobby talk. They had the easy rhythm and shorthand of people who had known each other their whole lives. Jessica found it fascinating to watch Bobby in his natural habitat, not trying to impress her or quiz her about Coach. He wasn't acting differently, so much, just less nervous.

Then the conversation evolved into a sort of one-upmanship of them trying to embarrass each other.

"So, Lee gets suspended for two weeks because he gets caught with his pecker out peeing all over the front tire of the principal's brand new Lexus," Bobby said.

Lee elbowed her. "Did you know," he said, pointing his thumb at Bobby, "that this guy once spent an entire year pretending to be a good little Baptist because he had a crush on Hannah Jordan?"

The tips of Bobby's ears were red. "It wasn't a whole year," he mumbled.

"Oooh," sang Jessica. "Who is Hannah Jordan? Did you ever make her see Jesus?" As soon as she said it, Jessica wished she could take it back. Probably making sexual innuendos about the guy you turned down wasn't the best move, and she had no idea if he'd be offended by her casual blasphemy.

Lee howled with laughter and shoved her shoulder, and she relaxed a little. "Aw, hell naw! If I remember correctly, he followed her to this lame New Year's Eve party at the church in tenth grade, just to watch her fawn all over some football player."

Bobby gave a tight smile. He seemed to shrink in on himself, like he wanted to dive under the table. This only inspired Lee to continue. Jessica was grateful. She really wanted to hear this story.

"He was totally smitten. Little fifteen-year-old Bobby, I don't even think his balls had dropped yet, following Hannah around with these cow eyes. If he thought she was going to be there, he was there. He dragged us all over the place. We went to the damn mall, we went roller-skating. Xbox had just come out and Marc Friedrich, lucky little shit, got one for Christmas. We all decided to hang out at Marc's house for New Year's Eve to play it. Old Bobert here tries to convince us that the First Baptist Church Teen Party is where the real action's at."

"Lee, stop," Bobby said. His face flamed red.

"Come on, Bobby, no one gives a shit who you had a crush on when you were fifteen. Man up. Jessica thinks this is funny, don't you, Jess?"

Jessica felt for Bobby and his abject humiliation, but her desire to hear the rest of this story won out. "Don't leave me hanging, Lee!" she said, grabbing his arm and shaking it.

Lee continued. "Not a one of us wanted to eat M&M's out of a bowl and pray on New Year's Eve with adults in the room. We wanted to play Xbox and shoot aliens and shit and sneak upstairs to steal some of Marc's dad's beer. So that's what we did. Not Bobby, though, nope. He combs his hair and puts on a nice shirt and gets his mom to drop him off at the church so he can fawn all over Hannah."

Jessica gave an exaggerated "aww," and Bobby finally cracked a grin. "This story is so adorable I might melt," she said.

Bobby said, "This story is so embarrassing I might melt."

"That's not even the best part!" Lee said. "So, we're just fifteen-year-old assholes, and we figure whatever, Bobby can have a boring-ass time if that's what he wants. We're down in Marc's basement shooting aliens, and the next thing we know it's like ten thirty. Bobby comes shuffling down the stairs looking like he wants to cry, whining about how he fucking hates football players. I think it was the first time I ever heard him say 'fuck.' But his voice hadn't finished changing, so it came out all squeaky, like 'fuck!'" Lee made his voice as high and falsetto as he could.

The expletive echoed off the walls of the Waffle House, making a gray-haired woman at the opposite end of the restaurant look disapprovingly at them. Jessica involuntarily sank into the booth, trying to hide from the reproving glare. As she did so, her foot slipped forward on the greasy floor and landed on one of Bobby's under the narrow table. Bobby sat up immediately, yanking his foot away. *My foot still likes your foot*, she thought, looking down at the remnants of her smothered and chunked hashbrowns and concentrating on finding a bite large enough to justify carrying to her mouth.

"We couldn't get much out of him," Lee continued, seemingly oblivious to the drama that had just played out, "but apparently he was following Hannah around like a little puppy, and she's following some football player around. He finally realizes there's no way prepubescent Turnbull can compete with jock-meat. So, he calls his mommy and gets her to pick him up and drive him over to Marc's house. He hit puberty later that spring, but I think"—Lee pointed his finger at Bobby, then tapped his forehead—"Bobby still thinks of himself as that scrawny little kid."

Lee and Jessica turned toward Bobby, who flexed into a bodybuilder's pose. He adopted a bad Russian accent. "I am strong like bull. Not scrawny like child I was. Please to talk about other person now." Despite the bravado in his voice, he was clearly trying to change the subject.

Lee took pity on Bobby and said to Jessica, "Okay, now you have to say something embarrassing about yourself. We need leverage in case you spill our beans."

"I feel put on the spot," Jessica said. "I have no idea what to say."

"Do I need to call Diane and ask her?" Bobby asked, his eyes twinkling mischievously.

Jessica balked. "Oh, God, I don't know," she said, quickly shuffling through the stories in her head. "This isn't funny, but it's funny. It's kinda gross. No, not that one. Let me think."

"Gross is good," Lee insisted.

"No, I'm sorry I said anything." Jessica sat there, her jaw hanging, her mind a frozen tundra: blank, featureless, and white, except for this one, inappropriate story.

"You have to say something," Bobby urged.

Jessica groaned in frustration. She had no other options. She had to tell it. "Okay, fine," she said, prepping herself for embarrassment. "So, when my mom was sick, I was taking care of her, and she got to the point where she had trouble showering." Both men looked at her with very serious faces, which she waved off. "I promise you this will get funny. So, I had to help her, and it was no small task. She was so stubborn and kept telling me to leave her alone, that she could do it herself. I ended up getting soaking wet every time. So finally, right near the end, it just made more sense for me to get undressed and get on in there with her. I wanted her to sit in this shower chair I'd bought especially for her, but she refused. She wouldn't let me hold her, but I was afraid she'd fall. It was super awkward, because my mom and I hadn't been naked around each other since I was, what, five? Six? But, hey, you do what you have to do when the situation calls for it. Well, then one day we're in the shower and she starts to fall and I grab her. She starts yelling at me that I'm pushing her. I'm like, 'Yeah, I am pushing you, I'm pushing you upright so you don't fall down and kill us both.' But she pushes back, and nearly knocks me over. And I lose my grip on her and I see her going down. I get scared, and the only thing I can think to do is block her fall with my leg. It works, except now my knee is jammed up her butt. Like *up* her butt, I swear. She starts screaming that there's a pole up her ass, and I'm like, 'Lady, it's not a pole, it's my leg.' Now I have to amputate my leg, because what other choice do I have?" Jessica laughed at the memory. So did Lee and Bobby, only she suddenly realized that they were probably both picturing her completely nude and dripping wet. A cold wave of nausea swept over her, and she found herself unable to find the humor in the story anymore.

"That's a really good prosthetic," Lee deadpanned, pointing to her lap. "I had no idea you had one."

"The technology is amazing these days," she replied, knocking on her thigh. "Very lifelike."

"Anyway, I should probably get home," Lee finally said. "Buster's gonna chew up the couch and shit in the living room."

"Buster's your dog?" Jessica asked.

"No, my roommate."

Jessica was about to ask him what grown man still called himself "Buster," when he said, "Just kidding. My dog. German shepherd mix. Sweetest boy in the world. Hates being alone."

Jessica sat in her car in the Waffle House parking lot with the engine running, checking her phone. She'd been off the grid for a good hour: something life-changing might be in her email or texts or on Twitter. She was just reading a thread about whether the proper spelling was "ketchup" or "catsup" when Lee tapped on her window.

"Hey, what's up?" she asked as she rolled the window down. The sun was right behind Lee's head. She had to shade her eyes to see his face.

"I didn't want to say this in front of Bobby, because I'd embarrassed him enough for one day, but God, I've known the guy for most of my life and he's like my brother. I look out for him."

Jessica could only think of one thing that Lee meant by this, and it both terrified and excited her. "Sure, go ahead," she said, wanting him to get it over with quickly.

"Right. Well, there's only one other time I've seen him moon over a girl the way he mooned over Hannah Jordan. And that's you. I don't know why you kicked him to the curb, and I'm sure you had your reasons, but you ripped my boy's heart out. Judging from what I can see? Neither one of you are over it. None of my business, I know, but you might want to reconsider." Lee knocked on the roof of her car. "This car is a piece of shit," he said, and walked away.

"I know," she said to his retreating back, her heart beating so loudly it drowned out all rational thought.

CHAPTER
TWENTY-FOUR

There were papers spread out all over the conference table, organized in a way that only Jessica understood. If she were to drop dead on the spot, no one else would be able to understand her system, ever. It was trial prep time, crunch time, her least favorite part of the lawyering game. In about five minutes, Tripp Wishingham would arrive for witness prep, the worst part of the worst part.

At least she wasn't hungry. Diane, always the good southern woman, had brought in her famous chicken cordon bleu casserole for lunch. There wasn't much a good southern woman's casserole couldn't make better, and all of Diane's casseroles were good, even if Diane herself wasn't always.

Diane. How could she do anything without Diane? Their relationship wasn't always smooth, obviously. They fought like sisters, and loved like sisters too. Apologies came in gestures more than words. A casserole. A donut. A "let's do this your way instead of mine." It would be hard to imagine someone who viewed the world more differently than she did, but somehow their worldviews fit together more than they clashed. They were yin-yang, interlocking puzzle pieces, symbiotic creatures. Jessica knew that Diane wanted the best for her, even if they didn't always agree on the best way to get there. She knew that it was

LORI B. DUFF

important to have someone who wasn't afraid to challenge her. The worst thing would be to become complacent in her thinking.

Jessica also knew that she didn't tell Diane how much she appreciated her nearly enough and made a mental note to do so, if not directly, then indirectly. Maybe a gift card? A big bouquet of flowers? Fancy chocolates? *Use your words*, she heard in her mother's voice, but dismissed it in favor of working on trial prep.

Jessica had spent the rest of the weekend after Waffle House cyber-stalking Sarah James, looking for anything she could use in court. Any weakness. Anything that showed an ulterior motive. Sometimes you didn't know what would be useful until you got into court and heard the testimony and something triggered a memory. Luck, as they say, favored the prepared. According to Sarah's Pinterest board, Sarah liked making casseroles and cute holiday cookies. Or at least, she fantasized about making cute holiday cookies. She could crochet and was partial to baby blankets. She didn't tweet, or if she did, her name was too generic to find. Her Facebook account was semi-private, though a number of pictures of Sarah and Francesca were public. Jessica scrolled through the photos, watching Francesca grow up through the years. Francesca's face was luminous. Coach showed heavily in her bone structure. It was what Francesca did with her features that distinguished her from her father, though. Where Coach had an inward intensity, Francesca shone. Everything about her looked friendly and delightful. Jessica studied the pictures of Francesca and her mother, trying to figure out whether they had filters on them or if Sarah and her daughter were just that beautiful. Jessica also learned that Francesca and Sarah attended the Methodist church. Sarah referred to her book club as her "wine club." They read bestsellers, picks from Oprah and Reese Witherspoon. Occasionally, men populated the pictures, but Jessica noticed they never stayed for long.

Jessica knew from the formal paperwork Eric had sent her

– 207 –

that Sarah worked in the marketing department of the distribution center and had gone to Georgia State. She made a decent income and, overall, had done okay for herself and Francesca despite the inauspicious beginnings of their little family. Jessica wanted to ask her about that night at the party with Coach. About those details. About how she felt starting college pregnant, how it felt taking an econ final with a baby at home and no father to help. She wanted to know what Sarah thought of Coach. She could have asked her those questions in a deposition, but the answers would only satisfy her own prurient curiosity. They wouldn't do her client any good. In fact, they might harm her client, so she didn't dare ask. She wondered about the ethics of taking Sarah out for a glass of wine when all this was over. Or if Eric would tell her.

Bobby had told her that he worked for a local paper because people interested him. So why hadn't Bobby asked Sarah those questions instead of just calling her out in his #MeToo column? Maybe he'd tried and she refused. For a moment, Jessica considered texting him to ask. After Saturday's Waffle House trip, maybe their relationship was mended enough. Just the thought of that afternoon sent a series of images through Jessica's mind: Bobby at the Waffle House. *My foot still likes your foot.* Lee telling her, "You ripped my boy's heart out." Nope. There was too much swirling in the air when Bobby was around.

She shook Bobby out of her head and resumed pre-marking exhibits and cross-referencing them on a master list. A few minutes later, Diane brought Coach in. Jessica rose to shake his hand, then sat back down, noting again that he waited to sit until she did.

"Charlie Kicklighter says you are suing him," Coach before Jessica could speak.

"Well, I'm not, personally," Jessica said defensively, wondering what business it was of Coach's. "Kaitlyn is, but yeah."

"Not cool, Jessica."

"What do you mean?" Football season was over, and Jessica knew that Coach blamed Charlie on his loss at State. Why did Coach give any craps about him? Besides—Coach's shenanigans had harmed her business enough. She had to take what she could. The pink pussy hat brigade had, thankfully, been short-lived in Ashton's public memory, but you never knew what went on behind everyone's polite, friendly veneer.

"He's just a kid. He's dealing with all kinds of stuff as a senior— did you know he's trying to get nominated to West Point?"

Jessica nodded.

"How is he supposed to focus with this giant distraction?"

"I mean, not for nothing, but perhaps he should have thought about that nine months ago when he failed to put a condom on it."

Coach shook his head. "You're always blaming the guy. Like she didn't spread her legs for him."

Jessica clenched her fists under the table, took a deep breath, and then tried to let all her aggravation go. "No, in this case, I'm not blaming Charlie for anything. Kaitlyn and Charlie are in this together, and they should handle the consequences together. He doesn't get to go on with his charmed life while she stops everything she was doing to take care of a baby they created together."

"It's not his fault biology is the way it is. It's not like he had the option of getting pregnant," Coach said. He looked like he'd just scored a touchdown.

Oh, how Jessica wanted to tear him down, but this wasn't the time or the place. They had to be a team next week in the courtroom. The better they got along, the smoother it would go. She tried as best she could to channel Diane. *What would Diane do?* Maybe she should get bracelets made that said that. Or maybe she should tattoo *WWDD* on her inner wrist. Objectively right or wrong, Diane was more diplomatic than she was, at least with men like Coach, and diplomacy got the job done. Jessica shrugged her shoulders and pasted on her version of a flirtatious smile. "Cut me some slack," she said. "Girl's gotta make a living, and Kaitlyn's a paying client."

This seemed to make sense to Coach. He nodded and peered over at the papers spread across the table. "Is all of this my crap?"

"All of it."

"That's a lot of crap." Coach let out a low whistle. Clearly, he hadn't realized what had been going on behind the scenes.

"Yup."

"What do you need from me?"

"You're here today so we can talk about expectations and get you ready to take the stand. This is it. The final hearing. The trial. The be-all-and-end-all done with it. They won't come off the idea of visitation, and you won't agree to it. Without including visitation, they won't commit to the financial agreement. Whatever happens on Tuesday is what's gonna happen, end of story. It's the championship game, the last game of the season; there is no more after this." Jessica stared at him, trying to gauge his comprehension.

"Can't we appeal if we lose?"

"Yes and no," Jessica said. This was going to be a long afternoon. "You can only appeal a legal error. You can't appeal because you don't like the outcome. Judges have a lot of discretion in these cases. So, unless Judge Brandywine abuses that discretion—if his decision goes totally against the evidence, or if he ignores the law—we're stuck with what he decides."

Coach shut his eyes and wrinkled his forehead, checking in with his inner coaching staff. "Why aren't we having a jury trial?"

"Well, for one, a jury trial would never end. Rather, it would never start. This is a small county, and we only have jury trials once or twice a year. They go in order of oldest cases first, so it would be like two years from now before this got heard."

Coach looked horrified. "Oh, God, no. This has to end."

"Right. Plus, juries don't get to decide custody and visitation, just numbers stuff like child support in these cases, and that's not what we're fighting about." Jessica shuffled through a stack of papers to her left and pulled one out, handing it to Coach. "I emailed you a copy of this. Did you get it?"

He glanced at it. "I think so."

Jessica filled her lungs before speaking. It irritated her to no end when clients didn't bother reading what she sent them. "This is their final proposal. Last chance to work it out before Judge Brandywine gets to decide what's in the order."

"Phil's a good guy," Coach said. "He's an Ashton Devils fan—I'm not worried."

"'Phil' *is* a good guy," Jessica agreed. Calling a superior court judge by his first name felt about as appropriate as inviting the pope out for a beer. "That's sort of the problem. He's a good guy who does his job. That means he follows the law no matter what he personally thinks of you, me, or Satan himself."

"What are you saying?"

"I'm saying that the fact that you are the much beloved Frank Wishingham III, golden boy and football god, isn't going to mean shit inside Judge Brandywine's courtroom."

"I'm not looking for favors," Coach said, clearly offended.

The truth of this statement rang loud and clear. He wasn't. Jessica understood this, maybe for the first time. He was so used to favors landing at his feet that favors weren't something he asked for. They appeared as the normal course of business. They were just there. All the time. The absence of favors was unthinkable. That was life as Coach. "I know you're not," Jessica said, the most sincere she'd felt with him since he'd arrived in her office all those months ago.

Jessica took a sip of water, then put the glass down, deliberately centering it on its coaster, and said, "Look, I know where you're coming from. We've been over this a thousand times. You and I are on the same page. You're not budging on the visitation thing, and neither are they. Okay. Fine. That's what courts are for, for resolving the stuff we can't resolve on our own."

"So?" Coach was in his usual stance, leaning back, his hands behind his head, elbows out, with his legs sprawled in front of him, looking completely relaxed. Jessica knew by now how meaningless that was.

"So that means all bets are off. We're really close to resolving this. I think we've got things good, financially. We agree on things, money-wise."

Coach grunted his agreement.

"The only thing you don't agree on is this visitation thing." Coach grunted again. "But it's a package deal. If we don't agree to visitation, then they don't agree on the financial thing."

"Their loss," Coach said. "If they don't want my money, that's not my problem."

Jessica huffed a breath out through her nose. "It doesn't quite work like that. Judge Brandywine can—and will—order you to pay money. I'm not worried about the money, though. He'll probably order you to pay something similar to what we've agreed to. I'm not too worried about visitation either. Remember, as we've already gone over, he can order that you *get* visitation, but he can't order you to take advantage of it. If you don't show up on your appointed weekend, or whatever day is agreed upon, nothing he can do. The worst thing that happens is the judge says you've lost the right to see Francesca, which is what you want. Visitation is a privilege, not an obligation. You can't get in trouble for not taking advantage of it."

"So we're good then," Coach said. He made a move to get up.

"No, we're not."

"How so?"

"Well, we're good legally. But I know how concerned you are about PR. And I get it. Your job depends on people trusting you with their teenagers. You're good with them—I've seen it. You aren't just teaching them the game; you're involved with their lives. Like you said. You're family."

"Damn skippy," Coach said. He sat up a little straighter, his pride evident.

"Here's what I'm afraid of," Jessica said, wishing she had a real drink in her hand. This would all go down easier if she had a rum and Coke. "They're going to try to crucify you."

"What? How?" Coach was in predator mode again, leaning forward, ready to pounce.

"Let's try it this way," Jessica said, stacking a pile of papers and clipping them together with a binder clip. "If I'm Eric Crabtree, the first thing I'm going to do to try my case is put you on the stand. I'm going to ask you questions before I ask anyone else questions. So, let's do some role-playing. Pretend I'm Eric Crabtree, and let me ask you the questions I think he's going to ask you."

"Okay . . ." Coach's eyes narrowed into a laser focus on Jessica. It unnerved her, but she tried her best not to let him know.

"So you've been sworn in, and the first question I ask is this: You're Francesca's father, right?"

Coach said nothing. Jessica thought about what a turd he must have been as a teenager. His poor mother.

"We're role-playing, so you have to answer the question."

"This is stupid. Just tell me what he's going to ask and what I should say."

"No, it isn't stupid. You of all people should know that practice makes perfect. You can't just sit in the locker room and tell your guys how to run plays. They have to actually do it."

Coach grunted something that Jessica took for assent.

"Again: You're Francesca's father, right?"

"That's what the DNA test says."

"Wrong answer."

"What do you mean, wrong answer?" Coach threw his log-sized arms up in the air, and Jessica involuntarily flinched. "That is what the DNA test says."

"It's *technically* the right answer. But it sends the message that you're nothing more than a sperm donor and you don't give any shits about this girl."

"Well," Coach said, smiling. "I swore to tell the truth, right?"

Jessica fought the urge to slap the smirk off him. "Don't be a smart-ass. You can tell the truth without admitting to the world that this poor girl's feelings are irrelevant to you."

Coach mimicked Jessica's voice. "'This poor girl's feelings.' Whose side are you on?"

"Yours!" Jessica said, louder than she'd intended. "It's my job to make sure your answers don't piss off the judge deciding your fate. Don't forget the reporters sitting in the back of the room. You want to inspire them to write an article about how cold-hearted and horrible you are?"

"Reporters? It's none of their damn business!"

"Maybe so, but they'll be there, and there's nothing I can do to keep them out. God bless America, we have open courts and anyone who wants to can sit in there to watch."

At this, Jessica realized that *anyone* included Bobby Turnbull, who would be staring at her backside the whole time. She made a mental note to buy some new Spanx. She glanced at Coach, whose muscular posture was folded over in an adolescent sulk.

After a moment, he said without his usual bluster, "So what should I say?"

"The answer to 'Are you Francesca's father?' is a simple 'Yes.' 'Yes' is a full sentence. That's the general rule. Use as few words as possible. Only answer the question you're asked, without editorial comment. You're not being asked to entertain anyone or display personality; you're being asked to deliver information. Are you Francesca's father? Yes. End of story."

Coach nodded.

"So, let's try this again. Coach Wishingham, you are Francesca's father, correct?"

"Yes."

"When did you learn that you were Francesca's father?"

"When the deputy came knocking on my door at zero dark thirty in the morning to hand me this lawsuit."

Jessica raised her eyebrows at Coach. He was being deliberately obtuse to try to maintain whatever power he could, but she knew she was in charge for now and it felt good. "Try again."

"When I was served with this lawsuit."

"Excellent. How come you didn't know?"

"What do you mean, how come I didn't know?"

"Okay, that was great," Jessica said, clapping her hands together. "Do you know what you did there?"

"Huh?" Coach looked genuinely confused.

"You didn't understand the question and so you asked for clarification. That's another rule. It's okay to ask what the question means. You want to make sure you are answering the question that is being asked, not the question *you think* is being asked."

Coach nodded and smiled, proud of the gold star he'd earned.

"Let me rephrase the question: How was it that between conception and Francesca's sixteenth birthday, you didn't know that you had a daughter?"

"How would I know? What's her name, Sarah and I weren't friends, we didn't hang out in the same circles. I didn't even know she was pregnant. We graduated and I never saw her again. If she didn't tell me, how was I supposed to know?"

Jessica rubbed her face with her hands. This was going to be a tedious afternoon. She wished again that she could dampen it with alcohol, but took a sip of her water instead and reminded herself that she billed this torture out at $250 an hour. A little over $4 a minute. She felt comforted. "Okay, again, you're telling the truth, which is great. There's nothing worse than having a liar for a client, and you are definitely not a liar."

Coach grinned at her, showing wolfish teeth, thinking he was earning another gold star.

"*But,* there's a way to phrase the truth that doesn't come across so . . ." Jessica sought for professional-sounding words to phrase what she was thinking and came up short. Blunt would have to do. "When you say, 'How the hell would I know if she was pregnant?' some people will hear it as, 'She was just some chick I fucked at a party one night when I was half lit and never spoke to again.'"

Coach laughed. "That's kind of what happened."

Maybe it would be better if he were a little less *honest.* "So how can we phrase that so it sounds a less harsh?"

"You tell me. Isn't that what I'm paying you for?"

For once, Coach was actually right on this count. Jessica acquiesced, and said, "The boy I was at eighteen is not the man I am at thirty-four. I'm not proud of everything I did while I was testing my wings and waiting for the decision-making portions of my frontal lobe to develop. High school is a strange place, socially, and the things we do under the influence of alcohol are not the things we'd choose for ourselves sober. That's why the drinking age is twenty-one, and we, as kids, should have been supervised better. I did an irresponsible thing with someone I didn't know that well, and I was too immature to follow up. She didn't contact me either, so I just assumed I'd gotten away with something and buried it in the giant pile of mistakes I made when I was a kid."

Coach whistled through his teeth. "Damn. That's good. Can you write that down so I can memorize it?"

"Yes and no." Jessica passed him a legal pad and a pen. "Take notes. But don't memorize little speeches word for word, especially not *my* words. For one, we have no idea what Eric's questions are going to be exactly, so the answers might not fit. Also, that sounds like me, not like you. You have to rephrase it so it sounds like Coach, not Jessica. That's just the idea of it."

Coach nodded and began scribbling on the pad. His eyebrows knit together in concentration. Suddenly, Jessica could see him in a physics classroom, absorbing complicated concepts. Jessica saw the eager little boy he must have once been. She saw how he could be attractive. To some people. Still not her.

"Okay. Next question."

They volleyed questions for a couple more exhausting hours. It was tiresome but not entirely unpleasant. Coach was a good student, and by the end they were even high-fiving each other for every emotionally intelligent answer Coach came up with on his own.

At around five o'clock, Diane knocked and peeked her head into the room. "I'm about to leave. I just want to make sure no one needs anything before I go."

"We're good," Jessica said, smiling up at her. "Thanks." Jessica tried to impart as much sincerity and meaning into the word "thanks" as she could.

"Sounds like things are going well in here," Diane said.

"Your girl's a good one," Coach said, wrapping his arm around Diane's waist and hugging her to him in his glee. "Smart."

If it had been Jessica he'd done that to, she'd have slapped his hand, but Diane seemed to be enjoying it, so she put the fantasy to bed. She was considering how to translate "Grown women in positions of authority shouldn't be called 'your girl'" into Modern American Jock when, letting go of Diane, Coach patted the side of her hip—*the side of her ass!*—and all Diane did was giggle. How did his fiancée put up with his nonsense?

Diane sat down in the chair next to Coach and before spinning her chair to face the table—did Jessica actually see this?—crossed her legs more slowly than normal. *Good Lord, Diane, did you just flash your panties at him?* Jessica had to take control of this situation before all the goodness and light she and Coach had built up over the last few hours floated out the window. Or up Diane's skirt. Jessica cleared her throat to get everyone's attention.

"Yes, everything went very well," she said deliberately. "Coach, in addition to being a great teacher, is a great student. I think he will do fantastic on the stand."

Now that Coach had an audience, his face went from little-boy-with-a-gold-star to its normal arrogant arrangement, and Jessica wanted to vomit on him.

"No kidding," Coach said. "They love me."

"Maybe so, maybe so," Jessica said, "but I still think we should find a way to settle."

"Why?" Coach asked. Diane looked skeptical.

"Look, I think you're going to do just fine answering Eric's questions. I think the outcome of the case is going to be pretty much what we want it to be—the money isn't going to fluctuate much because the law sets that. Judge Brandywine can order whatever visitation he wants, but you don't have to take it, so it doesn't matter."

"So you said. What's the problem, then?"

"The problem is your buddy Phil." Jessica glanced at Coach. She'd tried every other trick she knew to convince Coach that the optics for refusing visitation were bad. Now she had to hammer him over the head in a last-ditch effort. She didn't like putting Coach on the defensive any more than she had to—he didn't take to it well. "Phillip Brandywine is not an idiot. He's been on the bench for more than a decade, and he's seen it all. He's pretty cynical. You can put on a fabulous show for any spectators in the room. You can probably even convince Sarah James herself— you're that good." Coach's barrel chest swelled up a few inches more. "But let me tell you what Judge Brandywine is going to say. I'm even going to tell you what he's going to do. He's going to cock his head to the right like this, and raise his right eyebrow—just his right eyebrow—I can't really do it, but you get what I mean. Then he's going to stroke his goatee with his left hand." Jessica brought her left hand to her chin and began to stroke it.

Diane smiled wide and her body shook as she laughed silently. Coach just stared at Jessica, analyzing her as he might a video from last year's championship game.

"Then he's going to say this." Jessica dipped her voice down as low as she could and in her best old-southern-money accent said, "Ahrr yew tryin' tah tell me, Miz Fischah, that yawh client defiled this poowah guhl's honah all those yeahs ago and now won't so much as send huh a Christmas cahad?"

Diane dabbed her eyes with a tissue. "Sweetie, if you're trying to make a serious point, you have simply got to stop trying that accent. It is dreadful. Hilarious, but dreadful."

"Thank you, Diane," Jessica said. "But the point is fair: Judge Brandywine is going to cut to the chase. He's that kind of guy. Whatever you say, however diplomatically you say it, Judge Brandywine is going to hone in on that fatherless sixteen-year-old girl and how rejected she feels."

Coach slapped his hands down on the table, making Diane flinch. "Dammit, Jessica, every time I think we've gotten somewhere, I go back to thinking you'd rather be representing Sarah. I'm going to ask you one last time: Whose side are you on?"

Jessica opened up her mouth to fire back, but Diane silenced her with a hand. "I'm going to field this one," she said. "Listen, Coach, you've known Phil Brandywine for how long now?"

"Forever. He and my daddy were in the same Rotary club."

"Right. Now who is he married to?"

Jessica watched, impressed that Diane was getting all Socratic with his ass.

"What's her name . . . Linda? What's that got to do with it?"

"What do you know about Linda?"

Coach looked up and to the left, as if that was where his information storage system was housed. He flicked through a few mental cards and then said, "Pretty lady. Dark hair, dark eyes. Lotta hours in her hourglass, if you know what I mean."

"I don't mean what she looks like, I mean her background."

Coach looked at her quizzically. "I don't know. I mean, she's from here, good family. What else is there?"

Diane flicked her eyes over to Jessica and then back to Coach. Jessica had no idea where Diane was going with this, but she knew it would be somewhere good and couldn't wait to see. "Linda Brandywine used to be Linda Hope. Linda Hope was a few years younger than me. I knew her older sister in high school. Anyway, Linda married right out of high school, had a daughter, Laura, I think her name was. Linda's husband Greg left her when Laura was two. Just left. Disappeared. Left town, never came back. Never paid child support, never visited. Phil and Linda got married, and Phil took on the role of Laura's father. He never adopted her, though, because he felt strongly that Laura *had* a father and that father should be responsible for her. They sued him for back child support, even had him arrested a few times for nonpayment."

Jessica was torn between being glad to have this information and being pissed that Diane hadn't told her earlier. She worked on keeping her face arranged to give the impression that this was old news to her.

Coach took two deep breaths and then said, "Shit."

"Yeah," said Jessica. "That's the thing about courtrooms. You never know. You cannot ignore anyone's backstory."

"How did I not know that?" Coach asked.

"You didn't need to know it," said Jessica. "It had absolutely nothing to do with your life until now. You are not required to know everydamnthing about everydamnbody."

"But I usually do."

"I doubt that." Coach raised his eyebrow, challenging her.

"Okay, where did I go to law school?"

"Emory."

Jessica pressed her lips together. "That one was easy. My diploma is on the wall in my office. Um, are my parents alive?"

"Your dad lives in Arizona or New Mexico or someplace like that, and your mom died your third year in law school."

"Damn," said Diane. "Even I didn't know that until recently."

"What was my first boyfriend's name?"

"Oh, hell," Coach said. "How am I supposed to know that? What were you, fourteen?"

"See? You don't know everything."

"I know a lot," Coach replied. "I make it my business to know a lot."

"I wouldn't have taken you for a gossip."

"It's not gossip," Coach said. "Gossip is yah yah yah woman-speak. I'm talking information about important things. Information is power. The more you know, the more power you have. That's how you get things done around here."

"He's not wrong," Diane said.

"Okay, look," Jessica said, feeling uncomfortable for reasons she could not explain. "Now that you do know what you know about Linda Brandywine, do you see why going to court is a bad idea?"

Coach scratched the back of his head. "Sort of. The outcome is still going to be the same, right?"

"Probably. I mean, I don't guarantee anything, but it will be close."

"So Phil yells at me. Who cares? I've been yelled at before by better men than Phil Brandywine."

"In a vacuum, yeah. But remember: he's going to be yelling at you in front of the *Ashton Post*, who may quote every word he says."

Coach scowled, his blue eyes growing dark and cloudy. "I can't. Don't you understand? I can't agree to visit with this girl. It's not on the table. Brandywine can order it if he wants, but I will not sign my name to any piece of paper that says it's a good idea."

They all three sat in silence, each stoking their own personal fires.

"The *Post* is going to crucify you," Jessica said quietly. "I hope you have a good reason."

"It's not the *Post* that's going to crucify me," said Coach through gritted teeth. "It's Bobby Turnbull. Why don't you knock on his door and offer to start fucking him again so that he'll write decent articles about me. That used to work. Aren't I paying you enough for that?"

"Get. Out," Jessica hissed, with white-hot heat threatening to burst her words into flames. Anger and disgust competed for prominence in her chest. She stood up and pointed at the door. When he didn't move, Diane touched Coach's elbow and silently guided him out of the room.

When Diane came back, Jessica roared at her. "Why do you let him manhandle you like that? Why do you put up with him? He's gross. He's disgusting. He's . . . he's . . . he's . . ." Words failed her. She threw herself back in her chair, and a primal noise escaped her throat. She did nothing to stop the tears of frustration that slid down the side of her face.

"If you're mad at him, don't take it out on me," Diane said, standing beside her.

"No, seriously, I want to know. I want to know why you reward that asswipe with giggles and Sharon Stone leg crossings and letting him touch your ass. God! I want to throw up!"

"I don't reward him with anything," Diane said. "I'm rewarding me!"

"What the fuck are you talking about?" Absolutely nothing made sense to Jessica.

"Tripp is an idiot."

"Huh. We agree on one point."

"But he is a good-looking idiot. I am going to be fifty soon. Any minute now I'm going to be too old for anyone to want to smack my ass or see my panties. I've explained this to you I don't know how many times: I'm never going to get another David, not someone who loves me for me, who knows me on the inside. I don't even want that, truly. I had my love, and I'll always have that—just not in the day-to-day. But I can feel pretty and wanted for five minutes at a time, and you can *not* take that away from me. If he gets something out of it? I don't care. This is all about me, babycakes." Diane was crying now, too, looking down at Jessica, something she could only do while Jessica was sitting and she was standing. The nail of her acrylic forefinger was poking into Jessica's chest.

Jessica stared into Diane's face. She didn't understand where Diane was coming from, not really, but she got that Diane meant what she said. She needed to have a good think about what Diane was talking about—there were some points in there worth considering. Just because Jessica couldn't relate didn't mean they weren't legitimate. In any event, she had hurt her friend, and that she didn't want to do. Jessica grabbed Diane's hand. "I'm sorry," she choked out.

Diane yanked her hand away, causing Jessica to gasp. This wasn't how it was supposed to work. They argued and then it was spent as quickly as the anger flashed up. That's how it went. Jessica didn't know what to do with this refused apology.

"You might still be twenty-nine and think there's everything out there for you waiting, but I'm here to tell you there isn't. You go ahead and live by principle, thinking you're doing the right thing. But there are things out there more important than principle. You're pushing away love and happiness and fun and pleasure and all the good things just so you can go to bed thinking you're

right. That's . . . that's just bullshit. Stop it. Go hug your principles at night. Go grow old with your principles."

Diane's blue eyes locked onto Jessica's hazel ones. Tears
blurred Jessica's vision. She couldn't think of what to say.

"I'm going home," Diane said, whirling around and leaving.

"I'm sorry," Jessica said again, after she heard the front door
slam shut.

CHAPTER
TWENTY-FIVE

When Jessica got to the office in the morning, she walked past the debris in the conference room, remnants and reality from the evening before that she'd been too shocked to clean up. There was no avoiding it if she wanted to get to her office and, more to the point, the coffeepot.

She made herself a cup and buried her nose in the rim of the mug. She inhaled the dark smell of it, letting the earthiness ground her. *Mindfulness*, she reminded herself. *In this moment, there is coffee. I smell the coffee. I feel the heat of the mug in my hands.* She took a sip of it and held the liquid in her mouth. *I taste the bitter and the nut and the sweet and the joy that is coffee.* She squeezed the mug with both hands as if to imprint everything it contained in her body.

Jessica sat down at her desk and deleted some spam about improving the speed of her Internet service. She heard the front door open, then Diane's heels clicking along the hallway in their familiar rhythm. She braced herself. She had no idea what to expect. When Diane peeked around the corner of her office and said, "You okay, sweetie?" Jessica put her coffee cup down, her eyes welling at the softness of Diane's words, and just nodded. Diane put her purse on the floor and sat across from Jessica. "Yesterday was rough."

"Was it?" Jessica said, wiping away tears. "I hadn't noticed."

"Tripp isn't mad at you. He's mad at something else and he's taking it out on you."

Jessica silently thanked Diane for graciously ignoring their own argument. "Believe it or not, I know that. There's something he's not telling us. I disagree with ninety percent of what the guy says, but there's a logic to it. A twisted, sexist logic, but a logic you can follow. There's no logic to his refusal to meet with Francesca, or even to sign a meaningless piece of paper that says he has the right to meet with her. I don't know what his reason is, but we must be getting close, which must scare him. So he's covering it up with all this macho bluster and bullshit."

Diane nodded, impressed. "You've given this some thought."

"It's not like I was sleeping last night. I had plenty of time to think. About a lot of stuff." This was an invitation to Diane to talk about their own argument, but Diane ignored it. "I know it wasn't personal intellectually. But to hear someone you've got to champion in public basically say he's paying you to whore yourself out so he can get some good PR is rough."

"That's not exactly what he said."

"Isn't it?"

"Well, Bobby isn't some random guy. You did go out with him."

"Did. Past tense. And I didn't do what I did for anyone's PR or any other reason beyond the fact that I liked Bobby," Jessica said, knowing as she spoke that her affection for Bobby wasn't entirely in the past tense. She shook her head and kept going. "What I need to do is find a way to quit giving a shit here." She tapped her chest.

"So what are you going to do about it?"

"What can I do?" Jessica banged a gavel-shaped stress ball on the desk, rendering a final verdict. "I will put on my big girl panties, swallow my personal feelings, and represent the guy. I'm just glad it will be over next week."

Diane shook her head. "I don't know how you do it. It strains the limits of my southern raising. I mean, I can be polite to anyone and paste a smile on, and Lord knows he's pretty to look at, but to go into a room and tell the world he's right? Whoo-ee, I'm glad you're the lawyer."

"That's why I get paid the medium-sized bucks and will have a bleeding ulcer before I'm forty."

"You can have it." Diane bent over and dug into her cavernous purse. "I brought you something."

Jessica took the container she'd been handed. "Um, Cool Whip?"

"Stop it, no. That's just the container. Open it."

Jessica opened the lid slowly, as if tarantulas might be inside. When she got it about a quarter of the way open, she tore it off and hooted. "Cheese straws! You do love me!"

"You know I do. Despite yourself. Give me one." Diane leaned across the desk, plucked one out of the container, and popped it in her mouth.

Jessica chewed on hers. "Oh, God, I love these things. When I was little, I thought you were only allowed to have them at weddings."

"They're just comfort food. A pain in the ass to make, but honestly, I was a little keyed up yesterday, and I had some energy to burn. Besides, you're my favorite pain in the ass, so there was some symmetry there."

Jessica tossed the gavel at Diane and hit the shelf behind her, knocking over a picture frame instead.

Each time the phone rang that day, Jessica wondered if it was Coach calling to apologize for his rude behavior. But of course it wasn't. He'd done a good job of learning to craft emotionally intelligent answers for the limited purpose of one day in court.

That did not mean that he could be taught how to actually *be* emotionally intelligent. Empathy wasn't his game. Gaming was his game. Unless emotional intelligence served the overall strategy, it was irrelevant. People interested him to the extent that knowing about their lives helped him. The boys on his team interested him because them being a cohesive unit made them a better team. Whether they became better people or what happened to them once they left the team may not even cross his mind. Likewise, her purpose extended only as far as she could help him in the courtroom. He saw no connection between his behavior and the job he'd hired her to do. He didn't care if what he did helped her or hurt her in the long run. He would never apologize. Which was just as well. The thought of hearing Coach's voice made her vaguely ill.

Jessica was filing the last of Coach's papers when Diane came into the conference room. "Eric Crabtree is on the phone for you."

Next to Coach, Eric's voice was probably the last Jessica had any interest in hearing. She hated arguing with someone when she knew she was wrong. "Tell him I'll be there in a sec; I just need to untangle myself from this pile of papers."

Diane teetered off on her heels. Jessica took her time putting the file away and sitting down at her desk so she could gather up the strength for the conversation. She picked up the phone. "Hey, Eric," she said. "And no, we're still not agreeing to visitation."

"Didn't think so, but, believe it or not, that's not why I'm calling."

"Really?" she asked, suddenly intrigued. She could not imagine why else. "Then why?"

"Oh, it could be a lot of things."

Eric was clearly enjoying the tease, and Jessica resented him for it. "Well then," she said, "I'm just going to assume you're calling because Sarah James has decided to get married and move to Oregon. She wants to do a stepparent adoption for Francesca and never bother Coach or Ashton, Georgia, again. Great news. Great talking to you."

"Funny," Eric said in a monotone.

"I'm a funny gal."

"That's not it, though."

"Of course it's not. That would make my life easy. What is it?"

"You'll never guess who called me."

This game was getting tiresome. "Taylor Swift."

Eric laughed so loud Jessica had to pull the phone away from her ear. "Taylor Swift? What in the hell made you say Taylor Swift?"

"Well, you know, she has that song that talks about how teenagers are stupid, and if someone says *I love you* just to get in your pants, you're gonna believe it because you want to? That seems like the theme of all my cases these days." She attempted a few bars.

"Lord, Jessica, you cannot sing."

"No, I cannot. Just tell me who called you; Coach should not have to pay me for your delay tactics."

"Testy, testy," Eric said, taking an audible slurp of coffee. "Charlie Kicklighter."

"No kidding." The smallness of Ashton felt like it was closing in on her.

"No kidding. He told me that Coach Wishingham, of all people, told him to call me. Coach said that I was a giant pain in his ass, which meant that I must be a good lawyer."

Now Jessica laughed. It felt good. Her rib cage loosened a few degrees. "So? What does Charlie want to do?"

"Turn back time, mostly. Absent that, he's a good kid. He wants to do the right thing."

"Thank God," Jessica said.

"Yeah, well, don't get too relieved too fast. The problem is, he can't do the right thing, and if you and your girl have any kind of compassion for him whatsoever, you won't make him."

Jessica's eyes rolled around in her head so exaggeratedly she suspected Eric could hear them rattling in her skull. She couldn't believe Eric was about to ask her to have compassion for Charlie at Kaitlyn's expense. "Oh, don't even start down that 'poor Charlie's future is derailed' road with me."

"Hear me out, Jessica."

"Eric, I am not in the mood for—"

"Hear me out."

"Fine." Even to her own ears, Jessica sounded obnoxious. So be it. No doubt, whatever Eric had to say was going to be obnoxious.

"It's no secret that Charlie has his sights set on West Point. He's a straight A student, JROTC, quarterback of the football team, all that jazz. His grandfather was a one-star general in the army, did you know that?"

"I did not." Jessica wondered what this had to do with the case and why she should care.

"So I'm told Charlie's dad refused to join the army because he didn't want to move his family around every couple years, like what he'd grown up with. This caused a huge rift between him and the general. Charlie is named after the old guy, though, and Charlie always admired him. The general pulled a few strings and got Senator Buggs to nominate Charlie to West Point. No small thing, you know."

"No, it's pretty impressive." Impressive, yes, but still irrelevant to the matter at hand as far as she could tell.

"Right. So. What I'll bet you didn't know, because I didn't know and even Charlie himself didn't know until recently, is this: you cannot attend West Point if you are married or subject to a child support order."

"What? That's bullshit!" Jessica liked to think that she would have known this had they gotten a little further in the case, but she hadn't even filed it yet, so she cut herself some slack.

"Maybe it's bullshit," Eric said, "but it's also true."

"I don't believe that."

"Hold on." Jessica heard Eric clacking away on his keyboard. "I'm sending you a link."

Jessica clicked the link in his email when it appeared. There it was, on the front page of West Point's admissions website. The rule was in the top four: you had to be a US citizen, not married, not pregnant, and not subject to a child support order. "That is some seriously sexist crap. So a male cadet can knock up a woman—or women—but so long as he doesn't have to pay child support, he can stay. But if a female cadet *gets* knocked up—"

"Hey, Jessica, I don't make the rules; I'm just pointing them out."

"I mean, what if she gets raped and thinks abortion is murder, then her rapist gets to steal her career at West Point too?"

"Jessica!" Eric yelled. "Focus. I'm not here to debate military policy with you. We're only talking about Charlie and Kaitlyn."

"Fine."

"Seriously, Jessica, if you don't want to burn out, you cannot take these cases personally. I mean that as a friend. You're a good lawyer and I like you, but you're going to drive yourself nuts. It's just a job."

Jessica considered what Eric said. He was right in a way. None of what happened to any of her cases affected Jessica's own life. So long as she did her best, all was well, right? But what she did or didn't do had long-term consequences for people like Kaitlyn, Coach, Francesca, and Charlie. She heard her mother's voice, indignant about this horrible, sexist policy, refusing to allow her to kowtow to it no matter how it would affect the people in front of her. This was a bigger philosophical point than she could resolve in the few seconds allotted to her, so just to move things along she said, "Noted. So what are you proposing?"

"Look at this long-term. Baby Charles is better off with a daddy who is a career army officer who graduated from West Point. Phenomenal military insurance. Job security. Good income. Unlimited potential, especially given Granddaddy's connections."

"And? Who is stopping him?"

"You are. You and this child support suit. What part of 'He can't go to West Point with a child support order' is confusing you?"

Jessica ignored Eric's snark. "I'm just trying to process this. You know, Kaitlyn has dreams too. It's not like her fondest wish was to give birth her senior year in high school, then sit around waiting for her baby daddy to do everything he wanted to do. Meanwhile, she gets to clean up baby shit and baby puke and put her own life on hold. She is a straight A student too. Captain of the cheerleading squad. Did you know she wanted to be a pediatrician?"

"No." Eric at least sounded a little contrite.

"Well, that's on hold now. She could have gone to an Ivy League school or one of the Seven Sisters, but now she can only go to the community college within commuting distance of this backwater bullshit town so that her mother can help her out with the baby. A mother, I'll point out, she doesn't especially get along with but who she desperately needs. Who else is going to help? Not future General Charlie Kicklighter who gets the privilege of having a completely normal four years just like he dreamed of."

"Jessica, that's not his fault."

"Well, it's not her fault." Jessica realized she was being petulant, but she stood by it.

"It's nobody's fault!" Jessica had never heard Eric so keyed up. "Not everything is somebody's fault. Sometimes things just *are*. You're right. It is one hundred percent not fair. But you know what else isn't fair? Life. Not one damn fair thing has happened in my life. I'm not in the fair business; I'm in the law business. Same as you. Only I've been doing it about three times longer than you. Therefore, I have much lower expectations for righteous outcomes."

Jessica laughed. She hated every word he'd just said but couldn't argue with one of them.

"You'll get over that eventually, Jess. Here's the reality. These two kids are in a shit of a situation, but they didn't do anything special. They had sex. Just like most of their classmates. Hell, there isn't much else to do in this town if you're seventeen but smoke a joint and screw. And if you think you're in love, like they do, you don't have much incentive to find something else to do. They were dumb about contraception—Kaitlyn got pregnant—and they made their choice to keep the baby. I'm not here to judge; I'm just here to tell you what happened. You with me so far?"

Jessica nodded, then realized Eric couldn't see her nodding and said, "Yeah."

"Okay, so it sucks. There's this kid, and he's a gift from God or whatever, but he's also got to be dealt with. Someone's got to feed him and change his diapers and teach him not to put shit in his mouth that will choke him and all that crap. We still good?"

"Yeah." Eric was lawyering her, she knew. He was a good lawyer, and this was how he did it. He said stuff you couldn't disagree with in cross-examination, then *wham*, hit you with a natural conclusion you didn't want to agree with, but he led you to a point where you had no choice. Mostly she was curious where he was taking her, and she considered taking notes.

Eric slurped his coffee again. "So, I assume that Kaitlyn is not interested in giving Charlie primary custody, correct?"

"Oh, God no. Her mother would drop dead on the spot and take me with her for suggesting it. Anyway, Kaitlyn's breastfeeding and has some pretty strong feelings about that. She can't be away from Charles for any real length of time."

"That's what I thought," Eric said. "So, *by her own choice*, Kaitlyn is in charge of the majority of the baby stuff. Which, by definition, leaves Charlie with more free time to do his thing. Right now, Charles needs his mommy on a more full-time basis than he will when he goes to school during the day."

There it was. She could see his destination. She didn't like any of it, but for the life of her she could not come up with a counter-argument on the spot.

"So riddle me this, Jessica Fischer, Esquire, lawyer extraordinaire: If one of the parents has the opportunity to fulfill his dreams, dreams that will ultimately benefit the child, why shouldn't he? Why should both of them stop what they're doing and ruin their ambition? Kaitlyn can still go to medical school after Charlie gets out of West Point. She'll be done before she's thirty—that's still young. She's not foregoing what she wants to do, just delaying it. They're taking turns. Charlie goes first, that's all."

"It's not fair."

"Nope, it's not. But there's no reason why they should both suffer when only one of them has to. And who says that Kaitlyn is suffering? Is that not devaluing her worth as a mother if this is something she wants to do? Charlie tells me she's on board with this plan. Who wins that way? Not the baby."

"So what are you saying? Practically speaking, I mean." Jessica poked the tip of a pencil into the eye of a purple stress ball with a happy face printed on one side.

"I'm saying you need to dismiss this lawsuit."

"We haven't filed it yet."

"Then don't file it. You file it, you completely change the trajectory of this kid's life, and his son loses out just as much as he does."

Jessica plunged the pencil in deeper until it went all the way through. "So you're saying that not only does Charlie get to go first with his ambitions, but he doesn't have to take any responsibilities for his kid either? He leaves Kaitlyn holding the bag?"

"Jessica. You know that's not what I'm saying."

Eric was right. She knew. It just didn't feel right to her. Jessica pulled the pencil out of the stress ball and stabbed it repeatedly in its stupid, perpetually smiling face. "I don't like it."

"No one's asking you to like it. Look, Charlie will help when he can. I'm pretty sure his mother is going to fork over more than what he'd be required to pay in child support and buy the kid sailor suits and beg for MeeMaw time. I've talked to the family. This is not a deadbeat situation. What we're talking about is damage control. Let's not ruin these kids' lives any more than necessary. Blessing from God, right?"

Jessica said what she always said to opposing counsel when she didn't know what to say. "Let me talk to my client and I'll get back to you." It sounded a whole lot better than, "You might be right, but I'm not ready to admit that."

"Great," Eric said. "So, I take it from the way you answered the phone that we have to go through with this farce of a trial on Tuesday."

"Unfortunately."

"Your client does know what I'm going to do to him, right?"

The stress ball had taken a beating and was little more than a misshapen mass of foam. Jessica plucked off bits of it and piled them into a pyramid on her desk. "He knows, doesn't care. We all know what the outcome is. Can't we just cut to the chase and get there without going through the whole charade?"

Eric laughed like Santa, *ho ho ho*. "And miss out on all those juicy billable hours? I don't think so. Oh, young, sweet Jessica. You really don't know how to run a business, do you?"

CHAPTER
TWENTY-SIX

—◦—

J essica insisted on meeting with Kaitlyn and Denise as soon as possible after her call with Eric, eager to talk to them before Kaitlyn and Charlie had too much time to talk to each other about the matter. The less time that passed, the less time Denise had to spin herself into a tornado of crazy that Jessica would have to untangle. More to the point, Jessica had no interest in spending her weekend fretting about this *and* the upcoming trial.

So Diane arranged for them to come in late afternoon on Friday. She promised to sit in the room while they had the conversation, for Jessica's sake as much as anyone else's. Jessica feared not just Denise's crazy—she was afraid of letting Kaitlyn down. *Sorry, kid. Your dreams get put in a diaper pail while baby daddy goes on to military glory.* They were meeting in the conference room so they wouldn't have to cram into Jessica's office, which was good, space-wise, but it deprived Jessica of the comfort of her belongings. She wanted to be able to look at her certificates and photographs and figurines in their familiar disarray instead of the rows of display books with their uncracked spines and the hotel-quality art on the walls of the conference room.

Surprisingly, Jessica's level of dread turned out to be in opposite proportion to the outcome. Jessica showed them the West Point admissions website and explained the situation in as neutral a tone as she could muster. She told the women it was entirely up to them how they wanted to proceed and braced herself for Denise's tirade, probably one about deadbeat men.

That was not, however, how Denise reacted. Instead, she said, "If you will recall, that is exactly what I said in the beginning."

"Come again?"

"I sat in your office and said that Charlie had no way of paying child support and we shouldn't expect it of him. You were the one pushing us to do this. I never wanted anything from him. I want him out of C.B.'s life." Denise cut her eyes toward Kaitlyn, who studiously ignored her. "This lawsuit just makes him a formal part of it. Frankly, I'm just thrilled for him to go off to school and then Afghanistan or wherever and leave us alone. I just hope he doesn't get shot in some friendly fire training exercise." Sarcasm dripped like acid.

Although Jessica blanched at the thought of Denise wishing death on Charlie, especially in front of Kaitlyn, Denise had named her greatest fear for Kaitlyn: that Charlie would move on with his life and become, essentially, un-servable and unreachable overseas, living a nomadic military life out of reach of civil courts and his son who would never have a real relationship with him.

Kaitlyn's foot, rocking Charles's car seat, sped up a few clicks of the metronome.

"Denise," Diane said quietly. "You don't mean that."

"I do. I *don't* want him to get shot in some training exercise," she said, quite obviously deliberately missing the point.

Diane looked at Jessica. Jessica looked at Kaitlyn. Kaitlyn looked at the ceiling, blinking rapidly to keep the tears from brimming over.

"Kaitlyn?" Jessica said, keeping her voice gentle. "It's really up to you, kiddo."

"If it were up to me, not that anything is, Charlie and I would be living together with C.B. and making this all work somehow.

Apparently," she said, tilting her head toward her mother, "that is not happening any time soon. Everything is just so completely messed up. I had this great life, you know? I was in high school, having a good time. Who doesn't have a good time in high school? Everyone says it's the best years of your life, you know?"

No one who has survived high school says that, thought Jessica, but she just nodded in response and handed Kaitlyn a tissue.

"And now I can't go away to college, my boyfriend isn't welcome at my house, and—"

Denise interrupted. "What are you talking about? It seems like that boy is in our home more than ever."

"*That boy* has a name, Mom. His name is Charlie. His son's name is Charles, not C.B., and he has a right to see his son whenever he wants. Just because he's *at* our house doesn't mean he's welcome in our house." Kaitlyn blew her nose and held her hand out for another tissue. "Here's what I think," she continued. "Charlie and I messed up a lot of things. But there's no reason why we have to mess up every single thing. I mean, if you think about it? He's the one who has to suffer being away from Charles. If we're meant to be together, we'll be together when he graduates. If we're not, we won't. In the meantime, I know he's not going to forget he has this little guy, cuz he loves him, and he loves me, and Ms. Kicklighter will kill him if he does."

"Are you sure?" Jessica asked.

"I mean, I'm gonna miss him so much, but it isn't like him paying me seventy-five dollars or whatever a month is going to change anything on my end. Things are still gonna be the same kind of messed up or whatever."

Jessica had to remind herself that it wasn't her place to give personal advice, though she so desperately wanted to. It was her place to lay out the options, explain the pros and cons, and let Kaitlyn decide. She looked at Kaitlyn, love-blind, clearly determined not to let him off the hook. Jessica felt skeptical that

Charlie would stay connected once he found his own life in the masculine, regimented world of West Point, but knew it wasn't her call to make. Denise was on board with it, and that Kaitlyn had made a decision that differed from the one Jessica would have made didn't matter.

"Okay then. I'll let his lawyer know we'll let it sit. I do wish there were a way to legitimate Charles without having to deal with child support. There are benefits. Not just military stuff, but if, God forbid, something were to happen to Charlie, Social Security and inheritance rights and that kind of stuff. I know none of our judges will let us do it without dealing with child support too. I'll talk to Eric Crabtree and see if he knows something I don't. Maybe there's some way to do it in New York when Charlie gets there, or we can put it in writing that the minute he graduates we'll get it done."

"He hasn't been accepted yet," said Denise.

"He will," said Kaitlyn. "I mean, who wouldn't want Charlie?" The tears in her eyes sparkled with stars.

CHAPTER
TWENTY-SEVEN

In the middle of the night on Saturday, Jessica woke with a start. She grasped at the edges of her dream, but it slipped out of her hand. She blinked at the ceiling, her heart pounding. She felt wide-awake. Should she try to go back to sleep or get up and drink a glass of water? She reached over to the night table and pulled her phone off the charger to see what time it was: 2:43 a.m. Out of habit, she pulled down her notification menu. Junk emails. Tweets she might be interested in. Diane's name was listed in the endless sea of Facebook notifications.

Diane. Jessica put her phone back on the charger and closed her eyes. She wished she understood the complicated mess her relationship with Diane was. Diane was at once comforting and confusing. She pushed Jessica toward Bobby in the same breath as explaining why she herself wouldn't take men seriously after David's death. That couldn't be what she meant. What did she mean? Diane wasn't generally a hypocrite. If she knew how great love was that she wanted it for Jessica, why didn't she want it for herself? Because she'd already had it? Was she such a romantic that she thought a new love would taint David's memory but a roll in the hay wouldn't? Or maybe it was something else. She felt on the edges of understanding but not quite there. Jessica was grateful Diane hadn't brought their argument back up yet, but it needed finishing. No doubt it would come up again.

Bobby flashed across her sleepy mind. What if she'd done what Diane had told her to do instead of what she'd thought was right? Would she now be head over heels in love with Bobby, swimming in joy just thinking about him? And what if he got sick like David had, like her mother had? She put Bobby in David's place, caring for him like she'd cared for her mother. She dragged him into the shower. Washed him like a child, making sure he didn't fall. He was a good boy, sat obediently in the shower chair. She soaped his bald head, his dark curls burned away by chemotherapy. The water pounded his stooped back.

She knelt on the tiled floor of the shower, hugging him to her. "Don't go," she whispered to him. "Don't go." He was shrinking in the chair and she scooped him up, cradling him like a baby. She stood and the water from the showerhead hit their bodies. The water eroded his fragile form, breaking off pieces and sending them toward the drain. She bent over, sweeping him away from the drain, trying to block it with her foot. *My foot likes your foot. My foot will save you.* Her hands scrambled to turn off the faucet.

When she woke up for real at seven, Jessica had an irresistible urge to call Bobby to make sure he still existed. It was too early to call, though, so she didn't. Plus, she wasn't sure she could explain why she was worried. She had flashes of a dream, of Bobby swimming away from her, something about water, but not enough she could make a story out of. She couldn't quite get hold of the dream, but she could get hold of Bobby's image and the desire to hear his voice. The thought was ridiculous. Calling him at all would be ridiculous; even texting him this early would be awkward. She slapped her cheeks, trying to jar the images in her brain loose.

Knowing she couldn't remove these thoughts, she sought to replace them. She busied herself making coffee and a spinach omelet, and watched videos on YouTube as she ate. After breakfast, she laid a yoga mat out in her backyard and sat on it, her legs crossed. She tried to center her mind to meditate, but her thoughts were coming fast and furious. Her fight with Diane, Coach's upcoming trial, her confused thoughts about Kaitlyn, *Bobby*—all of them whisked together in a jumble. She imagined herself batting them away with a spatula. When that didn't work, she plucked each thought out of the air, said, "I acknowledge you," to it, then told it to move on.

None of them moved on.

She gave up and lay face up in the sunshine. She was just going to have to think through these thoughts and be done with them. She didn't want to. They were difficult thoughts.

Where should she even start? There was no beginning or end, just a giant bundle of heavy things, and not enough time to process it all. She felt herself start to cry. Not because she felt sad but because she felt overwhelmed. There was too much inside, and it came out in the form of tears. All she tried to do, she tried to do correctly. She wanted to do right. By herself, by her clients, by everyone around her. But that was so hard—and sometimes impossible to do. She couldn't always do right by herself and her clients at the same time. Was there even such a thing as an objective right?

What *was* right? Doing right by assholes like Coach squared with the lawyers' code of ethics. But doing right by Coach made her get rid of Bobby. That wasn't doing right by herself, and maybe not doing right by Bobby. What about Kaitlyn? Ultimately, she'd done what Kaitlyn had wanted her to do. That was the right thing to do, wasn't it? She had represented her client's interests to the best of her ability. But she didn't think what Kaitlyn wanted was right—she thought it let Charlie off the hook, gave him an easy way out. Wasn't her own version of "right" at all relevant? What was right there? Was messing up Charlie's future right? Even if it stood up for the principle that Kaitlyn was equally entitled? She was so sure it was, but she seemed to be the only one that thought so.

Maybe that's the problem, she thought, *thinking*. She was always thinking. Always trying to reason herself out of every situation, as if the world were one giant logic problem and people were nothing more than fleshy computers. *What if I didn't think?* She took a deep breath, chuckling to herself at the irony of the thought itself. *What if I just felt instead of thinking? What do I feel?*

She started a guided meditation. *What do my toes feel? What do my feet feel? My shins? My knees?* Then she skipped ahead. *What does my heart feel?* She felt a sense memory of her hands gliding along the back of Bobby's shirt, his lips on her neck and her nose buried in the pleasant musk of his hair. She felt warm there, safe, cared for. Her instinct was to throw the memory away, toss it across the yard, over the fence so she couldn't access it. Frustrated, Jessica made a decision. She set a timer on her phone for a half hour. She would give herself thirty minutes to wallow in whatever feelings she had for Bobby. She would let go of inhibition and be done with it.

She gripped the grass at the bottom of her mat with her toes and hit start on the timer.

What do I want? She closed her eyes and felt the sun's heat bathe her face. *No thinking. Feeling. What pops in my brain, unbidden?*

Bobby. He appeared in her imagination, reaching out toward her with his pale fingers with the tufts of dark hair on the first joints. She wanted to stop fighting it and curl up against him. To laugh at his jokes and know what kind of shampoo he used.

To come home from a long day and find him already in the living room with his feet up on the coffee table, drinking a beer, scratching the head of their one-eyed, three-legged rescue dog. She wanted to kiss him.

Why was kissing Bobby wrong? How could she think that Bobby needed limits? If ever there was bullshit, that was shit from the prize-winning bull. Coach was the one who needed to be limited. Bobby understood limits. She could explain to him where the lines were. Coach didn't know, didn't care. He'd be out of her life in a few weeks anyway. She thought about the story Lee told in the Waffle House. Hadn't she done the same thing that Hannah Jordan had done? Thrown Bobby over for some asshole football player? No wonder he reacted the way he did. Bobby himself had told her that in her conference room. Why hadn't she listened? She remembered leaning her head on his chest, his arms circled around her back. If she knew what cologne he wore, she would buy a bottle for herself just to have his smell with her.

She curled up into a ball, rolled onto her side, and cried. She missed Bobby. She missed him, and it was all her fault. They'd be four months into a relationship now, but she was an idiot, just like Diane said, living lonely and unhappy on useless principle, coasting on two dates' worth of memories. She lay there, feeling miserable, swimming in the depths of it, knowing she deserved it, until the timer went off.

She made a plan in the shower. After she put on clean clothes, she felt a bit better. Her hair dried and lips glossed, she called Bobby before her nerves got in the way of execution. It went to voicemail. She hung up without leaving a message. "Shit, shit, shit," she whispered into the void.

She composed a text message, typing and deleting it several times, finally landing on *Call me when you get a chance, please. It's important.* She hit send before she could chicken out.

Then she stood there. Her grand plan did not include killing time; it included action. She looked around. She didn't want to do anything that would make her too grubby in case Bobby called, so yard work was out. She'd already cleaned the house yesterday. There weren't even dust bunnies to chase—damn her efficiency. Her mind was racing too fast to make reading a possibility. She thought about yoga but was afraid of sweating.

She gasped as it occurred to her that he might not call. What if he saw her text and decided that she wasn't important enough to bother with? The possibility sent her to the sofa where she hugged a throw pillow. What would she do if he didn't respond? She started to panic. Should she call Diane? Diane would definitely talk her out of this spiral. Hell, Diane might just call Bobby herownself and take care of things. She might know where he lived, and then Jessica could drive over there.

Then a new thought entered Jessica's panicked brain. What if Bobby wasn't alone? What if he'd moved on? It wasn't like anyone would necessarily tell her. Except maybe Lee, but only if he'd known. Bobby might not report in on every new date he had. He didn't seem like the kind of guy who would just take a woman home for a little something-something, but neither did he seem like the kind of guy to kiss and tell. Maybe she'd misread him. Maybe they hadn't gone all that far because he liked talking to her but didn't find her physically attractive. That was possible. She didn't like it, but it was possible.

She went into the bathroom and looked in the mirror. Her blue shirt tinted her hazel eyes blue. Should she put on more makeup? She didn't usually wear much, especially on the weekends. Just a swipe of mascara, maybe a touch of eyeliner, and lip gloss. Maybe he wanted more glamour. The more she looked at her face, the more she saw its flaws. The slight bump on the bridge of her nose. Her too-large eyes. The mole on her right cheek. This whole thing was ridiculous. An exercise in futility.

She needed to stick with what she was good at. She was a

good lawyer. She should spend the day preparing for Tuesday's trial, not running this stupid emotional errand. Emotions only led her nowhere and distracted her from the business at hand. There was a reason why she thought things through instead of diving into her feelings. That's what she was good at.

Jessica turned off the lights in the bathroom and headed toward the garage to pull Coach's file out of her car. She had her hand on the door to the garage when she heard her phone ringing. She went tearing off to get it before it went to voicemail.

"Hello?" she said breathlessly, not even bothering to check and see who it was.

"Hey, Jess." Bobby's warm brown voice filled her ear, and she wanted to hug the phone. "You wanted me to call you?"

"Yeah, um, I need to talk to you about something. It's kinda important." She was breathless, and the words tumbled out.

"Is everything okay?"

Jessica realized how dire her last few sentences must have sounded and cringed. "Yeah, I guess so. I mean, no one's dying or anything. I'd rather talk in person. Is there anywhere in this godforsaken town we can meet for coffee where the entire gossip patrol isn't going to report in on what they heard?"

Bobby paused. "Is this business or pleasure?"

"Honestly? I don't know yet."

"Then no. There is nowhere in this godforsaken town we can meet for coffee where the entire gossip patrol isn't going to report in."

"Dammit," said Jessica.

"Look," Bobby said. "If you trust me, you can come by my house. There's no one here but me and my cat, and she's not talking."

"You have a cat? Why didn't I know you have a cat?"

"There's a lot of stuff you don't know about me, Jessica. There's a lot of stuff I don't know about you." This sounded ominous, and it made Jessica want to tell Bobby to forget the whole thing, but she didn't.

"What's her name?"

"Come over," he said. "I'll introduce you formally. Assuming she comes out from behind the couch."

On the way to Bobby's, Jessica stopped by Dunkin' Donuts and picked up a box of assorted Munchkins and a couple of coffees to sweeten her peace offering. Bobby's house was a brick ranch with a neat yard and red shutters. Azaleas bloomed along the walkway to the front door. It all looked so homey and inviting, but she still felt like an intruder. He opened the door before she got a chance to knock.

He led her to the kitchen and gestured to a seat at the table. She sat, nervously setting the box of Munchkins down in front of her, and looked around. His kitchen was appealing and better equipped than she would have guessed. A block of Japanese knives sat on the counter next to a Ninja blender. Copper-bottomed pots hung on a rack above an island with a cooktop. He had a spice rack, and the bottles were varying degrees of empty. This was a place where food was made.

She spilled the bag of creamers and sweeteners out on the table. "I wasn't sure how you took your coffee, so . . ." She trailed off, realizing it made her sad that she didn't know how he took his coffee.

"Black's fine," he said, grabbing a cup and taking a sip. She tried to read his tone, but she'd never seen him look like this before, not that she'd seen a whole variety of his looks. His lips were pinched together, and his eyes seemed impenetrable. "As are the jelly Munchkins."

"Where's the cat?" she asked, for lack of a better opening line.

"Hiding. She doesn't like strangers."

"Hey, I'm not that strange," Jessica said, hoping to get half a smile out of him. "Will you at least tell me her name?"

"Bast."

"The Egyptian cat goddess!" Jessica said, proud that she knew this bit of trivia.

"She certainly thinks she is a goddess to be worshipped," said Bobby, finally giving her a crooked grin, though not quite making eye contact.

It occurred to Jessica that while she knew exactly how she wanted the middle of this conversation to go, and how she hoped it would end, she had no clue how to begin. She took a long sip of coffee, and then followed up with a blueberry Munchkin. So long as her mouth was filled, she wouldn't have to talk.

"So what did you want to tell me?" he asked, losing patience.

Well, that was one way to start. "The other day, I was getting ready for Coach's trial next week, and, well, long story short, Diane and I got into this big fight. She was flirting with Coach, and it made me mad that she was letting him get away with being such an ass. She said she was just making herself feel good by having a good-looking guy react to her. I said it was gross because he was gross. He was looking at her like she was a nice piece of steak."

"He is gross," Bobby said. "But what does that have to do with you being here today?"

"Right. Well, that wasn't where it ended. Or her only point," Jessica said, taking a long sip of coffee, hoping it would give her strength. "She said I was worse."

"Huh? I mean . . ." Bobby drummed his fingers on the tabletop. "I can think of a few things I'd rather you hadn't done, but none of them quite sink to that level of disgusting." He smiled weakly.

Jessica looked down at her lap. She simply could not look him in the face. "According to Diane, she didn't actually *give* Coach anything, she was giving *herself* a good time by making herself feel attractive, and if he got anything out of it, well, that was purely coincidental and none of her business. Honestly, it took me a good thirty-six hours to get what she was talking about."

"Okay . . ." Bobby said, still looking confused. "But still, what does that have to do with you texting me like there was some kind of emergency?"

Flustered, Jessica nodded. "Right, right, right. So, Diane's out there getting what she wants, and to hell with anyone else and what they thought or got out of it. Me, on the other hand? I'm so busy trying to do the objective right thing, whatever that is, that I never bothered wondering what was right for *me*. I was having a good time. With you, I mean. I did something good for myself, and I threw it all away. Why? Because of some abstract professional code of ethics that doesn't benefit anyone except for Coach. He doesn't deserve what he already has, much less anything else."

Bobby stared at her, his face still unreadable. His eyes were intense, boring into hers. She felt like he was searching her soul for something that might not be there. "One of the things I liked about you was that you had that strong sense of right and wrong," he said. "That you were willing to sacrifice yourself for a cause you believed in. I liked how you went all in, even though I ended up losing because of it."

Jessica wanted to grab Bobby and shake him. He wasn't going to let her get away with being subtle. She put her coffee down so Bobby wouldn't see her tremble. Everything, absolutely everything, rode on her ability to be precise in what she said next. "I can handle my clients ethically and still have a personal life. I understand now that those things are not mutually exclusive."

Bobby's mouth was a straight line. Jessica watched his chest expand and contract as he breathed. "Sometimes," he said when he finally spoke, "those things overlap and when they do, you have a history of not handling it well."

"I know. But what's that quote? 'Those who do not learn history are doomed to repeat it'?"

"George Santayana."

The fact that Bobby knew who said it made her fall just a little bit harder. This raised the stakes. "I learned history. I learned from history. So I'm not doomed to repeat it."

Bobby narrowed his eyes. "What are you trying to say?"

"That I'm sorry. That I wish I could take back what I said. What I did. I was trying to do the right thing, and maybe I *did* do the right thing—ethically—on paper, but I don't live on paper or in an ethics textbook, I live here, in Ashton, in the real world, and dammit, Bobby, I miss you," she said, her voice breaking a bit.

Bobby just stared at her.

"You have to say something," she said. "You can tell me to fuck off, but you have to say something."

"You broke my heart in half last year." Bobby sounded a thousand miles away.

Jessica looked down at the plastic lid of her coffee cup and picked at the edge of it with her thumbnail. "I'm really sorry. If it means anything, I broke my own heart too."

"Don't be sorry," he said, coming back to the present with a long sigh. "I know why you did. I was really mad for a long time. If I were a different kind of guy, I would have shown up at Coach's house and thrown a punch. Instead, I punched him in the way that I could. In the paper. I'm not proud of that."

"Nothing you said was untrue!" Jessica had no idea what Bobby was talking about. If that article wasn't a punch at her, what was it?

"I know, but that article didn't serve any purpose other than to let me try to hurt him. My motive wasn't to tell the truth. I realized that later. *I* was the one with a conflict of interest. You're better than me. You realized you had a conflict of interest, and you stepped away no matter what your personal feelings were. I just blindly plowed ahead. I threw my sucker punch and hid behind the paper like a coward."

"You're not a coward. You were hurting," Jessica said.

"Yeah, and I handled it like an adolescent asshole."

"For what it's worth, I thought you were punching at me, not Coach. I thought I deserved it too. Even so, I really liked the article. It told the truth, and the truth needed to be told. No one was saying it, and that was starting to piss me off." Hope bloomed in Jessica's chest. If all these months he hadn't resented her like she'd thought but was mad at himself for acting a fool, well, she could reassure him he hadn't. She'd done nothing but miss him, hadn't been mad at him at all. That was a sitcom-worthy misunderstanding that could be cleared up in a single conversation.

Bobby seemed to consider his options before saying, "Do you want to know something?" He fished another jelly Munchkin out of the box and chewed it slowly before continuing. "Remember that story Lee told you about that New Year's Eve in high school?"

Jessica nodded.

"Let me fill in the details Lee doesn't know. Yes, I had a monster of a crush on Hannah Jordan. Yes, I followed her all over town like a moron. Yes, I heard that she was going to the New Year's Eve party at the church. I wanted to go to that party. I even convinced myself I thought the party was going to be more fun than Marc's basement with his Xbox and my best friends. I can be a real asshole sometimes."

The tips of Bobby's ears were bright red. She wanted to kiss them but was afraid to move.

"Tripp's mom was one of the chaperones at the party. She was a super sweet lady. Pretty too. Looked a whole lot like him, except narrow. Willowy. Nothing hard about her. I didn't really have any friends at that party. So, I followed Hannah around, and Hannah kept following Mrs. Wishingham around, asking when she thought Tripp would get there."

Two and two equal four, Jessica thought, though why it hadn't occurred to her before this moment she had no idea. Bobby and Coach were about the same age, and they'd both grown up in Ashton. Of course they would have been in high school at the same time.

"Mrs. Wishingham was so nice to her; she was so nice to everyone. She just kept saying, 'I don't know, dear, he said he might show up later.' I knew there was no way he would come to a lame church party on New Year's Eve. He was a senior and a football star, and we were a bunch of freshmen and sophomores. All of us were losers."

"Bobby!" Jessica said.

"Look, I'm not a loser now, but in tenth grade? The late-blooming intrepid reporter for the school paper? Not exactly A-list material in the high school cafeteria.

"So anyway," Bobby continued, "I keep following her around like a stupid puppy. She's not even making eye contact with me, just talking to her friends, and every fifteen minutes asking Mrs. Wishingham about Tripp. Finally, Mrs. Wishingham takes pity on me and says, 'Hannah, dear, I don't think Tripp is going to make it. But Bobby is a nice young man. Why don't you talk to him?' And for like three seconds I felt like maybe I was going to get somewhere until Hannah turns around and looks at me with such utter disgust. She doesn't say anything, just looks at me like the thought of speaking to me makes her want to throw up on her patent leather shoes. Right then and there I went from being madly in love to hating her. It was all I could do not to just burst into tears.

"Mrs. Wishingham saw the whole thing. As soon as Hannah walks away, she asks me if I'm okay. I ask her if I can call my mom, and she takes me into the church office. We call my mom, my mom brings me to Marc's, and, well, you know the rest."

Jessica thought she might die if she didn't get to hug Bobby, not the adult Bobby sitting across from her but the fifteen-year-old boy still hurting inside him. She knew that she had to be still and let him finish. Even the rise and fall of her chest as she breathed seemed an extravagance.

Bobby cleared his throat. "So yeah. You are the second person in my life to throw me over in favor of Tripp Wishingham."

"Bobby, I . . ." Jessica trailed off when he put a hand up.

"I'm not done. I found out the next day that Mrs. Wishingham stayed at the church until one thirty in the morning to make sure everyone's parents picked them up and to clean the rec room from all the shenanigans. Nobody knows what actually happened between one thirty and when she was found at four o'clock with her car up against a tree. She was dead. It's kind of ridiculous, but I blame Tripp for that, always have. If he'd been there that night, Hannah never would have looked at me like dog shit on a shoe, and he could have been there with his mom to either drive her home or go get help or something. She wouldn't have died alone, anyway.

"He didn't deserve Hannah, he didn't deserve his mother, and he sure as shit doesn't deserve you. But he got all three of you, and here I am."

Bobby stood up and went to the sink. He splashed water on his face and dried it off with a kitchen towel. As he did so, Jessica got up and hugged him from behind, resting her face on his warm back. "Bobby, I'm here now. I'm sorry. I didn't know any of this. But even so, I was wrong." He turned around and she looked up at him, expecting him to bend down and kiss her. Instead, he put his hands on her shoulders and gently pushed her away. As soft as the motion was, she felt like he'd pushed her off a skyscraper.

"I'm glad you're here, I am," he said. "I'm glad to know what you're telling me. Part of me wants to just let go and be relieved and kiss you. But I can't, Jessica, I can't. It took me too long to get over you, and that was only after two dates."

Jessica's entire chest felt hollow. "I don't know what to say."

"I don't either," he said. "I don't even know what I want to hear. But I think maybe you should go. You keep looking at me with those beautiful eyes of yours, and the light hits them and they look blue and green, and there's all that gold shining in them. I only have so much willpower, and right now I am coasting on fumes."

"I . . ." she began.

"Please go," he said, walking over to the door and opening it.

Jessica drove home on autopilot. Somehow, she found herself in her house where she crawled into bed. She'd done a lot of crying already this weekend, and it seemed like she wasn't close to finished. She tucked the comforter under her chin, saying a quiet prayer of thanks that she had done most of her trial prep the week before. She would be useless today, and tomorrow's purpose would be to pick apart every line of what had happened at Bobby's house with Diane.

Jessica rolled onto her side, feeling the coolness of the pillow beneath her cheek. It was so different from Bobby's warm back against her face just an hour before. A chill ran through her. She felt like she'd never be warm again.

CHAPTER
TWENTY-EIGHT

Finally, it was Tuesday, and the high drama of Coach's trial forced Jessica to focus outside of herself. Jessica had spent a good bit of Sunday and Monday experimenting with foods to settle the acid churning in her stomach. White foods worked: plain rice, milk, and nonfat vanilla pudding. It was possible that full-fat vanilla pudding would have worked as well, but she didn't have any and she didn't feel like going to the store. She didn't feel like going to court either. If she'd had her druthers, she'd be wearing yoga pants with unwashed hair and wallowing in her own misery with a half gallon of Breyers vanilla bean and a spoon.

Court started at nine, but Jessica told Coach to meet her at eight thirty. Waiting for him to arrive, it was all Jessica could do to breathe in a normal, human way. Her typical pre-trial nerves were compounded by knowing that Bobby would be in the room. She had read somewhere that Barbra Streisand threw up every time before she went on stage. Somehow that kinship gave her comfort. It would pass; this she knew too. As soon as the testimony started, she would get in the zone and all would be well. Until then, however, it was something to swallow. Picturing herself hurling all over Coach's neatly pressed dress pants and tasseled loafers helped a little.

She made small talk with Coach, asking him about his weekend and whether or not he felt ready. He grunted a few answers, so she gave up and started scanning around to see who else was in the room. She spotted Emily in the first row of benches. Her long hair fell in shampoo-commercial dark waves with expensive butterscotch highlights. She had flawless skin and eyebrows with precise edges. Jessica would have to wake up at 4:00 a.m. to achieve such perfect casualness. Jessica decided Emily was too depressing to look at, and busied herself with spreading her papers on the defendant's table. Coach drifted away from her, and just hearing his booming laugh as he shook hands with and backslapped the bailiffs was all too much. Jessica got out of her chair and wandered over to Traci Stephens, the court reporter. Traci had always been kind to her.

Traci greeted her and said, "Well, at least I get some eye candy today."

Jessica rolled her eyes. "Not you too!"

"Look at him! Tall, dark, and handsome! Lucky you, all that late-night trial prep alone with him. I'm surprised Emily allowed it."

"Believe me, Traci, it was all work." She smiled at Traci to hide the fact that she couldn't stand her client. Hiding this information from a woman who had the ear of the judge ranked high on her to-do list. Jessica looked over at Coach and tried to pretend like she'd never met him before. He was tall, he was dark, and, personality aside, he was objectively handsome. She allowed that he did have a certain magnetic charm, even if it was skin-deep.

"I couldn't believe those girls from the school were protesting him. If he'd been my teacher . . ." Traci gave Jessica a knowing wink that Jessica had no idea what to do with.

The door to the courtroom opened, and the movement distracted her before she was required to respond. It was Bobby

Turnbull, in a pair of khaki pants, a pink button-down shirt, and a blue tie printed with small flowers. He caught her eye before she had the chance to turn back to Traci. *Dammit.* Her already churning guts gave another lurch.

"Oooh, Jessica," Traci whispered. "The ex."

Bobby smiled at her and waved. She waved back. She turned to Traci, wondering how *she* knew about their two dates.

"Can't we import some new people in this town?" she said, forcing a laugh.

Traci laughed too. "Other than a good football team, thanks to your guy over there, we don't have that much to offer."

Roderick Blalock, the judge's law clerk, came out of the back door, a sure sign that court would start soon. Jessica said, "Wish me luck!" to Traci and pulled Coach away from his thoughts on the baseball season. She sat down, looked over at Eric, nodded a greeting, and then turned to Coach. "You ready?"

"Ready as ever," he said smugly. She wanted to snatch the arrogance off his face with her fingernails, leaving bloody trails. He swiveled back toward Emily, who shaped her hands into a heart and smiled. He returned a toothpaste-commercial smile and said, "Love ya, babe."

"You got this, babe," she said, blowing him a kiss.

Jessica filed that away as a necessary detail in the story she would tell Diane later.

"All rise! The Court of the Honorable Phillip J. Brandywine is now in session!" Deputy Everett's voice boomed as Judge Brandywine came through the back door of the courtroom.

Judge Brandywine held his hands out and motioned for them all to sit before they'd had a chance to fully stand up. "Good morning, everyone," he said, arranging himself in the big leather chair on the bench, his black robe flowing around him. He looked down at Traci and then over to his left at his law clerk. "Ms. Stephens, Mr. Blalock."

They beamed at him, basking in the attention, mumbling, "Morning."

"For the record," he continued in his officious judge voice, "we are here in the matter of Sarah James versus Frank Wishingham the Third, Civil Action File Number eighteen dash zero two five eight dash one. It appears that all parties and their counsel are present and you wish to have the matter taken down, is that correct?"

Both Jessica and Eric half stood at their tables and said, "Yes, sir." Eric added, "We will share in the cost of takedown of the transcript by the court reporter." Jessica nodded her consent.

"I've read the pleadings and relevant documents in the file. This seems rather straightforward to me. Have you been able to work any of this out?"

Jessica said, "Yes, sir," and Eric said, "No, sir," at the same time.

Judge Brandywine looked from one to the other of them. "Which is it?"

Jessica turned to look at Eric, pleased that she got a leg up so early on. She knew good and well they hadn't worked anything out, but she wanted the judge to know that they had worked everything out but the visitation, only it was a package deal for the James camp. Since the financial matters were more or less inevitable, trying them would only waste Judge Brandywine's time, and Jessica wanted the judge to know whose fault it was. She said, "We worked out the financial matters, Your Honor, but not the visitation. I think it may be a package deal, which explains the um . . . confusion."

"Your Honor, my client was willing to compromise on certain issues if Mr. Wishingham was willing to do the same," Eric said. "He wasn't, and so we were unable to come to a meeting of the minds. That's where we stand, ready to proceed with trial."

"I need counsel to approach the bench."

Coach raised his eyebrows at Jessica. Without words, his face shouted, *What the hell?*

She patted his shoulder. *Don't worry, I'm in control.*

Eric and Jessica lined up in front of the judge's bench, which was designed to make them look and feel small. They had to crane their necks upward to see the judge towering over them.

Judge Brandywine cleared his throat and, sparking jealousy in Jessica, took a large sip of his coffee. Litigants were only allowed water in the courtroom. "What exactly is the issue here?" he asked.

Jessica and Eric looked at each other, each daring the other to start. It was Eric's turn, since she started the first time. Neither spoke until Judge Brandywine said, "Mr. Crabtree?"

"I don't know that child support is going to be a problem, since we agree on income and insurance. There are disagreements, however, about back child support obligations. The big area of contention is visitation."

"Does Mrs. James not want Coach Wishingham to visit?"

"Actually, it's the opposite."

Judge Brandywine tilted his head to the right like he always did. "Come again?"

"Coach Wishingham refuses to visit."

Judge Brandywine lifted his right eyebrow, just like Jessica had predicted. "Ms. Fischer, why does your client refuse to visit his daughter?"

She had prepared for this question. "That's not exactly how he would phrase it, Your Honor. I'll let him address it more deeply in testimony, but, in a nutshell, he believes that it would be disruptive to the minor child's life to introduce a new parental figure at this stage of the game."

The judge bit his lips together. As predicted, he wasn't buying this line. "Have you discussed with him my generalized philosophy on parent-child relationships?"

"I have, Your Honor." The advantage of knowing the judge—and having him know her—was that without anything showing up on the record, she had just communicated to Judge Brandywine that she had tried to talk some sense into her client and he hadn't listened to her good advice. Whatever followed was not her fault, and the judge wouldn't blame her for it.

"I'm not prejudging the case, of course, but I do usually believe that there is a benefit to children having a relationship with their biological parents if there is no adoptive parent in place and the biological parents are essentially fit. You are claiming that he is essentially fit, aren't you?"

Jessica supposed this was what passed for a joke in judge-world. She presented him with a courtesy laugh. "Of course."

"Okay, then, let's try this case and get it over with." Jessica felt good knowing that the judge felt the same way about this case that she did.

After they thanked the judge and walked back toward their respective tables, Jessica got her first look at Sarah James in person. Sarah sat as if she were balancing books on her head, her hands folded neatly in front of her. Her hair was pin straight and pulled back in a barrette. She neither repelled nor drew you in: she was the sort of person you generally wouldn't notice. Jessica tried to imagine her at Kaitlyn's age, drinking warm, shitty beer or Kool-Aid punch, maybe for the first time. What a swirl of confused thoughts must have piled in her disordered mind when a high school luminary like Tripp Wishingham climbed on top of her. Of all the people in this room, Sarah intrigued Jessica the most, and it was her story she was least likely to hear.

Eric's questions to Coach were all variations on ones Jessica had role-played during trial prep. Coach, good student that he was, responded to each question brilliantly and charmingly. He played, it seemed, directly to Emily. *Look how great I am! Lucky you, to be marrying your emotionally intelligent, brilliant, prepared husband-to-be!* His eyes were twinkling, and his chin dimple was reminiscent of Cary Grant. His voice modulated like he'd taken years of drama classes instead of spending years pushing drama kids into lockers.

Jessica was wholly focused on the happenings in the front of the room. She filled page after page on a legal pad with notes, listening intently to what everyone said. She gauged the reactions of the judge and the people the judge would talk to later, like Rod and Deputy Everett.

Eric asked a simple, straightforward question: "Mr. Wishingham, can you explain your insurance benefits to the court?"

Then the clouds rolled in.

After an hour and a half of fielding difficult questions like he was playing a casual game of catch, this softball seemed to stump Coach. "I, uh, I . . ." He began to cough, though it didn't sound like there was any real cough there. "Can I have a drink of water?"

Jessica, who'd been sailing smoothly in the zone for all this time, suddenly felt like her boat would capsize. What on earth was happening? Why would such a simple question stump him? She narrowed her eyes at Coach, then looked at Eric, then back at Coach. Something was going on that she didn't understand, and until she got a grip on it, she could not get back in the zone.

Deputy Everett poured water into a cup and handed it to Coach. He sipped it slowly, then balanced it on the rail of the witness stand. Coach coughed again. "I, uh, can I have a second to talk to my lawyer?" He peered at the judge. Every inch of him transformed into an eight-year-old boy with wide blue pleading eyes.

Judge Brandywine sighed and glanced at Eric, who shrugged.

"We've been going for a while," he said. "Let's take a five-minute recess."

"All rise," said Deputy Everett, and everyone stood as Judge Brandywine slouched out of the courtroom.

Jessica made her way to the witness stand, glad for the opportunity to ask directly. "What's going on?"

"I've got to talk to you." Coach stared at his feet. She'd never seen him so meek.

"So I gathered." Jessica looked around for a private place to talk. "Here. Come with me." She touched his elbow and he shuffled around the railing, still focused on the ground. "Let's go in the jury room." They sat down at the large conference table ringed by twelve comfortable armchairs. "What's up, Coach?"

"What the fuck is she doing here?" Coach growled, coming slightly back to himself now that they were alone.

"What the fuck is *who* doing here?" The adrenaline was cresting in Jessica's body, and she did not feel the need to try to control it alone with Coach.

"Francesca. What the *fuck* is she doing in the room? She walked in just now."

Jessica started to run her hands through her hair, then remembered how much hair spray was holding it together and refrained. "I didn't see her. She was behind me. Is it a problem?" *Okay*, she told herself. *This is a solvable problem.* The Francesca in the room part, anyway. The getting Coach back on track part might be more difficult. She closed her eyes and took a deep breath, trying to calm herself as the panic drained before she could set about calming the large beast in front of her.

"Is it a problem? Is it a problem?! Jesus! Fuck! Jessica! What have I been saying for the past months? I do not want to meet her. Have I not made that clear enough? What is wrong with you?" Coach sprang up and began pacing around the table, his volcanic energy too much to be contained in a chair.

Jessica's thoughts spun out like a marlin hooked on an inadequate reel. She'd been right, she knew it. There's something he wasn't telling her, but she'd never really pressed him for more. Seeing how much of an effect Francesca's presence had on Coach only made Jessica more curious. Still, she knew she couldn't solve this problem now, not in the middle of trial. The best she could do would be to calm him down and get through this. She inhaled, counted to ten, and breathed out. She saw now that she should have done a motion *in limine* to have the judge decide beforehand that Francesca would be excluded from the room, but Jessica had never considered that she'd show up. Who brings a sixteen-year-old girl to a fight between her parents about whether or not her dad wants to meet her? At that thought, Jessica breathed a sigh of relief. That was it. She'd say that exact thing to the judge to get her out of the room on those grounds, and Coach could deal with his own psychology around the whole thing some other time. That wasn't her problem. And, with any luck, Coach wouldn't be her problem much longer either.

She poured herself a cold cup of water from the water cooler, drank from it, and then turned to Coach. "Okay, look. I didn't know she'd be here. There's no good reason why she needs to be in the courtroom. I'm pretty sure I can get the judge to make her leave. I'm glad you told me. How else would I know, right?"

Coach's nostrils flared. She walked around the cooler and put her hand on his arm, petting him lightly. "You okay?"

He stopped his pacing and stared her directly in the face. She willed herself not to look away. His intensity was a bit much. "It's a lot, you know?"

Jessica patted his arm, then stepped away from his gravity. "I know." She took a few breaths and added, "For what it's worth, you were doing fantastic on the stand. You're a great student."

"You're not a bad teacher," he said. "Where's the bathroom? I've got to take a leak."

— — —

"Your Honor," Jessica said when they were all back in place, "it appears that Francesca James has entered the courtroom." Everyone reflexively looked toward the witness gallery. As the only young woman in the room with Coach's dark hair and luminous blue eyes, they all knew who she was. Francesca, feeling the power of so many eyes on her, focused on her lap.

Jessica turned back to the judge. "Francesca is a girl of tender years. She is, of course, the subject of this litigation. A lot of things are going to be said in this room that she may not be mature enough to understand in a broader context. We have invoked the rule of sequestration, so witnesses are excluded from the room. I know this court does not generally allow the children in domestic cases to be present during litigation, and I don't see any reason to make an exception here."

Judge Brandywine looked at Eric. "Mr. Crabtree?"

"Your Honor, Francesca is not a small child. She will be seventeen in just a few months. At seventeen in the state of Georgia, she will be old enough to be tried as an adult if she commits a crime. This is her life we are talking about. The adults are litigating it for her, but she has the right to hear what people are saying. We do have open courts here."

Jessica could have spit venom in Eric's eye, simply because she agreed with him.

"Any response, Ms. Fischer?"

After a moment of panic, a rush of adrenaline gave her the answer. "Your Honor, obviously Francesca's mother has not yet testified, but we expect based on her discovery responses that she will state that Francesca wants to visit with my client. That is abject hearsay *unless* Francesca is available for cross-examination. In order for Francesca to be available for cross-examination, I have to be able to call her as a witness. If she is available to be called as a witness, she is subject to the rule of sequestration. Therefore, she has to leave the room."

"Do you really expect to call a sixteen-year-old girl to the stand?" Eric said.

"You can't have it both ways," Jessica said, hitting her stride. "Either she is too young to be called to the stand and participate in the hearing, in which case she is too young to sit through the trial and process what she hears, *or* she is old enough to be called to the stand and participate in the hearing. In that case she must be excluded from the room due to the rule of sequestration."

Judge Brandywine smiled his first genuine grin of the day. "I think she's got you, Mr. Crabtree. I'll give you a moment to explain to your client and her daughter why she can't be in the room."

Coach, who was sitting close enough to the bench to have heard the whole conversation, whispered a prayer of thanks.

When they broke for lunch, all Jessica wanted was to go back to her office and breathe for a moment in her own space. She would do a halftime recap with Diane, and then her head would be able to return to the trial, refreshed. On her way out, Coach grabbed her by the shoulders and inclined his head toward hers. Their foreheads didn't touch, like he did with the boys on his team, but close enough. "You're rocking it," he said. "See you at one thirty."

She felt the magnetic glow of his praise on her skin. She wanted to earn it again. That knee-jerk desire to please him gave her a flash of insight into why those boys on his team worshipped him. He was an awful person, but he had a chemical appeal. You wanted to make him happy. What on earth was it? That was the "it" factor, she supposed, whatever charm was. She shoved that train of thought in a waffle square and set her mind back on the trial.

CHAPTER
TWENTY-NINE

Testimony wrapped up at about four. Judge Brandywine gave them a fifteen-minute recess to gather their thoughts before closing arguments. Jessica wished she didn't have to bother. Closing arguments were for juries. Judge Brandywine already knew what he was going to do. She could say nothing that would change his mind.

Sarah James had taken the stand, but Jessica's opportunity to ask her all the interesting questions had gone away when they stipulated that Coach was indeed Francesca's father. No point in talking about Francesca's conception if you could skip ahead sixteen years. Sarah insisted she didn't know who the father was until she got the DNA tests back, which was why she waited so long. No, she hadn't named Francesca after Frank Wishingham—she'd named the girl after her grandmother, Frances. She said everything with a bland expression and a monotone. Jessica guessed she'd cried and screamed out all the emotions years ago and was only trying to get this over with.

Francesca's testimony was more dramatic. She shared her father's magnetic presence, though rather than use it to command a room, like he did, she was more coy and flirtatious. Everything she said came behind her false eyelashes, which served as excellent frames for her striking blue eyes. Jessica studied her face as she spoke, looking for any traces of her mother and finding none. Where Sarah was beige, Francesca was vivid colors. Where Sarah's voice was a lullaby, Francesca's was a dance number. Jessica watched with intense interest as she stared Coach down, telling the world that she spent her entire life wanting a father, and now that she'd found hers, she wasn't going to let him slip away. Anyone in the room would have thought Coach was taking intense notes; instead, he was coloring in a rather detailed rendition of the Ashton "A," complete with serifs and traditional shading. Jessica wished she could bore into that thick skull of his and get at what he was thinking. No, she wanted to bore into that barrel chest of his and get at what he was feeling. Surely he had feelings. The way he'd reacted when Francesca had walked in the room proved that.

But she couldn't do that. Now all she could do was figure out how to sum it all up and end this fiasco. Jessica scribbled some notes on a legal pad, her third of the day, and glanced at her client, who was standing with Emily, his arm possessively curled around her shoulders. Emily looked just as perky and perfect as she had at eight thirty in the morning. Who knew what magic tools she kept in that cavernous Burberry handbag of hers. Jessica had wilted, for sure. The last time she used the restroom, she'd blanched at what she saw in the mirror. Her hair looked slightly crazy—she could only keep her hands out of it so much. Despite her best efforts, her mascara and eyeliner had raccooned under her eyes.

It's for him, she thought. The dog and pony show was entirely for Coach. Both Emily's and the one she was about to give. The thought made Jessica slightly ill—she didn't want to do anything for Coach's benefit alone. Her closing argument would not win or lose this case. It would not influence anyone in the room. But it would prove to Coach that he spent his many thousands of dollars on a lawyer who cared, who believed in his cause, and who had good arguments to make on his behalf. *Barf.*

Truth be told, she was just tired of the whole thing. She was tired of being proud of coming up with creative arguments that sounded plausible and legally sound for a cause she didn't believe in or entirely understand. If it were up to her, she'd go home and take a nap. Let Judge Brandywine issue a written decision whenever he got around to it. The judge knew the law. He was a good judge. But even if he weren't, it was still his call to make. *Not an option*, she told herself. *Get on with it. Finish your job.* She shook herself and refocused on the task at hand.

Judge Brandywine returned to the bench, and everyone else took their seats. He looked as tired as Jessica felt. "Are we ready for closing?"

"Yes, sir," Eric and Jessica chorused.

"Mr. Crabtree, you're the plaintiff. You may begin."

"We will waive opening and reserve closing."

Asshole, thought Jessica, though she expected this and would have done the same. She stood and gathered her notes to walk over to the podium. As she did so, Coach whispered, "You got this." Jessica half expected him to pat her on the butt, professional athlete style.

"Your Honor, there is nothing complicated about this case. I won't waste your time going through the financial matters in detail, as they speak for themselves. Your Honor has the exhibits that show the parties' income, the health insurance information, and the child support worksheets that calculate the amount going forward.

"As for back child support, I present to the court the case of *Medley v. Mosley*. May I approach?" The judge nodded as Jessica handed him a stapled-together packet of papers, then walked over to Eric and handed him a copy of the same stack. "Which stands for the proposition that although the court can order back child support in some circumstances, it has to be based on the actual expenses incurred in raising the child. The child support amount is irrelevant. No evidence was presented about actual expenses. So, in addition to the laches issue, that is, why Ms. James waited sixteen years to establish paternity and ask for child support, she is now asking the court to guess at the amount she spent over the years.

"Now, moving onto visitation. I have been in this court countless times during divorces and other custody cases when the children at issue were fourteen and older. And I have heard you say time and time again that once a child is of a certain age, it's pointless to force them to go to visitation if they don't want to. To do so is just asking for trouble. This is the same situation, just in reverse. Why are we forcing visitation? How could that possibly benefit Francesca?

"Frank Wishingham is not some deadbeat loser. He is a man who has built his career and his reputation on being the 'teenager whisperer.' He knows how teenagers operate. That's the secret sauce in his recipe for success. He knows them. He knows what motivates them, what de-motivates them, what makes them tick. He's got a master's degree in education. I daresay if we tried to have him qualified as an expert witness in adolescent behavior, the court would accept him due to his extensive training and experience.

"It is his deeply held belief, as he testified." Jessica strode over to the witness chair, trying to get Judge Brandywine to conjure up the image of Coach sitting up there. He had seemed so sincere. She waited until everyone looked at the chair before continuing her sentence. "That Francesca has a sixteen-year-old understanding of the world. That doesn't compare to his thirty-four-year-old understanding of the world. He knows that in the long run, his disruption of her life will do more harm than good. I know that this court is not in the business of letting teenagers run the show. Parents, adults are authority figures for a reason.

"The bottom line is this, and this is just reality. The court can order visitation, but the court cannot order Coach Wishing-ham to exercise that visitation. Here's what I've never been clear on: why we are here pushing for something that no one can force. I know this is a court of law, not church, but sometimes the Bible says it best. Ecclesiastes tells us to everything there is a season. Right now, it's baseball season. This is not the right season under heaven for this meeting to happen. Thank you."

Jessica sat down. As penance for her impassioned speech, she promised herself to donate money to the Court Appointed Special Advocates or some other group that helped children with troubled parents.

Coach gripped her hand. She whipped her head toward him. His face radiated sincerity. "Thank you," he whispered, squeezing her fingers. She nodded at him, smiled, then turned toward Eric, who was beginning his closing argument.

She snuck a look at Sarah James. Sarah was sitting the same way she was at the beginning of the trial: her back straight, her hands folded on the table. Her features were tighter, however, almost concentrated in the center of her face, as if she were holding them together for fear they'd go flying off her skull if she didn't clench them in. *I'm sorry, Sarah*, Jessica telegraphed. *I promise you. I'm really, really sorry.*

Jessica tuned back into Eric's argument. ". . . have not had a chance to fully read the *Medley* case, and with Your Honor's permission, I'd like to have until Friday to provide a written brief on that issue."

Oh, bullshit, thought Jessica. Eric knew as well as she did that she'd typed in "back child support" in her legal search engine and that case had just popped up. *Whatever.* She didn't care whether or not Coach's abundant stashes of money got depleted, so this was the least of her concerns. She wrote "written brief on the issue" on her pad, just to appear busy.

"It's absurd to say," Eric continued, "that getting boys to

run plays on a football field is the same as understanding the complex emotions of a girl whose father has rejected her. Sarah James knows her daughter because she has spent every day of Francesca's life with her. Frank Wishingham does not know his daughter because he has callously refused to so much as share a meal with her. How much psychological damage that is doing, I cannot say."

Jessica spent her mental effort on not hating Eric. It was irrational to hate Eric. All he was doing was making an argument she agreed with. Why Coach wouldn't suck it up like a big boy and have dinner with Francesca she would never understand. *It's not your job to understand*, she reminded herself. *It's your job to represent your client. That's how the system works, and you believe in the system. He deserves representation; the judge makes the call.*

She could feel the heat emanating from Coach beside her. His broad shoulders and barrel chest were more than the fake leather chairs were intended to contain. Because of his height, his long legs folded upward and didn't quite fit under the table. He looked out of place, something he surely wasn't used to. She tried as hard as she could to feel empathy for him. It must be odd, she decided, to be that powerful, that in control of every situation, and be suddenly thrust into one in which you had to submit. Coach might not know how to submit.

Jessica checked back into Eric. Truth be told, it didn't matter what Eric was saying. She had said her part, and now Eric got the final word. Then they'd be blessedly done, whatever the outcome. Eric pointed at Coach, who studiously ignored him.

"This man is all for the greater glory of Frank Wishingham the Third. He knows he did wrong seventeen years ago, and he just wants to sweep that little mistake under the rug. That little mistake has a name, Coach Wishingham. She has a name, and feelings, and a whole life you know nothing about." Eric walked over and put a picture of Francesca on the table in front of Coach.

"Look at your daughter, Francesca." Eric stared at Coach, who stared back at Eric, refusing to look down at the picture.

Eric gave up, walked back to his table, looked at the judge, thanked him, and sat down.

The courtroom was silent for a few beats. Jessica looked over at Traci, who raised her eyebrows. Jessica wished she could communicate back, but Judge Brandywine would see her, so she settled for just maintaining eye contact for a few extra moments. She wasn't 100 percent sure what Traci was trying to say, but she thought it was, *He's got a point*, and she wanted to communicate back, *I'm paid to say what I say. You know that, right?* She exhaled and went back to focusing on the judge along with everyone else. He was scribbling something on a piece of paper. Whether he was signing an order in a completely different case, finishing up his notes, or completing the crossword puzzle from the Sunday *Post*, no one had any way of knowing.

"Okay," said Judge Brandywine, putting his pen down and making eye contact with each of them in turn. "As for child support, I've got your worksheet here, and it looks in order. We'll just go ahead and follow that going forward. This is April second. Is there any reason why I can't order that child support begins this month? I do not want to go another month without it."

Jessica looked over at Coach, who shook his head. "No, Your Honor," she said.

"All right then. Now. As for the back child support, I'll give you both until Friday at 5 p.m. to give me a written brief on the issues. The *legal* issues, mind you. I've heard plenty of the moral issues. I just want to hear about what the law has to say."

Eric and Jessica both nodded.

"As for visitation." Judge Brandywine scribbled some more on a piece of paper, and Jessica noticed that Coach turned Francesca's picture over with one of his panther-quick movements. The judge looked up and said, "Ms. Fischer, please ask your client to stand."

Jessica touched Coach on the elbow, but he was already unfolding himself from the chair. Jessica stood next to him in solidarity, pad and pen in hand so she could take notes.

Judge Brandywine worked his mouth around the words before letting them out. His head cocked to the right, and his eyebrow lifted in his familiar lecture pose. "I'm going to assume, Coach Wishingham, that you and your lawyer have had many conversations about this issue before you set foot in my courtroom."

"Yes, sir," Coach said, hanging his head and doing his best to adopt a humble posture. Humility did not fit his frame.

"Then I'm sure she explained to you my general philosophy about how children need to have a relationship with their parents."

Coach nodded.

"See here now," the judge continued. "I'm a lawyer by training, not a psychologist, and my power is somewhat limited. Unfortunately, Ms. Fischer is right. I can order that you have the right to visitation, but I cannot order that you exercise it. That's one of the limitations of this robe. But I do have the advantage of this bully pulpit, and by God, I am going to use it. I may not be able to get you to act right, but I can make you listen to me, at least for a little while.

"I am going to order standard visitation. Every other weekend, every other holiday, that sort of thing. You can take it or leave it; that's your privilege. I can only give you the opportunity to do the right thing; I cannot force you to do it. But I will tell you this. You can fool yourself that you are doing this for Francesca's good, but you have not fooled anyone else in this room. Your behavior is cruel and selfish. I cannot even imagine the damage it is doing to this poor girl's psyche. But hey, that's what freedom is, is it not? The freedom to be a horse's posterior.

"I'm not mincing words, Coach Wishingham. I'm not going to pretend this situation is anything other than what it is. You can appeal me if you like. I doubt you'll be successful since I am following the law. No doubt Mr. Turnbull, who has sat patiently throughout this entire proceeding, will quote me in tomorrow's paper. I also have no doubt he has come to the same conclusion himself." Judge Brandywine stroked his goatee with his left hand. Pyrrhic victory that it was, Jessica mentally called "bingo" in the Judge Brandywine prediction card.

"Put yourself in Francesca's shoes, if you are even capable of feeling for the girl. Imagine being sixteen years old and having no idea who your father is. Suddenly, you find out, and he's not just any gentleman, but he lives very close to you, and he's a local celebrity. Never mind the questionable circumstances of her conception. She suddenly has this opportunity to meet her father, to ask him questions, and to get to know a whole other side of her family. Maybe he has the same set of freckles on his arm. Maybe he makes the same face as she does when he is concentrating. She's just curious. And he says, 'No.' As hard as it is to be a sixteen-year-old girl in general terms, now she's got to handle the rejection of her absent father on top of all of that.

"Pat yourself on the back for a winning football season if you think that's what matters in this life. But nothing, I mean *nothing* you do will ever make up for what you have inflicted on this poor girl. I ought to make you put enough money to cover her therapy bills going forward in a trust fund. If I can find a legal justification for doing so, I will."

Judge Brandywine tapped his hands on the bench, spending nervous energy. Traci typed furiously on her stenotype. Deputy Everett stood with his back to the wall, impassive and unreadable, standing guard. Rod Blalock stared at Judge Brandywine, his mouth agape. Jessica didn't dare see what Eric and Sarah were doing. Judge Brandywine stood, his robes billowing around him like a cape. He left the courtroom without another word, Rod on his heels.

The courtroom was quiet enough to hear the door latch as it closed. As soon as it did, everyone collectively exhaled. Jessica continued to focus on the bench where the judge sat, afraid to move until someone else did. She heard Coach breathing loudly through his nose to her right and, finally, Eric shuffling papers to her left. Traci finished her typing, then began clearing up her equipment.

Jessica turned to Coach, who was still standing, stiff and tall as a redwood. She felt obligated to speak to him, but she could not for the life of her figure out what to say.

"Not now," he growled, his expression and posture not changing.

"Got it," she said. She turned to the not insignificant business of packing up her papers in some coherent order. A few moments later, she saw Coach leave the table out of the corner of her eye and head over to Emily.

She took her time getting things together. The lobby and the parking lot needed to clear before she left. The only person she had any interest in talking to was Diane. Little by little the room emptied. Before Eric left, he came over to her and shook her hand.

"You made some decent chicken salad out of the chicken shit you'd been handed," he said. "Too bad Judge Brandywine doesn't like chicken salad."

"I don't blame him," she said. "I hate the stuff, myself."

"Go home," he said, walking backward out of the court-room so he could still face her, the tails of his shirt pulling out of his pants and his tie already loosened. "Pour yourself a glass of Scotch and then go to bed."

"Scotch tastes like furniture polish."

"Chardonnay then. Whatever. 'Night, Jessica."

"Good night, Eric."

Jessica spent the next few minutes arranging her pens in a

line, waiting until everyone else had left so she wouldn't get cornered into a conversation in the parking lot. When the courtroom was empty except for Deputy Everett, she swept the pens into her briefcase, left the room, and sat down on one of the benches in the cavernous lobby of the building. She checked her emails and text messages to make sure nothing pressing had come up over the day. Seeing nothing that couldn't wait, she put her phone away and began to summon the energy to stand and walk all the way to her car.

Just as she rose, a door from the side hallway opened and closed. Jessica shut her eyes, praying that the person who would emerge from that hallway in a matter of seconds wasn't one of the dozens of people she had no interest in speaking to.

It was Bobby Turnbull. Shit. Jessica didn't have the emotional energy to deal with Bobby right now. How she felt. How he rejected her. How he smiled at her. It was too much.

"Hey, Jessica," he said, striding over to her. "Crazy day, huh?"

"No," she said, "I will not give you a quote for the paper. My brain is too scrambled. There's no telling what I would say."

"Nah, I don't need one. I've already filed the article. That's why I'm still here. The whole thing kinda spoke for itself. Judge Brandywine gave me the best quote I've had in a while."

"I think you can only get away with saying 'horse's posterior' without irony if you have that Foghorn Leghorn accent."

Bobby laughed. "Speaking of horseflesh, I'm kinda craving tacos. Wanna meet me at El Toro?" He held his hands up in a defensive position. "No pressure. Not trying to be weird. It's just dinnertime, we both gotta eat, and I want tacos. I'm not secure enough to eat at a restaurant by myself."

Jessica considered his suggestion, her stomach flipping in about twenty different directions. There was much she did not have the energy to talk to Bobby about. The very last complete sentence he'd said to her before this conversation was "Please go."

But tacos did sound good, and Bobby was usually good company and he knew exactly how her day had gone. Surely he would not have asked her to go if he wanted to make her day worse. Did she dare hope he wanted to make it better? El Toro, "The Bull," was an appropriate choice given the enormous amounts of bullshit she'd shoveled today. She realized she was cocking her head to the right, Judge Brandywine style. Was her eyebrow raised? She straightened her head and took a leap.

"Sure. No harm in tacos."

"Burritos either. Watch out for the chimichangas, though. See you there."

CHAPTER
THIRTY

—

Jessica called Diane on the way to El Toro and put her on speakerphone because she owned the last manufactured car without Bluetooth. She gave Diane the short version, promising the longer version in the morning. She purposely left out the fact that she was meeting Bobby for dinner and hung up just as she pulled into El Toro's gravel parking lot.

She pulled open the front doors, and there was Bobby telling the hostess there would be two for dinner. "If at all possible," he said, "we'd like a booth all the way in the back."

The hostess watched Jessica greet him and replied, "Oh, sure, honey, I'll give you a booth in the back," with an exaggerated wink.

As she led them toward their seats, Bobby said, "I asked for a booth in the back so the fewest number of people would see us. I tried for what passes for privacy in this town."

"Thank you," Jessica said, sitting down and busying herself with unwrapping her silverware, tucking the napkin on her lap. She wondered if Bobby would mind if she grabbed the entire salsa bowl to herself so she could double-dip. She looked at the flip menu of colorful margaritas. "I'm sad I have to drive. After today, I want one of each."

"If you trust me, I'll drive you home. You can get your car in the morning." Bobby broke a chip into tiny pieces on a napkin. "With an Uber, I mean."

A server walked by carrying a fishbowl margarita on a tray. Jessica wanted to dive into it and drink her way to the top. "Really?" Everything about this seemed like a poor idea, but Jessica was beyond caring.

He held his hand up in the Scout's honor gesture. That made Jessica feel nostalgic on top of everything else. "Yes. Of course."

Tabitha, or someone wearing Tabitha's name tag, came over to their table. "Can I get your drink order?"

"I would like a large Texas margarita, with salt, and a shot of Patron. Maybe two, but one for now," she said, perhaps a touch too enthusiastically.

Tabitha grinned wide, showing a missing molar on her upper right side. "Yes, ma'am." She looked at Bobby. "Anything for you, sir?"

"Unfortunately, or fortunately, we'll see, I've got to get this one home. I'll take a Dos Equis and a glass of water."

"Unfortunately?" Jessica raised an eyebrow when Tabitha walked away.

A spot of color showed on Bobby's cheek. "I meant unfortunately I can't match you shot for shot. Not unfortunately I have to take you home."

Jessica nodded and pointed a chip in his direction. "Before we talk about today, let's lay some ground rules. You have to promise me that every single word, every single gesture, every single everything that I say or do from this point forward is off the record."

"Forever and ever?"

"I meant just tonight when I said it, but let's go with until I say otherwise."

"You got it."

"Promise?"

Bobby held up three fingers again. "Scout's honor."

"Did you make it all the way to Eagle Scout?"

"No, I never made it out of Cub Scouts. Why?"

"Because you do that a lot." She held up her fingers. "Scout's honor."

Bobby looked at his hand. "Really? Huh."

"You did it twice just now."

"Huh. I guess you just make me swear to a bunch of stuff."

"I'm very demanding," Jessica said, right as Tabitha came back with their drinks.

"As you should be," said Tabitha.

Jessica pointed at Tabitha. "See? This lady knows how to get a good tip."

Bobby looked up at Tabitha. "She hasn't even started drinking yet. Just wait."

Tabitha walked away. Jessica picked up her shot with one hand and the slice of lime with the other. "You've never seen me drunk. What do you know?" What was up with Bobby? Was he flirting? Was he just showing that they could be friends? Was he trying to prove to God knows who that he had insider information about her?

"Nothing," Bobby said. "I'm waiting too."

Jessica lifted the shot glass. Screw Bobby and his motivations. She needed a drink. "To motherfucking Frank 'Tripp' Wishingham the Third."

Bobby clinked his beer bottle against her shot glass and sipped it. Jessica shot the tequila, sucked the lime, and shook her head. "Oh, the burn. It burns so good."

"Francesca was freaky," Bobby said, after they'd both taken significant swallows of their drinks.

Of all the million comments that Bobby could have made about today's trial, this was not the one she expected to lead the pack. "Freaky? Freaky how? I thought she was beautiful. Graceful."

"She is. I mean, she is the spitting image of Tripp's mother. It was like seeing a ghost walk in the room."

"Really?"

"Really. And get this. I did some research over the weekend, because, apparently, I like to torture myself. I got to thinking after our . . . conversation . . . on Sunday." Bobby took a long pull on his beer, and for the first time, Jessica realized that there must have been an aftermath to that conversation for Bobby, too. She knew what his reaction to what she'd said was—how did he feel now that he'd had time to think about it?

Bobby wiped his mouth with a napkin and continued. "How does a guy like Tripp spawn from a woman like Mrs. Wishingham? I called my dad, got him talking. You know, if you think Ashton is small now, imagine it thirty years ago or more."

Jessica pictured Bobby with actual, living parents. A pang of guilt stung her. She should have been more curious about him and his life. Instead, she just worried about how he made her feel. Oh well, it didn't matter anyway. She'd more or less thrown herself at him the other day like he'd been sitting around for a third of a year waiting for her to come to her senses. He'd just told her to go home.

"So Dad said that Tripp's father, Junior, was the same kind of asshole as Tripp, which made it even weirder that a real lady's lady like June Wishingham would find herself hooked up with him. I kinda wondered if it wasn't like one of those royal marriages, where the Spanish princess married the Bavarian prince for some political or financial alliance, and no one really gave a shit if the Spanish princess and the Bavarian prince could hold any kind of conversation. Mrs. Wishingham was a Marable before she married. You know how many streets and parks and whatnot around here have Marable in the name."

Jessica's fish tacos had arrived at the table. She was experimenting with how to eat them without dripping them all over her lap, no small task when the majority of her focus was on what Bobby was saying. She felt like she should respond, if for no other reason than to give Bobby the chance to eat his dinner. But she enjoyed the sound of his voice and his storytelling, and halfway feared she may never get to experience it again.

"Then Dad said that they married in November, and Tripp was born in May. He was as big a baby as you'd guess him to be, so you do that math."

Jessica laughed, and as she did so, coleslaw flopped out of her taco, and onto her blouse. "Dammit!" she said, wiping at the stain, trying to do so without looking like she was manhandling her left boob. Bobby stopped talking and watched her perform this action with a curious look on his face. "I'm going to go to the ladies' room. I'll be right back."

She cleaned the mess off her blouse in short order, then arched backward under the hand dryer to dry it. As she stood under the hot air, a theory occurred to her. She checked the damp spot in the mirror, thought, *Good enough*, then hurried back to the table.

There was still a good half left in her margarita glass. She drank several large gulps of it, then said, "I have an idea."

"What's that?"

"I've been thinking the whole time that there has to be a reason why Coach refuses to meet Francesca. Not for dinner, not for five minutes, not to give her a Christmas present. Not for nothing. I was starting to think maybe it was because she looks just like his mom, and that was too much for him. You know, like he missed his mom and that made him sad and all."

Bobby knit his eyebrows.

"I know," she continued, gaining enthusiasm for her own fantastical theory. "That's giving him too much emotional credit. But something you said earlier—consider this. What if he really is just like his dad. Or more to the point, his dad is really like him." Jessica nodded, encouraging Bobby to follow her train into the station. When his eyes sprung open, she knew she had him. "What if his *dad* did the same thing to his *mom* that *he* did to Sarah James? Only his mom wasn't letting his dad off the hook for sixteen years: she shotgunned him into a wedding."

"That's totally plausible," Bobby said.

"Yeah, yeah it is." Jessica licked the salt from the side of her margarita glass and sucked deeply on the straw, finishing the drink with a loud slurp.

Bobby shook his head. "I don't know. I just don't know. I'm thinking you should just write fiction."

"I get that I'm completely pulling this out of my ass. But wouldn't it be poetic, though? His sainted mother dies and then *bam*, right afterwards he creates his mother's absolute clone?"

"It's a little southern gothic," he said with a lopsided smile.

"We live in the South, baby!" she said, flinging her arms wide, nearly clipping Tabitha as she walked by. "Oh! I'm so sorry!" Jessica wasn't sure which embarrassed her more, impulsively calling Bobby "baby" or almost smacking Tabitha in the stomach. She supposed she was at the point where she could blame everything she did from this point forward on draining adrenaline and adult beverages and decided not to care.

"It's okay," Tabitha said, patting her on the shoulder. "Can I get you another margarita?"

Jessica looked at her glass, then at Bobby, who appeared amused. "That's probably not wise."

Bobby said, "Give her another shot for the road."

Tabitha left to get the shot and the check before Jessica could protest. Jessica grabbed Bobby's water glass and drained it. "The rule is," she said, "if you're gonna drink a lot of alcohol, then you hafta drink a lot of water or you get a headache in the morning."

"I'll keep that in mind," he said.

"I'm still mad that Coach's life isn't going to change now that he knows he has a daughter. Someone should make him meet

Francesca. It's not fair that he can punch her in the heart and no one can do a thing about it, not even the judge. Truth, justice, and the American way my ass."

"More like what's good for General Bullmoose is good for the USA." Bobby saluted.

Tabitha came with the shot and Jessica downed it.

"Li'l Abner," Jessica said. "I played Mammy Yokum in high school."

Bobby looked bashful. "I played General Bullmoose."

Jessica looked at him with more sobriety than she'd displayed in at least a half hour and said, "You're still trying to impress me. Why?"

"Did I? Impress you?"

"Actually, yeah."

"Good. Look, your problem is that you expect the world to behave in rational ways. It doesn't. The good guy doesn't always win. Sometimes he goes home broken and wounded and just has to regroup and get ready for the next battle."

Jessica tried and failed to figure him out. The world was fuzzy around the edges.

"You're the good guy," he said. "Let me rephrase that. You're like a colonel in the army. You've got some rank, and you get to make a lot of decisions, but you don't always get to choose the wars you fight in. Hitler took Poland and France for a good long while. The Polish and French colonels or whatever the hell they call them there lost those battles. It didn't make them any less right. Letting Hitler steamroll over Poland and France would have been the wrong thing to do."

Jessica pointed at him. "You watch too many documentaries. I'm not the good guy. You know what I did today? I was fucking Hitler's colonel. I fought his battle for him, and I won. Coach got everything he wanted except for a lecture from the judge. Just following orders! That's me!" She felt herself starting to cry.

Damn. That second shot of Patron was probably not the best idea.

Bobby slid out of his side of the booth and into Jessica's, putting his arm around her. Her head flopped against his shoulder, the heat of his body warming her soul.

"Jessica," he said softly. "Sweet, sweet Jessica. I'm sorry I went down that road. You're right. I watch too many documentaries. That was a bad analogy." He hesitated, then stroked her arm. "Someone had to represent him. Frankly, I'm glad it was you. Do you know what an asshole attorney like Chris Carmichael would have done with Tripp as a client? He would have gone on the offensive and attacked poor Sarah James. He would have called her a slut. He would have accused her of hiding this information from Tripp for her own nefarious purposes. He would have seen to it that she had to pry every penny out of Tripp's hand, then he would have charged him double what you did for the privilege.

"You, on the other hand, made him actually pretend to be humble on that stand, offer to give her money, and give some cock-and-bull story about not wanting to see her being in her best interest. You didn't just fuck with her, and you didn't let Tripp do it either. You tried to work it out, I know you did. Chris wouldn't have tried."

Jessica knew Bobby was saying nice things, but her brain was too fuzzy to follow all of it. His voice felt like a warm blanket folding over her, and she hoped he would never move his arm. He warmed her outsides as the tequila warmed her insides. She pulled her napkin off her lap and dabbed at her eyes with it. Then she said, "Ow. Dammit. I just got salsa in my eye."

Bobby reached over to the napkin holder and pulled out a clean one, handing it to her. She wiped at her eye. "Do you feel better?"

Jessica squinted up at him. "I got the salsa out of my eye, if that's what you're asking."

"You goof."

"Yeah," she said, smiling. "You're good at this."

They stared at each other in silence. *If this were a movie*, Jessica thought, *now's when he would find me irresistibly awkward and kiss me.*

Instead, Bobby took his arm back with a deep breath and returned to his side of the table. Why? Why didn't he take advantage of the moment? "I'm actually good at a lot of things."

"Oh yeah? Like what?"

"I can solve a Rubik's Cube in under a minute."

"Seriously?"

"Yes, seriously."

"Prove it."

"Do you happen to have a Rubik's Cube in your purse?"

Jessica opened and closed her purse. "Nope."

"Then I can't. You'll just have to trust me."

Jessica put her elbows on the table and her chin in her hands, capturing his gaze. "I think I do."

"Good," he said. "Are you ready to go? It is a work night, and I think we've done about as much damage as El Toro will let us do." With this, Jessica's heart broke. She had come to him at his house and laid bare her feelings. Now here she was, drunk and vulnerable, and he wasn't biting at that hook either. Clearly, he was done with her. She was officially friend-zoned. The thought took away all the warmth of the last few minutes like taking off a parka in a snowstorm. She felt chilled to the bone.

They had a brief squabble over the check. Jessica won, her argument being that since they talked about work most of the time she could ethically justify it as a business expense and have Coach Wishingham indirectly pay for the meal.

When they pulled into Jessica's driveway about twenty minutes later, Jessica sat there awkwardly for a moment, not wanting to end her time with Bobby, but also wishing she could figure out a way to ask him what he was thinking without sounding desperate.

"Are you okay?" Bobby asked, jerking her out of her stupor. "Can I walk you to the door?"

Jessica opened the car door and climbed out. She held on to the car's frame and looked at Bobby over the roof. "I probably could have driven myself home, you know." This was a lie, she knew, but she wanted to sound stronger than she was at the moment.

"Maybe, maybe not. Why take chances?"

"Why not take chances?" she said quietly as he came around the car. He took her elbow to guide her along the walk. She fought the urge to lean into him. Jessica unlocked the front door and dropped her purse inside. "Thanks for driving me home," she said.

"You're welcome."

He didn't move. Neither did she.

"Do you want to come in for a cup of coffee?" she dared ask, her heart pounding in her ears.

Bobby stood there frozen, long enough that Jessica suspected he hadn't heard her invitation. She contemplated asking him again when he spoke.

"I do," he said.

Neither one of them moved. Then Jessica sneezed into her arm.

"I'm sorry. Pollen. April in Georgia!" she said, smiling shyly as she opened the door.

They headed into the kitchen and she saw it how he must see it—so sterile compared to his. Her countertops were white and the appliances stainless steel. An uncluttered island sat in the middle of the room. It was perfectly neat and perfectly lifeless. What did it say about her? What was he thinking as he leaned against the island and watched her make coffee?

Jessica remained silent as the Keurig heated up, feeling Bobby's gaze on her back. She didn't say anything, afraid that if she spoke she'd say the wrong thing and he'd find a reason he had to leave. He didn't say anything either, which only made her more nervous. Once the cups were brewed, Jessica led them into the living room where they sat on opposite ends of the sofa. It was a comfortable, plush piece of furniture, but it seemed as bare as the kitchen to her refocused eyes. She wished she had throw pillows, an afghan to toss over the back. Something to give it the homeyness it lacked.

And still, neither one of them spoke. When she could stand it no more, Jessica broke the silence. "Can we just shoot this elephant in the room? He is seriously harshing my vibe."

Bobby laughed, pointed a finger gun into the middle of the room, and said, "Bang."

"Come on, Bobby," she said. "I need to know what you're thinking. No beating around the bush here. Two days ago, you were telling me to leave your house."

"I don't know," Bobby said. "Not exactly. I just know that I watched you all day today working so hard to make Tripp Wishingham look good. You were so good at what you did. I sat there knowing how you really felt about him, and I was just amazed. I started to get mad all over again at Tripp for all the shit we talked about on Sunday and more. I was jealous that he got to sit next to you. Then I just got mad at myself because I was too scared to say yes to you on Sunday. I could have . . . I was a coward, and then—"

Bobby was cut off by someone pounding on her front door.

"What the hell is that?" she said, her heart skipping at least two beats.

"I have no idea. If this were TV, any second now we'd hear, 'Police! Open up!'"

"Jessica!" a man's voice shouted from outside. "Jessica! Please tell me you're there!"

No. "Is that Coach? It sounds like Coach." Jessica started to rise, but Bobby motioned for her to stay seated.

"Let me get it. He sounds drunk." Jessica lowered herself back onto the sofa, wondering what in the hell Coach was doing pounding on her door like that.

Bobby opened the front door a crack. Jessica heard Coach's voice.

"Jesus Christ, Turnbull, it's you. What the fuck are you doing here?"

"I could ask you the same," Bobby said, his voice even and calm.

"You gonna let me in?"

"You gonna be nice?"

"Let me in." Jessica instantly felt like a piece of meat tossed between two fighting dogs. This was *her* house. Why wasn't anyone asking her if *she* wanted Coach in?

Bobby must have opened the door wider because Coach barreled into the living room. He had changed out of his court clothes and was wearing his standard khaki pants and an Ashton red polo shirt. He sat down next to Jessica on the couch. He pointed a thumb at Bobby, a ref's gesture of "yer out." "Make him leave. I need to talk to you."

"Hi, Coach," she said. "Welcome to my house. Make yourself at home. Feel free to tell my guest to leave just because you feel like it. Don't worry at all about what you're interrupting." She sat on her hands so no one would see them shaking.

Coach scowled, then bull-snorted clouds of brown liquor. Jessica reared back at the smell.

"Did you drive here?" she asked, horrified and incredulous.

"Yeah."

"You seem pretty drunk." Jessica looked over at Bobby to see how much backup she had. She didn't think Coach would hurt her no matter how hard she pushed him, but then again, she'd never seen him drunk before. Bobby was pacing back and forth in the small space between the love seat and the coffee table, cracking his knuckles.

"So what? I can hold my liquor and know all the cops between here and my house. There isn't one of them that wouldn't just tell me to be safe and let me be on my way." As strong as the bourbon smell was, his tone was casual and arrogant, like usual. Jessica relaxed.

Jessica wasn't surprised. "You do know that a DUI isn't just about the tickets, right? It's also about the people you could have killed between there and here."

"I got here, didn't I?" Coach said, as if that proved his point.

Bobby perched on the edge of the love seat next to the sofa and gently asked Coach for his keys. He spoke meekly—it sounded like an admission to being a beta, but it did wonders to lower the temperature in the room. Coach puffed up his chest like the anole lizards that populated her porch, sticking out his chest and pumping its dewlap in an aggressive display. Jessica suppressed a giggle.

"What do you need my keys for?" Coach scoffed.

"I just want to move your truck. It's blocking mine."

Coach dug into his pocket and tossed his keys at Bobby. "Don't fuck with my mirrors or scratch it."

"Got it. Never fuck with another man's truck." Bobby saluted Coach, and Coach turned back to Jessica. Over Coach's head, Bobby winked at Jessica and pocketed Coach's keys before going outside. She realized how hard it must have been for Bobby to bow to Coach like that, and how masterfully he had defused a potential tinderbox of a situation. Her heart surged with affection for Bobby at the same time it sank with the realization that it meant that Coach wasn't leaving any time soon.

"So," Jessica said, "why did you break traffic laws to come to my house at night? How do you even know where I live?"

"I told you," Coach replied, "I know what I need to know. I was so pissed off after today that after I got home, I had a few glasses of some very good bourbon. I said some things to Emily she might not have been so happy with. She told me to get the hell out until I could sober up." Judging from the way he was speaking, he was correct—Coach could, in fact, hold his liquor. You had to smell him—and know him—to know how drunk he was.

"That explains why you left," Jessica said slowly, still swimming out of her own alcohol fog—she could not hold her liquor as well as Coach. She was trying to figure out how to get the answer she wanted without setting him off. "It doesn't explain why you are here."

"Because you and Emily are the only two people who a) know how my day went and two, are on my side."

On your side, Jessica sneered internally, and prided herself for being sober enough not to say it out loud. She hoped her face didn't give her away. Coach's own drunken belligerence was sucking the tequila out of her cells.

"And now *that* asshole is here," he said, pointing toward the front door, which had opened and shut only moments ago, "and anything I say is going to be reprinted in the paper. I thought you weren't fucking him anymore."

Apparently, Coach hadn't heard the door opening over the sound of his own voice. Bobby caught Jessica's eye conspiratorially before saying, "I asked you to be nice. Do I need to ask you to leave now?" Jessica's gut lurched between gratitude that Bobby was dragging her on his side in the turf war and being miffed that Bobby felt like it was his job to protect *her* turf, as if she couldn't do it on her own. It finally landed on gratefulness—she wasn't used to having someone on her team who would take the lead like that and fight her battles. It felt good that he wanted to fight for her. She was too tired to fight anyway.

"Dammit, Turnbull, you know what I mean." Coach swiveled toward Bobby, then said, his voice taunting, "I *meant* I thought you were no longer engaged in your courtship, m'lord. Just asking a goddamn question. Jeez."

"To answer your question," Bobby said, his voice measured, "I'm not, as you so poetically put it, fucking her, not that it is any of your goddamn business."

Coach stood up and faced Bobby. "It's my business what you put in your paper about me, which seems to be tied to your relationship with her."

"One thing has nothing to do with another," Bobby countered. "Both of us have too much integrity to compromise our ethics over a prick like you. If I write something unlikable about you in the paper, it's because there's something unlikable about you."

Coach edged closer, forcing Bobby to crane his neck to hold eye contact, a power move designed to intimidate if ever there was one. Bobby, God bless him, stood his ground. "Unlikable about me? How many times have you walked into a stadium and had people cheer?"

"That's because of what you do, not because of who you are," Bobby said. "My job is to show people who you really are."

Coach clenched and unclenched his fists. Jessica suddenly realized she ought to be fearful for Bobby. She'd been watching this like she'd watch a rom-com but found herself in her own living room. Coach was a head taller than Bobby and easily outweighed him by seventy-five pounds. But all she could do was laugh. The more she tried to stop, the more she laughed. Soon, her silent laughter turned into a full-throated belly laugh. Bobby scrunched up his features quizzically, but Coach whipped around with a face full of fury.

"What the fuck is wrong with you?" he sneered.

"Both of you," she said, through peals of laughter. "Pants down."

"What?" said Bobby.

"You have lost your mind," said Coach.

"I'm serious," said Jessica, calming down a little, just an occasional giggle breaking through. "Take down your pants, boxers too, and I'll get out a measuring tape. We'll see whose is bigger. Not that I give a shit. That's what you're doing, isn't it? Trying to figure out whose dick is bigger?"

They both stared as her laughter picked up steam again. "Wouldn't that solve so many problems?" she shrieked. "My God! How many court battles would be settled if we could just make men whip 'em out!" She doubled over and wiped her eyes on her sleeve, then suddenly sat up straight when she realized she might have just peed herself. But still, it felt good, God, it felt good to just laugh. She hadn't felt this relaxed in weeks, months, maybe. Not since . . . well, not since her dates with Bobby.

"I'll tell you what," she said. "For some idiot reason, I'm still wearing my pantsuit. I'm going to change into play clothes. You boys find a way to get along. Coach, you obviously can't be on the road, and we can't drive you home until you're sober anyway because apparently Emily doesn't want you there. So, you have run of the house. Except my bedroom. I'll be back in a few moments." She took a few steps toward her bedroom, then turned around. "I don't care what you do to each other, but, Coach, if you get blood on my carpet, you are paying for the carpet cleaning service to come out. For the whole house, not just spot cleaning."

CHAPTER
THIRTY-ONE

By the time Jessica had changed into an old pair of jeans and a T-shirt, splashed her face with water, and summoned the courage to check on the two men down the hall, they had left the living room. She heard them in the kitchen before she saw them. She paused to eavesdrop to see how things were going before she alerted them to her presence, curious to hear what they'd talk about without her in the room.

"So, why *aren't* you going out anymore?" Coach was saying. Jessica heard the refrigerator door open and close, and then a cabinet door.

Bobby sighed loudly. Would he admit to pining for her after being dumped? Would he go all macho and say it was just a quick fling? Would he say anything resembling the truth?

"You want to know the truth? The God's honest truth?" he said. Jessica held her breath so she could hear every word that followed.

"Look, Turnbull, I know you think I'm an asshole, but one thing I don't do is lie. Don't you lie to me either."

The two men were silent as the ice dispenser rumbled.

"It was you," Bobby said after a moment, his voice low.

"Me? What do I have to do with it?"

"Jessica felt like she couldn't go out with me and represent you at the same time because I was writing about you in the paper. Even though we kept that completely separate, you never thought we did. She takes her job really seriously. She felt like she couldn't do it and be with me at the same time. So yeah, she left me for you."

"Jesus Christ," Coach said.

"Yeah," said Bobby.

"No wonder you hate me."

"I don't hate you. I just hate that you get every damned thing you want, and I get to be the designated driver and the whipping boy. And you still find reasons to complain."

Jessica heard the clink of ice rattling around in their glasses and the crack of the seals being opened on the plastic caps of bottles. He'd told the truth. Poor Bobby. He sounded small and defeated. Why would he admit that to Coach?

"I *don't* get everything I want," Coach said, sounding genuinely confused.

"Bullshit."

"There's a lot you don't know."

"I know enough."

Jessica decided it was time to make her entrance. She couldn't bear hearing Bobby sound so sad. She coughed so they'd hear her coming and walked around the corner. "I see you found my cranberry juice and vodka," she said.

"Signature drink of the house, I thought," Bobby said.

"Girly drink," Coach said, but Jessica noticed that his glass was nearly empty.

"My house," Jessica pointed out. "I'm a girl."

"So I noticed." Coach looked her up and down. "You seem to have all the girl parts in the right places."

Jessica opened her mouth to reprimand him, but Coach steamrolled on before she could gather breath. "Turnbull here tells me that you restricted his access to your girl parts because of me. I may be a lot of things, but one thing I am not is a cock-block."

"Tripp," Bobby said, looking humiliated. "Please don't help me."

"No, Turnbull, I'm gonna fix this. I screwed up two major things, and I can fix one of them. I respect the hell out of you, Jessica. You might not know that, because I'm not always the nicest to you, but believe it or not, feeling like I don't have to be nice to you is a compliment." He took a sip of his drink and made a face. "How do you drink this sweet shit?"

Jessica shrugged. "I like it." She liked his compliment, too, though she'd never admit that to him.

"Anyway," Coach said, dumping his drink in the sink and getting more ice from the dispenser, "that's not what I meant to say. This guy here? He actually likes you, and he tells me that you dumped him because of me, and that I will not stand for." Coach poured what had to be a triple shot of vodka over the ice, then sipped it. "That's better."

Bobby shrank into himself like he wanted to disappear into the pantry. Jessica wanted to protect him, but she couldn't figure out how—it seemed like Coach was working in her interests and she didn't want to stop him.

"Don't I get a say in any of this?" asked Jessica, knowing if she sounded too eager Coach might give up his mission and wanting to send a message to Bobby that she was trying to stay on his side, whatever that was.

"Do I?" said Bobby.

"No," Coach said. "You guys forget I teach physics. You think I don't recognize an irresistible, powerful magnetic force when I see one? You got a dry-erase marker? I'll write you out a formula on this sliding glass door." He took another sip of the vodka. "You got a lime in that refrigerator?"

"Should you be drinking more?" Jessica said. "How were you

planning on getting home?" He was actually holding himself together fairly well, but he smelled like a distillery and his eyes were bloodshot. He'd nearly finished the vodka he'd poured himself and was reaching for more. This was a guy who was clearly accustomed to being drunk and holding his own.

"Hadn't really thought that far ahead," he said. "Things work out. They always do."

Jessica and Bobby looked at each other, and she knew they were thinking the same thought: *For you they do, Coach.*

The three of them stood in silence for a few beats until Bobby asked, "What's the second thing?"

Jessica furrowed her brows, and Coach said, "What second thing?"

"You said you screwed two things up and you could fix one. What's the other?"

"You know," Coach said, gesturing at Jessica with his glass and then draining it all in one motion. "The bullshit I had to hire you for." Coach poured more vodka before saying, "I'm sitting down," and led them into the living room. This time, he let Bobby sit next to Jessica on the sofa, and he sat on the love seat, his knees touching the arms on either side and his shoulders obscuring the backrest. He balanced the glass of vodka on his knee. Jessica noted that somehow Coach had become the host in her home. She wanted to resent it, but she found herself too entertained. "Can you not make me look like a total asshole when you write about the trial in the paper, Reporter Boy?"

"You make it hard," Bobby said, and Jessica snorted a laugh.

"Fuck you."

Suddenly, "Cruise" by Florida Georgia Line started playing from somewhere in the love seat.

"Um, Coach?" Jessica ventured, trying not to giggle; all of a sudden everything was funny to her. "I think your ass is ringing."

He stood up as he dug into his back pocket to get his cell

phone. "Fucking Emily," he said, handing the phone to Jessica. "You answer it."

"I don't know her, but I'm like ninety percent sure she doesn't want another woman answering your phone." She passed it to Bobby, who answered it.

"Tripp Wishingham's phone . . . Yeah, he's here . . . Yeah, even drunker than when he got here . . . This is Bobby Turnbull, but actually this is Jessica Fischer's house . . . Would you mind? Do you need the address? . . . Thanks, Emily." Bobby passed the phone back to Coach, who slipped it in his pocket. "Emily is going to pick you up. She says she'll be here in about fifteen minutes, okay?"

Coach nodded.

"Seriously, Coach. Why are you here?" Jessica asked, picturing how stricken he'd been when Francesca had walked into the courtroom earlier that day.

"Because I wanted to talk to you about today. That's it. How was I supposed to know you were about to get laid?"

"I think it was something else," said Jessica.

Coach looked at Bobby. "Will you tell your girl to shut the fuck up? Her and Emily, man. Neither one of them know when to keep their mouths shut."

"She's not my—"

"You're an idiot," Coach said. "If you're not fucking within a half hour of when Emily gets me out of here—"

"Coach!" Jessica shouted, shocked that he'd say such a thing out loud but wishing it would be true all the same.

"I don't know who's worse," Bobby said, turning to Jessica. "Him or Diane."

Jessica considered. "It might actually be Diane. At least he's honest about his intentions."

CHAPTER
THIRTY-TWO

B y the time Emily arrived in her twee blue BMW convertible and they had wedged Coach into it, it was almost ten
o'clock. Not that late, but it was Tuesday: and a long, action-
packed Tuesday at that. Fatigue pulled at Jessica's bones.

Jessica and Bobby watched Emily pull out of the driveway,
then went inside, taking their places back on the sofa. Neither of
them had wanted Coach to interrupt their earlier conversation,
but now that he was gone it felt like a giant hole was in the room.
Jessica wanted to remind Bobby that he was in the middle of saying how wonderful she had done at trial and how he was jealous
of Coach for sitting next to her, and maybe combine that with
Coach's suggestion that they get on with making love, but she
didn't dare be that bold.

Bobby took Jessica's hand. "Well. That was an unexpected
turn of events."

It felt like all of her nerve endings traveled to her hand. She
could feel every ridge of his fingerprints, every line of his knuckles, the rim of his nails. Warmth flowed directly into her heart
and down into her stomach. How could he not feel this? She
stared into his eyes, trying to read his thoughts.

"I kinda feel like it's late and I should go," Bobby said, not making a move to get up. "But so much happened in the last couple of hours that needs deconstructing."

"And so many conversations that need finishing," Jessica agreed. "I'm so tired I'm afraid I'm going to fall asleep while we're talking. I wish we could both just go to sleep and sync up our dreams and talk there."

"We can't go to sleep," Bobby said. "I'm pretty sure that Coach is going to call us in a half hour to see if we are fucking."

The relief of his casual joke unlocked Jessica, and she started laughing so hard her belly ached with the effort.

"Do you wanna talk about Coach and why he came over here to interrupt our conversation? What he really came over here to say?" Bobby said when she'd calmed down a bit.

"Not really. Truth be told, I don't want to talk about him at all. I'm tired of him."

"No?" Bobby said. "But there is unlimited depth to the subject of Tripp Wishingham and his mommy issues."

"There's unlimited depth to other subjects too."

"Oh yeah? Like what?"

At the risk of having a heart attack, Jessica forced herself to say, "Like the subject we were talking about when we were so rudely interrupted by he-who-shall-not-be-named."

"You're right." Bobby closed his eyes and pressed his lips together. Could he possibly be as nervous as she was? He squeezed her hand tighter, like he was afraid she'd bolt if he didn't hang on to her. Without opening his eyes, he said, "Look, Jessica, I stand by everything I said last weekend. You really did break my heart. I fell hard for you so quickly, and you pulled the rug out from under me. All those teenage insecurities came flooding back—it wasn't just being dumped by you, it was being shoved in line behind that undeserving prick once again. I felt like a little unloved boy, and—well, my pathology is not really the topic of conversation tonight." He opened his eyes and stared intently at her, causing her insides to liquefy. "All that shit I thought I was over got churned up. I blamed you for my own bullshit. When I finally got through it, finally got to the point where I understood what you'd done and could appreciate it, thought maybe we could be friends, you came over with blueberry Munchkins and an offer to try again and I panicked. My own peace was so fragile, and I was too afraid that you'd disturb it."

Jessica had no idea what to say. Her own breath came out in ragged streams—his ultimate conclusion could still go in either direction. She wanted to reassure him, but how?

"But then I saw you today and I thought what a fool I was. I was proud of you for the job you did. I wanted to be the one sitting next to you, claiming some special connection to you. I wanted to take you to dinner afterwards and toast your victory. Then, when it was over, you didn't even turn around to see if I was still in the room. As hyperaware as I was of you all day, I realized you weren't even thinking about me. You were thinking about he-who-must-not-be-named. And all my grand plans about getting back what I'd thrown away on Sunday went down the drain. I skittered out of the courtroom like a cockroach, convinced I'd lost my last chance."

Jessica blinked at him. Did he have no idea how hard it was to get in the zone for a trial? How hard it had been for her to forget that he was there behind her the whole day, watching her? She was stunned into silence realizing how different their perceptions of the day had been.

He continued talking. "I found a conference room, filed my article as quickly as I could, then went to go home so I could drink in my living room and feel sorry for myself. Then there you were, just sitting there, like you were waiting for me." The serious look on his face softened, and his features melted as if she were seeing him through a lens covered in Vaseline. "I thought, *This is it. This is the universe giving me one final chance. Don't fuck it up,*

Turnbull. Seize the day, or the evening, no matter how scary it is. So I did. And now here I am. And if you end up disturbing my peace, well, I guess it's worth disturbing."

Jessica was afraid to move. Everything about this moment was perfect, and she felt like anything she said or did would be imperfect and, therefore, ruinous. She wanted to put her hand against his cheek and promise to spend every minute making sure his peace was undisturbed, wanted to show him with her body how sincere she was about making him feel nothing but good. She took a deep breath, trying to think of something suave and perfect to say, only coming up with a lame joke about how "disturbing the peace" was a city ordinance and not a real crime.

Before she ruined the moment with a bad joke, Bobby spoke. "I feel like if we just had some good rules about work and life and what we can and can't do and talk about—if it's not too late—we can make this work."

Rules, Jessica thought. *That, I can do.* Her brain, short-circuiting on all the emotion, jumped into lawyer mode. It would basically be like a relationship contract, and they could write it out that way. All they had to do was think about what could go wrong, what scenarios would trip them up, and figure out on the front end how they would handle it. Whose interests would take precedence in which scenario, taking into account ethics rules and . . .

"Jessica," Bobby said, breaking her out of her reverie. "You have to say something, or I'm going to die here."

"You're going to think I'm crazy, but I was thinking that we could kind of structure it like a parenting plan—in divorces, when people do custody agreements they make it so you can look at your watch and know exactly where the kid is supposed to be at any given moment. So we could do something like that where we know in any given scenario what we're supposed to do and what we can say and what we can't, and in that way we won't . . ." She knew she was babbling, but now that she had started talking she couldn't stop vomiting words.

Bobby had a crooked smile on his face. "Are you talking about our inevitable divorce?"

"No, no! I'm just saying we should draw up some kind of relationship contract to head problems like Coach off at the pass and . . ."

"Stop talking," Bobby said, closing the gap between them by pulling her against him. He pressed his lips against hers, parting her mouth with his tongue. His sandpaper chin scraped against her cheek, and he held her close with his long arms. She pushed up against him, melting into him. She was beyond rational thought; she just *wanted*. He kissed her neck and bit her earlobe and explored every inch of her back with his large hands. She held on to him tightly, lacing her fingers through his hair with one hand and grabbing fistfuls of his shirt with the other. She hung on, afraid that if she let go this time, he would not come back to her. She was never taking that chance again.

He came up for air, pulling away from her with a soft moan. He cupped her cheeks and kissed her forehead before looking at his watch. Her heart froze. *Is he really checking the time?*

"It's eleven," he said, his deep voice even huskier than usual. "We're only a half hour past our deadline."

"He's a good coach," she agreed, "but he didn't teach you this play, did he?" She planted kisses in his palm, then folded his fingers around them so he could keep them there.

"You've got two choices," Bobby said. "You can kick me out now, or you're stuck with me. If I don't go home right now, I won't be able to."

Jessica locked her hands around the back of his head and pulled him in for a deep kiss. Then she whispered in his ear, "Stay."

— — —

Jessica lay with her head on Bobby's chest, his arm around her shoulders. He fell asleep before she did: she listened to his soft snores. She put her hand on his belly, running her fingers over a small scar. What was the story behind it? She had so much to learn and couldn't wait to do it. She watched his chest rise and fall with his breath, felt the wiry hairs underneath her palm as she drifted off.

She woke in the morning to her alarm. Bobby curled around her back, the big spoon to her little. She reached over the pile of books on her night table to stop the incessant peal of the alarm, then slipped out from beneath Bobby's arm, the pressure from her bladder forcing her up. Out of habit, she took her phone with her. She covered herself with a bathrobe, suddenly very conscious of her nakedness.

"Come back," Bobby called after her. "I really need you to come back." Every part of Jessica's body lit up with her smile.

As she sat on the commode, Jessica scrolled her new messages and saw one from Coach. It had come in at exactly 10:30 the night before: *U FUCKEN HIM YET?*

Her bark of laughter echoed off the bathroom tile.

She came back to the bed and resumed her position, nestling against Bobby. He pulled the hair away from her neck and kissed her softly at her nape. "Good morning, my little blueberry Munchkin," he rumbled in her ear. "What were you laughing at?"

"Mmm," she said, not quite ready to form words. She passed her phone over to him.

Bobby glanced at the screen and muttered, "God. I can't stand that asshole. Get him out of this bed." He tossed the phone on the carpet, then swung his leg over her hip and dragged her closer to him. "Why are you wearing this? Suddenly coy, are we?" He pulled the shoulder of her bathrobe down and kissed the newly exposed skin.

She felt utterly naked, more so than before despite the thick velour that still covered most of her body. He had called attention to what they had done. It was now the light of day, and the sun shined through the window on their messed-up hair and the sleep creases across their faces. She was suddenly shy. They had been in the moment last night, that unreal place where sex happens and passion covers a multitude of sin. What had she said to him last night? On what parts of his body had she mindlessly, desperately put her hands, her face, her tongue? Her face felt a thousand degrees hotter as the memories flooded back, both embarrassing her and arousing her in turns.

"Kiss me," Bobby whispered in her ear, his hand snaking underneath her robe and cupping her breast. He stroked her nipple with his thumb. All her hesitancy disappeared.

She turned toward him and kissed him, regretting that she hadn't paused to brush her teeth while she was in the bathroom. He broke away, replacing his thumb with his mouth.

Jessica pressed the back of his neck and held him there. Her eyes closed as she focused on the line of electric pleasure reaching across her body that he drew from her as he suckled.

Before she was ready, he lifted his head. "Jessica. I don't want to stop, but . . ."

"But I know," she said, tracing his jawline with her finger. "It's a workday, and you have to go."

He dropped his head on her shoulder and laughed. "No. Not now. I mean, I hate to interrupt, but I'm going to enjoy this more after I go to the bathroom."

She kissed the top of his head and said, "Go. Hurry." She pulled the bathrobe around her in a facsimile of his warmth and waited for him to return.

CHAPTER
THIRTY-THREE

B obby drove Jessica to El Toro to get her car. The building was gaily painted with a mural of a bullfighter and his red cape taunting a bull. As many times as she'd been to El Toro, she'd never noticed the artistry in the painting, the bright, happy colors in it. Her car looked dirty and abandoned, colorless and scuffed by comparison in the empty parking lot, and she thought maybe it was time to get a new car after all. Bobby got out of his car and kissed her soundly, begging her to make a thousand promises to call later that day. He waited until her car started and she pulled out of the parking lot before leaving himself.

When she got to the office, Diane was on the phone, so Jessica just waved hello, then made herself some coffee to take to her desk. She was there, checking emails, when Diane flounced into the client chair. "Well, girlie?" Diane said. "I'm way behind. Your five-minute recap in the car about the trial of the century hardly satisfied my curiosity."

Jessica swiveled her chair from her computer screen so she was facing Diane. Yesterday's story was too jumbled to tell easily. Memories she wouldn't relate flashed across her mind and she smiled.

"You are positively glowing," Diane said. "It must have been a greater victory than you let on. Hold up." Diane leaned forward

0LORI B. DUFF

and took Jessica's chin in her hands. "That's not a victory glow. That's nookie. You got some! Do I know who the lucky boy is?" Diane teased, and threw laughter at the ceiling.

Jessica wanted to crawl under her desk and cut an escape hatch in the floor with a pair of scissors. Instead, she sat in her chair, blushing and trying to shrink. As if on cue, her cell phone, lying in the middle of her desk, buzzed and displayed Bobby's name.

Diane yelped. "Bobby! You did the nasty with Bobby Turnbull!"

Jessica's eyes flashed. "No. Stop that right now. I did not do anything *nasty* with Bobby."

"What did you do? 'Make love?'" Diane used her fingers to make air quotes.

"Maybe." Jessica felt foolish. "Making love" sounded goopy and part of a Hallmark movie. But why should she be ashamed of falling so hard? It had been a long time coming.

"Give me a break. You haven't gone out with the guy in months, and then you hop in bed with him after a stressful day. I'm supposed to think 'love' has anything to do with it?"

Jessica knew being annoyed with Diane was unreasonable, but she couldn't help it. It felt too dumb to say out loud, but she felt like she and Bobby had invented the very concept of romance, and to hear Diane diminish it with her typical jokes set Jessica's teeth on edge. "Yeah, Diane, you are. I'm not saying I'm in love with Bobby, but I hope to be soon. What we did was an act of love. Everything he said and did made me like him more. It was all part of getting to know him. I felt good and safe and cared for. I wanted to make him feel good because he's a good person and he deserves good feelings, and I think he feels the same way about me."

"Oh, please," said Diane. "Look, I'm glad you hooked up with him. Sex is a fabulous release, and you and Bobby are an adorable couple. But let's not get ahead of ourselves. You didn't invent the concept."

Jessica lifted her hands into the throttle position, shook them without actually wrapping her fingers around Diane's neck, and then put them back down. Diane's talent for mind reading and being absolutely correct was maddening. "Hold up now. You get all pissy with me because I broke up with Bobby over principle because you think I'm denying myself the pleasure of love. Then when I actually get with him, you think I'm making too much of it. In the meantime, you've been denying yourself the pleasure of love for fifteen years."

"Denying myself?" Diane laughed again. "What the hell are you talking about? I have had more boyfriends this year than you've had since I've known you."

"No, Diane, you haven't. You haven't had a single boyfriend. You've just had sex." Jessica immediately wished she hadn't said this. She had, though. There wasn't anything she could do about it.

"That was low," Diane said, dramatically tossing her immobile hair. "It's not my fault that men find me attractive."

"Nope. It isn't. It's entirely to your credit. It's your fault that you push them away the minute they decide they like you too."

"You don't know what you're talking about."

"Don't I?"

Diane left Jessica's office in a huff. Jessica knew what would happen. They'd both bury themselves in work. A few hours later, they'd both pretend they hadn't had a fight. This wasn't how she wanted this morning to go. She hadn't meant to fight with Diane—she wasn't even mad at her, not really. She just couldn't understand for the life of her why—or how—Diane could get a taste of what she'd experienced last night over and over again and then keep swatting it away when it started to get reliable.

Jessica sighed and picked up her phone to read Bobby's

message. *I finally got the girl and I can't stop smiling. Meathead jock 0, Late bloomer 1.*

She texted back, *It's about time you bloomed. Smiles here too.*

The exchange filled her with enough confidence to go for round two with Diane. Jessica got up from her desk and turned the corner out of her office into Diane's. The extra chair was piled with paperwork. "I'm sorry," she said, and sat on the floor, her back against Diane's desk.

"Humph," said Diane, not looking away from her computer.

"I shouldn't have said what I said. Not the way I said it, anyway."

"No, you shouldn't have."

"You may not remember, but a while ago, we got into a little argument. You said I had no business advising you about your sex life until I got laid."

The corners of Diane's mouth turned up. "I may have said something like that."

"Well, I got laid."

Diane's smile reached across her face. "Okay. You got laid. And Bobby was the one doing the laying?"

"Yes, ma'am."

"Good for you. I trust he knows how to adequately lay the pipe?"

"Diane!"

"I'll take that for a yes. And you're going to do it again, or he wouldn't be texting you so soon afterwards, yes?"

Jessica's grin answered the question.

"Excellent!" Diane clapped her hands. "Do I get any romantic details?"

"No. Well, yes. Well, some. Not right this minute. There's something I have to say first. Better this time, I hope."

Diane gave her a wary look but gestured for Jessica to continue.

"Look, Diane, you are one of the most amazing people I know. You're smart and funny and caring. To top it all off, you really are a hot little number."

"You're off to a pretty good start," Diane said.

"It makes me sad that you want the best for everyone else but not yourself. It's like when David died, part of you died too—the part of you that knows how to receive love. I didn't know you then, and I don't know all the details of what happened. But I know what I see. As soon as men start seeing you as more than that pretty body you're in, you make them go away."

"You don't know," Diane said.

"You're right, I don't know. There's a lot I don't know because you don't talk about it. But I do know that you're a whole lot more than a sex toy. I do know that nookie is fun for some body parts, but making love is something you do with your whole self. Yeah, that sounds corny, but I can tell you from personal experience, very recent personal experience, mind you, like, this morning—"

"We get it," Diane said. "You got laid this morning. Good for Bobby. Good for you."

Jessica opened her mouth to respond, and Diane cut her off. "Baby girl, look. Here's the thing you don't understand. I had my Bobby. Everything you feel for Bobby, I felt for David and then some. I *feel* for David." Diane swiveled her chair so she faced Jessica.

"David and I were in the same kindergarten class, did you know that? Mrs. Hawkins's class. That's how long we knew each other. In sixth grade, I was still taller than he was. By eighth grade, he'd shot up. We didn't start dating for real until ninth grade. When we got married, he was the only boyfriend I'd ever had, the only boy I'd ever kissed. The only boy I wanted to kiss. I still love him and I always will.

"I've had that. I don't need to do it again, and I don't want to. I receive plenty of love. I get it from you and your pain-in-the-ass sass, from Kaitlyn and Denise, from my high school friends who I still have dinner with once a month, from my church, from lots of places. My life is full. I don't need to overfill it with some less-than-David guy. I like flirting. I like sex. I enjoy feeling attractive. I like boys. You honestly think I kick men to the curb when they start to get serious? No, no, no. I kick 'em to the curb when they start interfering with the fullness of my life and taking time away from the people and things I love."

Jessica felt punched in the gut. "I'm . . . I'm sorry," she said, unfolding herself from the floor so she could hug Diane.

"Make sure you're sorry about the right thing," Diane said. "Be sorry because you think you know more than me. I'm always right." Diane stood up so the hug could be more complete. Against Jessica's shoulder, she said, "You mean well, I know. You just have to remember that your job—as a lawyer and as a friend—isn't to get everyone what *you* want; it's to get them what *they* want."

Jessica hugged her harder, feeling how small and birdlike she was underneath the shell of hair spray and acrylic nails and colorful, ballooning skirts. This woman was the mother, the big sister, the friend she craved. Her uncanny ability to hit the nail square on the head with every stroke of the hammer made her not just necessary but loved. She'd just hit Jessica with a sledgehammer, whether she knew it or not, square between her eyes, and it would take some processing to get the feel for all the things she'd knocked into place.

"Okay," Diane said after a moment, pulling away and sitting back in her chair. "Now you know. David's dead. Boys are good for toys. And you pay me to work for you, not yammer on about things in the past neither one of us can change."

"You are amazing. You really are. Just keep reminding me, in case I forget."

"I will," said Diane. "Like when you get mad at me for

scheduling Tripp Wishingham at eleven thirty. He wanted to come in on his lunch break."

When Coach showed up a few minutes early for his appointment, Jessica let him come straight back. Diane wanted to sit in on the post-trial conference, but this time it was Coach who asked for privacy. "I need to talk to my lawyer," he said. "Privileged stuff, you understand." He winked at Diane and patted her hip, causing Jessica to roll her eyes and groan.

Jessica hardly had a chance to shut her office door when Coach said, "You didn't answer my text. Did you fuck him?"

Jessica sat down hard in her chair and pointed directly at Coach. "That is none of your business."

"I'll take that for a yes. Good. The two of you were driving me crazy with the sexual tension. You could cut it with a pair of dull scissors."

Jessica breathed in slowly through her nose to the count of ten. "Why are you here?"

"So rude!"

"I'm sorry," Jessica said, with mock pleasantness, adding a few bats of her eyelashes for effect. "How might I help the great Coach Wishingham?"

"Look, there's a reason I came to your house last night that I didn't get to tell you because *he* was there."

She had learned over the years that sometimes the best way to get information was to be silent. She took that tack.

Coach shifted in the chair, not knowing where to put his arms—he tried his behind-the-head relaxed posture and rejected it, but didn't tense up for his high-alert stance either. It suddenly struck Jessica that he felt vulnerable, and he had no idea how to behave. Coach cleared his throat. "I wanted to tell you what my deal was with Francesca—why I didn't want to visit with her, why she freaked me out like that. I thought I . . . I thought I owed you that much."

Jessica's instinct was to tell him that he didn't owe her anything, but she choked it off before she ruined the story. She smiled instead, tried to look warm and harmless, absolving, how a priest might look as he sits in a confessional booth.

Coach coughed again. He was nervous! The all-powerful Tripp Wishingham was nervous talking to her! Oh, how she wished she could travel back to tenth grade and tell fifteen-year-old Jessica that one day a famous football star would be afraid to say something to her. "I think I told you when you first showed me her picture that Francesca looked a little bit like my mother."

"You did."

Coach leaned to the side to get his wallet out of his back pocket. He pulled a small picture out of it and handed it to Jessica. "This is my mom's high school graduation picture."

Jessica took it from him and looked at it. The resemblance was uncanny. If Coach had told her this was a picture of Francesca, she'd have believed him. "Wow."

"I know. The spitting image." He took the picture back from Jessica and put it back in his wallet. "I adored my mother. She was kind and good. A real lady in the true southern sense. I was a mama's boy when I was little, but as soon as I hit puberty, I admit I turned into a bit of an asshole. I guess a lot of teenagers do. I know it's normal. Part of the growth process, learning to separate yourself from your parents, yada yada."

Jessica nodded, wondering where he was going with this.

"I looked mostly like my mom, but I was big like my dad, and as much as I admired my mom's demeanor, I was wired like my dad. We were a lot alike, and the things that drove my mom insane about my dad also drove her insane about me. She did her best to steer me in another direction, but like I said, I was an asshole. You couldn't tell me shit. What are you going to do?" He looked at Jessica as if she could answer the question, so she shrugged. She tried hard to keep her face serious and concerned-looking, but so much of what he said lined up perfectly with her theories from last night.

Coach took a deep breath and sighed. "The night she died— it was New Year's Eve. She was big in the church ladies' club, and they were big on saving young souls from the perils of assholes like me. They had a party at the church for all the losers who either couldn't find a real party to go to or whose parents wouldn't let them go to a real party. She begged me to go. Begged me. Tried to forbid me from going anywhere else, but my dad, well, he was the man of the house and his word was the final word, and his word was that no son of his was going to be with the lesser social strata on New Year's Eve against his will. He understood the power of networking—that it's your buddies who will bail you out and stand behind you."

Coach put his elbows on his thighs and his head in his hands, a folded-up posture Jessica had never seen him in before. Without lifting his head, he said, "Mom kept begging me to 'just stop by.' If I couldn't come for the party, to help her clean up afterwards. Just to shut her up I told her I'd try."

Coach didn't say anything for a long moment. Jessica said, "You okay?"

He looked up, still hunched over. "Goddamn, her eyes. They just lit up, you know. Like she was some gimp and I'd agreed to go to the prom with her. That sparkle made me feel so good. I honestly thought at that moment that I'd try to go and help her clean up. Make sure she got home safely. Be a gentleman and all that bullshit." His chest heaved as he breathed in and out. Jessica knew generally what happened next, but she was riveted nonetheless.

"I meant to go, I really did. But my buddies and I, we got drunk, and we found some girls who also got drunk, and, well, helping my mom clean out the church social hall became less and less of a priority if you know what I mean." He gave a sheepish smile that made Jessica see beneath his bluster. He took another deep breath; this one came out raggedly. "And I don't know what happened next. No one ever will, I guess. Maybe she was tired from all that cleaning she had to do without my help and she fell asleep. I know for a fact she wasn't drunk—that woman never let alcohol pass her lips. All we know is that she ran her car into a tree and her beautiful face into the steering wheel sometime in the middle of the night."

Coach didn't look like he wanted to be touched; until this very moment he hadn't asked for any kind of sympathy, hadn't really even asked for it now, and Jessica had no idea how to react to him. She wanted to put her hand on his arm, give him comfort, but he seemed as if his nerves were so raw any touch might be too much, so she sat still, silent, letting him speak.

"I pretty much stayed drunk the rest of my senior year. Football season was over; I'd already signed with college. All the teachers felt so bad for me that they passed me whether or not I turned in homework. I basically fucked up until graduation, and I don't remember much of it. I don't know that I want to. I believed that it was my fault my mom died. I still do, kinda. She used to warn me that I was too much like my dad. Too charming, too good-looking for my own good. That I'd talk my way into trouble I couldn't get out of one day, just like he did, then I'd be stuck in a life I didn't want. I didn't know what she was talking about.

"Now I do. I couldn't spend one hour of my life helping a perfectly nice lady who loved me sweep up some goddamn potato chips, and now she's dead. I talked my way into God only knows how many pairs of panties. And let me just say here, I know what you think." He pointed two fingers at his forehead then, in a cockeyed parody of a salute, pointed them at Jessica. "And I appreciate your never saying it out loud. I really don't remember Sarah, but I know my technique, and I never would have if I thought for a second she didn't want it, too. I had an MO which worked every goddamn time, and it is an absolute fucking miracle that Francesca is the only kid that resulted from it. And she looks just like my Mom. Her absolute fucking clone." Coach met Jessica's gaze for the first time in this conversation. "I cannot look in her eyes, Jessica. That picture—she stared out of it with my mother's eyes. I cannot see her happy. I cannot see that same goddamn spark that my mom had when I told her I would try to come help her at the church. She looks exactly the same, and she will break me. I cannot let a teenage girl break everything I have built up, do you understand me?"

Jessica nodded slowly. It would have been nice to have all this information on the front end—to understand him this way, to get his motivations. But she knew. People came to things in their own time. She felt honored, in a way. How many people had ever seen Coach in this way? Still filling the room with his presence but allowing himself to show the chinks in his armor, the places where arrows had already pierced through? He didn't appear to be crying, but his eyes were wet. "Can I hug you?" she said.

"The fuck you're asking for?"

Ah yes, the king of consent. She laughed and came around the desk, putting her arm around his shoulder and leaning her head against his.

"You're not telling Turnbull any of this, are you?"

"No, no, of course not. This is all privileged information."

"I still don't trust him." Coach snuggled his head in deeper against the crook of her shoulder—was he trying to get at her boob? "But I trust you, and I'm glad you're fucking him. Let me know if he's not good to you. I'll punch him in the nuts."

Jessica slapped the shoulder she had previously been petting and broke away, smiling. "You'll never change, will you?"

"Couldn't if I wanted to."

CHAPTER
THIRTY-FOUR

After Coach left, Jessica cradled her head on her arms on her desk and lay there for some time. Between the trial, Bobby, Diane, and now Coach, she was too overwhelmed to do anything but try to process the maelstrom of thoughts fighting their way to the front of her mind. Shoved to the back were all the clients she'd ignored in the past week while prepping for Coach's trial and the pile of paperwork next to her elbow that needed tending to. She wanted to go home and crawl under her comforter and let her brain process everything while she slept. Thinking of her bed made her think of Bobby, and she smiled, thinking that knowing she could find comfort against him made everything else seem surmountable.

She had climbed so deeply into the recesses of her thoughts that she didn't hear Diane come in and sit in the chair opposite her until she coughed to get her attention. Jessica lifted her head off her arms in surprise. "How long have you been here?"

"Long enough."

They sized each other up for a moment before Diane said, "You gonna tell me what Coach told you?"

"Sorry, I can't."

"What do you mean, you can't?" Diane seemed genuinely scandalized. "I mean, I understood Kaitlyn, but Coach?"

"He asked me not to." Of all the things Jessica had said to Diane in the past, the things that were, objectively, unkind and even mean, this was the first time Diane looked truly wounded. "I'm sorry, but . . ." Jessica searched for a way to tell her without telling her. "We had a moment. He actually peeled back his asshole shell and talked to me like a real human being for the first time."

Diane squinted at her, examining her.

"Do you want to hear about Bobby?" The details of this would serve as a very juicy peace offering.

Diane clapped her hands. "You know I do!"

Jessica gave her the rundown, starting with their dinner at El Toro, and ending with their kiss, implying the rest with a "Then, well, you know."

Diane threw her hands in the air and swiveled her hips. "You got well laid!"

Shaking her head, Jessica said, "Very well. And that's all the details you're getting about that."

"That's enough. I'm so happy for you. You deserve to be in love."

"You know I love *you*, Diane."

"I'm very lovable," Diane said.

"That is exactly what I have been trying to tell you all day, you know." Jessica reached into her stress ball basket and grabbed one. It was from a cardiologist's office and shaped like a heart. She threw it at Diane and, for the first time ever, Diane caught it, her hands crossed over her chest.

Diane stood up, staring at the red foam heart in her hand. "I think I'll keep this one," she said, pocketing it and heading back to her own office.

Book Club Questions for DEVIL'S DEFENSE

1. What are some of the ethical dilemmas that Jessica encounters as a lawyer? How would you handle them if you were in her position?

2. How does the setting of small-town Ashton influence the plot and the characters?

3. What are some of the advantages and disadvantages of living and working in a small town?

4. Do you think Jessica wins or loses the trial, or somewhere in between?

5. How does the book explore the themes of personal discovery, truth, and justice? What are some of the lessons that Jessica learns by the end of the book?

6. How does the book compare to other courtroom dramas you have read or watched? What are some of the similarities and differences?

7. What role do you think Diane plays in Jessica's life?

8. How do you feel about Coach? Do you think Jessica gives him a fair shot? Is anything about him sympathetic? Why or why not?

9. What assumptions does Jessica make about Coach that turn out to be true? What assumptions does she make that turn out to be untrue? Did you share those assumptions early in the book?

10. How does Jessica's relationship with Bobby affect her professional and personal life? Do you think she makes the right decision by dating him?

11. Jessica says that Eric Crabtree is her friend, but she spends most of the book arguing with him. Do you believe her? Is that something unique to lawyers? If you had someone in your life with whom you constantly argued, do you think you could consider them a true friend?

12. What did you think of the ending of the book? Were you satisfied by the outcome? Surprised? Why or why not?

ACKNOWLEDGMENTS

Writing a book seems like it would be a lonely experience, but it's not. In fact, it's rather crowded. It may look like I'm sitting in a room by myself typing away, but my head is full of the thoughts and shouts of my characters. They wake me up at night to tell me things. Then, when they've had their say, a whole bunch of real, live people get involved.

My mother passed before she got to read this book. In fact, I got a lot of the first draft written while caring for her during her last month. So she's a huge part of it and informed some of the scenes where Jessica takes care of her mother. I hope she's somewhere to know it. My father did get to read it before he died, though not the final version. When we were cleaning out his house, I found the printed-out manuscript feathered with Post-it Notes, and it made me cry.

So. On to the living. I'm hesitant to name names, because I will inevitably forget someone very important. Not because I forgot them but because they are so much in the forefront of my mind that it seems obvious that they're there, even when they're not.

Thank you to Laura Horton, my first reader, who, for reasons unknown, seems to like the shitty first draft of all of Jessica's adventures. Dr. Daniela Gitlin is an *amazing* beta reader who isn't afraid to tell the truth and keep my characters psychologically honest. Y'all get you a good friend who is both a talented writer *and* a psychiatrist *and* who is willing to spend untold hours quibbling about every single word in your book. It will make your book better. Rachel Stout of New York Book Editors took the book to the absolute next level. Diane Hale, the *real* Diane, who is nothing like the Diane in the book except for her job, accent, and dislike of f-bombs, gets all the praise for being my right arm and my keeper and my friend. Also, for not minding that I stole most of her family names.

I owe a debt of gratitude, payable in, unfortunately, nothing but glory to the Walton Writers, who patiently listened to me read this out loud over the course of three or so years and encouraged me in untold ways. Friends with Words—y'all make me feel like a legitimate writer just by allowing me in your august company, and I am grateful.

Thank you to Brooke Warner, Shannon Green, and the team at She Writes Press for taking me seriously and making this book legit and for having such a streamlined process, which soothed my anal-retentive heart. I always felt like I was in the hands of someone who knew what they were doing.

Thank you to all the people who will most assuredly NOT be named whose personalities I stole pieces of to make my characters seem real.

A shout-out to everyone who has ever read something I've written and told me it was good. You keep my impostor syndrome, that saucy minx, at bay. Y'all are the ones who will find all the Easter eggs I sprinkled liberally throughout.

And my family. My children, Jacob and Marin, who are by far my greatest creations. I couldn't write characters as perfect as you in my books—no one would think they were believable. What real people have your talents, intelligence, and damn good looks? And my husband, Mike, who gives me time and space and support to write as much as I want and never gives me grief about it.

My heart, she overflows with gratitude and love.

ABOUT THE AUTHOR

Lori B. Duff is a lawyer, municipal court judge, and award-winning writer. An empty-nester, she lives in Loganville, Georgia, with her husband and rescue puppy.

Looking for your next great read?

We can help!

Visit www.shewritespress.com/next-read
or scan the QR code below for a list
of our recommended titles.

She Writes Press is an award-winning
independent publishing company founded to
serve women writers everywhere.